BAYSIDE

Fantasies

Bayside Summers
Love in Bloom Series

Melissa Foster

ISBN: 978-1-948868-42-6
ISBN: 1-948868-42-3

Cover Design: Elizabeth Mackey Designs
Cover Photography: Regina Wamba

PRINTED IN THE UNITED STATES OF AMERICA

A Note from Melissa

I love writing about characters who aren't perfect and taking them on a journey neither one expects. Tegan Fine and Jett Masters definitely fit the bill. I hope you enjoy their steamy, thrilling, roller-coaster ride of a love story as much as I enjoyed writing it. If this is your first Love in Bloom novel, all Love in Bloom stories are written to be enjoyed as stand-alone novels or as part of the larger series. Dive right in and enjoy the fun, sexy ride. For more information on Love in Bloom titles, visit www.MelissaFoster.com.

If you're an avid reader of my Love in Bloom series, you'll remember first meeting Tegan in *Surrender My Love* (The Bradens at Peaceful Harbor), and you may have seen her in other Braden books as well as in The Whiskeys series. You also will have met Jett in many of the Bayside Summers books.

I have more steamy love stories coming soon. Be sure to sign up for my newsletter so you don't miss them. www.MelissaFoster.com/Newsletter

FREE Love in Bloom Reader Goodies

If you love funny, sexy, and deeply emotional love stories, be sure to check out the rest of the Love in Bloom big-family romance collection and download your free reader goodies, including publication schedules, series checklists, family trees, and more! www.MelissaFoster.com/RG

Bookmark my freebies page for periodic first-in-series free ebooks and other great offers! www.MelissaFoster.com/LIBFree

Chapter One

TEGAN SQUINTED TO see past the blur of pummeling rain and whipping windshield wipers as she drove toward the gas station. Gripping the steering wheel so tight her knuckles blanched, she yelled over her rattling defroster in the direction of her cell phone. "This is insane! You could have warned me I was moving to the *arctic* for half the year." She raised her voice an octave, mimicking her friend Chloe Mallery's voice. "'You'll love it!' you said. 'There's nothing like Cape Cod in the spring!'"

"In my defense, everyone knows April showers bring May flowers."

"It's the first week of April, and it's *freezing*. I'm pretty sure all the flowers are digging their way to China right now. I'm starting to rethink the other promises you made, like hot eligible bachelors coming to the Cape in *droves* over the summer."

"That *is* true," Chloe said.

"Says the single girl who uses dating apps to find men. What was I thinking?"

Chloe laughed. "You were thinking of your favorite uncle, and of me, Harper, and Daphne, of course. Your new besties!"

A pang of sadness moved through her. Tegan had lost her

great-uncle Harvey Fine, an eccentric retired-actor-turned-amphitheater-owner, last summer. He'd left her his house, the amphitheater business, and enough money that she could walk away from it all and never work a day in her life. But she'd adored her uncle, and two weeks ago she'd left her hometown of Peaceful Harbor, Maryland, and come to the Cape to see if she could make a go of it. For the next seven months, Brewster, Massachusetts, would be *home*. But while Tegan was used to traveling alone on short vacations, the seven-month move was still a little jarring. She wished Jock Steele, her uncle's caretaker for the past decade who had also become her trusted friend, had stuck around. At least then she'd have company in the rambling old mansion and someone to help her understand some of the ins and outs of her uncle's business. But Jock was off trying to figure out how to move forward with his own life.

As she drove through a puddle at the gas station's entrance, spraying water up to her windows, she was convinced her uncle had known the move might be difficult and had pulled strings from the heavens above, bringing Harper Garner, a local screenwriter, into Tegan's life. Harper had not only proposed a joint venture that would expand the offerings of the amphitheater, but she'd also introduced Tegan to Chloe and several other of her closest friends, each of whom had welcomed her with open arms.

"Think of this storm as one of your adventures!" Chloe said excitedly.

"My life has been one big adventure for as long as I can remember." Tegan had worked three jobs for years. She never knew what the day would hold, and she took a solo vacation at least once each year to someplace new and exciting. But this would be her biggest adventure yet because it was the one she cared most about. The house that had once felt joyful and like a second home now felt too empty, and the wicked weather felt like a sign.

She glanced out the window at the driving rain whirling with the wind, the ominous and angry-gray sky gave the nearly deserted gas station an eerie vibe. "Don't worry, Chloe. I'm not hightailing it out of here. Even with this crazy storm, it feels like I've been dropped into a whole new world that I was *meant* to discover."

She pulled past a row of pumps where a black SUV was parked—or maybe *abandoned*—and into the next row. "I must have been nuts coming out in this, though," she said more to herself than to Chloe. She'd been weeding through her uncle's belongings for a week and a half, and she'd needed to get out of the house before she lost her mind. "After I get gas and hunt down a place to grab lunch and work on a plan for the amphitheater, I'm going to hibernate until the storm passes."

"Think of all the reading you'll get done. Did you start this month's book for the club yet? If not, be forewarned, it is definitely *not* safe to read in public." Chloe was an administrator for an assisted living facility, and she also ran an online erotic romance book club. This month they were reading a book from one of Tegan's favorite series, Nice Girls After Dark by bestselling author Charlotte Sterling.

Tegan cut the engine, and her old Corolla, Berta, sputtered and coughed before finally shuddering to silence. Her uncle had left her a fancy Lincoln Town Car, but like his house, without him in it, it felt *wrong*. Besides, she wasn't ready to give up Berta just yet.

"I just started the book," she said to Chloe. "And I realized it was NSFW on the *third* page. Holy cow, talk about dirty!"

"I know. It's a good one. That should keep you nice and warm when you're hibernating."

"Good. Now tell me where I can get some food if I survive pumping my gas."

"Oh gosh, that's a toughie this time of year. Other than the grocery store, there are only a couple places that open before Memorial Day. My friend Gabe's coffeehouse, Common Grounds, is open year-round, but it's in Harwich. There's the Sundial Café between Brewster and Orleans. Where are you right now?"

The Cape was made up of several quaint small towns. Orleans was only about fifteen minutes from Tegan's property in Brewster. At least in good weather. It had taken her more than forty minutes to drive there today.

"I had to come to Orleans to find an open gas station. I passed the Sundial on my way here. That's perfect. But you could have warned me about nothing being open."

"If I had warned you, you might have thought twice about leaving your perfect little Peaceful Harbor, and then where would that leave Harper?"

"I would never let my uncle *or* Harper down by not even trying to make this work."

She took her phone off speaker and held it to her ear as she scoped out the gas station. "This place looks deserted. I see an SUV, but there are no signs of life. This isn't going to be like that movie where the stupid girl takes a wrong turn and ends up in the hands of a serial killer, is it?"

"*Hardly,*" Chloe said sarcastically. "But you might get swept away in the wind. I'll stay on the phone so if you get carried away like Mary Poppins I can call for help."

"Okay. Wish me luck—I'm braving the arctic." Tegan

grabbed her credit card and pulled the hood of her raincoat over her head. She tried to open the car door, but the wind slammed it closed, nearly catching her fingers and causing her to shriek. "The freaking wind pushed my door closed!"

"You're a badass book club girl. Go out there and show that wind who's boss!"

"Damn right I am." She used her shoulder to push the door open, struggling against the wind and rain as she stepped out of the car. The door slammed, and her hood flew off. Rain pelted her despite the shelter over the pumps. She tried to pull her hood on and turn her back to the wind and rain, but they seemed to come from every direction, and her hood kept flying off. "Can you hear the wind howling?"

"Howl back!" Chloe yelled.

Tegan tilted her face up and howled as loud as she could through her chattering teeth. A guy walked out of the gas station's convenience store while she was howling.

"Awesome mating call!" he shouted, with a wave. Then he howled as he ran toward a pickup truck she hadn't noticed parked around the side of the building.

She ducked her head, pressing the phone to her ear. "Oh my God! Some guy with a killer smile heard me and howled back!" She and Chloe roared with laughter as the truck drove out of the lot. She fumbled with her credit card. "My fingers are numb!" She inserted the card into the pump, bouncing on the toes of her rain boots to try to warm up, and her eyes caught on a tall, broad, dark-haired man coming out of the convenience store. His hair and expensive-looking overcoat were already drenched, and he strode unhurriedly through the driving rain with a phone pressed to his ear, looking serious. He moved with an air of authority, as if he could stop the rain and wind if he so chose, but it wasn't worth his time.

"I want to hear all about your plans for the amphitheater…"

Chloe's voice turned to white noise as the man's eyes sailed over Tegan for only a second before landing on the SUV in the next row. But in that second, the earth stood still. She watched him disappear behind his vehicle.

"Are you listening to me?" Chloe hollered, snapping Tegan from her reverie.

"Uh-huh. Hold on." She peered around the gas pump, trying to get one last glimpse.

He stood by the hood of the SUV, the phone still pressed to his ear. He lifted his face, catching her staring, and *winked*. She sucked in a sharp breath, but she was frozen in place. He had the bluest eyes she'd ever seen. A cocky grin appeared on his handsome face, and then he ducked into his SUV and drove away.

The air rushed from Tegan's lungs, and she realized she hadn't just been staring, but she'd been *gawking*—and smiling like an idiot. "Holy *fudge*. I take it back. You *do* have hot guys here. At least one or two."

"Please tell me the howler wasn't Justin Wicked. He's the biggest flirt around."

Their friend Justin was not only a flirt, but he was also a talented artist, co-owner of a stone distribution company, and a member of the Cape Cod chapter of the Dark Knights motorcycle club. He was protective over his friends in the same way the Dark Knights in Tegan's hometown were protective of their community.

"For the record, Justin is gorgeous," Tegan said. "But it wasn't him."

"A hot, unidentified howler? I love it!"

"I wasn't ogling the howler." Tegan wiped the rain from her face, still staring out at the road. "This guy looked like he dined on fine wine and caviar. But I could tell that he *knew* he was hot, which makes him good for only *one* thing."

"A night of awesome sex and then *see you later, alligator?*" Chloe asked.

"No." She rounded her shoulders against the cold and said, "He's the kind of guy that would probably check himself out in the mirror the whole time. I hate guys like that. This guy was only good for fantasies. *Dark, dirty* fantasies where he's the man I *want* him to be, not the arrogant jerk he probably is." She turned back to the pump and read the display. "Are you freaking kidding me? The stupid thing says *Card Error. See Attendant.*"

"It's an adventure, remember? Think positive. Maybe the attendant will be hot and single," Chloe said.

"There has to be a better go-to than hot guys," Tegan said. It had been a long time since she'd met a guy she wanted to date, much less sleep with.

"*Two* hot guys?"

Tegan pulled her coat tighter around her and said, "Only if they're bringing ice cream and pizza."

"You're no fun."

"I'm all kinds of fun. Like right now. I'm going to brave the monsoon to see the attendant so he can restart the stupid pump. I'll call you later."

"Don't forget the bachelorette party Saturday night! The theme is *the hotter the better!* So go full-on superslut!"

"I cannot wait! I have the perfect outfit for that."

After ending the call, she shoved the phone in her pocket, wrestled her wet hood back on, and held it there as she ran into the building. She wiped the rain from her face as she made her way to the counter.

The guy behind the counter lifted kind eyes from the magazine he was reading and said, "It's nasty out there, huh?"

"It is." She waved her card and said, "The pump won't take my card."

"This is your lucky day. Your gas is already paid for."

"Excuse me?" She must have heard him wrong.

"A guy who was in here earlier gave me a hundred bucks and said to fill up the tank for the next person who came in and to keep the change. You were pulling into the pump at the time, so you're the lucky winner."

"Really? He paid it forward—that's awesome." Tegan was a big believer in paying it forward, and she tried to do things for others as often as possible. But she'd never been the recipient of a true pay-it-forward effort. It felt as good as being the one who did it. "Well, that sure makes today a lot brighter."

She ran back to her car, thinking about the two men she'd seen leaving the building, immediately writing off the self-absorbed hottie. As she pumped her gas, she didn't think about the wind and rain or her icicle fingers. She was too busy wondering how to find her soul mate—the howler who had driven away in the pickup truck.

Chapter Two

TEGAN FELL IN love with the upbeat atmosphere of the Sundial Café the moment she arrived. Mint-green walls boasted autographed paintings by local artists, cool sundials made of wood, stone, and metal, and dozens of crayon drawings stuck to the walls with pieces of Scotch Tape. The dark hardwood floors were as marred and scuffed as the wooden tables, none of which matched and all of which were currently taken. Tegan sat at the counter on a red velvet-cushioned barstool, poring over her notes for the amphitheater. Her hair was soaked, and she probably looked like a drowned rat, but she didn't care. This was exactly what she'd needed: a warm cup of hot chocolate and a place that felt *alive*. Their no-cell-phone rule was an unexpected bonus. She'd have no distractions beyond the adorable sounds of seven-year-old Joni Remington chatting with customers, which was more of a joy than a distraction. Every few minutes Joni popped over to check out what Tegan was working on. Joni's father, Rowan, an insanely tall, shaggy-haired guy with a bohemian vibe, ran the café. In the first five minutes Tegan was there, he and Joni had introduced themselves and given her the lowdown on the area. Everyone in the café was talking about the chance of a nor'easter or a hurricane. Tegan couldn't imagine it getting any worse than it already was.

"Here you go, sugar." Rowan set the grilled cheese sandwich she'd ordered on the counter.

"Thanks." Tegan had noticed that Rowan called everyone *sugar*. He had soulful eyes and an easy demeanor, which reminded her of her late uncle.

"Joni would approve of your lunch. She loves grilled cheese."

Tegan took a bite of the sandwich and glanced at Joni, sitting at a table chatting with a young couple. She was wearing a blue sweater with a fuzzy pink bear in the center, a yellow skirt over blue leggings, a purple tutu, and gray-and-pink leg warmers with pink ruffles at the bottom. On her head she wore a blue knit hat with big owl eyes on the front and flaps that covered her ears. Joni had told Tegan the hat was her *hootie*.

She turned back to Rowan and said, "Joni's great. She seems to know *everyone*."

"My daughter has a knack for meeting people. She got that from her mother." He wiped down the counter and said, "As you've probably noticed, most folks around here don't keep their businesses open in the off season for the few customers who venture out in this weather, but I like knowing people have a place to go."

"You own the café?"

"Yes, but I only work in it during the winter and early spring. I run a food truck in the warmer months. Besides, when school is canceled, it's good for Joni to be around people instead of locked in a house with her old man all day."

"Sounds like you're a good dad. I'm glad you're open. The place is packed, so you must do well."

"We are remarkably busy today, but this isn't typical for this time of year. We usually see only a handful of customers all week. I think people are going stir crazy with all this rain. But winters and early spring can be lonely around here. I'm glad to keep it open for those who need a place to hang out." He ran his eyes over her wet hair and said, "Or dry out."

"I appreciate it. My house was far too quiet to get anything done. Does your wife work here, too?"

He glanced at Joni and said, "We lost Joni's mom to breast cancer a few years ago, but she wasn't my wife. She didn't believe in marriage."

"Oh." Sadness washed through her. "I'm sorry for your loss."

"Me too. Carlo—Carlotta—was the love of my life, and an incredible person. Joni and I do our best to keep her memory alive. Joni inherited Carlo's flair for outlandish clothing."

"I like her outfit." Tegan ate another bite of the grilled cheese and said, "Tutus are the *bomb*."

Rowan chuckled.

"Hey, Row?" A man waved him over from the other end of the counter.

"I'll let you get back to work." His gaze coasted over the plethora of notebooks and sticky notes littering the counter, and then he went to help the other customer.

Tegan nibbled on a piece of her sandwich as she surveyed her notes. Her uncle's amphitheater hosted local children's theater groups throughout the summer. When Tegan had inherited the business, she'd had no idea there were so many things that went along with keeping it afloat. She'd assumed theater groups called to schedule the amphitheater and all she had to do was book them. But that was just a small piece of what it took to run the programs. Luckily, the children's programs booked a year in advance and were already scheduled for this summer, leaving her mostly administrative work to wrap her arms around for that end of the business. But she and Harper were bringing a new aspect to the theater—episodic theater for adults. They were holding a *soft launch* of the program in late summer: one three-episode series, which would run for three nights each week, for the month of August. Harper was writing the plays and handling the productions, and Tegan was handling the marketing, website, and administration.

The bell above the door chimed, and Joni's cheerful voice rang out. "We have a no-cell-phone rule, peanut butter cup."

Tegan grinned. Joni called everyone by silly names and made up even sillier stories. She had already called Tegan *Tinker Bell*, *banana split*, and *brownie bite*, and when Tegan complimented her ruffled leggings, Joni said she'd gotten them from a gorilla at the park.

Tegan glanced over her shoulder, and her eyes connected with the sharp blue eyes of the trench-coat-wearing winker from the gas station. He raked a hand through his wet hair, pulling it back from his face like a Dolce & Gabbana model. It made his sharp jawline and aquiline nose appear even more striking. That arrogant smile he'd flashed earlier reappeared, sending heat rushing up Tegan's chest despite the warning flags waving in her head.

Joni had impeccable taste.

The guy was definitely as tempting as a peanut butter cup. The extra-large kind that required two hands to eat.

The man patted Joni on the head and strode to the counter, eyes locked on Tegan, cell phone still firmly pressed to his ear.

His piercing stare intensified the heat flaring inside her. She turned back to her work and stuffed a piece of grilled cheese into her mouth. She was not one of those women who lusted after assholes. The *howler* was more her type, happy and outgoing.

Winker stepped beside her, and she forced herself not to glance over despite the delicious scent of expensive cologne and the rugged outdoors wafting off him.

"The kid's got five mill to put in the game. We've got ten times that," he said with a bite of frustration. "We'll get the deal. The kid's just got stars in his eyes. Get the team on due diligence. You know the drill. And for crying out loud, shut down that magazine. I don't want to hear about it again."

Rowan approached with an annoyed look on his face. He stopped across from the guy and said, "Sorry, sir, but we've got a no-cell-phone policy."

Now Tegan couldn't resist stealing a glance to see his reaction.

The guy was rubbing his forehead. He held up his index finger to Rowan, speaking into his phone. "Put the meeting off until I'm in the office next week." He made a half-scoff, half-laughing sound and said, "Not in this lifetime."

Rowan arched a brow at Tegan like, *Get a load of this guy.*

Joni climbed onto the stool beside her. The fringe of her light brown hair stuck out from beneath her hat, framing her pretty little face as she said, "I told *Rude Dude* no phones."

Rowan nodded his approval. "Attagirl, Jojo."

"T, I've got to run," the guy said. He ended the call and set his phone on the counter. Then he splayed his hands in Rowan's direction and said, "Sorry, man. You know how it is. Work never ends. So, how about a cup of dark roast?" He shrugged off his coat as he turned to look around, shaking water on Tegan's notes. "Where can I hang this?"

"Hey!" Tegan grabbed a napkin, dabbing furiously at her papers.

"Damn. Sorry." He grabbed a handful of napkins from a holder on the counter and wiped it over her sticky notes, tearing them from their place on the counter and smearing the ink.

She slapped her hand over his and said, "*Stop*. I've got it."

He held his hands up in surrender. "Sorry, but maybe you should take whatever this is to an office."

"What are you, the counter police?"

JETT BIT BACK a curse, wondering if today could get any shittier. Between delayed flights and learning that one of the owners of Carlisle Enterprises was playing hardball, he was ready to lose his mind. Looking like a jerk to the woman whose animated behavior and sunny smile had seared itself into his memory when he'd first seen her was like a nail in his coffin.

The guy behind the counter set a coffee mug and a menu in front of him, his protective gaze moving between the adorable little girl and the feisty blonde who was frantically trying to rearrange her sticky notes. Jett wondered if they were his wife and daughter.

Great. In addition to sounding like a prick, he had been checking out the guy's wife—here *and* at the gas station. If that didn't scream *asshole*, he didn't know what did.

"I'm sorry," Jett repeated. "I've been traveling all day in that mess out there, I'm on the verge of closing a huge business deal that has hit a few snags, and I took it out on the wrong people." He glanced at the little girl with the owl hat and said, "I'm sorry, princess. I should have gotten right off the phone when you told me." He looked at the guy behind the counter and said, "I didn't mean to disregard your rules. I'm not really a jerk. Well, not that much of a jerk, anyway."

"That's okay, man. I'm Rowan." He extended his hand, and Jett shook it.

"Jett," he said. "It's nice to meet you."

Rowan nodded in the direction of the little girl and said, "Joni's my daughter. She's the captain of this ship. You'd be smart to listen to her."

"I will be sure to listen to Joni from now on."

"Listening is important!" Joni exclaimed. "It says you *care*." She bounced off her seat and pointed toward a row of hooks on the wall. "Your coat goes there, Inspector Gadget."

Jett chuckled and turned to thank her, but she'd already skipped off to sit at a table with an older woman. He hung up his coat and went back to the counter, admiring the blonde as he approached. Rowan was a lucky man. She was truly beautiful, with high cheekbones, a slim, straight nose, an insanely sexy mouth, and a long, graceful neck. She wore an oversized gray sweater and jeans tucked into knee-high forest-green rain boots. Her hair was damp, and though it looked dark brown, he'd noticed several shades of blond whipping around her smiling face at the gas station.

"I'm sorry about your notes," he said as he sat beside her, noticing that she'd cleared the counter in front of his seat. "And the office comment. It's been a day…"

"It's my own fault. I shouldn't have spread out so much." She picked up what was left of a grilled cheese sandwich.

"I could have been more careful, and more tactful. I'm really not an asshole."

Her big blue eyes sailed appraisingly over him as she ate the last of her sandwich. Jett was used to women checking him out, but this chick did *not* look interested. And why would she if she was married to the hippie dude behind the counter?

"I'm going to give you the benefit of the doubt," she finally said. "I think I know what your problem is. You need to loosen up." She reached over and tugged at his tie, loosening it. "And this definitely has got to go." She pushed his suit coat off his shoulders, tugging it down his arms.

He took it off and laid it on the counter, amused by the aggressive stunner. He glanced at Rowan, to make sure he knew he wasn't trying to flirt with his wife, and said, "Are you always this pushy?"

"Pretty much. I can usually tell if someone is trustworthy within minutes of meeting them, but I hate trying to talk *past* things to figure that out. You're so *buttoned up*, it's hard to tell if it's a costume or if it's who you really are. You should take the tie off and unbutton that choker of a shirt. You'd probably feel less stressed."

"My clothes don't make me stressed. And I assure you, I really am an Armani guy."

Her lips tipped up, and she said, "Maybe so. But *Armani* through and through? Or perhaps you're Armani when it suits you and something else the rest of the time?"

He caught sight of Rowan in his peripheral vision and said, "Do you scrutinize your husband this closely, too?"

"I don't have a husband, but if I had one and he acted like he had a stick up his butt, I would."

Feisty. He liked that. "I assure you, I don't have a stick up my butt. I've just got a lot going on right now." *Like figuring out if you're Rowan's girlfriend.*

She cocked her head, a shimmer of seduction sparking in her eyes. "That's a shame. A guy who dresses like you should be able to handle just about anything. Guess it's more of a costume, then?"

She was *good*. He wondered if she harnessed all that sass and let it loose in the bedroom, too, or if she was one of those women who knew how to rile a guy up but had zero follow-through.

Why the hell was he even thinking about that when she was probably Rowan's girlfriend?

He took a sip of his coffee to distract himself from the lust simmering inside him and said, "I never said I couldn't handle it. I've got a lot at stake right now."

She rolled her eyes, turning back to her notes, and said, "Don't we all?"

"What is all this that I almost ruined, anyway? Are you planning world domination? Revenge on an ex? Redefining the meaning of life?"

"Something like that." She rearranged a few sticky notes and said, "I'm creating a plan of attack for a business I inherited."

"A *plan of attack*. Is that anything like a business plan?" He scanned the sticky notes and notebooks, on which snippets of information were written. *Community theater group meetings? More word of mouth? Taxes? Schedules?*

"Yes, exactly."

Rowan sauntered over, eyeing them curiously. "Everything okay here?"

"Yes," she said. "The sandwich was delicious, thank you."

"Anytime, sugar." Rowan cleared her empty plate and walked away.

Sugar? *Girlfriend*, he deduced. "Have you *run* a business

before?" Jett asked.

She turned keen eyes on him, sitting up straighter as she said, "For your information, I run *two* businesses, and I'm quite good at it."

"I don't doubt that." Nothing was sexier than confidence, except maybe the combination of confidence and sass, which she had in droves. "You strike me as the type of woman who determines what she wants and goes after it with everything she has."

"I *am*." Heat sparked in her eyes again, and it felt like a challenge.

A very enticing challenge, though she could be playing him to get her man's attention. He hated chicks who did that. Giving her the benefit of the doubt, he took the bait and said, "What kind of businesses are you involved in?"

"I do photo editing, and I make children's costumes. I'm also a nip-and-tuck girl for a clothing shop in Maryland, which I had to give up while I'm here, but I'll return to it in the fall."

He had no idea what a nip-and-tuck girl was, but that didn't stop lewd innuendos about *nipping* and *tucking* from forming in his mind. He held them back and processed her response. If she was here only temporarily, maybe she wasn't Rowan's girlfriend after all. "What about the photo editing and costume making? Are those things you're doing while you're here, or are they on hold as well?"

"I can do those anywhere, so I'll continue doing them while I get up to speed with the business."

"You're very industrious."

"I don't like to be bored at work." Her voice turned low and seductive as she said, "Or *anywhere* else."

"That's something else we have in common."

"Else?"

He wanted to say they both knew something was brewing between them, but he held back just in case she *was* Rowan's better half and said, "We're both business owners."

Her lips curved up and she said, "What business are you in?"

"The business of making money." He glanced at her notes and said, "But if those notes are your idea of a business plan, then you've got bigger problems than a little smeared ink."

"Looks like I was wrong." Her eyes narrowed. "It wasn't the buttoned-up shirt or the tie choking out the kindness in your brain. You just aren't very tactful, are you?"

"The woman who practically undressed me has an issue with directness?" He grinned.

"I...*No.*"

"Good." He leaned closer and said, "Then tell me, are you and Rowan a couple, or are you single?"

Her brows lifted. "Me and *Rowan*? I just met him and Joni today."

"He seemed protective of you. I assumed you were together."

He knew better than to assume anything. He was a shrewd businessman who had built an empire taking over multimillion-dollar corporations and teaching starry-eyed business owners how to exceed their biggest dreams. He could negotiate circles around the toughest competitors, and yet this petite, sharp-witted, blond-haired beauty had thrown him off his game?

That was damn *refreshing.*

She gathered her things into a messy pile and said, "I think Rowan is just a nice guy who doesn't like people coming into his café, ignoring his daughter, and acting like they rule the roost."

"*Ouch.* Epic fail on my first impression."

"*Second* impression," she said lightly as she stuffed the notebooks and the pile of sticky notes into a messenger bag.

Strike two. She was right.

But he wasn't ready for their conversation to end. Hoping to score a little more time with her, he said, "Let me make it up to you. I can help you with your business plan if you'd like."

She ran an assessing eye over him as she pushed from her chair and fished money out of her bag. "I'm pretty sure I can handle it. But thank you for offering." She tossed the money on the counter next to her bag and walked away like she was on a mission. Her sexy hips swayed temptingly as she made her way to the hooks on the wall and snagged her bright yellow-and-white raincoat.

As she put it on, Joni raced across the café and said, "Where are you going, jelly bean?"

"Home, hootie girl."

Joni wrapped her arms around the blonde's legs, and Jett realized he'd been so taken with her, he'd forgotten to ask her name. She hugged Joni, and then she crouched before her, her whole face brightening as she said, "Maybe I'll see you here again sometime."

"I hope so! Will you bring the princess drawings you told me about? And can you make me a costume? I like mermaids, but I want wings on it, like a bird, and fur, like a lion."

"That sounds magnificent! I can try to make it, but it'll take some time."

"We got time!" Joni threw her arms around the blonde's neck and said, "Don't let the hurricane get you."

"Hurricane, shmurricane," the blonde said with a wave of

her hand. She pushed to her feet and said, "It can't get much worse than it has been all day. See you soon, raccoon."

"After a while, monkey butt!" Joni said as she ran behind the counter to her father, who scooped her up and kissed her cheek.

Joni was damn cute, but the woman heading his way in full rain gear, hood up, was even cuter, and sexy as *fuck*. He stood as she returned for her bag. He was used to getting lost in deals and negotiations, but he couldn't remember the last time a woman had held his attention beyond business or a quick and greedy tryst. Most women flirted with him like they'd never get another chance and would have made excuses for their drenched appearance, as if they could gain his interest if he'd seen them when it was sunny out. But this feisty woman hadn't fluttered her lashes, giggled, or made an excuse for a damn thing, much less her gorgeous, albeit drenched, appearance, and he freaking loved that about her.

"Would you like me to get your car and bring it around so you don't get soaked?" he offered.

"I won't melt," she said as she hoisted the messenger bag from the counter. It slipped from her hand, dropping to the floor and spilling its contents at his feet.

She crouched to collect them with a groan, and he bent beside her, gathering piles of sticky notes and helping her put them in her bag.

"Thank you. I'm such a klutz," she said, exasperated.

"Accidents happen."

Her gaze softened. "What did you say your name was?"

"*Armani*, when it suits me," he said coyly as they rose to their feet. "And yours?"

"Miss *Fine*," she said flirtatiously. Then she spun on her

heel and headed for the door.

"Damn right you are," he called after her, chuckling.

She looked over her shoulder, and when her baby blues hit his, another jolt of electricity arced between them. She winked, and in the next breath she was out the door, struggling against the wind and rain to keep her hood on as she darted into the parking lot. He could go after her, but he was in town for only two nights, and he had to deal with the Carlisle issues. The last thing he needed was a distraction. Besides, in his experience most women didn't live up to the impressions they gave.

But there was no denying that Miss Fine was an alluring little bird with the keenness of an eagle and the femininity of a dove.

Holy shit. Birds? He was losing it.

He sat on the stool and peered into his coffee cup, wondering if there was some hippie shit in there that had stolen his manliness and turned it into touchy-feely nonsense.

Chapter Three

JETT WAS STILL thinking about the blonde when he parked in front of the office of Bayside Resort in Wellfleet, the beachfront property his younger brother, Dean, co-owned with their buddies Rick and Drake Savage. They'd all grown up together in Hyannis, along with Jett's older brother, Doug, a physician working overseas, and Rick and Drake's sister, Mira, who was now married with two children and had recently moved closer to her son's school. Most of Jett's childhood friends were still living on the Cape, but the day he'd left to attend college, he'd known he'd never move back.

He cut the engine and gazed out at the driving rain. Winter had left a skeleton of the Cape behind for spring foliage to eventually nurture back to life. But instead of seeing the dismal sky and desolation of a land ravaged by weather, he saw images of the feisty blonde pushing off his suit coat and loosening his tie with a curiously sexy look in her eyes. He sank back in the driver's seat, in no hurry to push those images away. But he needn't have worried, because more visions rolled in. Like a movie playing in reverse, he saw her hair whipping across her face as she wrestled with her hood at the gas station as she peered around the gas pump, smiling at him like he was the best thing she'd seen all year.

And he'd never fucking see her again, which was probably for the best, but hell if it didn't leave him with a dull ache in his gut.

He grabbed the gift bag for his friend Daphne's daughter from the passenger seat and tucked it beneath his coat before stepping out of the SUV and climbing the porch steps to the office. He raked a hand through his hair and headed inside quickly to keep the cold from infiltrating the cozy space. As he closed the door, two-and-a-half-year-old Hadley toddled over carrying a stuffed bird in a nest. Her fine brown hair was pulled back with a pink barrette, which matched her pink hoodie with white letters across the front that read MAMA'S LITTLE TROUBLEMAKER.

She stared stoically up at Jett with her adorably chubby cheeks, lifted the nest in two hands, and said, "My bird!"

Jett had never known such a serious child. He heard Daphne, the curvaceous blonde who ran the office for the resort, talking with someone in the stockroom. She and Hadley lived in the apartment above the office. Dean had told Jett about Hadley's new favorite toy, and he'd come prepared. He crouched before her and said, "Hey there, pretty girl. What's your bird's name?"

"*Bird*," she said flatly, brows knitted.

"Do you think she'd like a few friends?"

Hadley nodded, watching intently as he withdrew the gift bag from beneath his coat and said, "This is for you."

"Hold bird!" She thrust the nest toward him.

He chuckled as they exchanged the nest for the gift bag. She plopped down on her bottom and shoved her grabby little hands into the bag, taking out the peekaboo fabric birdhouse and four stuffed birds. Even as she played, her brows remained knitted, and her lips pursed, like a discerning adult.

Daphne poked her head out of the stockroom and her eyes widened. "*Jett*," she said softly. She touched the ends of her long blond hair, and her eyes darted to her daughter, who was playing happily with her new toys.

Daphne was always a little flustered around him, which he found endearing. She was a beautiful, smart young woman, but she was also sweet as sugar and she had an amazing daughter, both of which made her the *wrong* person for Jett.

Cool quasi uncle he could handle. *Stepdad*, not so much.

He'd never had a great role model in that department. Jett's father hadn't been the easiest man to be around for most of Jett's life. He'd gone through cycles of being an attentive father and then an arrogant, self-centered prick. And though he'd been on the good side of that for the last couple of years, Jett didn't trust him to remain that way. While his brothers had made amends with their father, Jett and his dad were still trying to find their new normal. Things were cordial but not warm. He knew they might never be on solid ground again, but at least they were trying.

"Hey, Daph," he said, rising to his feet. "You look great."

She blushed. "Thank you. You didn't have to bring Hadley a gift."

Jett didn't know the circumstances behind Daphne's divorce, but he knew it must have been bad since Daphne had not only walked away from her marriage but had also left the *state* and moved back to her hometown. Daphne was a great mother, and she and Hadley deserved a man who would appreciate and protect their tender hearts. Someone who would love them forever and hopefully wash away any of the hurt Hadley's absent father had left in his wake. While Jett wasn't that man, he loved them like family. Did he have to bring a gift for Hadley? No. But he wanted to make sure that little girl knew that all men didn't suck.

"Yes he did!" The familiar voice came from behind Daphne seconds before Dean's wife, Emery, ran past Daphne and threw her arms around Jett.

"How's it going, spitfire?" Jett loved Emery. She adored his brother and she was good for him, but he had special admiration for the energetic brunette because she was the reason their father had begun trying to change his ways. Emery was a yoga-back-care specialist and she taught yoga next door at Summer House Inn, which was owned by Rick's wife, Desiree, and her sister, Violet. Their father had been less than accepting of her, believing his son could make more of his life without her by his side. One night he'd pushed too far, and Emery had lost her cool, telling their father exactly what she'd thought of the way he treated people—especially his family. She'd forced him to take a good, hard look at who he had become.

Emery stepped back and put her hands on her hips, looking Jett up and down, and said, "Gosh, I've missed your ugly mug. I'm so glad you're here!"

"I've missed you, too." Jett took off his coat and tossed it on a chair on his way to Daphne. "Get in here and give me a hug." He embraced her and said, "Good to see you and the little one, sweetheart."

Hadley scooped up her birds and pushed to her feet, toddling over to Daphne. "Birds!" she exclaimed. "*My* birds!"

"I see that." Daphne ran her fingers over Hadley's head. "Did you say thank you?"

Hadley turned around, arms full of birds, and said, "Thank

you *birds!*"

"You're welcome, Had," Jett said as she plopped down on her bottom to play.

Rick's office door opened, and Dean and Rick stepped out.

"We thought we heard you out here. Good to see you, buddy." Rick opened his arms to embrace Jett.

"You, too. How's Desiree feeling?" Jett asked.

Pride shone in Rick's eyes. "She's doing great. Due in July. Thankfully the morning sickness has subsided."

"And her breakfasts are even *better* when she's pregnant," Emery added.

Desiree made breakfast for all their friends during the warmer months, and from time to time in the winter and early spring. There was a running joke about her cooking being reflective of her and Rick's sex life.

"Glad to hear it." Jett shifted his focus to Dean and couldn't keep from rattling his brother's chain. "Hey, bro. I got a nice *long* squeeze from your beautiful wife."

Dean narrowed his eyes. They were both over six feet tall and athletic with blue eyes, but that was about as far as their similarities went. Jett was fit but not *ripped*. He spent too many hours traveling and confined to offices to be a thick-bodied powerhouse like Dean, who worked with his hands creating incredible landscapes and hardscapes. While Jett had their father's dark hair, Dean was fair-haired like their mother, and his thick beard gave him an even more imposing, Viking-like appearance.

"Keep your filthy hands off my wife," Dean said stern and low, his eyes darting to Hadley, who was completely absorbed in her toys. "What happened? You pop all of your blow-up dolls?"

"I've got dolls who *blow*, and I've *popped* a good number of them, but none quite as fine as that wife of yours," Jett teased, but his mind reeled back to Miss Fine. Why was he *still* thinking about her? The hell with it. Here for only two nights or not, he'd been an idiot not to pursue her.

Dean chuckled, his eyes shooting straight to Emery, who was beaming. He winked at her, then set a serious stare on Jett and said, "Don't make me kill you in front of our friends, man. It's bad mojo." He hauled Jett into a manly embrace and said, "Missed you, bro."

"You, too," Jett said. "But I've got to tell you, your wife is far more squeezable than you are."

Dean crushed him tighter against his chest.

"*Dick*," Jett choked out under his breath.

Dean tossed him away with a hearty laugh and reached for Emery.

"Does Jett look *different* to you?" Emery asked.

Dean looked him up and down. "Nope. Same old ugly bastard as always."

"I think he looks different," Daphne said. "There's a light in your eyes or something."

"I've had a strange day." *And that light is caused by a spunky, smart-mouthed blonde who was making a business plan on sticky notes.*

"From that smirk on your face, I'm not so sure I want to hear the details," Rick said.

"No, man. It's not like that," Jett said. "I just…" *Can't stop thinking about this woman.* He grasped for a subject change. "Where's Drake?"

"He and Serena went to check on the music store, in case the storm gets worse," Rick said.

"I just heard the weather report on the way here," Jett said. "The worst of it isn't expected until midweek."

Rick sat on the couch and said, "You know Drake, always overprepared. I was surprised to hear you were coming for the bachelor party, given the weather. You know Gavin's wedding isn't for two weeks, right?" Their buddy Gavin Wheeler was an interior designer, and he was business partners with Drake's wife, Serena.

"Are you staying until the wedding?" Dean asked. "Mom and Dad must be psyched."

"No. Sorry, Dean. I'm leaving Sunday morning. But since you eloped and ripped me off of the pleasure of throwing you a bachelor party, and our straitlaced older brother didn't want one, I don't have many chances left to enjoy bachelor-party debauchery."

"Gavin's not exactly the debauchery type," Daphne said a little sheepishly. "Something tells me you're not, either, Jett."

Hadley pushed to her feet and held a red cloth bird out for Jett. "Dett. *Bird!*"

"Thanks, baby girl." He took the bird and leaned down to say, "Can Uncle Jett get a smile?"

Hadley closed her mouth, giving him a deadpan look that made everyone else crack up.

"Aw, come on. You're giving me a bad rep." Jett swooped her up and lifted her over his head, earning a huge toothy grin and a sweet giggle. "Attagirl," he said as he lowered her to his hip and kissed the top of her head. "I feel like Superman, getting Hadley to smile."

"She's my *man meter*," Daphne said. "She smiles for you, which is why I'm not buying the whole debauchery thing. You just haven't found the right woman yet."

Hadley tried to wiggle free, and Jett set her on the floor. She snatched the bird from his hands with a tiny scowl and stomped back to the rest of her toys.

"I think your man meter is off, Daph," Rick said. "This guy's not ever going to settle down. But, Jett, you're barking up the wrong tree if you're looking for a debauchery-filled party. I'm sure most women around here are hunkering down with a good book in front of a warm fire like Des is."

"I know I am," Emery said. "Except for Harper's bachelorette party, of course."

"Me too," Daphne added.

Jett wasn't really interested in debauchery, unless the blonde from the café was involved, but he *had* heard that the party was going to be wild. "The bachelor party is at the Salty Hog. I heard it was going to be packed."

"Packed with *bikers*, not single women," Emery chimed in. "You grew up here. You know the Dark Knights hang out at the Salty Hog."

He might have grown up there, but he hadn't been to the Salty Hog in years.

"Maybe my brother is into big, hairy bikers," Dean teased, earning laughs from everyone.

Jett ignored the barb and sat on the edge of Daphne's desk thinking about the blonde from the café, who he was fairly certain would *not* be at the Salty Hog. He wondered how he could run into her again. She was a gorgeous single woman. Surely she'd be doing something fun on a Friday night besides reading. "What's open around here tonight?"

"*Nothing*," Emery said. "Colton is opening Undercover for Harper's bachelorette party tomorrow night. There will be plenty of women there, but no guys allowed. Sorry, Jett."

Colton was Harper's brother and he owned Undercover, a nightclub in Truro.

He might just have to make another visit to the café tomorrow. Maybe she'd make that place a habit.

"Jett, let's get your stuff over to the house." Dean snickered and said, "We got you noise-canceling headphones, so you can sleep this time."

"That won't be necessary." Jett pushed from the desk. "I learned my lesson when you and Em kept me up all night over the holidays. Daph's got me covered, right, babe?"

"I sure do." Daphne went to her desk and took out a set of keys, dangling them from her finger. "Cottage number seven."

"Seriously? You're not staying with us?" Dean asked.

Jett snagged the keys. "Thank you, Daph, and *yes*, seriously. You don't need a third wheel. Besides, I've got work to do while I'm here."

Daphne picked up Hadley and said, "I'm going to run my big girl upstairs for a try at the potty. It's great to see you, Jett. I'll see you at the wedding?"

"Definitely." He held up the keys and said, "Thanks for having my back."

"Jett, you know we love when you stay with us, and we really did put noise-canceling headphones on the guest bed. *Just in case.* I'll leave you boys alone to figure things out." Emery went up on her toes and kissed Dean, and then she headed up the steps to Daphne's apartment.

Rick grabbed his coat from the closet. "I'm heading to the inn to see Des. See you tomorrow night at the party."

After Rick left, Dean crossed his arms and lowered his chin, staring at Jett. "You know our family wants more time with you, not less, right?"

"Of course I know that, and at some point I'll make more time. But I'm knee-deep in preparations to acquire Carlisle Enterprises, which will be a profit *machine* once I get my hands on it, and I've got *Fortune* magazine breathing down my neck to do a feature on rich guys who give back, or some shit like that." He'd been featured in *Forbes* magazine a few years ago as one of five entrepreneurs who made it big paying it forward.

"Tough life," Dean teased.

"Hey, I didn't ask to be featured."

"Let me guess, you're trying to get out of it."

Jett clapped a hand on Dean's shoulder and said, "You do know me well, little brother. It's all bullshit. Let them give it to the guys who live for that stuff, like the kid. One day he'll be on there. I'm sure of it. The little starry-eyed bastard is going up against me for Carlisle."

When Jett first went into business, one of his favorite professors had asked him to take a graduating student under his wings and show him the ropes. Jett had enjoyed mentoring so much, he'd accepted several mentees since, and was currently mentoring a bright young man named Jonas Cross. But none of the people Jett had mentored had the arrogance, confidence, and skill that Zack Kingsley, aka *the kid*, possessed. Jett had mentored Zack for two years and Zack had been out on his own now for three. He was doing well, and Jett was proud of him. They kept in touch, and they had a fun, though competitive, relationship. Carlisle Enterprises would put Zack on the map, but he didn't stand a chance with Jett in the game.

"You always said the kid had brass balls," Dean said. "You know you deserve to be in that magazine."

"I'm perfectly happy staying in the shadows." What Dean didn't realize was that even with all that Jett did for others, it could never make up for the ways in which he'd failed his own family. Most of all Dean, who had been picking up the slack with their family when Jett was unable to make it home for family functions ever since Jett left for college. But Jett wasn't about to get into all that now, so he changed the subject. "How are things here? Business still good?"

"Business is great." Dean's expression turned serious and he said, "I thought you said you were working on things with Dad."

"Christ, Dean. Do you ever give that shit a break? I am working on it. I talk to him at least once a month. The fences are mending, but we're both busy."

"I get that, but one of you has to *give*. You can't fix things if you're not here, and Mom and Dad aren't getting any younger."

Always the peacemaker.

Dean hadn't just picked up the slack for Jett. Doug had already been away at school when Jett had left for college. With both of his brothers gone, and Jett barely speaking to their father, Dean had taken it upon himself to remain on the Cape to make sure their parents were okay and, more specifically, that their mother didn't feel abandoned. He made a point of attending events for the foundation their grandfather had started, in which their father was heavily involved, and he was always there when they needed him.

Jett pushed to his feet and grabbed his coat. "I appreciate your concern, and I owe you years of gratitude for picking up the slack for me. But it's not your job to make up for my shortcomings anymore. Dad and I are going to get through this at our own pace."

"Your own pace. I know what that means. If it's business related, you're in for the long haul, but when it comes to personal relationships, you're like a bad one-night stand—in and out before breakfast."

Chapter Four

"S.L.U.T." BLARED OVER the loudspeakers at Harper's bachelorette party Saturday night. Harper's sister, Jana, and sister-in-law, Cree, had done a great job throwing the party together. A black banner with gold letters that read SAME PENIS FOREVER hung over the bar. Pink helium balloons with LET'S PARTY BITCHES printed on them in black bobbed around the ceiling and danced from strings tied to chairs. A bra pong game hung on a wall by the dance floor—bras in several colors were hooked to a board, ready for the girls to toss Ping-Pong balls into them. Harper had refused to allow strippers, so Jana brought in life-size cardboard cutouts of scantily clad males and scattered them around the dance floor. She also gave each of the girls a pink-black-and-white eye mask with a cute tag in the middle. Harper's tag read HOT BRIDE, while the others said things like SEXY MAMA, NAUGHTY ONE, BADASS BABE, DIRTY TEASE, SINGLE SLUT, and WILD THING. Tegan had no idea what her tag said, because Jana wouldn't let them look at their own masks, and she warned them not to tell each other or there would be repercussions. Jana was as tough as she was beautiful, and Tegan was not about to go head-to-head with her. Desiree and Emery had made penis-shaped cookies. Much to Desiree's embarrassment, Violet, who was as dark and brazen as Desiree was blond and sweet, had added white frosting dribbled down the front of the cookies like semen.

Chloe hadn't been kidding about the theme of the party being the hotter the better. Thank goodness the bar was closed to the public, because they'd *all* gone full-on slut with their outfits. Tegan fit right in wearing the outfit she'd made last winter for a New Year's Eve party—a skintight, sleeveless gray velvet shorts jumpsuit with an open back and a plunging neckline that led all the way down to her navel. The gray choker and thigh-high peep-toed leather boots were the perfect accessories to ratchet up the slut factor.

"*Harper! Harper! Harper!*" Tegan chanted along with the other girls. They were doing blow job shots, a delicious mix of amaretto and Irish cream, topped with whipped cream, meant to be consumed *hands free*.

"Give me a second," Harper said, taking an exaggerated inhalation. She was decked out in a black lace shirt, unbuttoned to *below* her black bra, a black miniskirt, lace garters hooked to thigh-high stockings, and fuck-me heels. In addition to her BRIDE eye mask, she wore a sparkly plastic tiara and a white sash with BRIDE-TO-BE written in gold. "Okay, I'm ready!" She bent over the bar to pick up the shot with her mouth, her hands secured behind her back with fuzzy pink handcuffs, and her long blond hair tumbled forward, knocking off her tiara.

"Someone hold her hair!" Colton hollered from behind the bar, where he was dancing shirtless, his washboard abs and blue tattoos on display as he served them drinks.

Colton was gorgeous, with sharp features and spiky bleached-blond hair. He wore low-slung jeans, a black bow tie, and white cuffs around his wrists with penis-shaped cuff links. It was too bad he was wasting all that hotness on *them*, when he was into guys. But from the moment Tegan had met him last summer, it had been clear that Colton and his brother, Brock, would do anything for their sisters.

"I've got it!" Jana gathered Harper's hair in her hand. "This is payback for all the times you held mine when I puked as a teenager."

Harper looked at her and said, "Girl, you owe me *years* of this!"

Serena pulled out her phone and started videoing. "This is the moment of truth, my friends. Does Harper Garner soon-to-be Wheeler spit or swallow?"

"Of course she swallows," Colton said with a smirk. "It's one of the Garner *gifts*."

"Colton!" Harper scolded. "Do *not* make me laugh when I get this thing up to my mouth or I'll spit it out!"

"I hope you don't say that to Gavin," Violet said, smoothing her black halter minidress over her narrow hips. It had cutouts along the sides, revealing all her colorful tattoos.

Harper said, "Trust me, my man *never* makes me laugh when my mouth is down there." She sealed her lips over the rim of the shot glass.

Everyone chanted, "*Swallow! Swallow! Swallow!*"

Harper tossed her head back, downing the shot, and they all cheered.

Jana took the shot glass from Harper's mouth, then removed the handcuffs and said, "I'm borrowing these for tonight, sis."

"Like you don't already have your own?" Cree said. She had grown up with Tegan in Peaceful Harbor and had lived on the Cape for several years. She'd married Harper and Jana's brother

Brock over the holidays.

"One can never have too many handcuffs," Jana said. "Wait, does anyone *need* a pair?" She dangled the handcuffs from her fingers, offering them up.

Chloe shook her head. "I've got my own."

"Dean and I have *plenty* of toys," Emery said.

"Me too," Serena said. "*Several.*"

Jana waved the handcuffs at Desiree and Daphne, both of whom shook their heads, blushing furiously. "I'm not even going to ask Vi," Jana said. "I don't want to know what kind of dark shit you and Andre are into."

Desiree and Violet ran an adult-toy shop out of the back of their art gallery by the inn. When Tegan had come to the Cape for Cree's wedding, the girls had taken her on a tour of the impressive little shop. Tegan had been so busy wrapping up her life in Peaceful Harbor and preparing to come to the Cape, she hadn't had much time for dating. She'd bought a few toys from their shop to keep her company on long, lonely nights. Now that she had *Armani* to fantasize about, she just might put them to good use.

Violet grinned. "Dark, light, you name it, we probably do it."

"You're so *lucky*," Chloe said.

"Tegan? Handcuffs?" Jana offered.

Tegan wasn't into bondage, but a silk tie now and again with the right guy was a definite *yes*. "No thanks. I'm good."

"Steph?" Jana waggled her brows.

"To use those, I'd need a man," Steph said. "And there's no one promising on the horizon."

Tegan knew Steph from the book club. She was a poet and she ran an herbal shop in Brewster. She was always doing funky things to her brown hair, and tonight she had blue streaks in the front.

"No one promising?" Violet said loudly. "How about Dwayne?" Dwayne was Justin's cousin.

Steph rolled her eyes. "I've known Dwayne Wicked since I was a kid. Sometimes I help him with his dog rescue, but that's *it*. I'm *not* going there, thank you very much."

"Hey," Serena said. "I'm married to a guy I've known forever, and I can tell you it's the *best*!"

"Knowing a guy forever is not a reason not to date them," Violet added. "If not Dwayne, then how about Justin? Baz? Beckett? Zeke? Zander? Tank? Do I need to go on?"

Tegan tried to keep up. She'd met Justin and his brother Zander and Gavin's brother, Beckett, at Gavin's birthday party last year, but she had no idea who the others were.

"Do *not* set her up with Justin," Chloe said. "He's a total player."

"*All* those guys are yummy," Daphne said. "I'm not into bikers, like Justin or his brothers and cousins, but Gavin's brother, Beckett? *Delish*. And Jett?" She fanned her face. "He's *too much* man for me, but I do love to look at him."

"*Hello?* Single girl over here!" Tegan waved her hands. "You just rattled off a list of assumedly single guys, some of whom I've never met. I know Beckett, but he lives in Virginia, and Justin, who's hot, but I think Chloe's secretly wishing she could climb him like a tree—"

"Only if you duct tape his mouth shut," Chloe said.

Violet leaned over Chloe's shoulder and said, "Mouths are the second-best part of men."

"And *hands*," Tegan said. "I love big, strong hands." She'd noticed that *Armani* had big, manly hands, and last night she'd thought in great detail about all the things he could do with those strong hands *and* his sexy mouth.

"*Arms.* I love strong arms. Brock's are *perfect.*" Cree licked her lips and raised her brows.

"Can we *not* talk about body parts?" Daphne pleaded. "It's been a *really* long time for me."

"Aw, Daph. We're going to find you a man," Desiree promised.

"Who else is on the single-guy list?" Jana asked.

"Justin's brother Blaine and Dean's brother Jett!" Emery said.

"Blaine? Now, there's a tasty morsel. But Jett? He's technically single and definitely hot," Chloe said. "but totally married to his business."

"What I wouldn't give to be bent over my bar for that strappingly handsome man," Colton said, earning a wide-eyed look from Daphne.

"Is Jett *bi*?" Daphne asked.

"I wish," Colton said.

"You'd get a lot of women if you were bi," Daphne said more to herself than to Colton.

Colton patted Daphne's hand and said, "Baby cakes, I am straight-up gay. The scariest place I've ever been was in a vagina, and I got the hell out of there as fast as I could."

"Colton, you're here for *eye candy*, not *input*," Jana said. "Serve up another round of shots for us, please."

"Okay, bossy pants." Colton stepped away and said, "But for the record, I'd happily take *any* of those Wicked men for a ride."

Jana glowered at him.

As the girls talked about Justin's single brothers—Zeke,

Zander, and Blaine—and his single cousins—Tank, Baz, and Dwayne—Tegan's mind trailed back to the arrogant, handsome guy from the café. *Armani* had somehow managed to push her fantasy about her truck-driving, howling soul mate to the back burner.

"Justin and his brothers will be at the wedding," Harper said, bringing Tegan's mind back to their conversation.

"Let me ask you guys something. Have you ever met a guy and been totally turned off *and* turned on by him at the same time?" Tegan asked. "Is that even possible?"

"Babe, that's every man who walks on this earth," Colton said as he poured the liquor into the shot glasses.

"I agree. If they don't scare you in some way, they say weird shit," Violet said. "But if they were too much like us, we'd get bored."

"I've never been turned off by Gavin," Harper said proudly.

Jana gave her a deadpan look. "You're not married yet. Wait until he *Dutch ovens* you because he thinks it's funny. Hunter did that *once*, and he barely survived my wrath afterward."

"Gross!" Daphne said.

"What's a Dutch oven?" Desiree asked. "Is that code for something sexual? Rick's working hard to show me all the moves that go with the lingo, which is *so fun*." She whispered *so fun*. "But I don't know that one."

They all giggled as Violet explained the meaning to Desiree.

"That's disgusting!" Desiree exclaimed. "Rick would *never* do that."

"I didn't mean grossed out by him. I meant that he was a bit too arrogant. You know the type. Expensive suit, fancy car, assumptive," Tegan explained. "But he's funny, smart, and obviously sharp about business."

"Where did you meet him?" Serena asked.

Daphne squeezed closer to them. "I learn so much when you guys evaluate men. Does it matter where you meet?"

"It depends," Serena said. "A library says something very different than a bar, for example."

"Guys don't hang out at the library, trust me on that. I take Hadley there just about every week, and there are never any hot single guys."

"She didn't meet him at a library." Chloe looked at Tegan and said, "May I?"

Tegan had told Chloe all about *Armani* last night when they were comparing outfits for the party. Her leggy blond friend looked like a model in a little black dress that laced up the center, exposing *miles* of toned belly. She waved a hand of approval, giving Chloe the floor.

"Tegan saw him at a gas station, then talked with him at a café," Chloe explained. "There were definite fuck-me vibes going on between them. I told her she should have taken him home for the night, but she said she didn't need the distraction since she's got so much on her plate."

"So why are you asking about single guys if you don't want to be distracted?" Jana asked.

"Because I can't *stop* thinking about him. He's already become a distraction. I've only got about two months to get the schedules, website, marketing—basically *everything* I need for Harper's play—in place, and I caught myself *daydreaming* about this guy like some lame, hard-up woman, which I'm *not*." Tegan sighed. "Or maybe I am right now, but that's because I need to be. Forget it. It doesn't matter. We didn't exchange numbers or anything. I'll never see my sexy suit wearer again except in my fantasies. Let's do another shot. Maybe I can drink enough to forget him."

Chloe nudged her and said, "Sometimes fantasies are a heck of a lot better than the real thing."

"Darn right," Steph agreed.

"Hang in there, girls," Harper encouraged them. "There *are* good men out there, and several of us are testaments to that."

"I know I am." Jana patted the handcuffs and said, "I guess these babies are coming home with me tonight. My baby daddy is at home taking care of Kai, so when I get home, I'm going to take care of *him*." Kai was her four-month-old son.

Colton snagged the handcuffs and said, "Sorry, boss, but these are *mine* tonight. I've got a bear who needs to be taught a lesson." He hooked them to his belt loop, then pushed a row of shot glasses across the bar. "A round of deep-throat shots for the girls with partners. May your men all get lucky tonight. And for our single girls, a round of screaming orgasms." He picked up a shot glass in each hand and began clinking glasses with the girls.

"Why do you have one of each kind?" Desiree asked.

"Guys have needs, too." He winked and they all downed their drinks.

"Single Ladies" blared from the speakers, and Serena and Emery cheered.

"Come on!" Serena grabbed Emery's hand, and Emery grabbed Jana's. They ran to the dance floor with the rest of the girls on their heels.

They all danced around the cardboard cutouts of men. Tegan waved her hands, shimmying and wiggling her hips, singing along with everyone else.

"Watch out for Tegan!" Cree hollered.

"What do you—" Violet turned to look at Tegan.

Jana's jaw dropped. "Tegan, *what* are you doing?"

"*Dancing!*" Tegan said, arms flailing. "Cree's just jealous of my moves!"

Emery tried, and failed, to stifle a laugh. "Babe! You look like a fish out of water."

"I *know!*" Tegan spun around, and then she planted her feet, pointed her thumbs to the left, and bounced her upper body in that direction, then switched directions. "I totally suck, but it's okay! I *own* it!"

"Who's *sucking* and *owning* it?"

The girls spun around at the deep male voice booming through the bar.

It took Tegan a second to recognize the stocky guy with short blond hair and a lascivious grin as he stepped forward, opened his arms, and announced, "Dwayne Wicked at your service, ladies. Sucking welcome, swallowing appreciated, and those dresses…" He narrowed his eyes and made an "mm-mm" sound. "I must have died and gone to heaven. Who wants to revive me?"

Harper yelled, "Gavin!" and ran across the room toward her fiancé.

There was a cacophony of commotion as several of the other girls' significant others came into the bar. Some of the girls ran toward the men, but Tegan's eyes were now locked on her arrogant suit wearer walking through the door. His piercing stare rooted her in place as every dirty detail of her late-night fantasy came rushing back.

"*Armani,*" she said breathlessly as Chloe walked by.

"*Armani?*" Chloe followed Tegan's gaze and whispered, "Holy shit. Armani is *Jett?* Girl, you are one lucky bitch. Good luck. I have to go hammer Justin for crashing the party."

"Tell him *thank you* from me." Tegan heard the lust in her

own voice.

Heat blazed a path between her and Jett, but she didn't look away as he drank in her barely there outfit. She rolled her shoulders back, regaining control to give him a dose of his own medicine. She settled one hand on her hip and put on her best arrogant smile, openly admiring the man who looked anything *but* too buttoned up. His thick dark hair was windblown, and he hadn't shaved. *Boy* did he wear scruff well.

He shrugged off his black hooded rain jacket and tossed it on a chair, giving her a better view. The top two buttons of his deep-purple shirt were undone, revealing a dusting of dark chest hair she itched to touch. His sleeves were rolled up to his elbows, revealing muscular forearms, and as he closed the distance between them, his jeans stretched tight over his thick thighs.

He moved more aggressively than he had at the café, exuding raw masculinity that made Tegan's mouth go dry. His virility was not like Dean's, wrapped around sheer size. No, this man had an innately captivating presence driven by confidence. Every woman there was dressed for sex, and Tegan knew she was nowhere near the best-looking one of them, but his eyes never left hers.

When he reached her, he said, "Five minutes ago I was wondering how I was going to cut the night short without insulting anyone." He stepped closer. So close, his chest almost brushed hers. "Now all I want to do is make sure you don't run off again without giving me your phone number, because I've got to tell you, searching *sticky-note girl* on Instagram got me nowhere."

She laughed softly, enjoying this flirtatious side of him. "Sticky-note girl?"

"I tried searching *hot chick at Sundial Café*, but no luck there, either."

"You did *not*."

He flashed a coy smile that was so different from what she'd seen earlier, she could do little more than stare…and wonder how many other smiles he had yet to share. Did he have a wolfish one in the bedroom? Or was he *all business* there? Was there a carefree smile tucked away somewhere? One that came out when he wasn't being Mr. Suave or Mr. Business? He may not be her pay-it-forward soul mate, but she wasn't at the Cape looking for love anyway. She'd had a couple of flings in college, but it had been years since she'd done anything so reckless. She wondered if it would be considered reckless if her friends knew and trusted him? *No*, she decided. *It's just impulsive. An adventure.*

He was looking at her with a playful, sexy expression, causing her pulse to quicken even more. God, he wore that look well. Maybe a fling with the object of her fantasies would help her focus on the business she was supposed to be working on.

"I also searched *Miss Fine*, but you were nowhere to be found. What's a guy to do?" His brow furrowed, and he said, "I didn't think to search *Fuckable Flirt*. That's a nice surprise. One I can definitely attest to."

"Wha—" She gasped, then remembered her eye mask. She tore it off, quickly reading the tag. *Fuckable Flirt.* She was going to kill Jana.

"WE DIDN'T CHOOSE the masks," the blonde said,

clutching hers in her fist. "Jana made them *and* chose each of ours without telling us what they said."

She was adorably flustered, and he couldn't take his eyes off her. He took the mask from her hand and slipped it into his shirt pocket. "Well, that's a damn shame. I kind of got my hopes up."

"Who's up for a blow job?" Colton called out from behind the bar, where he was lining up shots.

Everyone cheered, including the blonde.

Jett grinned *hard*, earning the sexiest laugh from her. "Now we're talking. But I usually like to know a woman's name before we go that far." He offered her his hand and said, "Jett Masters. It's a pleasure to meet you."

Her whole face lit up as she shook his hand. "I'm Tegan Fine."

"An unusually beautiful name for an incredibly stunning woman."

"A little cheesy, but I'll take it," she said teasingly. "You have quite a fan club here."

"It's not just *here*. I'm a *worldwide* hot commodity." He nodded toward the bar and said, "Shall we go get down and dirty?"

"That depends." She crossed her arms and jutted out her hip defiantly. "Is your arrogance here to stay?"

He loved her directness and knew she'd walk away if he wasn't the man *she* wanted tonight. That level of self-respect was hard to come by, and it was even more of a turn-on than her gorgeous curves. He couldn't resist heating things up a notch. "Do you want it to be?"

"*Tegan!* Come on, we're going to do screaming orgasms next!" Cree hollered from across the room.

Tegan's gaze turned sultry, and her eyes remained trained on Jett as she held up her index finger in Cree's direction and said, "Do you *always* give women what they want?"

He stepped closer, and she inhaled sharply. "*Want, need,* it's all sort of intertwined, don't you think?"

"I find it best *not* to think when a man is pleasuring me." Her tongue slicked across her lower lip, leaving it temptingly wet.

"Then we'll get along just fine." He offered her his arm. "Shall we?"

She took a step forward and stumbled over her own feet. He turned just in time to catch her around her waist. She blinked up at him, wide-eyed and breathing hard.

He tightened his grip, bringing her flush against him, and said, "Do I fluster you, Miss Fine?"

"My fuck-me boots fluster me. *You* amuse me." She arched one thinly manicured brow and said, "Are you going to hold me captive all night while everyone else enjoys *blow jobs* and *orgasms*? Or are we going to join the party?"

"It would be rude not to join the others." He leaned closer, inhaling the scent of sweet citrus and sunshine despite the storm brewing between them, and said, "I'm only in town for one night, but you can be my willing captive once we're done."

"We'll see about that. The jury is still out on you." She stepped out of his embrace and slipped her arm around his. "Show me your *fun* side, and then we'll decide if you can be my *master* for a night."

His cell phone rang, and he pulled it from his pocket, seeing TIA STRONG on the screen. Other than his friends from Bayside, there was only one woman in Jett's life who ever called him on his shit, and that was Tia, his long-time assistant. She worked out of his New York office and never hesitated to bust his balls, as she'd done last night. They'd been going over his schedule for next week and he'd asked her to track down a *Miss Fine* who was new to the Cape and, based on the sticky notes he'd seen, might be taking over some sort of entertainment company. Tia had asked if he was thinking of taking over her company, and when he'd hesitated, eventually saying, *Not exactly*, she'd heard something in his voice and had figured out his reasons, immediately refusing to help track down a booty call. Tia would *love* Tegan, if only because she'd enjoy another woman giving him shit.

Tegan leaned closer and said, "Never check your phone or take a call at a party, especially when you've got a lady on your arm. That's strike one. See you later, *Armani When It Suits You*." She sauntered over to the girls, who were huddled around the bar giggling and doing shots, and she didn't even give him a second glance.

Well, damn.

The woman dropped things, tripped over her own feet, danced like a nightmare, and still she had more class than the Gucci-wearing models and upper-echelon executives he knew. She was utterly mesmerizing, and like the best deals he sealed, he wanted to figure out what made her tick.

He sent Tia's call to voicemail and turned off his ringer. He was in town for only one night, and he didn't care if he *scored* with Tegan or not, but he sure as hell wasn't about to strike out.

Justin shoved a shot glass into Jett's hand and said, "Drink up, dude. By the looks of things, this might be the only blow job you'll get tonight."

He didn't give a rat's ass about a blow job. There were plenty of women who would dole them out like candy if that's all he wanted. But Tegan was clearly not one of those women. Or maybe she *was*, but he had a feeling one night with Tegan Fine would only whet his appetite.

He and Justin clinked glasses and drank their shots as Dwayne sidled up to them.

"I didn't know you knew Tegan," Dwayne said. "Guess that explains why you weren't interested in picking up chicks at the Hog tonight. She's one fine piece of—"

"*Don't* go there, Dwayne," Jett warned. "It's not like that. I didn't even know she knew Harper."

"No?" Dwayne looked lustfully at Tegan and rubbed his hands together. "Perfect. That outfit will look great on my bedroom floor."

Jett glowered at him, his hand curling into a fist, surprising himself by the vehemence with which the possessive urge hit him.

Justin put a hand on Dwayne's shoulder and said, "Get out of here before the man kills you."

"What? He said—"

"Get a clue, cuz," Justin said sharply. "She's checking him out like he's *hers*."

Jett turned, catching Tegan watching him with confidence and desire. Once again she didn't look away. *Hot. As. Sin.*

Violet grabbed Dwayne by the arm. "Is your big mouth getting you into trouble again?"

Before Dwayne could get a word out, Steph yelled, "Spice Girls!" She and several of the other girls ran to the dance floor to dance to the fast-paced song. Beckett, Drake, Rick, and Desiree brushed past Jett, following them.

"Let's go, playboy. There are a few single ladies who need dance partners." Violet winked at Jett as she dragged Dwayne toward the dance floor.

"*Shit*," Justin ground out. "Beckett's moving in on Chloe and Daph. You're on your own, dude."

Jett was anything but on his own. Tegan's eyes were still trained on him. He tilted his head toward the bar and mouthed, *Buy you a drink?*

She lifted a full shot glass, as if to say, *No thank you.*

He tried to ignore the pang of disappointment in his chest.

Tegan grabbed a cookie from a tray on the bar and held it up, showing him the penis-shaped treat. Her eyes narrowed, and she dragged her tongue along the iced cookie. Heat rushed to his groin. *Christ, this woman...* She put the cookie in her mouth. *That's it, baby, show me what you'd like to do to me.* He hoped to hell none of the other guys were watching her, but he refused to look away to check. Tegan raised her brows, then *chomped* into the cookie, her eyes never leaving his. *Fuuck.*

He knew a warning when he saw one, but the sinful glimmer in her eyes relayed a different type of warning. She was on *fire*, and he wanted to dive into the flames. She lifted her glass as if to toast, then downed the shot and set the empty glass on the bar without looking away. A flirtatious smile appeared on her beautiful face, and he realized she was totally playing him, gaining the upper hand.

"Who wants to challenge the bride and groom in bra pong?" Harper yelled, jarring Jett from his thoughts.

"We do!" Emery pulled Dean across the room.

Tegan arched a brow, her eyes briefly darting toward Emery and Dean. He nodded, accepting the challenge to be her partner in bra pong, whatever the hell that was.

She sauntered toward him in those fuck-me boots and that slinky skintight outfit, stopping only inches away to say, "Ready to show them who's boss?"

"I'd rather show *you*," he said, earning a pretty blush, which was surprising, and adorable, after the show she'd just given him.

"You can show *me* who's boss," Colton offered. He pointed up to the SAME PENIS FOREVER banner and said, "That was Jana's doing, *not* mine. I'm all for variety!"

Brock laughed as he, Cree, and Andre walked past Jett, toward the dance floor.

Jett chuckled and shook his head. "*Fools.*"

"That's what you get for crashing a bachelorette party," Tegan said as they went to join the others in the game.

"Next to stopping at Sundial yesterday, crashing this party is the best thing I've done since I got to the Cape."

"Wow," she said, taking his arm. "Just like that you wiped that first strike clean."

"I like a woman who doesn't hold grudges."

"And I like a man who can stop flirting long enough to play the game," Dean said, tossing Jett a Ping-Pong ball.

The damn thing bounced off his hand and skittered across the floor. He shook his head, ignoring his brother's and buddies' taunts about not being good with his hands. Dean tossed him another ball. He caught it this time and eyed the colorful bras hanging on the board.

"Any of those yours?" he asked Tegan.

"Wouldn't you like to know?" She took the ball from his hand and said to the others, "Who's ready to lose their shirts?"

That started a round of lewd comments about playing *strip* bra pong, which continued throughout the game. Jett couldn't believe how quickly he and Tegan fell into sync. She was wild and funny, and as competitive as he was, challenging every snarky comment from the other teams and focusing on every throw as if her life depended on it. They cheered and high-fived, laughing like college kids who didn't have a care in the world. When they won the final round, Tegan jumped into his arms, her eyes glittering with joy, one fist shooting up toward the ceiling as he spun her around. He fought the urge to kiss her, knowing that once he got his mouth on her, he wouldn't want to stop there. He couldn't remember the last time he'd laughed, much less enjoyed a woman's company so immensely.

As the evening wore on, Colton cranked up the music and dimmed the lights, giving the party a night-on-the-town vibe rather than a crashed-bachelorette-party feel. Everyone danced, mingled, and drank, except three of the girls who were the designated drivers. Jett and Tegan traded scorching innuendos, growing closer by the minute, despite the girls constantly dragging her away for one thing or another.

Jett stood by the bar with Justin, Andre, and Violet, trying to concentrate on what Andre was saying about his and Violet's last trip overseas. It was a futile effort. He couldn't tear his eyes, or his thoughts, off Tegan. She was dancing with Chloe and Steph. There was nothing sexual about the way her body flailed and jerked, but Jett was spellbound. *Off* the dance floor Tegan was an unusual mix of playful and sensual. But *on* the dance floor? He was pretty sure everyone else saw her as a hot mess, but all he saw was a beautiful, carefree woman bursting with confidence. He'd never seen anything so enticing.

Man, he missed being that kind of happy. It seemed his thoughts, actions, every business deal, every frigging *step* he took, was weighed down by the ghosts of his past. When he was on the Cape, he couldn't wait to leave—and when he was gone, guilt ate at him. But tonight, being with Tegan, kept that ugliness at bay.

He thought back to earlier in the evening when they were toasting Gavin and Harper. Colton had offered Tegan a glass of champagne, and she'd set her sexy eyes on Jett and said, *Thanks, but this tall glass is all I need.* Then she proceeded to pick up his champagne glass and lift it to her lips, like that drink was all she was after. But she'd stopped short of taking a drink to lick her lips, and he swore he'd felt her hot, slithering tongue on his flesh. She was bold and confident, but she had an underlying sweetness that he couldn't wait to get to know more intimately. He was usually excellent at reading people, but he couldn't decide if Tegan was simply dipping her toes in the sexual teasing pool and pulling back before she got too wet—or if she was a master seductress.

Justin nudged Jett and said, "Why aren't you out there dancing with Tegan?"

"I will be. *Soon.* I'm enjoying watching her." He took a sip of his drink. Tegan stumbled. His gut clenched, and he pushed from the bar, but Emery caught her, and the two of them burst into hysterics. He chuckled and said, "She's so fucking cute."

"She is," Justin said. "Every time you two are near each other you look like you're ready to tear each other's clothes off, but you might not want to get too close when she's dancing. You could get a black eye."

Jett met his amused gaze and said, "I'll take my chances."

Andre pulled Violet closer and said, "The best women dance to their own beat. I know mine sure does."

"Come on, big boy. Let me show you my moves." Violet dragged him toward the dance floor.

Jett had known Violet for years. When she'd first come to the Cape, she'd been tough as nails and had walls as thick as stone. Despite being half sisters, she and Desiree had barely known each other, but they'd committed to running the inn together for the chance to rebuild their relationship. He'd been amazed at Violet's transformation. She was still badass, but she was softer and more loving toward her sister and friends, and of course, now Andre. Every time Jett saw her, he thought of his own family, and in the back of his mind he wondered if he and his father could ever come that far.

But those were thoughts for another day.

He had watched Tegan dance long enough. He needed to be closer to her, to hear her laughter and see the sparks in her eyes when he touched her. He looked across the bar and said, "Hey, Colton, think you can queue up 'Sex on Fire'?"

"Queue it up? Dude, look at me. I'm the *stoker* of heat." Colton began dancing and said, "Sex with me is *always* on fire."

Justin chuckled.

Jett gave Colton a deadpan look.

"*Oh*," Colton said dramatically. "You mean queue up the *song*." He pointed at Jett and said, "Gotcha. I'll follow it up with 'Slow Hands' and other sex-inducing songs for the rest of the night. I've got your back, even if I'd rather you had mine."

Jett laughed and shook his head.

"Jett is *finally* making his move," Justin said.

As Colton queued up the song, Jett strode toward the dance floor. Tegan's back was to him. Her arms reached for the ceiling as she flung her head and ass from side to side. Chloe looked over Tegan's shoulder, and Jett held a finger up to his lips. Chloe grinned and nudged Steph, and the two of them took a few steps away, allowing him to move in front of Tegan. Her eyes were closed, like she was lost in the music. In his mind, Jett unraveled that thought and dragged it into a bedroom, seeing her naked beneath him, eyes closed as their bodies moved to their own wicked beat.

He reached up, catching her hands with his. Her eyes flew open, but as he guided her arms around his neck, her baby blues turned dark as night. He didn't want her to think he didn't like her dancing, but he *needed* her in his arms. The music was too fast for a slow dance, which made it perfect for them to find their own rhythm.

"What took you so long?" she asked sassily, her hips still moving erratically.

"I was savoring the view. Nothing good comes from rushing—in business *or* in pleasure."

He held her gaze, enjoying the flames simmering in her eyes as he trailed his fingers along her arms from her wrists to her shoulders, where he slipped his fingertips beneath the thin material of her outfit. He was vaguely aware of their friends dancing around them, but he was already too lost in Tegan to pay attention to anyone else. He slid one hand down her torso. Lust pulsed hot and urgent inside him with the feel of her curves. He slipped his arm around her waist, drawing her closer and slowing her down. Her eyes widened just a hair, then narrowed seductively as the song changed to a slower beat.

Appreciative sounds rose around them as couples and friends came together, unleashing their sensual sides. But there were no sounds coming from Jett and Tegan as the music pounded through them. Her soft body conformed to his hard frame, her heart beating rapidly against him. He held her there, one hand pressed to her lower back, his fingers resting on the curve of her ass, guiding her hips to the same grinding, swaying rhythm as his. His other hand moved down her hip, teasing over her bare thigh. The pounding of the music and the lust swimming in her eyes coalesced with the feel of their bodies moving as one, drawing him in even deeper.

TEGAN'S BODY WAS on fire. Jett's hands were strong and possessive. His hungry gaze drilled into her like he sensed her desires and wanted to satiate every blessed one of them. He threaded one hand into her hair. His scruff scratched her cheek tantalizingly as he pressed his warm lips beside her ear. He tightened his hold on her, crushing her to him, his lips trailing down to her neck. Her knees *weakened.* Lord help her, her heart was going to explode. She was going to die from sexual tension, she just knew it.

One sexy song bled into the next, their hands moving hungrily over each other's bodies, sending rivers of lust coursing through her. His hard heat pressed temptingly against her as they danced. In her sky-high boots she was almost tall enough to take the kiss she'd been wanting all evening, but despite her aggressiveness with Jett, she wasn't usually that forward with men, and she held back. He was seduction *personified,* making her feel bold and sexy, making her *want, need,* and *crave* in ways she never had. She felt safe with him. For the first time since she'd come to the Cape, she wasn't overthinking the work she had to do or the life she'd left behind. In fact, she was having trouble holding on to any one thought beyond *wanting Jett,* and that felt amazing—and a little dangerous since he'd consumed her thoughts for the past twenty-four hours. But she couldn't help wondering, if they *didn't* hold back, if they let themselves enjoy one perfect night together, maybe *then* she'd be able to get him out of her system and she'd have no future distractions to deal with. Well, except maybe the night of the wedding when she'd see him again, but that would give her time in between to focus on work. *And if we connect in bed like we have tonight, I might be ready for a repeat by then.*

"You're so fucking sexy," he said gruffly into her ear.

A thrum of warmth invaded her core. "If you keep saying things like that, the dance floor is going to go up in flames."

"Is that a complaint or a compliment?"

"*Compliment*," she said breathily. The lights flickered and the music hitched, jolting her head from her Jett-induced trance, though her body was still threatening to combust.

"Guess the storm is rolling closer," Colton said.

Tegan had been so busy trying to stop thinking about Jett earlier in the day, she hadn't followed the weather forecasts.

Jett stroked his hand down her back, keeping her close as he spoke into her ear. "Did you drive here tonight?"

The desire in his voice made her thoughts stumble. "I...I came with Jana and Cree."

The lights flickered again, and a few curses sailed up from their friends.

"I am so sick of rain," Jana said.

"No kidding!" Harper said. "As long as it stops before the wedding, I'll—"

Thunder boomed, drowning out her words. The lights flickered, and then the room went pitch-black and the music silenced. Jett crushed Tegan against him as gasps, shrieks, and more curses rang out from their friends.

"I've got you," Jett said reassuringly.

Everyone else spoke at once, panicked and frustrated, using their cell phones as flashlights as they rushed off the dance floor and began gathering their things. But Jett was calm, his heart beating steady and strong against Tegan's shoulder. He placed his hand gently on her cheek, and with the help of the lights from the others' cell phones, his eyes found hers.

"I'd like nothing more than to take you home," he said, studying her face. "But I'm leaving tomorrow, and I can't promise you anything beyond tonight."

She understood, even if she couldn't form the words to tell him so.

"I'll walk you to your door and then leave if you want me to," he offered. "But I'm not ready for our time together to end."

"I'm not, either," she said as more thunder rumbled overhead. The intensity of their chemistry made it difficult to think, but she managed, "My house is in Brewster. It's a bit of a drive."

He brushed his thumb over her lips, his eyes boring into hers as he said, "I'd drive to Boston if that's where you lived."

Justin appeared beside them with one arm around Steph, the other around Chloe, and said, "You got Tegan?"

"Yeah. Where's Daphne?" Jett asked, his eyes moving around the dark room. "Does she need a ride?"

Tegan warmed all over knowing he was watching out for her friend.

"Daph's in the ladies' room with Violet. We've got her," Rick called from a few feet away, where he was helping Desiree on with her coat.

"The storm wasn't supposed to get bad until midweek," Colton said.

Chloe flashed her phone light in Jett's face and said, "You'd better be good to my girl, Jett Masters. If I hear one bad report,

I'll kick your ass."

Jett chuckled. "I think you know me better than that." He looked across the room and said, "Colton, you want us to stick around and help you get things under control here?"

Colton waved and said, "Nah, I'm good. Thanks. Although I have no idea why my emergency lights haven't come on. Maybe it's a short in the electrical system."

"I'll stick around and check it out," Brock said. "Listen up, everyone. You never know about these storms. Stock up on water and nonperishables, make sure you have plenty of candles on hand, and we're around if you need anything."

"Yes, *Dad*," Jana and Harper teased in unison.

Harper and Gavin thanked everyone for coming and doled out hugs. When Harper embraced Tegan, she lowered her voice and said, "Jett's great, but he really is married to his work. Just keep your expectations in check. Don't get hurt."

Once again, Tegan was thankful to have close friends there. "I won't. I'm going to be married to my work for a while, too. This is just, *you know*, fun for a night." She couldn't believe she was admitting that, much less intending to do it.

"That's what I said about Gavin, and now we're getting married." Harper reached for Gavin's hand. "Call me once you get the schedules figured out for the theater, and be safe in this weather."

Tegan promised to call as soon as she had things under control. After they said goodbye to their friends, Jett fetched their coats and they made their way outside. Cold, stinging rain hit her cheeks, but even that did nothing to diminish the heat between them. Wind howled across the power lines, gusting so forcefully it was hard for Tegan to walk forward. Jett's arm circled her waist, drawing her against his chest. He put one hand on the back of her head, using the other to shield her face as if he could *be* her umbrella, as they hurried across the parking lot, and when she stumbled, he held her up.

"I'm such a klutz!" she said as he helped her into the SUV.

"It just gives me a reason to hold you tighter."

He leaned in, blocking the rain that was pounding on his back from hitting her, and brushed her wet hair from her face. It was an intimate touch, another chivalrous effort. His eyes met hers, and her name slipped roughly from his lips. "*Tegan…*"

She leaned forward and touched her lips to his, taking that first kiss she so desperately wanted. There was no time to adjust to the hard press of his mouth, no testing of the waters as he took control. He clutched her wet hair, angling her mouth beneath his as he intensified the kiss. His tongue delved deeper, his lips were warm and insistent, and he tasted of alcohol and dirty promises. She couldn't wait to have those unspoken promises fulfilled. She clutched at his head and shoulders, craving *more* of him. His hand moved under her coat, caressing her breast. She arched against his hand and he pushed beneath the fabric, rolling her nipple between his finger and thumb. She moaned into their kisses as he climbed farther into the front seat. Cold air whipped around them, but she didn't care. His kisses roared through her, every swipe of his tongue taking her higher. She was blinded with desire, panting and pawing, utterly lost in him. She'd never been kissed so thoroughly, so *possessively*. He was relentless, and oh, how she loved it! When he tore his mouth away and sealed it over her neck, "Yes!" flew from her lungs.

He sucked hard, squeezing her nipple, sending flames scorching through her. The pleasure was so intense, she saw stars. She pushed her hands into his hair as he blazed a greedy path down her neck, licking and kissing along her breastbone. He pressed a single kiss to the swell of her breast, and she felt him lifting his head, but she didn't open her eyes. She could feel his heart beating frantically as she waited for another touch, another kiss. When it didn't come, her eyes fluttered open.

His gaze was as fierce as it was caring. Her nerves hummed like live wires, whipping and sparking dangerously, and yet somehow she also felt a sense of calmness and safety in his arms.

"Not here," he whispered as he carefully righted her jumpsuit, covering her breast.

He brought his magnificent lips to hers, kissing her so tenderly she felt like she was in a dream.

Chapter Five

THE RIDE HOME was a blur of wind, rain, and anticipation. They stumbled through Tegan's massive front door, kissing and stripping off their drenched coats. Jett backed her up against the door, and it shut with a loud *thud* that echoed off the high ceilings and hardwood floors.

Her eyes flew open, and she said, "*Upstairs.*"

They stumbled toward the grand staircase, kissing as they made their way up the steps.

"You *live* here?" he asked hurriedly.

"Mm-hm," she said as his lips reclaimed hers in another delicious kiss.

When they reached the second floor, he pinned her against the wall, feasting on her mouth, his big body boxing her in. He took her hands in his, spreading them out to her sides, grinding his hard length against her. Without breaking their kisses, he nudged her legs open with his knee, then even further with his foot, until she was spread-eagle against the wall, his willing captive. Lightning traveled up her core with every grind of his hips. She'd never been with a man who knew how to take control like this. But she wasn't scared. She was *intrigued*, and so turned on her chest heaved with anticipation. His mouth moved down her neck, and he dragged his tongue enticingly slowly, just above her choker. His head dipped lower, and he bathed her chest in openmouthed kisses, until every inch of her pulsed with desire. She bowed off the wall, rubbing against him, mewling and panting as his mouth moved lower, tasting the exposed and sensitive skin near her belly button.

He drew back with a wicked glint in his eyes and rose up, lightly brushing his lips over hers. "It's been a long time for me, and I've been hard half the night thinking of all the things I want to do to you, so if I get too rough, tell me. I don't want to do anything you're not comfortable with."

The demand and the care in his voice turned her on. "Okay," came out as a heated whisper.

His eyes darted down the expansive hallway. "Anyone else live here?"

She shook her head and the visceral *hunger* in his eyes made her sex clench. He released one of her hands and dragged his fingertips from her wrist to her shoulder. He didn't say a word as he hooked his finger into the material at her shoulder and pulled it down to her elbow, freeing her breast. His eyes never left hers as he did the same with the other side, leaving her bare from the waist up.

He cupped her face and brushed his thumb over her lower lip, gazing deeply into her eyes as he said, "You can trust me. I'll never hurt you. I only want to make you feel good."

She wasn't worried, but his reassurance comforted her.

His gaze moved lower, and her nipples pebbled and burned under the heat of it. He ran his hands down to where the material bunched at the crook of her arms. His fingers circled her there, holding her against the wall. His head dipped lower, and he traced circles around one nipple until it ached with need.

He moved to the other breast, and so began a maddening rhythm as he revved her up one tantalizing lick at a time. When he sealed his mouth over the swell of her breast, electricity radiated out from her core.

Her eyes slammed shut and she panted out, "*More.*"

He dragged his tongue over her nipple, and she was so ripe, so ready, she couldn't hold *anything* back.

"*Oh God. Yes...Again,*" she pleaded.

He did it again and again until her thoughts spun. When his mouth came down over one taut peak, rivers of pleasure sliced through her. He sucked harder, wedging his knee against her center, creating mind-numbing sensations. Every rub of his knee brought her closer to the edge. She was trembling, breathing in ragged gasps, chasing an orgasm that was just out of reach.

"More," she cried out. "*Harder.*"

He didn't miss a beat, giving her exactly what she wanted until she was a bucking, needy mess of desire, spewing greedy sounds she'd never heard before. In the space of a second, his hot hands moved her legs closer together, and he stripped her outfit to the floor. Her thong came off next. She should be nervous, standing naked in the hall in only her boots and choker while he was fully dressed. But there was no room for that when he was taking off his shirt, revealing a broad, gorgeous chest and lean, lickable abs.

"Eyes up here, gorgeous," he said.

Her eyes flicked up to his, and holy moly, he was looking at her like she was the most beautiful creature he'd ever seen. He moved like a panther on the prowl, running one hand up her thigh as he said, "Shaved bare," in a guttural voice that sent a shudder of anticipation through her. He made an appreciative sound as his fingers moved across her inner thigh and over her sex. "*Exquisite*," he said into her ear, sliding his fingers along her wetness torturously slowly, his thumb pressing on her most sensitive nerves.

She reached out and palmed his cock through his jeans. "I want to play, too." The huskiness of her own voice surprised her.

He lifted her hand to his mouth and kissed her fingers. "I promise you will have all the time you'd like, sweetheart."

He laced his hand with hers and covered her mouth with his, kissing her long and so sensually, she would have done anything he asked just to be kissed like that again. She closed her eyes as he lowered himself to his knees and brought his mouth to her center. The first slide of his tongue sent pinpricks up her limbs. The second sent the air rushing from her lungs, and then he was *feasting* on her. His scruff tickled and scratched. His hands and mouth worked with such mastery her thoughts fragmented. She clawed at his shoulders, rocking her hips. There was no holding back the animalistic sounds climbing up her throat as he sent her racing toward the clouds. Her hips bucked, her sex pulsed, and just when she started to catch her breath, he became rougher, more possessive, catapulting her into renewed ecstasy. The world careened around her. She clung to his shoulders, trying to steady herself, but she was no match for the erotic haven he'd created, and she surrendered to the glorious sensations.

She lost all sense of time and space. When she finally started to come down from the clouds, he rose to his full height and lifted her into his arms.

"Bedroom?" His voice was gruff, but his eyes were softer, like a beast who had taken the edge off his hunger.

She pointed down the hall and wrapped her arms around his neck, pulling his mouth to hers. She didn't care that he tasted of her; she needed him more than she'd ever needed anything. He broke the kiss when they entered her bedroom long enough only to locate the bed, tear the blankets down, and lower them to the mattress. Rain pounded against the windows, but Jett's mouth was on hers again, exploring and demanding at once, and everything else failed to exist. His kisses were magical and addictive, like finding her favorite candy buried in the world's best ice cream sundae. Just when she got used to the roughness, he'd slow them down, kissing her tenderly. He made love to her mouth with the same intensity and focus as he'd pleasured her. How could a man she'd only just met make her feel so much?

He lifted her leg at the crook of her knee as they kissed, and then he kissed his way south again, slowing to devour her breasts and to kiss her belly, which tickled. She couldn't stifle her giggles.

He chuckled and said, "*Damn* I like you." Honesty resonated in his eyes as he took off her boots and his shoes.

She reminded herself that this was only one night and not to read too much into whatever he said or did in the heat of the moment. She waved at his jeans and said, "Get those clothes off and show me how much."

"In a *hurry*?" He came down over her and pressed his lips to hers. "What if I said I didn't want to have sex, that I just wanted to spend all night pleasuring you?"

She felt herself grinning. "I'd say you're really good at *that*."

"I'm even *better* at the real thing," he said cockily.

"Then I'd say you should get to it so I can judge where your best skills lie."

He pushed his hands beneath her, grabbing her butt like he owned it, and said, "I like your bossiness."

"I like your *mouth*," she said sassily.

"You're probably going to hate what comes out of it next," he said a little seriously. "I wasn't expecting to hook up when I left the house tonight. I'm usually prepared, but I don't have protection. I don't suppose...?"

The regretful look in his eyes made her laugh. "Mr. Armani isn't prepared? Let me alert the media."

"Aw man. You're killing me," he said as he rolled off her.

She tried to put on a straight face, but her laughter kept bubbling out as she straddled his lap. "I wonder if your friends know you're a tease," she joked, loving that Mr. Perfect was human after all.

"I'm just not the kind of guy whose goal in life is to have sex."

"Oh, *hm*. I kind of thought that was our goal tonight."

"Yeah, well, that's different. I didn't leave the cottage to-night *seeking* sex."

She put her arms around him and said, "Are you clean, *Armani*?"

"Absolutely. How about you, sticky-note girl?"

"I wouldn't have let you put your mouth all over me if I wasn't." She kissed him softly, then wiggled lower on his lap and started opening his belt. "I'm also on the pill."

"You tortured me for no reason?"

She whipped his belt from the loops and tossed it across the room. "It was fun watching you squirm." She unbuttoned and unzipped his jeans, licking her lips at the sight of his thick erection outlined by dark cotton. She was being so much bolder than ever before, but once again she didn't care. If she had this big, beautiful man for only one night, she wasn't going to waste a second of it.

Her pulse quickened as she climbed off him and pulled down the top of his briefs, revealing the broad head of his erection. Her mouth watered with the need to taste him, to feel his desire pulsing in her hand, to *possess* him as he'd possessed her, but she didn't want to rush. She leaned forward and licked the head of his arousal.

He groaned and shoved his jeans and briefs down. Together they made quick work of taking them off. She pushed him flat on his back and licked him from base to tip, eliciting another appreciative noise. She wrapped her fingers around his cock and licked all around the crown.

"*Fuck.*"

"Don't come," she said softly, and then she lowered her mouth over his shaft.

"You're playing with fire. I told you it's been a while." He gritted his teeth as she worked him with her hand and mouth. He ran his hands over her hair, moaning, his hips pulsing with every stroke.

"Tegan, *baby*," he warned huskily, bringing her eyes to his.

The salacious look in his eyes made her want to drive him even crazier. "Don't come," she reminded him, and his jaw clenched.

With her eyes locked on his, she made a dramatic show of swirling her tongue around the head and down his shaft, making him groan again, before she finally took him into her mouth. She sucked and stroked, tight and fast, feeling him swell within her grasp. He reached down and grabbed the base of his cock.

"You've got to stop. I need to be inside you." He swept her

beneath him and said, "You make me crazy."

"*Good.*" She played with his damp hair.

His lips curved up, different than she'd seen before, warmer, more intimate. He skimmed his hand down her side and said, "You really are beautiful. I wasn't just blowing smoke."

He said the sweetest things, and she tried not to let them affect her, but that was like trying to ignore the sun breaking through a cloudy day. She knew she shouldn't make tonight into something it wasn't, regardless of how much fun they were having and how right they seemed, so she said, more casually than she felt, "You're not so bad yourself."

He lowered his mouth to hers, kissing her deeply as he aligned their bodies. The way he kissed her, passionate and thorough, made her even more aware of the rest of him. His powerful thighs pressed down on her, his cock nestled against her center, and his strong arms cradled her. His chest hair tickled, and his scruff scratched her cheeks as alluringly as it had her thighs. He smelled like sex and man, and he tasted like heaven. She'd never felt so *aware* of another being in her life. She held her breath in anticipation, but he didn't thrust into her. He drew back, dusting kisses on her lips and cheek, all the way up to beside her ear. Every touch sent tingles skittering over her flesh.

He tucked his face beside hers, teasing the head of his cock along her center. When his hips finally pressed forward, he entered her slowly. She felt her body stretching to accommodate him as he took her inch by inch, until he was buried to the hilt.

His arms tightened around her, and he exhaled a long breath, saying, "So good," into her ear. He pushed in impossibly deeper as he leaned up, causing her to inhale sharply at the new angle. Their eyes connected and she felt the impact dead in the center of her chest. His brows knitted, as if he'd felt it, too, and like a flash of light, she saw the same curious confusion she felt rise in his eyes. She didn't have time to ponder the thought as his mouth claimed hers, and they began to move, quickly finding their rhythm and giving themselves over to their passion. They ate at each other's mouths, groping and clawing, moaning and pleading for more. She wrapped her legs around him, anchoring her heels against his hamstrings as he drove deeper, *faster*. Every thrust took her higher, sending her closer to the peak.

"Hold me tighter," she said breathlessly.

He reclaimed her mouth—*God, your mouth*—as he pushed his hands beneath her ass, crushing her hips to his, and quickened his efforts. Blood pounded through her veins, whooshing in her ears. She dug her fingernails into his flesh as her orgasm crashed over her, and she cried out. He swallowed her sounds, continuing his masterful movements, keeping her at the peak so long she was sure she'd pass out from sheer ecstasy. And just as she started coming down from the peak, he slowed his pace, stroking over the secret spot that made her toes curl and her eyes clench tight. Electric shocks torched through her as she lost herself to another intense climax. His every muscle flexed, and he tore his mouth away with a *growl*, giving in to his own intense release. He pounded into her, making the sexiest noises she'd ever heard.

His thrusts slowed, and his head dipped beside hers, both of them breathless as their bodies carried them through the very last aftershock. She couldn't let go, didn't want him to roll away just yet. The way he held her, like she was precious and *his*, and the way their bodies fit perfectly together, made their connection feel soul deep.

Oh no, no, no. Where did that come from?

Her thoughts were still too hazy to figure it out, so she forced a lie to try to regain control of her stupid head and said, "I can't breathe."

"Sorry, babe."

He rolled off her and she instantly missed the weight of him. This was silly. She wasn't a clingy girl. She didn't need or want a boyfriend. The man had literally fucked her senseless. She pushed herself up and said, "I'll be right back," and hurried into the bathroom.

God, Tegan. Get a grip!

After going to the bathroom and freshening up, she stared at herself in the mirror. Her heart was still hammering, and her hands were shaking. Her hair was a mess, her skin was flushed, and her makeup was smeared. She looked *well fucked*. She needed to snap out of the blissed-out state he'd left her in and reclaim reality.

She took a moment to scrub off her makeup and gave herself a good talking to.

It was a fuck.

That was all it was.

A fuck. A fling. Nothing more.

She inhaled a deep breath and blew it out slowly. Feeling a bit more in control, she went back into the bedroom.

"You are so damn sexy," he said as he stepped from the bed and gathered her in his arms. "My turn. Keep the sheets warm."

She watched his fine, naked ass as she climbed into bed. A slew of horrible thoughts sailed through her mind. What if he was trying to figure out how to get the heck out of there? *He wouldn't have said to keep the sheets warm if that was the case.* Great, now she was even more nervous. Should she sit up? Lie down? Try to look sexy? She quickly shifted in a few different positions, all of which felt awkward and posed. She was just sitting there, probably appearing as worried as she felt when he came out of the bathroom looking beyond gorgeous, all lean and handsome, his thick shaft hanging temptingly between his legs. She couldn't have held on to a single thought if she'd wanted to as he joined her beneath the sheets and pulled her closer, kissing her softly. He shifted them lower on the bed, so they were lying on their sides, his arms around her.

"That was amazing," he said with a hint of awe.

"Yeah," she agreed. "You really are good at *everything*."

He leaned up on his forearm, gazing down at her with a sinful and somehow also *mischievous* grin. "That's a two-way street, beautiful."

"*We're* really good at everything," she said as he lowered his lips to hers, kissing her so deeply, all her best parts tingled with anticipation.

He drew back and nipped at her lower lip. He grazed his teeth along her jaw, and she felt him go hard against her as he said, "We're *excellent*, in my opinion."

His warm breath sent goose bumps over her flesh. She was not going to let her head get carried away this time. She needed to take control. She pushed his chest, taking him down on his back, and said, "Maybe we should go for round two," as she straddled his hips. "Just to see if we can elevate our status from *excellent* to *mind-blowing*."

He grabbed her waist, his hips rising as she sank onto his hard length. They both moaned. Sparks ignited in his eyes as he ground into her.

"We're going to need *much* hotter words than *excellent* and *mind-blowing*," he said in a gravelly voice. "Because we are on *fire*."

Chapter Six

JETT AWOKE TO the sounds of angry weather pummeling the windows and soft sighs coming from the warm, and wonderfully naked, beauty sleeping in his arms. He couldn't remember the last time he'd woken up with a woman in his arms, but he knew for certain it wasn't with anyone like the sexy, funny *vixen* cuddled up beside him.

Tegan made a sleepy sound and threw her leg over his, snuggling closer. He pressed a kiss to the top of her head and ran his hand down her back, cupping her ass. She made another sexy sound and palmed his erection.

"Well, good morning to you, too," she said groggily.

He chuckled for the millionth time since he'd met her. "Good morning, sunshine."

She lifted her face, blinking sleepily. She was even more beautiful than he remembered. She sighed dreamily and said, "I love being in bed, don't you? It's so toasty and comfy."

He had a feeling the foolish smile he felt on his lips would be there all day, on his way to Boston and on the flight to Chicago. The thought hit with a pang of regret. "I'm usually up with the sun," he said a little absently.

She pressed a kiss to his chest and said, "That's because you don't have a *Tegan* in your bed."

"That's the damn truth."

She got up on all fours, her golden hair tumbling around her face. "We *could* get out of bed if that's what you want." She crawled toward the edge of the bed, giving him a glorious view of her ass.

"Like *hell* we can." He snagged her by the waist, sweeping her beneath him, both of them laughing.

He moved down her body, cherishing and devouring the dips and curves he'd memorized last night. She fisted her hands in the sheets as he took his fill. Her heels dug into the mattress as he focused on the spot that had driven her wild last night. She came hard, clawing at his shoulders and crying out unabashedly. He got as much pleasure out of making her writhe and plead and from hearing his name sail wantonly from her lungs as he did from having her hands and mouth on him. He loved his way back up her body, slowing to taste and tease her belly and ribs, earning sexy giggles. *Man*, he loved that sound. He kissed a path to her breasts, taking his time cherishing each one, turning those giggles to sultry moans as he brought her to the verge of coming again. He held her there, on the edge of release, until she was begging, rocking beneath him, the need in her voice too much to deny. Their bodies came together fast, and there was no holding back. They were breathless and greedy, and he wished he could freeze time and revel in the all-consuming *oneness* that carried them both over the edge.

They collapsed to the mattress, sated and spent, their hands joined between them.

"We should win a gold medal for that," Tegan panted out.

Sex had never been so fun. "Hell, yeah, we should."

"What time's your flight?"

"Twelve forty, out of Boston." He reached for his watch, which he'd put on the nightstand sometime during the night. "*Shit.* I've got to get going. It's almost eight." He couldn't remember a time when he didn't want to face the week ahead, but all he wanted to do right then was bask in Tegan, enjoy her sweet, sinful body, devour her hot, willing mouth, and revel in her sunny disposition. He wanted to spend the day joking about stupid things and volleying sexy banter, not driving to Boston, flying to Chicago, and spending hours preparing for a meeting.

Which was exactly why he needed to leave. He couldn't afford to be sidetracked.

He gave her a chaste kiss and climbed out of bed. "You're a dangerous woman. I've got to shower and pack." He moved swiftly around the room, snagging his clothes from the floor, chastising himself for getting so caught up in her. In this weather it would take forever to get to Boston. "Shoes...?"

Tegan pointed across the room as she got out of bed. Her hair was tangled from his hands, and her lips were pink from their kisses. She didn't even try to cover up her nakedness, and he really liked that, too.

She stood with one knee bent, her toes curled under, twirling the ends of her hair around her finger, looking as innocent as she was sexy. "You could save time and shower here," she said sweetly. "With *me.*"

His chest constricted. He dropped his clothes and said, "Fucking *dangerous* isn't the right word." He strode across the room and hauled her over his shoulder. She laughed as he carried her into the bathroom. "You're the *worst* and the *best* influence I've ever met."

"Tell me something I don't know," she said cheekily.

He bit her butt cheek as he turned on the shower, causing

her to shriek and kick her feet. As he lowered her down his body, she wrapped her arms and legs around him, clinging to him like a monkey to a tree.

"We'll be quick," she promised.

He carried her beneath the warm water. He was already hard, and as she slid lower, taking every inch of him into her tight body, he practically growled, "The hell we will."

THEY WEREN'T QUICK, and they were *very* dirty. Jett was still half hard as they hurriedly dressed, thinking about Tegan on her knees in the shower sucking him off. Those big blue eyes staring up at him, challenging him to thrust deeper. *Fuck.* He was going to lose it just thinking about her.

"Hurry!" she said as she pulled on a sweatshirt. She grabbed his phone and shoved it in his back pocket as they rushed down the stairs.

He stopped at the bottom of the stairs and wrapped her in his arms, slowing down long enough to kiss her the way she deserved to be kissed, deeply and appreciatively. She was standing on the bottom step, which made her closer to his height, but she still went up on her toes. His hand slid to her ass. The thin material of her leggings only added fuel to their raging inferno. She made one of her sultry noises, and his freaking cock throbbed to attention.

"I'm never getting out of here if you keep making those noises." He brushed her wet hair away from her face and said, "We should do this again sometime."

"When are you coming back to the Cape?"

"In two weeks for the wedding."

She pressed closer and said, "Do you have a date?"

"No. I don't really date."

"Oh," she said with a hint of disappointment. "Well, I don't have time to date, either, with the move and the business and everything. But maybe we could do this again after the wedding?"

Damn she was cute when she was nervous. He touched his lips to hers and said, "What are you proposing? Another hookup?"

She shrugged one shoulder. "Well, we *are* friends now, and we're both busy. I kind of like these *benefits*…"

"Miss Fine, are you asking me to be your *fuck buddy?*"

"*No,*" she said, her cheeks turning crimson. "I hate that term."

"So, you've had an arrangement like that before?"

"Oh my gosh, *no!*" She tried to pull away. "Forget it. It was a dumb idea."

He tightened his hold on her and pressed a kiss to her forehead, bringing her eyes back to his. "I was *kidding.* I haven't done a friends-with-benefits relationship before, either. How would that work, exactly? No commitments? We just get together when I'm in town?"

She shrugged. "I don't know, but I know people do it. I can ask my friend Izzy back home. I think she has that kind of arrangement with a guy she knows from Boston."

"You're so fucking cute. Do *not* ask your friend. We can make our own rules, but we've got to be quick or I'll miss my flight."

"Okay. Well, um…obviously no commitments."

"Right. I'm good with that. But I don't share. If you're

sleeping with me, you're sleeping with *only* me."

She laughed softly. "I bet you must have been fun in the sandbox. That would be a very *possessive* friend-with-benefits setup, which is called a *boyfriend*."

"Whoa, *no*. We can't go there. I am definitely not looking to get tangled up with those kinds of strings." He looked at his watch.

"How about no asking for details about other guys or women, and sex with others *only* with protection," she suggested.

The thought of her with another man made him want to punch something. "That means a *condom*, *not* just the pill, right?"

She rolled her eyes. "Of course."

"Okay. Sounds good." He looked at his watch. "I've got to go."

He kissed her, and when she wound her arms around his neck, he couldn't *stop* kissing her. She was heaven and hell all wrapped up in one beautiful, effervescent package.

They kissed their way to the door, and when he finally found the strength to peel his lips away, he said, "This storm is supposed to get nasty midweek. As Brock said, stock up on essentials: food, water, matches, candles. Does this house have shutters? Do you know how to put them on?"

"I've been through storms before." She patted his chest and said, "Be careful driving to Boston, and have a safe flight."

He kissed her again, hating that he had to leave, and at the same time, irritated at himself for feeling that way. "Should we exchange contact info?"

She nibbled her lower lip, her eyes contemplative. "No. That's a recipe for disaster. We're not boyfriend-girlfriend. It's not like we should be touching base or sharing our days, right?"

"Right. I'll see you at the wedding, then?"

She nodded.

He gave her one last kiss and said, "I look forward to seeing you *naked* afterward."

"Me too." She blushed.

He pulled open the door, and the wind blew rain into the foyer. "Shit." He pushed the door closed, hating the thought of her out there all alone. "Maybe you should come to the resort and stay in one of the cottages so you're not out here by yourself."

"I'm *fine*. I've lived alone for years. I'm a grown woman. I can handle a little rain and wind." She nudged him toward the door and said, "Now *go*."

TEGAN CLOSED THE door behind Jett and wiggled her butt, pumping her fists and spinning in a little happy dance, whisper-shouting, "*Yes! Yes! Yes!*" She darted up the stairs, taking them two at time, and dove onto the bed. She flopped onto her back, beaming up at the ceiling, arms out to her sides, legs kicking, as she yelled, "That was *so* freaking fun!"

Her pulse was going crazy, and she might be losing it, but she didn't care. She couldn't wait for him to go through security at the airport and find the red lace thong with the little metal heart charm on it that she'd stuck in his coat pocket in the middle of the night. What she wouldn't give to be a fly on the wall when the metal detector went off!

How did she get so lucky to find a guy who was funny, sexy, smart, *and* good in bed? She rolled over and pressed her face into the pillow he'd used, inhaling his manly scent.

Jett Masters.

Even his name was hot.

She reached for her phone, rolling onto her back as she scrolled through her missed texts. She read one from Jock that he'd sent last night—*There's a storm heading your way. You okay?*—and one from Chloe that came in this morning—*I'm dying! You and JETT! Call me!* Tegan was glad she'd turned her phone off before the party.

She sent a quick response to Jock. *Hi. I'm fine. It's just rain and wind. How are you? Have you gone to see your family? Are you writing? Where are you?* Then she called Chloe.

"*Girl,*" Chloe said when she answered, "please tell me he did not drop you off at the door with a peck on the cheek."

"Oh my gosh! I don't even know where to start, except to say that Jett Masters can be my *master* any day of the week!"

They both shrieked.

"I want *all* the details. Starting with the very first kiss!"

"That man does not *kiss.* He *claims,* with every single touch. *God,* Chloe! I'm *giddy!* Why didn't you tell me you knew a sex god? And why haven't *you* scooped him up? Or Daphne? I can't even imagine how that incredible man is still single! But I'm so glad he is, because guess what?" She didn't give Chloe a chance to answer and yelled, "We're going to be friends with benefits!"

"*Wow!* I'm so happy for you," Chloe said, though she didn't sound all that happy. "Is that what you want?"

"Are you kidding? It's *perfect.*" A text rolled in and she glanced at her phone, saw Jock's name on the bubble, and decided to read it later. She popped to her feet and said, "*No* commitments. *No* worrying over feelings, or if he's going to call, or any of that nonsense. I get to do my thing, and he does his.

When he's in town we'll hook up. I'm going to be so busy getting the business ready to go for Harper's productions, I won't have time for dating. This makes it easy to have fun *and* focus on work." As Tegan paced, she caught sight of Jett's briefs sticking out from beneath the bed. The thought of him going commando made her stomach flutter.

"Well, Jett's certainly a great guy," Chloe said.

Tegan looked out the rain-streaked window at the trees bending with the wind, contemplating the hesitation in her friend's voice. "*But…?*"

"I don't know if this means anything at all, *but* as long as I've known Jett, I've never seen him with a woman."

"Trust me, he's *not* gay."

"I know that!" Chloe exclaimed. "I'm just thinking this through, playing devil's advocate. If he asked you to be his fuck buddy, don't you think he might have more *buddies* out there? Maybe it's his MO. It would make sense. He travels all the time."

"Can you please call it friends with benefits? It sounds nicer."

"Okay, FWB it is."

"Thank you. I know this is going to sound weird, but it was *my* idea, and neither of us have had an arrangement like this before."

"Wow, really? You asked him?"

"Yes, and honestly, I'm excited about doing this with him. It's perfect for my life right now, and Jett isn't just hot and amazing in bed. He makes me laugh, and you know how I feel about that." Her uncle's daily goal was to laugh as often as he could, and because of him, Tegan had always done the same. It was good for her soul and made the entire world look brighter, no matter what was going on around her. "It's a good feeling knowing that once every few weeks I'll have fun with a great guy. I don't know why *everyone* doesn't do this. Think about it, Chloe. No pining after a guy who inevitably messes up all the time."

"Or going through horrible dates with guys you meet on dating apps who say they're smart and funny, but really they're juvenile and dull."

"Exactly! See? You need an FWB, too!"

"God knows I need something better than what I have. But you said every few weeks. Did Jett actually *tell* you that he comes here every few weeks?"

"No. But his family is here, right? Didn't you tell me that you, Dean, Rick, Drake, and I can't remember who else grew up in Hyannis, or near there? Dean is Jett's brother, so I assume Jett grew up with you guys, too. It seems like he's close to everyone, so he must come back to see them."

"His family lives on the Cape, but he and his father aren't very close. I don't know the whole story, but things are tense there. And I don't want to burst your bubble, but Jett comes to town only three or four times *a year*, and he stays for only a day or two."

"*Oh.*" Three or four times a year? She wasn't sure what she'd expected, but it was definitely more than that. They'd gotten along so well, she'd been as excited about the friendship as she had about the sex. She tried to mask her disappointment and said, "That's *unexpected*, but it's not the end of the world."

"That won't bother you?"

"Of course not," she lied. "That's more sex than I'm having now, and I'll have more time for work. I'm still making costumes for the princess boutique, and I'm doing Cici's photo editing. I've got loads of stuff to do." Cici, Tegan's older sister, was a photographer living in New York with her husband and their two young children.

"And don't count out meeting a real boyfriend," Chloe reminded her. "Someone who can be there when you *want* him, not just when it's convenient."

"You just told me that dating sucks."

"I never said I was giving up. Finding the right guy is hard."

"But finding a *hard* guy is *easy*," Tegan said, and they both laughed. "Don't worry, I'm leaving that door open. We agreed that we could still have safe sex with others." Her stomach twisted at the thought of Jett in bed with another woman. She tried to shove that thought away, but it hovered like a dark cloud, impossible to ignore. She closed her eyes, remembering what it had felt like when he was lying on top of her, inside her, saying dirty things. It worked. Her body tingled all over, wiping out the distressing thought of moments earlier.

Except now she was turned on again, and that wasn't good, either, so she said, "Tell me what you're doing today, because I'm starting to miss having that man's hands all over me."

"Oh boy, here we go…"

"Shut up! You have no idea how incredible…Never mind. I can't think about him or I get all hot and bothered, and I have work to do."

"You can always whip out your battery-operated boyfriend."

"You are *not* helping. Distract me, please. Just tell me what you're doing today, or sing a stupid song, or *something*. Because if I don't stop seeing Jett's face, I'll never get any work done."

"Don't use his name, Teg. Trust me, it helps. Anyway, I have a very exciting day planned. I'm battening down the hatches. Have you been outside? The storm is heading directly for us, which reminds me. Justin is stopping by later to help me with my shutters. Do you want me to have him come by to help you?"

Tegan pushed to her feet and headed downstairs. "Why does everyone think I need help? I'm *fine*." She went into the kitchen, which was the size of half the house she rented in Peaceful Harbor. "What I need is breakfast." She pulled open the fridge and scanned the nearly empty shelves. "*And* a trip to the grocery store."

"Stock up on water and food that doesn't need to be cooked in case you lose power. This storm could get nasty."

Tegan grabbed a yogurt and tore it open. "It's already nasty." She pulled a spoon from the drawer and said, "But don't worry, the grocery store is on my list right after I get my arms around some things for Harper's productions."

"Everyone is excited for that to start."

"I am, too. I think it was smart to start with a small pilot program this summer and make sure we've got things under control before we go hog-wild. I just hope we can pull it off."

"You can, and we're here to help if you need it."

"Thanks. I'd better get started. Please don't tell anyone about my arrangement with Jett. I don't mind the girls knowing, but it might be weird if the guys find out."

"Girlfriend, I hate to tell you this, but after last night's mating dance, you and Jett have *no* secrets."

"Great. I guess I should have expected that. Wish me luck, then."

"You already got lucky. You should be wishing *me* luck."

"You don't need luck. Justin's gorgeous, he's a great friend, and he's coming to your house today. That's a prime FWB op right there."

"I don't do *bad boys*, remember? And look at you, pimping out the whole FWB thing like you're an expert on the subject."

They both laughed, and they harassed each other for a few more minutes before finally ending the call.

Tegan carried her yogurt down the hall toward her uncle's office, where she'd worked on her ideas for the theater yesterday. As she passed the elegant living room, she became painfully aware of the burgeoning silence, broken only by the eerie sounds of wind whipping against the old manor house and rain slapping the expansive windows. Had the odd creaks and groans of the six-bedroom house always been there? In the past, when her uncle was napping or out with Jock, she heard his laughter in the silence, or his craggy voice telling one of his tales that always made *her* laugh. But now it was Jett's laughter she heard, his deep voice masking the sounds of the storm. He was front and center in her imagination, as if he belonged there. As if he were invited by her uncle because he thought Jett's laughter would make her happy.

She pondered that thought as she entered his office. Her uncle's presence was everywhere, too strong for even images of Jett to obliterate. She could still see Harvey sitting in his wheelchair behind the stately desk and herself sitting in one of the two plum-colored chairs across from him, mesmerized by everything and anything he said. He'd always seemed bigger than life, like it was he who belonged on his stage, even in his wheelchair. She remembered sitting on his lap when she was young as he read to her out of one of the books from the shelves that lined the wall behind the desk. She'd give anything to see him one more time, to hold his frail hand and listen to his beautiful stories about his beloved wife, Adele. Longing brewed dark and forsaken inside her. She glanced out the nearly floor-to-ceiling windows, which usually offered impressive views of the amphitheater, but it was too stormy and gray to see that far across the yard.

She turned away, looking over the piles of her uncle's things scattered around the room. She'd started to go through them, but when sadness had swamped her, she'd set them aside for another day.

Today was not that day.

She had no idea how she'd worked on her plans for the theater in his office yesterday, but there was no way she could do it today. She wondered if her encounter with Jett had sparked these raw emotions, but if anything, he'd brought renewed life into the lonely mansion. *Maybe that's it. His absence magnifies the silence.*

She didn't know if that was why she felt lonelier now than she had yesterday, but she gathered her things and hurried to the kitchen, one of the only rooms where her uncle's presence didn't overwhelm her. It made sense, since he'd had a cook come several times each week to prepare and stock meals that Jock would later heat up for him.

The kitchen was brighter than the rest of the house, with winter-white walls and light maple cabinets. There were fireplaces in almost every room, including the kitchen, which made it feel homey and old-fashioned, despite the newer finishes. She set up her supplies on the large kitchen island and table to begin mapping out her plan of attack, then realized she'd never read Jock's message. She navigated to it on her phone and read his clipped response. *Glad you're fine.*

"Oh, Jock," she said sorrowfully. It had taken years for Jock to confide in her about how he'd met her great-uncle at the lowest point of his life, after suffering the loss of his girlfriend and newborn baby. She'd never learned exactly how Jock had met her great-uncle or how Jock's position as caretaker had come about. But she knew Jock had been a bestselling author before suffering the heart-wrenching loss, and he'd never gone back to writing. Jock had always said that her uncle had saved him, but her uncle had said they'd saved each other. Neither man had ever elaborated, and she'd never pushed. But in his will, her uncle had left Jock an old-fashioned typewriter *and* two million dollars that Jock would only be able to claim if he published something. Her uncle was a jokester, but he was also the most loving man she knew. She was sure that was his way of forcing Jock to get back to living his life for *himself.*

But some things couldn't be forced.

Jock didn't talk about his family much, but she knew they lived on Silver Island, not far from Nantucket and Martha's Vineyard, and ran the Top of the Island Vineyard. Tegan knew he had rarely gone home to visit over the past few years because of caring for Harvey full time, but she had a feeling there was more to it than that. She had met his parents, three sisters, and his brother Levi when they'd stopped by to visit him over the summers. But she had never met Jock's twin brother, Archer. Once when she'd asked about how close Jock and Archer were, Jock had made a comment that sounded like there was trouble between them. But he'd promptly changed the subject, and once again, she hadn't pushed. He'd put his belongings into storage and left the Cape shortly after her uncle passed away. She'd asked if he was going home, and he'd said he didn't want to burden his family with his grief. That worried her. She considered Jock family, and she could no sooner let him grieve alone than Jock could have let her uncle go without proper care. But Jock was a stubborn man, like her uncle had been. It was no wonder they'd gotten along so well.

She decided to call Jock rather than texting.

"You didn't have to call," Jock said when he answered.

She heard the smile in his voice. "If you didn't want me to call, you would have answered my questions."

"I'm good, Teg. Are you okay? I've been watching the weather. It doesn't look good."

"I'm fine."

"Don't forget to stock up on water. The freezer in the basement is big enough to hold..."

As Jock detailed Storm Prep 101, Tegan thought about Jett doing the same. She wished they'd exchanged phone numbers so she would know if he reached Boston safely. *God...*She was doing exactly what they'd been trying to avoid.

She forced herself to focus on Jock instead of Jett and said, "Jock, I'm fine. It's a storm, not Armageddon. Where are you? In the States? Overseas? Are *you* okay?"

"At the moment I'm sitting in a café enjoying a cup of coffee and reading a newspaper. You know what that is, right? Those things they made back in the day that stain your fingers?"

"Ha ha, smart-ass." Jock was an expert at circumventing questions. "Let's forget the *where* and go with *how*. Are you trying to write?"

"I am, and I'm staring at the same blank page. How about you? Have you fleshed out that business plan you've been thinking about, and putting off, all winter?"

"I had a lot to take care of with my other businesses, but I'm working on it." She leaned over a large piece of poster board and drew an enormous circle. "But we're not talking about me. Have you reached out to your family? You were with my uncle *all* the time. You can finally spend some time with them. I bet they miss you."

"How was Harper's party?"

"*Jock.* Have you at least reached out to Archer? He never came to visit you when I was here."

"Teg, drop it, okay?"

"It would help if I knew what we were *dropping.*"

He was quiet for a long moment, and then he said, "He doesn't want to hear from me. Next subject?"

"Are you at least going to see your family when we're on Silver Island for Harper and Gavin's wedding?"

There was another long stretch of silence.

"*Jock...*"

"You never answered me. How was the party?"

"Next subject," she teased, and he chuckled. "Well, if you're not writing or with your family, you should come back and stay here with me. This was your home for more than a decade, and I'm lonely here."

"Even with all the friends you've made?"

"I don't mean here at the Cape. I mean in the house, on the property. Besides, I could help you find writing inspiration and you could help me with the business."

"I can't be there right now, Tegan. It reminds me of how much I've lost."

She sighed, unable to argue with that. "Tell me about it," she said softly.

"You don't have to carry on your uncle's legacy. He wanted you to be happy, and he said you were meant to find your happiness at the Cape."

"He said that?"

"Many times. That's why he gave you a reason to be there. But you don't have to stick with it. He'd never want you to be lonely."

"I know. I just miss him. I want to make the theater work and I want to carry on his legacy. I believe in the same things he did, paying it forward and spreading joy. It's just this huge, lonely house that has me in a weird place. I'm working in the kitchen," she admitted. "And I'd better get back to it, actually."

"Is your fridge full? Do you have candles?"

"Jock, *please* stop acting like an overprotective brother. I'm a big girl."

"A lighter? Wood for the fireplace?"

"Goodbye, Jock."

"Tegan, I'm serious. New England storms are monsters compared to what you're used to."

"I'm saying goodbye now, but I love you and wish you were here."

"I love you, too, Teg."

"Then come back."

"If I can't be overprotective, you can't nag."

"What*ever*. I worry about you."

"Let's get back to the things you need to have on hand for the storm."

"*Ugh!* Goodbye!" She ended the call feeling happy at having heard his voice.

As she pushed up her sleeves and picked up a pen, her phone vibrated with a text from Jock. She opened and read the message. *You could find a boyfriend to keep you company.* She wiggled her shoulders thinking about her new FWB situation. Who needed the headaches that came with boyfriends when she had Jett?

She thumbed out a response. *No time for a bf. I've got a business to plan.* She set down her phone and went to work with thoughts of Jett dancing in her mind. There was no better motivation to get the job done than knowing that after two weeks of hard work she'd be rewarded with a night or two of *hard* Jett.

Chapter Seven

THE THUNDEROUS ROAR of the waves echoed in Jett's ears as he flew through the front door of his cottage at Bayside Resort, trailing water all the way to the bedroom. Wind and sheeting rain had slowed traffic to a crawl. The normally short drive from Brewster to Wellfleet had taken Jett more than an hour. He grabbed his suitcase from the closet, tossed it on the bed, and shoved his clothes into it. He heard the door to the cottage open. *Shit.* He didn't have time for long goodbyes.

"Jett?" Dean called out.

"Bedroom closet," he hollered as he put his suit in the garment bag.

Dean's coat and hat were drenched, and he had a pinched look on his face.

"It's a shit show out there, and I'm late." Jett zipped the garment bag and said, "I've got to get to Boston."

"I've been calling you all morning. Tia called *me* trying to track you down. Why didn't you answer your phone?"

Jett ground out a curse and pulled his phone from his back pocket. "I turned it off last night and forgot to turn it back on." He fired up the phone and it vibrated like a nymphomaniac's sex toy. He'd missed five calls from Tia, a handful from his clients, and one call from his brother Doug. "Tia's going to slaughter me."

"Wait. You turned your phone *off?*" Dean asked as Jett pushed past him with the garment bag. "And *forgot* to turn it on?"

Jett was too busy grinding his teeth to respond. He'd been so fucking caught up in Tegan, he'd forgotten *everything* else: the phone, the time, the calls he'd needed to make that morning, *and* the reports he'd hoped to review before the flight. He tossed the garment bag on the bed and began scrolling through Tia's messages, most of which were warning him about the impending storm.

"You must have had a hell of a night with Tegan." Dean squinted, reaching for Jett's coat pocket. "What's that?"

Jett looked down as Dean pulled something red from his pocket. His brother dangled—*a red lace thong?*—from his fingertips with a laugh.

"Damn, bro. I've known you my whole life and never realized you were a trophy guy."

"Give me that." Jett snagged the thong and shoved it back in his coat pocket. He hadn't taken the thong, which meant Tegan had put it there. *Holy hell, that's hot.*

"That explains a lot. I guess you two hit it off."

"Yeah, she's great," he said as he hurried into the bathroom to gather his toiletries.

Great didn't even begin to describe what he thought of Tegan. He'd spent the first half of the drive back to Bayside fighting the urge to say *fuck it,* turn around, and drive right back to her. He'd spent the second half of the drive convincing himself not to. But he wasn't about to start spouting off about how amazing she was. That would make him as messed up as he'd been that morning, and he couldn't afford to be side-tracked. He had a plane to catch.

"So why are you running off?" Dean crossed his arms, staring Jett down as he came out of the bathroom with his toiletry case. "There's a fricking storm blowing in, and you'd rather risk your life to run away than get stuck seeing a woman for a second time?"

"Cut the shit, Dean. Business doesn't stop because of a little storm."

"Actually, it does. But *you* don't, do you?" Dean followed Jett as he stalked into the living room to grab his computer and briefcase.

"I don't know why you're so pissed off, but I don't have time for this." He put his laptop in his briefcase and headed back into the bedroom.

"I'm pissed because for the first time that I can remember, *something* came before work in your life, and you're acting like she was *nothing*."

Jett gritted his teeth. He was irritated enough for allowing himself to get so caught up in a woman. He didn't need his brother hammering him, too.

"Tegan is our *friend*," Dean said. "She's going into business with Harper, and hopefully she'll be around for a long time. You can't screw her over and leave us to clean up the mess."

Jett set down his briefcase and closed the distance between them, anger boiling inside him. "When have I *ever* left you to clean up my mess with a woman? For that matter, when have you ever seen me hook up with someone around here? You *know* I don't fuck with women's heads."

"That's my *point*," Dean said, drawing his shoulders back.

Jett was on his last nerve, and it was fraying fast. "What's your fucking point, Dean? Spit it out clearly or I'm going to miss my flight."

His phone rang with Tia's ringtone, and when he reached for it, Dean said, "I know what your messes look like, Jett. You may not have left this particular kind of mess before, but that doesn't mean I don't see the writing on the wall."

"There's no *mess*, Dean. I know how to handle women."

"Mom's a woman. If you handle Tegan anything like you handle her, then I'd better bring tissues."

Jett's phone stopped ringing, and he stifled another curse. "I know I let Mom down, and I appreciate everything you've done for me."

"*Do*, Jett. Everything I *do* for *her*."

As if Jett needed a reminder of the guilt he lived with? Jett couldn't keep his voice from escalating. "When you had trouble with Dad, who had your back? Who dropped *everything* to be here for you when shit hit the fan?"

"You did."

"Damn right I did," he fumed. "Don't act like I don't do shit for this family. I might be severely lacking in the *time* department, but there's so much damn water under the bridge, it's all I can do to tread water."

"I know," Dean said a little less angrily. "I get that. All I'm saying is, if you gave half the amount of time to your family that you do to your clients, maybe you wouldn't be so stressed all the time."

"I'm not stressed all the time. Coming *here* is stressful."

Dean's eyes narrowed.

"Not because of *you*. It's hard to be away from my office, that's all."

"That's *all*...?" Dean nodded, with a sorrowful look in his eyes. "You've got friends and family here who love you. Maybe one day you'll realize that just because you look like Dad doesn't mean you have to act like he used to."

Jett's phone vibrated with another text, giving him a reason to avert his eyes from the painful truth in Dean's. It was from Tia. *Call me!*

"You're a great guy, but your priorities are seriously fucked up." Dean glanced out the window and said, "I've got to get shit done, too. Have a safe flight."

Jett ground out a curse as Dean left the cottage, and he called Tia.

"Are you *okay?*"

The panic in Tia's voice only reminded him of the mistake he'd made. "I'm fucking *perfect*. Sorry for worrying you."

"What happened? Did you lose your phone?"

"No. I turned it off."

There was a long silence.

"Tia, you there?"

"I'm picking my jaw up off the floor."

"*Christ*, not you, too. What's the story with my flight?"

"What's the story with turning off your phone? Did someone have a gun to your head?"

"No."

"Ah, a *knife* then?"

The amusement in her voice made him chuckle. "I was with someone. Now can we drop it?"

"No effing way! There's only one woman who could get you to turn off your phone. I didn't know Mila Kunis was in town. How'd you score that action? Kill off Ashton Kutcher? Oh man, I'd better get my sister to find you a criminal attorney, stat!" Tia's older sister, Aida, was an entertainment attorney.

"Are you done?" he asked flatly.

"Not even close. I wonder if she was silently critiquing you, comparing you to her husband. Did she accidentally call you Ashton? What's she like? Sweet and sassy, or was she everything you hoped for? Naughty, nice, and down to party?"

"Can you be done busting my balls now, please? I don't get on your case about the guys you go out with."

"No, you just have them followed and report all their dirty deeds to me," she said sarcastically.

"Someone's got to watch out for you." There was only one reason Tia wouldn't be freaking out about his flight, and as that reality sank it, it pissed him off. "My flight was canceled, wasn't it?"

"If you'd had your phone on last night, I could have gotten you on a night flight. But you had to go get your freak on."

He laughed. "Enough, Tia."

"I want her name so I can sic Reggie Steele on her." Reggie was a private investigator whom they'd used several times over the years.

"Not happening."

"You're a buzzkill."

"I think she'd disagree." He looked at his bags and thought about spending another night with Tegan. His cock cast its vote with an excited twitch. They'd had amazing chemistry, and he wanted to know more about her. And *that*…was dangerous.

Therein lay his answer.

As enticing as Tegan was, Jett needed to tackle the work he'd put off and get started on the due diligence for the Carlisle deal. If he drove into Boston and worked at the airport while he waited for a flight, he could review the reports and make the calls he hadn't made that morning. "Tia, when can you get me out of here?"

"Did you not hear the message about the storm heading for the Cape? Or did she literally fuck your brains out?"

She did. "*When?* Tomorrow?"

"Hopefully. I'm on it, but you'd better keep your phone on this time so I can reach you, even if you can't keep your pants on."

"*Enough*, T." *Tomorrow.* He'd put the hours in now, get his work done, and leave at the crack of dawn to get to the airport. "I'll be right here working with no distractions, phone on, nose to the grindstone."

LATER THAT AFTERNOON, with his vehicle packed and ready to go, Jett was still trying to get his nose to that grindstone, but thoughts of Tegan continued to distract him. He'd returned his brother Doug's call. Catching up with him was a pleasurable fifteen minutes, during which they talked about Doug and his wife's station overseas. Their station changed with each assignment. They didn't talk about their parents, and since Doug came home only once or twice a year, he didn't resent Jett the way Dean seemed to. After speaking with Doug, Jett called his grandmother Rose to check on her, hoping that maybe she could help take his mind off Tegan. They talked weekly, and she could usually take his mind off anything. But today even his funny, sweet grandma Rose couldn't thwart his thoughts from Tegan, though he was glad she was safe in the storm.

After the call, he glanced at his coat, thinking about the red lace thong Tegan had put in his pocket. He'd never forget how beautiful and sexy she'd looked last night when he'd stripped off her black thong and she'd stood nearly naked before him, save for her choker and boots, wearing confidence like a second skin. He had no idea when she'd had time to sneak that tempting piece of lingerie into his pocket, but the fact that she had was a major turn-on.

His phone rang, and *The Kid* flashed on the screen. Jett had wondered how long it would take him to reach out. He answered the call and said, "Hey, kid, how's it going?"

"Can't complain. I just got back from two weeks in Bali with the redhead I met last summer. I told you about her. Likes to surf, owns a bar in Manhattan?"

Zack was always boasting about one woman or another. Jett couldn't keep them straight, but he wasn't in the mood to talk about the kid's sex life, especially when he couldn't stop thinking about his own, so he said, "Sure. Glad you had a good time."

"*Good time* doesn't even begin to describe how great the trip was. It's amazing what sunshine and a good woman can do for your spirit. Anyway, now that I'm well rested, I'm ready to crush the competition for Carlisle Enterprises. Just thought I should call you first, you know, give you a chance to back out gracefully, save your reputation."

Jett chuckled, imagining the twenty-seven-year-old pacing by the windows of his Manhattan office, dreaming about being as successful as Jett was. Jett could buy and sell Zack many times over, but Zack was an excellent businessman and a smart investor. With his drive and determination, he'd make his own mark on the world—even if it wouldn't be by crushing Jett. "I see you still have those stars in your eyes."

"A wise mentor once told me that if I didn't strive to be the best, I was just wasting everyone's time."

"Sounds like a smart guy. Let me know when you're done dipping your toes in the investment pool and are ready to give up the ladies and wild nights to play with the big boys."

"You mean give up my life?" Zack laughed. "Never gonna happen, man. You might need to give up those things in order to sit on your throne, but that just means I'm a better business-man. See ya in the trenches, Jett."

"Have fun in those trenches, kid. I'll be the man on the throne."

As he ended the call and pocketed his phone, a loud crack of thunder boomed, sounding like it was right outside the cottage. The storm had become white noise when he was thinking about Tegan, but now the sounds of wind and rain—and shouting—traipsed in. He grabbed his coat—giving the pocket with the lingerie a little squeeze—and went outside to investigate.

Dean and Rick were hustling toward the supply shed.

Jett ran into the driving rain after them and hollered, "What's going on? Need a hand?"

"A tree fell on the gallery!" Rick shouted over the wind.

Shit. The girls. "Everyone okay?" His mind raced to Tegan. There were trees all over her property. He could kick himself for not getting her number so he could check on her.

"Yeah," Rick said. "I won't let Des leave the house in this weather, and Vi and Andre were in their cottage."

"We can definitely use a hand. Streets are flooding, causing all sorts of trouble for retailers," Dean explained, weeding through keys for the one to the shed. "Drake and Serena took off to help in town. Violet and Andre started to get the artwork out of the gallery, but there is a ton of it. We need to cut the branches off and clear the roof so we can tarp it."

As Dean unlocked the shed, Rick said, "What about your flight?"

"Canceled. Tia's trying for a later one." He followed them into the shed.

"I thought you had work to do," Dean said with a bite of tension.

Jett held his stare. "I got a verbal ass kicking from my whiny brother. I'm not about to make that mistake again. You need me. I'm here to help."

Dean handed him a chain saw. "Think your delicate hands can handle real work?"

"You mean *after* I kick your ass?"

They loaded supplies into the back of Dean's truck, and as they drove next door, Jett asked if anyone had checked on Daphne and Hadley. Thankfully, Dean had, and they were safe and sound in their apartment above the office.

Dean parked in front of the gallery, which was located in the first of three cottages leading up to Summer House. The tree had fallen from the backyard, crushing the right side of the structure. The gallery looked like it had been swallowed by the spidery branches.

As they piled out of the truck, Violet came out of the gallery carrying a box covered with plastic and met them on the walkway. "The sex shop is demolished. We're putting the merchandise in the empty cottage." She peered at Jett from under the hood of her black raincoat and said, "You're still here?"

"My flight was canceled. Sorry about your stuff. Did you get pictures for the insurance company?"

"Damn it. No. I didn't think about it." Violet turned to go back inside.

"I'll do it," Jett offered. "Has anyone talked to Tegan?"

Violet smirked. "Weren't you the last one to crawl out of her bed?"

"We didn't exchange numbers."

"Nice move, *rookie*," Violet said. "Chloe talked to her. She's fine."

Thank God.

Violet took off toward the empty cottage, and the men sprang into action. Jett hiked a thumb over his shoulder and said, "I'm going to take those insurance pictures."

"We need to make sure the structure is safe," Rick said. He was an architect by trade and had owned a design-build company in DC for several years. "Then we'll empty the place and deal with the tree."

Dean retrieved a ladder from the truck as Rick and Jett jogged around to the back of the cottage.

"You and Tegan didn't hit it off after all?" Rick asked.

"What do you mean?"

"You didn't exchange numbers."

"I was rushing to make a flight."

"Uh-huh."

"Seriously. She's incredible, and we were great together. So great that I forgot to turn my phone back on." Not to mention he'd slept better, and later, than he had in years.

"If that's the case, then you're an idiot for not getting her number," Rick said as they inspected the stability of the fallen tree, which was leaning against the crushed wall and roof.

"I've spent the last few hours debating driving out to check on her. But when I made a comment to her about taking care in the storm, she gave me a hard time and said she could handle herself. Think it'll look clingy if I check on her?" Jett asked as

Dean rounded the corner of the house carrying a ladder.

Dean leaned the ladder against the rear of the house and said, "Did you just say *clingy?*"

"Should we get our *Teen* magazines and take a quiz to see if you're clingy?" Rick chuckled.

"*Fuck* off." Jett didn't like the idea of Tegan being out there all alone, with no neighbors in sight. He didn't care how long she'd lived alone; if a tree fell on her house she could get hurt.

They didn't talk about Tegan or anything else as they inspected the fallen tree, which thankfully appeared to be lodged in place and stable for now. Jett took pictures of the damage from the back and sides of the cottage, then headed inside. Rain poured through the open roof on the right side of the cottage. Tangled branches shot out in all directions. Tables were demolished, the pieces scattered on the wet floor among shards of broken pottery and torn paintings. Andre stood in his rain gear among the rubble, piling paintings into boxes.

"What a nightmare," Andre grumbled.

"I'm sorry, man." Jett grabbed as many pieces of artwork and pottery as he could hold and put them in another box. Then he got busy taking pictures.

"Vi and I are supposed to take off after the wedding to open another clinic, but we can't leave Des and Rick to deal with this mess on their own." Andre ran Operation SHINE, an international humanitarian organization similar to Doctors Without Borders. He and Violet traveled to open three clinics each year in newly developed areas.

"Rick's got the experience to handle it," Jett reminded him.

"He has a resort to run and a baby on the way." Andre picked up handmade cards Desiree had painted, which were now ruined, and said, "The girls worked so hard on this stuff."

"It sucks that they've lost artwork they poured their hearts and souls into, and the income from their hard work, but at least they weren't in here when the tree fell. I don't want to diminish how awful this is, so I apologize if this sounds cold, but at the end of the day, art is still just an accessory," Jett said as Violet stepped into the cottage. "The girls are irreplaceable."

Andre hoisted the box into his arms and said, "You're absolutely right. I can't imagine a single day without Vi."

"You know I love you, Andre," Violet said. "But can we stop the touchy-feely shit and get moving before that tree flattens us all?"

"That's my girl." Andre gave her a chaste kiss on his way out of the cottage.

I'd like to know how my woman is.

Jett uttered a curse. Tegan was *not* his woman, and that was exactly how he wanted it to remain.

"What's going on with you?" Violet asked. "Why do you look like you want to kill someone instead of like you just enjoyed a night of fuckery?"

Because I have no idea where the urge to go check on her fits into the damn rules.

HOURS LATER, JETT was frozen to the bone, they'd managed to salvage a few pieces of artwork, and the guys were all heading into Summer House, where the girls had a fire going and hot food on the table.

"You coming?" Dean asked Jett.

"Nah. I've got work to do."

"Thanks for all your help today. It was nice having you around."

Jett nodded. As cold and drenched as he was, he'd enjoyed pulling together with Dean and the guys, too. He'd been relieved when he saw Daphne a while ago on her way to Summer House with Hadley to join the girls and she'd mentioned that she'd seen a post from Tegan on some book club forum. Tegan had said she'd stocked up on food for the storm and was planning on staying inside until the sun came out. At least he knew she was safe.

"In case I don't see you before you take off, have a safe flight." Dean gave him a quick slap on the back and went to join the others.

Jett headed for his cottage, chewing on a twinge of regret that his brother knew he wasn't big on goodbyes. A quick *See ya next time* text was usually all Dean got from him.

When Tia's text rolled in, Jett was glad for the distraction.

I've got your flight details.

He typed out, *Great, email them,* sent it off, and pulled out his car keys, circling back toward the resort office to drop off the key to the cottage.

Chapter Eight

BETWEEN THE COLD stinging rain and hellacious winds, it was nearly impossible for Tegan to see, much less push her cart across the grocery store parking lot. It took all her might to keep the darn thing from careening into a parked car. When she finally made it to her vehicle, she pushed the cart against the side of her car and held on to it with one hand as she transferred the groceries into the back seat. The trunk had long ago stopped functioning.

After wrestling against the wind and rain to return the cart, she flopped into the driver's seat out of breath and soaking wet, feeling like she'd been to *war*. She rested her head back, laughing at the ridiculousness of her day. If she hadn't spent half the day dreaming about Jett, she might have left the house earlier and beaten the crazies to the grocery store. The storm was far worse than she had thought. There were trees down *everywhere*. Her car had rattled and shaken the whole way as she'd followed detours around flash floods and accidents, and when she'd finally arrived, the shelves had been nearly bare. The checkout lines were so long, she had time to text her sister, her mother, and a few friends back home. She'd even had time to post on the book club forum and read all the posts she'd missed the last couple days. What felt like a *lifetime* later, she had finally checked out. At least the madness had cured her from thinking about Jett as anything more than a good-time friend. She didn't have time for daydreams. He had his life, and she had hers. Now that she had her head on straighter, she *totally* had this FWB thing under control.

The gallon of mint-chocolate-chip ice cream I bought is just backup, in case I fall off the FWB wagon again.

She started her car, but it coughed and sputtered to silence. She patted the dashboard. "Come on, Berta. I believe in you." She turned the key again, and it sputtered again, rattling around her, then *died*.

"One more time, girl. You can do this." She cranked the engine. It wheezed, shuddered, then *caught*. Tegan let out a celebratory *whoop!*

She turned up the heat, fastened her seat belt, and drove out of the lot, crawling along behind a line of endless vehicles. The police rerouted traffic around a fallen tree, and she followed the other cars, stopping for long stretches of time and then moving at only five or ten miles per hour down unfamiliar roads. They were detoured two more times, and she hoped she was still heading in the right direction. Her mind drifted to the work she'd done earlier in the day. She'd made progress on the business plan, but since the amphitheater was no longer going to be used solely for children's productions, she needed to give it a new name. After spending far too long doodling potential names and writing *Jett* more than a dozen times with swirls, hearts, and other ridiculous scribbles, she'd given up and started designing the furry, winged mermaid costume for Joni. But that had reminded her of her chat with Jett at the café, so she'd headed upstairs to try to finally rid her brain of thoughts of him.

Cleaning usually helped clear her head. She'd cleaned her entire bedroom and washed all the laundry, including the sheets and Jett's forgotten boxer briefs—which didn't help her escape her thoughts of him.

Then or now.

She wondered where he was going on his flight from Boston. What did he have on his schedule? Meetings? Did he work in an office? From home? Chloe said he traveled a lot, so she assumed he was going to a business meeting. Those thoughts led to more specific ones about Jett. What was he like on a regular day when they weren't at a party and when he wasn't working? Where did he *live*? Did he really come back to see his family only a few times each year? She swallowed hard and asked herself the most painful question of all. Would he be with other women over the next two weeks?

Oh man. She was totally *chicking out* again. She needed to stop.

She gripped the steering wheel tighter and focused on the road. How long had she been driving? An hour? Longer? She had no idea where she was and hoped the car she was following as they turned onto a larger road was heading to Brewster, too. She looked around. Power lines swayed, and massive trees keeled in the wind. Potholes rippled like ponds in the road, and the white-gray skies surrounding her looked more like winter than spring. She continued following the car ahead of her onto what looked like a main road, and eventually she recognized her surroundings.

Thank goodness.

Her fingers unfurled, aching from the white-knuckled grip she had on the steering wheel. She hunched forward, using her hand to wipe the foggy windshield as she navigated toward home. She breathed a sigh of relief when the long private road that led to her house came into view. She made the turn, splashing through the puddled pothole she normally avoided. Her car bottomed out, lurching right into a rain-filled ditch and sending her groceries flying forward. She *yelped*, slamming on the brakes. The car shuddered and shook, rattling to silence.

"No, no, *no!*" Tegan pleaded, throwing the car into park. She tried to start it up again. "Come on! Come on!" She peered out her window into the driving rain, unable to see more than about a foot away before everything became a blur. But that foot was enough to see that the car was half in and half out of the ditch, resting at an awkward angle.

"Damn it!" She cranked the engine again. *Come on, Berta. Start already!* The wheezing of the engine sounded like a man struggling with his last breath, which made her think of her uncle. She could just see him shaking his head in amusement because she hadn't taken his fancy car. His voice sailed through her ears, *Laugh it off, darlin'*, followed by his familiar and comforting low chuckle.

God, she missed him.

She closed her eyes against the burning tears that she refused to let fall, remembering how her uncle had once told her that crying wouldn't help any situation—unless she got pulled over by the police. *In that case, you pull out all the stops to avoid a ticket. Go right for his ego and flutter those lashes. If that doesn't work, collapse into tears.* Laughter tumbled from her lips with the memory. She'd been sixteen when he'd said it, and she'd been afraid to drive by herself in a new area. Of course he'd made her laugh, and then he'd sent her off to pick up something *very important* from a gallery. He'd given her the keys to his car and said, *Roll down the windows and turn up the music. Fears are no match for Cape Cod air.* On the way to the gallery, she'd driven too slowly, windows up, radio off, just like her mother had taught her. *No distractions.* She'd arrived white-knuckled and feeling like she'd held her breath the whole way. On the way home she'd cracked the window and turned the radio on low. Soon she'd gotten lost in a song and turned it up, rolling down her window and enjoying the calming sea air. She'd felt so good, she'd stopped for ice cream, driven to Breakwater Beach and taken a walk there. When she finally got home, her uncle's wrapped package in hand, he'd asked her to unwrap it for him. In it was a small, hand-carved wooden jewelry box with *There's nothing you can't do* engraved in the top. Apparently her mother had forewarned her uncle about her fear of driving, and he'd had the whole excursion planned all along.

She still used that jewelry box, and she almost always drove with the windows down and the radio on.

Except in weather like this.

She looked at the groceries scattered around the car and had the funny thought that at least she wouldn't starve. She searched for her phone, finding it under the passenger seat, and debated who to call to help her get her car out of the ditch. She remembered that Justin was going to see Chloe, so she called her. The line crackled and her call went to voicemail, so she left a message. "Hey, it's me. I think I might need Justin's help after all. My car's stuck in a ditch. But, um, if you guys are having sex or something, don't stop. I'll try someone else." She laughed softly as she ended the call, thinking, *Go, Chloe!*

She stared out at the rain, pondering who else to call. Her phone made three violently angry beeping sounds, startling her. A dangerous weather warning appeared on the screen advising residents to stay indoors due to flash floods and downed trees.

"Gee, really?" she said as thunder rumbled overhead. A streak of lightning cracked too close for comfort and she *shrieked.* In the next breath, hysterical laughter burst from her lungs. She sent a silent thank-you to her uncle because he was right: Laughter was far better than tears. But she sure wished he could see his way to pull a few more heavenly strings and send a tow truck.

A tow truck!

She navigated to the browser on her phone and tried to search tow trucks, but the stupid blue bar stopped after a second, never fully loading. *Perfect.* The car rocked in the gale-force winds, and Tegan tried the engine again, but there was only a faint and ominous *click.* Berta had had enough, and as much as Tegan loved her car, she found herself laughing *again,* drunk on circumstance.

She thought about Chloe, Jett, and Jock trying to warn her about the storm and how she'd assured them she could handle it. *Damn right I can.* She didn't need to bother her friends. The house wasn't *that* far, even if it was a *really* long road. The house was down a ways, then around a bend, out of sight. She could make it in four or five minutes with the groceries and the rain, and she wasn't going to melt or blow away. Berta would be just fine until she could arrange to get her towed and hopefully fixed.

Tegan to the rescue, she mused, though she was in no rush to sprint through the rain carrying groceries.

She unhooked her seat belt and rooted around the back seat for the ice cream. If she had to brave the storm, she deserved something sweet first. Maybe the rain would let up while she enjoyed it. She tore off the top, and using two fingers, scooped out the creamy goodness and shoved it into her mouth. *Mm.*

She dug out another hunk and ate it.

This is even better than laughter.

Storms were kind of pretty when she wasn't trying to get somewhere. She sank back in the seat, eating ice cream and watching the rain.

A long while later, headlights flashed through her rear window. She turned and stared at the blurry lights. *Justin! Thank you, Chloe!*

A dark, hooded figure appeared beside her window, and she quickly rolled it down, but the bright blue eyes staring back at her stole her voice, and all that came out was a breathy and confused "Hey."

Jett's gaze moved to her sticky hand stuck in the nearly empty ice cream container, and amusement rose in his eyes. "Having a little party?"

"I..." *Jett. God, Jett. Look at you.* He was even more handsome than she remembered. And he was here! *Wait...what?* "I thought you were leaving town."

"My flight was canceled." He leaned his forearms on the window, blocking the rain from hitting her and bringing his handsome face close enough to kiss. He smelled rugged and delicious. "I'm flying out tomorrow morning instead. I know you can handle the storm on your own, and you obviously have everything under control, having chosen a ditch from which to watch it and all, but I thought you might want a buddy to hang out with. Is there room for two in this hot rod?"

She couldn't stop the grin from spreading across her face. "There is, but I'm not sharing my ice cream."

"That's a shame." He reached into the car and lifted her ice-cream-coated fingers out of the container. He licked them from palm to tip, then put her fingers in his mouth and sucked them clean, drawing them out slowly.

Tegan. Couldn't. Breathe.

He pressed a kiss to her fingertips and said, "I do love mint chip."

"Me too," she whispered.

He slid his hand to the nape of her neck, pulling her closer, and said, "Hello, friend," against her lips, then took her in a long, sensual kiss. She put her arms around his neck, practically pulling his big body in through the open window as she tried to *consume* him. The ice cream container tumbled off her lap. They both laughed as he drew back, but the second their eyes connected, heat flared again, and then he recaptured her lips, kissing her so long she came away dizzy.

"Anything else you'd like to *withhold* from me?" he asked.

"Uh-huh. *Everything.*"

He nodded in the direction of her house and said, "What do you say we take this party inside?"

"My car is dead. I need to get it towed, but I have no cell service. Can I borrow your phone?"

He reached down and retrieved the container of ice cream, handing it to her as he eyed the scattered groceries. "How long have you been out here?"

She shrugged. "A while."

"How about if you drive my truck up to the house, and I'll take care of your car."

"It's dead."

"Yeah, I got that."

A little thrill darted through her. She reminded herself he was just there to hook up, not to be her knight in shining armor. She didn't need a knight in shining armor anyway. She was perfectly capable of handling things herself. "I'll just call a tow."

"I've got that, too. My truck's warm and dry. I'll grab your groceries and meet you inside in a few minutes."

"You don't have to—" She stopped talking as he reached in, pulled her hood up over her head, and ran the back of his fingers down her cheek.

The softest smile appeared on his face, though it did nothing to diminish the lust in his eyes. If anything, it ratcheted it up a notch. "Fucking adorable."

*Oh God…*Chloe's reminder tiptoed through her head. *Don't you think he might have more buddies out there? Maybe it's his MO.*

This was the moment of truth. She could call off their arrangement, or she could pull up—or rather, *down*—her big-girl panties, take this FWB situation by the horns, and enjoy every hot second of it.

"What's it going to be, sunshine? Party in the ditch or someplace where we have a little more room to *spread out?*"

Her insides flamed. She put on her best in-control smirk and said, "We've got one more night together. Why waste it in a ditch?"

AFTER JETT ARRANGED for a tow truck, he gathered the groceries, kicking himself for not listening to his gut and checking on Tegan earlier. When he'd arrived, her hands and cheeks were freezing and what was left of the ice cream had gone soft as butter. What if she'd collided with a tree instead of a ditch? Anything could have happened, and she was calm, cool, and collected, eating ice cream like nothing had gone wrong. He sat back in the driver's seat of her car, wondering why she was driving that old clunker when she lived in a house that was probably worth a cool two million. He spotted her phone on the passenger seat and her purse on the floor. She really wasn't like any of the women he knew. Most women wouldn't be caught dead without their phones and purses. He tucked the phone into his jacket pocket and the purse into one of the bags. Then he placed the key beneath the mat for the tow truck driver, although they'd be lucky if the tow truck got there before tomorrow, as they were dealing with the mess from the storm.

He tugged his hood over his head and climbed from the car. The wind whipped his hood off as he reached into the back seat for the groceries, which were another source of curiosity. Was she feeding an army of bad eaters? He'd collected several boxes of sugary cereal, but no milk. In addition to the ice cream, she'd bought bags of candy and a dozen containers of yogurt with candies in the tops, packages of sliced cheeses, a box of micro-wavable buttered popcorn, several bags of sliced pepperoni, a loaf of sliced white party bread, which looked like the tiny slices of bread his mother used for finger sandwiches, a jar of mayonnaise and one of extra-crunchy peanut butter, a couple boxes of Teddy Grahams, crackers, chips, salsa, two six-packs of powdered doughnuts, and some olives—green and black. She'd also bought a copy of *Cosmo* with the headline ARE YOU SEXY ENOUGH IN THE BEDROOM? TAKE OUR QUIZ!

She didn't need a damn quiz. His loss of focus was a testament to her bedroom abilities.

His chest was wet. He zipped his coat up the rest of the way, and scanned the property as he trudged down the long road, shoulders hunched against the wind and rain. He couldn't put his finger on why, but the place felt familiar. As he climbed the porch steps, Tegan peeked out of one of the sidelight windows. His chest warmed at the sight of her beautiful face. She disappeared, and a second later the front door swung open.

"You must be freezing. I'm so sorry." She began patting his face with a towel.

"I'm fine." He set the grocery bags on the floor and crouched to take off his boots.

"Thank you for handling that." She stooped beside him, swiping at his hair with the towel. "Did the tow truck come?"

"They're tied up with the storm, but I left the key in the car for them. It might take a few days to get it fixed. If it's even fixable. We should see about a rental for you so you aren't stuck."

"I don't need a rental, but I hope Berta isn't dead for good," she said, a little panicked.

He set his boots by the door and said, "Berta?"

"She looks like a Berta, don't you think?"

He chuckled. "I guess. Hopefully you'll know in a day or two if she can be fixed."

"Fingers crossed. Gosh, you're soaked, and I don't have any dry clothes that will fit you."

"I've got clothes in my truck." He shrugged off his coat, and she tried to dry his shirt with the towel. He dropped his coat on his boots and put his hand over hers, pressing it to his chest. Her eyes flicked up to his, full of desire. He drew her into his arms and said, "That's better."

A blush crept up her cheeks. "Now we're both wet."

"Even *better*." He reached over his shoulder with one hand and tugged off his shirt.

Her eyes widened with appreciation as she ran her hot little hands over his chest, sending lust coursing through his veins. Christ, just that simple touch made him hard as stone. He pulled her close again, letting her feel what she did to him.

He felt her heart racing as she said, "Do you want to—"

He crushed his mouth to hers, and she went up on her toes, grinding against him. Her sexual confidence made him ache to be inside her. He tore his mouth away long enough to whip off her sweater and bra. "You're so fucking beautiful."

She reached for the button on his jeans, and he stripped them both naked as they devoured each other's mouths. She practically leapt into his arms, her legs circling his waist as he lowered her onto his hard length and captured her mouth *and* the entrancing moan coming out of it. She was tight and hot, her fingers digging into his scalp as they fisted in his hair, sending darts of pleasure down his spine. He leaned back, using the door for leverage, and clutched her ass, helping her move faster, *harder* along his shaft. She made a series of mewling sounds, her legs tightening around him, and he knew she was close. He was right there with her. What the hell had she done to him? He usually had impeccable control, but she made him so damn hot there was no slowing the rush of pleasure and need mounting inside him. He pushed one hand into her hair and tugged her head back, giving him access to her gorgeous neck. He sealed his mouth over her flesh, sucking and grazing with his teeth, as he'd learned she loved last night, and she went a little wild. Her hips bucked, her sex pulsed, and *"Jett"* sailed greedily from her lips, catapulting him into the throes of ecstasy. He clung to her, the room spinning away as he came so hard it felt like it was ripped from his soul. He ground out her name between gritted teeth, still working her along his cock, sending her reeling once again. She was incredible, beautiful, and so sexy, arching her back, and thrusting her breasts forward as she rode him.

When she collapsed boneless and trembling in his arms, he rested his head against her shoulder, trying to catch his breath and clear his hazy vision. The feel of her in his arms, trusting and spent, burrowed under his skin. "So. Fucking. Good," he panted out.

She nuzzled into the curve of his neck, sighing contentedly.

Neither of them said a word for a long moment.

She shifted in his arms, and her breasts pressed against his chest, her thighs tightening around his middle. He should be cooling off, but it was impossible to ignore her softness, her feminine scent, and how perfectly they fit together. He was still inside her, already half hard. She pressed a kiss to his neck, her tongue gliding slowly along his skin, and his cock rose to attention. *Fuuck.*

Her fingertips brushed the back of his neck, and she whispered, "Again?"

He was happy to comply, quickly getting lost in her sensual sounds, her greedy pleas, and all her sexy *benefits.*

Chapter Nine

AS TEGAN DRIED her hair after their *second* shower together in less than twelve hours, Jett went downstairs to take care of the forgotten groceries and to hang up the towel he'd used to run bare-assed to his truck when he'd retrieved his suitcase. He'd been too hot and bothered to notice the intricately carved railings on the grand staircase last night. He took a moment to admire impressive oil paintings hanging in the expansive foyer and hall. The dark hardwood floors, high ceilings, and elegant crown moldings reeked of class. None of this meshed with his impression of Tegan, though admittedly, he didn't really know her very well.

He snagged the groceries and towel from the floor and went in search of the kitchen, passing lavishly decorated rooms. The elegant rooms didn't jive with the woman upstairs, although the piles of papers and boxes scattered about did.

Each room was more luxurious than the next, until he came to the bright, salmon-floored kitchen with a massive stone fireplace. The farmhouse-style table and island that stretched nearly the entire width of the kitchen were both covered in sticky notes and littered with papers. Now, this room reminded him of Tegan. He chuckled to himself as he set the groceries on the counter and laid the towel over the edge of the sink. He imagined a large family gathered around the table and wondered if Tegan had many siblings.

He scanned the papers on the table. The notes were no less confusing then they'd been at the café. *The café.* He wondered how Rowan and Joni were making out in the storm. He scrubbed a hand down his face. His thoughts were becoming as scattered as Tegan's notes.

Moving around the table, he tried to piece together what she was working on. His eyes caught on a piece of poster board with a large circle drawn on it. There were lines bisecting the circle at clocklike intervals, with notes written all over it in different colors of ink. What went on in this woman's brain? His eyes swept over the smattering of papers covering the edge of the poster board, stopping on one with his name written on it several times.

"I see you found the kitchen."

He lifted his gaze as Tegan breezed into the room looking gorgeous in a baseball shirt with pink sleeves, white shorts, and fuzzy pink socks. *Fucking adorable.* "Aka your office?"

"Pretty much."

"Big house."

"Yeah. Too big for me. It's the one thing I'd change if I could."

"Do you get lonely here?" He lifted the paper with his name on it and arched a brow as she came around the counter.

She snagged it from his fingers. "I'm a *doodler.* Don't get a big head over it. I just didn't want to forget your name because, you know, you're not *that* important." She slapped it onto the table upside down and began turning over more papers.

He put a hand over his heart, feigning a hurt expression.

"And here I was planning our kiss behind the bleachers."

She rolled her eyes. "Get over yourself, Armani. I doodle about everything and everyone." She began unpacking the groceries. "I can't help it. I've always done it. My college papers were covered with names and ideas about random things."

"Uh-huh." He pretended to examine more papers and said, "I don't see anyone else's name written down."

Her back was to him, but he heard her sigh as she tore open a box of crackers. Her hands began moving fast and furious, doing something he couldn't see.

"Then you're not looking hard enough, and you shouldn't be nosing around anyway. I'm starving. Are you hungry?" Before he could answer, she said, "We're FWBs. Friends with benefits don't have the right to *snoop*."

He chuckled and came up behind her, putting his arms around her waist. She stiffened against him, her hands stilling. He knew he needed to nip the idea of *doodles*—which implied hopes of a *relationship*—in the bud, and he would in time, but right now he had to get her out of her own head so she could relax. He pressed a kiss to her cheek and said, "Take a breath, babe. I'm not snooping, and I'm glad you didn't want to forget my name. FWBs—is that what you called us?—should definitely know each other's names."

She exhaled one of those long, contented sighs and turned in his arms. "Try this." She held up a cracker sandwich.

He opened his mouth, and she shoved the whole thing in. He tasted pepperoni, cheese, and olives. Some of his favorites.

"I was working on my business plan for my uncle's theater and I realized it needs a new name," she said, turning back to the counter, where she was assembling about a dozen cracker sandwiches. "I was brainstorming, and we'd just spent hours in bed together, so…"

He finished eating and said, "I get it. You couldn't stop thinking about me. You wouldn't be the first."

She gave him a deadpan look.

"I'm pretty unforgettable. But for the record, I don't think *Jett* is a good name for a theater."

She shook her head, a smile playing on her lips. "You're a brat."

"That's not what you were screaming when you came in the shower. I'm pretty sure I heard you call me a *god*."

"I said, 'oh God,' not 'you're a God.'" She handed him another sandwich and said, "Although you're pretty good in the orgasm department. Now, put that in your mouth before I kick you out of my kitchen and into the storm."

He took the sandwich. "So it sounds like you inherited a theater, you drive a car that should have gone to the dump years ago, and you eat like a man watching football. What else should I know about you?"

"Not much. It's true I eat like a horse." She took a bite of a cracker sandwich and carried the plate to the table, shoving papers to the side to make room. "If you're worried about what you'll do if you come back to the Cape and I've gained ten pounds, you shouldn't." She hurried back to the counter and began putting the groceries away without pausing long enough for him to respond. "FWBs can end things at any time, with a text even. Just zip one off that says, *This isn't working for me anymore.* It's one of the greatest benefits of our situation." She opened the refrigerator and shoved the yogurts in so hard they rolled across the shelf. "I don't have to worry about you scrutinizing my muffin top or asking why I'm not working out more, and you don't have to worry about me nagging you about whether you're seeing other women."

The bite in her voice told him just how hard that was going to be for her, but he wasn't about to assuage that discomfort with empty promises. When she shut the refrigerator, he grabbed the front of her shirt, pulling her closer, and pressed his lips to hers.

"I like women who eat. Skinny, voluptuous, short, tall, black, white. None of that matters as much as what's in here." He touched the side of her head. "I like beautiful women of any size, but what I find most attractive are smart, interesting women who don't blow smoke to get into my pockets *or* my pants."

Her eyes narrowed, as if she didn't like what he'd said, but he was a straight shooter, and he wasn't about to pull a smoke-and-mirrors job on her.

He tugged her against him, gazing into her eyes as he said, "Trust me, Tegan. Your mouth is one of my favorite things about you, and not just because you know how to use it on my body like no other woman ever has. I like it because that wicked mouth of yours tells me what's in your head, and I find that—I find *you*—incredibly interesting."

Her gaze softened.

"I told you that I don't date. Our little FWB arrangement has already outlasted every woman before you." He brushed his hand over her waist and said, "Ten pounds won't send me running for the hills, but dreamy thoughts of white picket fences just might."

Her mouth drew into a tight line; then the edge of her lips lifted into a confident smirk and she said, "I'm a busy woman. I don't have time for dreamy thoughts any more than I have time for insecure men who bitch when they can't get ahold of me."

Damn, she was incredible. "Then we'll get along just fine. Now, tell me about all this." He waved to the papers. "And why is a woman with a house like this eating cracker sandwiches and driving a car that's clearly on its last leg?"

"You don't like my fancy food?" she teased.

"I actually love it, but I'm not sure it qualifies as *fancy*."

"I know," she said lightly. "Where do I start without crossing the FWB line?"

He scowled. "Tegan, let's not play games. I'm sorry if I hurt your feelings. We're both new at this FWB thing. I'm just trying to keep our expectations in line."

"You didn't hurt my feelings, and honestly, when I caught myself doodling your name, I gave myself a harder time than you ever could." She picked up a cracker sandwich and said, "We're on the same page, don't worry."

A sense of relief warred with a sense of something else inside him—disappointment, maybe? He wasn't sure what to do with that, so he ignored it.

"As for all this, and my car, it goes back to my great-uncle Harvey. Have you ever had someone in your life that you saw only a few weeks each year but you thought about all the time?"

Yeah, my entire family, and I don't even see them that much. He kept that to himself and said, "Sure. My grandmother."

"That's sweet. For me it was my uncle Harvey," she said with a hint of sadness. "He passed away last summer."

"I'm sorry to hear that." He took her hand, guiding her down to a chair, and sat beside her. "You must miss him."

"You can't imagine how much," she said softly. "I spent a lot of time with him here when I was growing up. He had emphysema and was in a wheelchair for the last several years of his life."

"You mentioned Maryland at the café. Is that where you grew up?"

"Yes, in Peaceful Harbor. I still live there, and so do my parents. I'm only here until fall. I've always loved coming here. My uncle made every day an adventure. He believed in laughter like other people believe in faith. He was very eccentric, as you can probably tell from the house—which, to answer your earlier question, I inherited along with his Lincoln Town Car, the Children's Amphitheater, and enough money to never have to work again. I probably shouldn't tell you that, because now you'll want me for my money."

He laughed. He couldn't help it. "You're probably right. You shouldn't tell people that. Especially *men*. We're all dicks, just looking for a rich woman to pave our way."

She rolled her eyes.

"Seriously, though, you should probably keep that under your hat. There are a lot of *takers* out there."

"I know, but I knew I could trust you. Everyone else does."

"You don't strike me as a follow-the-crowd type of girl."

"I'm not usually, but I trust our friends. And honestly, my uncle taught me to trust my instincts. He never cared what anyone else thought about him or how he lived his life, and he instilled that in me. You might have noticed that I'm not a great dancer."

The truth rolled off his tongue effortlessly. "I couldn't take my eyes off you on that dance floor."

"Because you wanted to get laid."

"Maybe, but don't fool yourself. Your confidence on that dance floor was a better aphrodisiac than a bikini-clad model tied to a bed."

Laughter tumbled from her lips. "Wow, you've sure thought

about that one, haven't you? Moving away from *that* image…"

She fanned her face, and he had to lean forward and steal a kiss.

"Don't think about it too long," he said. "It's an image I conjured as a teenager, and since it has never happened in real life, it stuck with me."

"Well, then, maybe one day we'll have to play out that little fantasy."

"Damn, Tegan." He took her hand and brushed it over his erection. "One sentence, and that's what you do to me."

She bit her lower lip as he rose off the seat, adjusting his jeans while she giggled and nibbled on a cracker. As he sat down, she said, "You good? All *situated?*"

"For now," he said evenly. "Tell me more."

"Well, I think I'd wear a *white* bikini, to instill that whole innocence vibe—"

He hauled her onto his lap and kissed her hard, but she continued laughing and wiggled off his lap.

"I need food before I'll let you have your way with me again." She reached for another sandwich. "And as far as my fancy food goes, I love to *eat*…" She dragged her eyes down his body, making his blood sizzle. "But I'm not big on cooking."

"I think I need a drink for this conversation." He got up and pulled open the fridge, taking out a bottle of Mike's Hard Lemonade he'd seen in it earlier, downing it in a few swallows. "Have anything stronger?"

"Perhaps. But if you can't take the heat, maybe you should get out of the kitchen."

He sat down and said, "Oh, I can take the heat. Eat up, baby, because you're going to need a great deal of sustenance to get you through the night. And while you're tanking up, I want to hear more about the uncle who thought it was a good idea to drag you up to the Cape alone."

"I'm not alone. I have friends here now, and from what my uncle's caretaker told me, my uncle believed this was where I *belonged*. Besides, it's not like he forced me to come. He knew me better than anyone. He knew I loved challenges and adventures. None of that scares me, and that's because of *him*. He taught me so much about confidence and taking life by the horns." She took a bite of a sandwich and said, "I came to visit the first time I got my heart broken by a boy. I was twelve, and I thought my world had ended because this boy asked me to be his girlfriend the last week of school, then two days later broke up with me to go out with my best friend. Obviously she wasn't a *real* friend. Anyway, I came here the following week, thinking my life was over." She shook her head and said, "So silly. My uncle volunteered at a hospital then, and I went with him to see the kids. When we got home, there were all these targets hanging on trees with the boy's name written on them, and buckets of water balloons in front of each tree. My uncle had set it all up for me as a way to get that boy out of my system, and it worked. By the time I was done, we were both soaking wet and laughing hysterically, and I could barely remember why that boy had seemed so special."

"Young boys are stupid, and young girls are sensitive. It's a dangerous combination."

"Girls are stupid, too, and some boys are sensitive. But we all live through it."

"When I was a kid, I'd storm into the house furious about one thing or another, and my mother would tell me to take it out on the basketball court in the driveway." He'd forgotten about that until just now. He'd also forgotten that when his father got home on those nights, he'd always taken extra time to throw a ball around in the backyard or pitch to him, so he could swing the bat until his arms grew fatigued.

"Well, I don't know much about your parents…" She paused, looking a little uncomfortable, and said, "Except that Chloe said you and your dad aren't very close."

"Thank you, Chloe," he said sarcastically. The last thing he wanted to do was talk about his family.

"Since you look like you're ready to kill her, we won't talk about *that*."

"Perfect," he said, trying to ignore the burn in his gut.

"My parents were always ushering me toward safety, in school, with friends," she said lightly. "They pushed me to go into accounting or nursing so I would always be able to find a job. But at the same time, Uncle Harvey was whispering in my ear about life being too short to miss any adventures and to follow my heart wherever it leads."

"Sounds like my grandmother."

"Maybe it has to be that way. Our parents were doing what they thought was *best* for us, to protect us from failure or from being hurt, and other generations, who have lived through so much, know the value of enjoying life. Who knows? But when I have kids, I hope I can find a balance and help them follow their hearts in a way that's safe. Anyway, getting back to my car, when I was afraid to drive, my uncle created an adventure for me."

She went on to tell him about her uncle baiting her to drive with promises of the magic of Cape Cod air and music. She mentioned a jewelry box he'd seen on her dresser upstairs. As she talked about her uncle and told the story, her eyes teared up. She was trusting him with cherished memories about a man she had loved and lost, and Jett wanted to take her tears away whether it was an appropriate feeling for an FWB or not. He took her hand, squeezing it gently, and moved closer so his knees rested on either side of hers.

"When I returned home to Maryland, Berta was waiting for me with a big red bow around it and a card taped to the steering wheel that said, *Roll down the windows and follow your heart wherever it may lead, but first get your parents' permission.*"

"He sounds awesome."

"He was. I wasn't allowed to take Berta on any road trips until I was eighteen, but on my eighteenth birthday, my older sister, Cici, and I packed our things, rolled down the windows, cranked the music, and drove from seven in the morning until eleven at night. It was, quite possibly, the best day of my entire life."

"Where did you go?"

"We drove to New York City, had lunch, and spent the day shopping and walking around. Cici *loved* the city even back then. She's a photographer, and she'd wanted to live in the city since she was probably ten or eleven. She brought her camera and took tons of pictures."

"Is she the one you do photo editing for?"

"Yes, for her and her husband, Cooper Wild, and his brother, Jackson, who are—"

"Famous photographers," he said, noting her modesty. The Wilds owned one of the most prestigious photography studios in New York City. "I did a photo shoot for a magazine and they were the photogs. Small world."

"I guess so. You must be a pretty important guy to have been in a magazine."

"Not at all. Tell me more about your road trip."

She looked at him quizzically, but she must have seen something in his eyes and understood that he didn't want to talk about himself, because she said, "Oh, it was just a day trip. We didn't have much money and couldn't afford a hotel room. But it was my first taste of freedom, and it sparked my love of adventures. I've made it a point to go on a trip every year since, and I've gone to some really great places." She finished the sandwich she'd started earlier.

"You take road trips in Berta? From what I've seen, that sounds dangerous," he said, reaching for a sandwich.

"I took most of my road trips in Berta when she and I were both younger. She's a little old to be rocking out on the highway like I do. Lately I've been traveling overseas. In the last few years I've gone to Ireland, Italy, Switzerland..."

As she listed the places she'd traveled, he wanted to ask if she went with boyfriends, but that wasn't an FWB-appropriate question. It bugged him that he wanted to know, since he'd never cared what the women he'd been with had done with other men, but he couldn't quell his curiosity, and he asked, "Do you travel with Cici, or with your girlfriends?"

"No. Cici has two kids now and, honestly, I prefer to travel alone. That way I can just pick up and go when my schedule allows."

She was even more impressive than he'd imagined, and she was brave. Although the idea of her traveling alone didn't sit well with him any more than the idea of her traveling with men did. Not that he thought she couldn't handle herself. He assumed she could, but a niggling of concern lingered.

"I'm not a big planner," she said, pulling him from those thoughts.

He glanced at the messy table and the clocklike poster board drawing and said, "Don't sell yourself short. Anyone who can make sense of all *this* has to be an excellent planner."

"Let me rephrase that. I'm not a big *vacation* planner in the sense that I know what types of things I want to see and do when I go away, but I don't create itineraries or that sort of thing. But I'm good at planning in general. I just don't go about it in a conventional way." She waved to the papers and said, "Believe it or not, I made great headway today."

"I don't doubt it. I mean, look at that clock drawing."

She rolled her eyes.

"I'm only teasing. You're a brave woman, Tegan, to travel alone, and to leave your family and your life behind to run a business that you're still trying to get your arms around."

"I don't know about *brave*. I'm just not afraid to try something that's important to me. I really want to make this work, for my uncle, for Harper and her dream of putting on episodic productions, and for myself. This theater already touches so many lives, and we have a chance to reach many more people, to make it something adults also look forward to attending each year. I've always done my own thing, but it's been on a small scale, which allowed me to have lots of flexibility and take time off whenever I felt like it. This will be very different."

"I wouldn't call photo editing for the Wilds small scale."

"But it is. I work behind the scenes. I don't take the pictures or meet the people who read the magazines and see the pictures that I edit online. There's a big difference between photo *editing* and being the photographer. I'm invisible, and I don't mind that at all. Cici and the guys are artists. But running the theater is an opportunity for that to change. I can carry on my uncle's legacy by not only running the business, but also being *part* of it. Attending the shows like my uncle did, meeting the actors, greeting the children and their parents, and taking part in the luncheons we hold afterward. When I attended productions with my uncle, each one was a fantastic event all its own. The actors were greeted with fanfare, buffets were plentiful, and the children's enjoyment was contagious. That's *magical.* I want to be part of that magic. And that's not all. Harper wants to bring her romcoms to live theater in episodic form. No one else is doing that with live theater. It's exciting. She even got an offer from Trey Ryder, the guy who runs the Movietime channel, to live stream the performances for big bucks. He said it was going to be the next big thing. But Harper turned that offer down. She didn't want to lose any artistic control or have to deal with television cameras at the productions."

"Wow. That's a huge deal to turn down. Do you realize how much of a gold mine you're talking about spearheading?" His mind had already taken off in fifteen different directions to help her succeed.

"For Harper's sake, I hope it is. Neither of us cares about the money, though, beyond making enough to live on."

"Why not? I know you have your inheritance, but why not shoot for the stars?"

"The money left to me is my uncle's. I will continue to earn my own keep, because that's what I believe in. Harper and I want to keep the productions special and sort of homey, so people feel like they're coming to visit old friends. We both feel like once people focus on money, they forget the little touches that make projects special and the reasons they started the business in the first place."

He chewed on that for a minute and realized how right she was. His driving forces were more profit oriented now than ever. He'd built his business helping smaller companies find their way, and nowadays he rarely put his energies into those buckets, because the profits were insurmountably bigger with larger investments and acquisitions.

"But she didn't close the door on Trey," Tegan said, bringing him back to their conversation. "He's still waiting in the wings, ready to make another offer if we do well and decide to move in that direction. But I doubt we will. It's not about the money, like I said. The idea that I can be part of something so cutting edge and exciting, right here on the Cape where my uncle lived and loved, is beyond incredible. I love the work I do, but this? This will fill me up in ways I never imagined possible. *If* I can pull it off."

Her excitement reminded him of himself when he'd first started his own business. He'd been full of determination, driven to be the person who not only helped business owners find their niche, but also guided them to surpass their expectations, taking them to unimaginable heights and experiencing the ride right along with them. He'd far surpassed that.

It had been years since he'd felt the thrill of building something from an idea, as Tegan was, and he knew that it had as much to do with her as the challenge at hand.

TEGAN WAS RAMBLING, and she felt a little silly for sounding like her head was in the clouds to a man who was supposedly *married* to his business. Though she wasn't really sure what business he was in. *The business of making money* hadn't given her any real clues.

"Let's change that *if* to a *when* and get started," he said.

"*Let's?* As in *together?* Because I can do this, you know."

"I don't doubt that, but if you're open to suggestions, figuring out how to make companies succeed is my specialty."

She sat back and crossed her legs. "Is that so, Armani? Tell me about it."

"There's not much to tell. I'm an investor with varied expertise. Venture capitalist endeavors, real estate, corporations. I take companies apart and rebuild them so they can achieve maximum success—"

"Well, I don't want my uncle's company taken apart. The children's productions pretty much run themselves, even if by archaic means. I'm planning for the *new* side of the business with Harper."

He cocked his head, looking mildly amused. "If you'd let me finish, I would have said that I didn't always take them apart. When I started investing, I partnered with small businesses instead of taking them over and worked with the owners to help develop winning business strategies and put them into play."

"And you probably took most of their profits, too. I shouldn't have told you about my inheritance. Thank you, but I'm not interested in giving away money when I can do this by myself."

He frowned, his jaw clenching. "Do you really think I'd take money from a woman I'm sleeping with?"

"Sure. Why not?"

"Because I'm not a dick." He sat back with a sigh. "We've got one night together before I take off, and as much as I want to spend every minute of it tangled in the sheets with you, the spark of excitement in your eyes and your determination to get this endeavor off the ground is even more alluring than the promise of an orgasm."

"*Why?*" she asked skeptically. "Because you think I can't do it alone?"

"No. Jesus, Tegan. You're clearly capable or your uncle wouldn't have left you with such an immense responsibility." He leaned forward and took her hand in his, holding her gaze as he said, "These last few years I've leaned toward large acquisitions, doing more of the taking over and restructuring I mentioned. I think it'll be fun to work with you and to get back to the nitty-gritty of launching a business. If we're half as good at doing this as we are in the bedroom, we'll have time for both business and pleasure."

A loud *crack* followed by a house-shaking *thud* brought them to their feet.

"What was *that?*" Tegan panicked as they ran to the windows. She'd gotten so caught up in their conversation, she'd forgotten about the storm.

Wind and rain battered the windows as they shielded their eyes and peered into the darkness.

"It sounded like a tree hit something."

"The amphitheater! I have to go see if it got hit!" She ran toward the hall to get her coat, and he grabbed her arm, pulling her to a stop.

"I'll go." The lights flickered, and he said, "Looks like we're in for a big one. Where do you keep your flashlights and candles?"

She ran across the kitchen and pulled open a drawer in a curio cabinet, retrieving a flashlight. "I'm not sure if there are more, but I have candles." She pointed to a candle on the counter. "The lighter is in the drawer."

"Great. Why don't you light that and look for more while I

check things out?"

"I hope it didn't hit the theater." She followed him to the front door. As he put on his coat, she said, "Be careful. What if another tree falls? What if you get hurt? What if the theater is demolished? I'm going with you."

She took a step toward the coat closet and he swept her into his arms, calm as could be, and said, "If you think I'll let you go outside in this, you're wrong. This is where I get to be a dick and tell you to stay inside. I know you're worried, but trees fall, property gets damaged, and there's *nothing* you can do about it during the storm except stay safe. You need to focus on finding the flashlights and candles."

"But what if *you* get hurt?"

"Don't worry, sunshine. Nothing will stop your FWB from performing his *beneficial* duties."

"I'm *serious*. It's awful out there."

"If I get hurt, you'll just have to nurse me back to health." He smacked her ass and said, "And I expect a sexy little nurse's outfit, complete with fishnets and heels." He winked and opened the door. Gusts of wind and rain bullied in as he stepped outside and closed it behind him.

Tegan ran around the house collecting flashlights and candles, slowing only to read a text from Chloe. *Just got your message. You okay? Need me to send Justin to help with your car?* Tegan sent a quick reply—*No. I'm good. All taken care of. Staying inside and out of the storm.*

By the time she got back downstairs, Jett was coming through the front door. She set everything on the floor as he shrugged off his coat, then reached for her hand. He reached for her often, and she found it reassuring.

"There was no damage to the amphitheater, but it was a

close call."

"Oh, thank goodness!" She put her hand over her chest. "I can breathe again."

"A big tree fell, taking down a number of smaller ones. Luckily, they landed a few feet from the amphitheater. But the storm is a lot worse than it was before, and other trees could fall."

"What if one hits the amphitheater?"

"Then we'll call the insurance company and get the ball rolling on a claim."

"It would have to be a *speedball*. The children's programs start Memorial Day weekend. What if the theater is hit and the insurance can't fix it in time? I'd hate to cancel the productions and let the children down. The kids' shows sell out a year in advance, with a large number of returning families every summer. With a storm like this, there will probably be tons of insurance claims. By the time they get to mine, it could be the middle of April."

He began taking off his boots. "Do you always borrow trouble? You don't have any storm damage yet."

"I know," she said. "But I *could*, and if they take forever to get the claim approved, it might delay the opening. I can usually take things as they come, but this would devastate me."

"That would be the biggest shame of all, such a beautiful woman, devastated. What would I do for an FWB?" He winked, and in a more serious tone he said, "If that happens, and it probably won't, it doesn't have to take that long. We would find out who the insurance adjuster is and see if we can get them out here fast."

"Is that even allowed? I guess I could just forget a claim and use my uncle's money to fix it."

"That's the biggest mistake small businesses make." He slung an arm over her shoulder and walked toward the kitchen. "Stick with me, *overthinker*. I'll teach you to bypass all those rookie mistakes."

"In one night?"

"Don't underestimate the *master*."

He said it seductively, and her pulse quickened for a whole new reason.

"Now, can you stop thinking up trouble?"

"Yes, sorry," she said, realizing she'd been rambling. "You have an answer for everything. No wonder you were featured in a magazine. Which one was it again?"

"I can't remember."

"Liar," she said as they set their supplies on the counter.

He chuckled. "Come on, sticky-note girl. We've got work to do."

Chapter Ten

CANDLES CAST DANCING shadows across the kitchen table as Jett reviewed Tegan's business plan. They'd long ago polished off the cracker sandwiches, downed a pizza, finished the six-pack of Mike's Hard Lemonade, and they were working their way through a bag of M&M's. The tow truck driver had texted Jett when he picked up Tegan's car, and she was hopeful the repair shop would be able to fix it. The storm raged on beyond the strong walls of the house, but inside, Tegan was toasty warm and more intrigued than ever by the handsome man beside her. Jett had worked through each and every one of her notes. He'd asked questions that led to answers she hadn't realized she'd had and to discussions about more of her ideas that she worried were too big to even entertain. He didn't thrust his opinions on her or make her feel naive or disorganized. She had never felt so completely accepted by, and in tune with, another human being. He'd taken a couple of work calls, but Jett's calls hadn't *consumed* him by any means. If anything, he'd spent less time on them than she'd spent FaceTiming with her parents and fielding texts from Jock and her friends back home. She had no idea why Chloe had said he was married to his work. He'd turned his phone *off* last night, and he'd told her he'd spent the day helping their friends because a tree had hit Desiree and Violet's gallery. Tegan liked imagining him jumping in to help, and she was glad no one was hurt. Maybe Chloe had the wrong impression of him. Either way, nothing had slowed him down. He made creating a business plan look easy as he reorganized her thoughts and ideas into a fashion that would make sense to anyone.

Jett stood back and pushed a hand through his hair, the candlelight catching his blue eyes. They'd lost power an hour ago, but they'd been having so much fun, and making so much progress, they'd barely noticed the disruption. His brows knitted in concentration, and it was easy to imagine him taking over a boardroom as he said, "We're missing a few things, but we're almost there."

"I can't believe you did all of this in one evening," she said with awe.

He blinked a few times with a confused expression. "What do you mean? I told you what I do for a living."

"Yes, but *this* is *fantastic*." She pointed to the reorganized table and the notebooks in which he'd written concise notes and schedules.

"Babe, you had most of the pieces. You just needed some help organizing them."

"You really think so?"

"Absolutely. I'll be interested in seeing the website when it's up and running."

"Evan Grant from the Geeky Guys is handling it, but he can't finish until I come up with a new name for the amphitheater."

"Right. We'll brainstorm on that. But there are a few gaps we need to close first." He took her hand, pulling her into a sweet, soft kiss. "Like that one." He cradled her face with his warm hand, brushed his thumb over her cheek, and said, "You're incredible, Tegan. Do you know that?"

She was too busy melting to think straight.

He lowered his hand, all business again as he said, "I work with a lot of business owners, and most of them have spent years following what seems like a wikiHow guide to developing a business plan, with zero originality. Even the company I'm working on taking over right now isn't up to par because the family members who are running it don't think outside the box. It's worth about ten million, and it's losing money every month. But if it were run correctly, it would be seeing huge profits and could easily be worth five times that in two years. You're creative, *innovative*, and from what I've seen here tonight, you've got a brilliant business mind. You just go about things in a roundabout way."

Fifty million? Her initial instinct was to tease him about blowing smoke up her butt to get her in bed, but the honesty in his eyes kept those words at bay. "Thank you. I know my brain works in weird ways. I can't get anywhere if I try to think in a linear fashion, but my sister is as organized and efficient as you are. She always goes from A to B to C, while my brain goes from A to Z to C to K and, well, you get the picture."

"I get it. Is that why you use the clock image?"

She nodded. "That was my uncle's idea when I was in school, and it really helps me get my thoughts started. As long as I know where I'm starting and where I want to end up, I can add ideas and things that I need to accomplish along the way. I usually have to draw five to ten renditions before I get all the pieces right because I don't only use that, as you saw. I'll forever be a sticky-note girl, but eventually I get there."

MELISSA FOSTER

"It sounds like your uncle understood exactly how your brilliant mind works. You're lucky to have had him. Lots of people who think unconventionally don't have that type of support, and they flounder." He picked up the notebook and said, "Let's talk about these last few items. The most important is your partnership with Harper. This is a cutting-edge endeavor you're working on."

"I know. It's exciting, but Harper is the brilliant one. The idea of bringing live episodic romcoms to theater was all hers." She'd already explained that if the soft launch went well, then next summer they hoped to run a different show every month, with three episodes each week. "As I mentioned, if this goes well, Harper wants to eventually run programs during the winter for locals. But we'd run only one production every other month since there are so few people in the off season. I'll have to hire someone to handle the winter administration since I'll be in Maryland during those months, but she knows people who might be interested."

"That's all great, but I meant the actual partnership, legally speaking. Who owns what percentage and how profits and expenses are going to be handled."

"Oh, I see. We don't have a legal contract, if that's what you mean. We're running this like the children's program with a few tweaks. Harper is paying a fee for the use of the theater. She's the one writing and producing the episodes, so she'll own all those rights, pay for those expenses, and keep the profits. I'll handle and pay for the marketing and administration of the theater. Easy-peasy."

"If only it were that easy, Tegs."

Tegs. She tucked that away in the things-not-to-overthink space she had started stocking with his furtive glances and tender touches, which he seemed to dole out naturally. "What do you mean?"

"The plan you have outlined is much bigger than just marketing the theater. You're marketing her shows exclusively. Is that what Harvey did for the children's shows?"

"No. The production companies handled all of their own marketing. In fact, the theater is so well known for the children's productions, he really didn't have to market at all. He just nurtured his relationships with the production companies, and he was friends with them all, so that wasn't a hardship for him. The buffets he hosted after the shows were his gift to the children, on his own dime. He was very wealthy, and like I said, he was all about paying it forward."

Jett blinked several times. "Tegs, you're talking about putting out big marketing dollars on a weekly basis. You're basically *building* Harper's name, her brand, handling all the marketing and PR. You should be compensated for that."

"She's my *friend*. I want her to succeed."

"I know you do, but I think you're listening to your heart a little too much here. Just for a second, take off your friend hat and put on your business hat. Do you want to remain friends with Harper?"

"Of course."

"Then you need to think about this a little differently. If you were hosting other shows and just marketing *your* theater, that would be different. But there are all sorts of complications that could result in hard feelings with this scenario. What if you do all of this and it takes off, and Harper gets another offer like the one from Movietime or to take her productions elsewhere?"

"Then good for her."

"Is it? Or will you feel like you've helped her build this

amazing business. You brought it to the public, and she walks away with millions. I know you don't care about the money. But won't you feel hurt that suddenly this business that you built together is gone? That Harper gets to live her dream and that you were part of that dream, but now you're not. What then, Tegs? Who's watching out for you in this scenario?"

"I don't...I didn't think about that."

"I know. That's your big heart clouding your business smarts a little, and that's okay. I'm only making suggestions. You don't have to take them. I just want you to think about these things. What if Harper gets pregnant and decides to be a stay-at-home mom instead of writing and producing shows? What if she gets a deal she can't turn down and wants to franchise her ideas? That would involve how the business is run, too, and you're going to be a big part of that. What if you have a following here and want to continue after she leaves? Can you hire writers and producers and maintain the same episodic structure without her involvement? Or if you decide you're sick of running this big house and the theater and you want to sell it? Have you thought about how that would impact *Harper* after both of you worked hard to grow a business she wants to continue running?"

"I've thought about some of those things, and although we haven't talked about them, I'm sure we'll work something out."

"Will you? You have other businesses and a whole life in Maryland, but it sounds like Harper's putting all her eggs into this basket, and it's a good one. Tegs, the best friendships, marriages, and partnerships often fall apart over differences of opinion, goals that change, or unspoken assumptions. No one ever sees them coming."

"You're kind of a buzzkill," she said, though she knew he

was right. Her sister had mentioned something similar when Tegan had first told her about the partnership, but Tegan had brushed it off.

"I don't mean to be a downer, but I'd just hate for either you or Harper to put your heart and soul into something only to have it ruin your relationship down the line. If you have these things worked out ahead of time, you can avoid possible problems."

"So, you're basically suggesting a prenup agreement, but for business, one in which I am compensated if I promote her shows exclusively. I guess that's a good idea. I'll talk to Harper about it."

"Great."

"What's next?"

"Marketing. You have a solid plan and budget for marketing on Cape Cod and the islands, and I completely agree with your new demographic of twenty- to forty-year-olds. Your idea about pulling in people from Boston, New York, Rhode Island, and Connecticut was spot-on. But why was it in the Dreaming Big section of your clock?"

"Because I'm not sure I can pull it off," she said honestly. "I've never done anything on this big a scale, much less with someone who was counting on me not to screw things up. I don't want to disappoint Harper, so I thought starting slower was better."

"Tegs, are you kidding me? Your ideas have the ability to double not only the income, but the value of the business. I know you're worried about the desire for profit overshadowing everything else, but I think if you and Harper are aware of that up front, it's something else you can discuss and put into writing so you never lose focus on those goals. Increasing the value of the business can only help Harper, which is why you should have that legal agreement in place." He stared deeply into her eyes and said, "Partners complement each other in different ways. She's got the creative side down, but you've got impeccable business sense and vision. Don't ever sell yourself short."

She didn't need approval from anyone, but his praise made her feel all sorts of wonderful. "You're not just blowing smoke to get in my pants?"

"I don't play games with business. Trust me, I'd have no problem telling you if I thought you should think smaller, or even back out of the deal, if I thought you couldn't handle it. Business comes *first* and *last* in my book. You're good, Tegs. *Own* it." He winked, and then he said, "But there's always room for improvement. You might want to consider shorter programs, for those people who come up only for the weekends."

She told him some of her other ideas, like hosting special shows for girlfriend/couple getaways. "But this is *episodic* theater. The idea is that there are three episodes to each romcom. We run the same three shows every week, so if a couple is here for two weeks, they don't have to cram their viewings into one week, although the option is there. Weekends are too short to make that happen."

"I understand, and that makes perfect sense. But at some point you might consider expanding to include one complete show on a Saturday to capture that audience, too. You never know what will entice a person into coming back. It's just a thought. Maybe hold on to it for the future."

He grabbed a notebook and opened to a blank page. He drew a circle and bisected it with a line. On one half he wrote TO-DO, and on the other he wrote FUTURE IDEAS. She pressed her lips together to keep from telling him how much she loved that he drew her a circle instead of trying to change the way she worked to his way of thinking.

"Did I do it wrong?" he asked.

"No. It's perfect. Thank you."

They talked about a few more things as they filled out the circle. When they were done, he said, "We've covered all the bases except one. *Contingencies.* What about rain? It can be pretty rainy here in August. You might have light rains that last an hour or two, it could pour for days, or you could get wicked storms that roll through fast and furious. What happens to the productions in those cases?"

"My uncle always used tents with light rain. He worked with the local high schools and college drama and arts clubs for so many years, there's a team of volunteers that sign up for the summers and set up for the events. If we get bad storms, we'll reschedule the children's programs. But Harper and I decided that it would be difficult to do that with the adult events, since it's a serial program. We're still trying to figure out how to deal with that. There's a company that specializes in making permanent tentlike structures, and some of them are gorgeous. I'm looking into those, but I'm not sure if I want to do something that permanent. Part of the ambience is being able to see the blue skies, or for the adults, the moon and stars. It's also outrageously expensive."

"I think you're right about the intrigue of the outdoors. Tenting is a solid idea, even if a little cumbersome for on-and-off rain. But you mentioned the importance of visitors feeling like they're coming to see old friends."

"Ideally that's what we're going for."

"You also said you didn't love staying in the house because

it's too big. I don't know how you feel about this, given how many memories you have here, but I saw a carriage house behind the amphitheater."

"You mean the caretaker's cottage?"

"I guess so. I only caught a glimpse of it in the storm. Have you considered staying there and holding the productions here in bad weather? It would take a bit of remodeling to open it up, but it might alleviate the headaches of putting up tents and such. When the weather's good, you can hold the productions outdoors, but on those days when you'd need a tent, you could move it indoors instead."

"Here? In the big house?" She stood up and looked around, mulling it over. She loved the caretaker's cottage, which had once been a carriage house. It was cozy, like her place in Maryland, and it had three bedrooms, which would be perfect for her sewing and photography. But she still considered it Jock's cottage. She had thought he might come back and settle in there to write, but she was realizing that losing Harvey might have been too painful for him to ever come back for good.

"It's something to consider," Jett said.

"It's not a bad idea. I just hadn't thought about it." She leaned against the counter, thinking of how lonely she'd been in the house. She knew she wouldn't lose her memories by moving to the cottage, but could she allow *strangers* into her uncle's house?

Jett got up and went to her. "Harper is writing romcoms, right?"

"Yes. She's really talented."

"You said laughter was sort of your uncle's thing," he said as he moved between her legs, guiding her arms around his neck. "It might be nice to bring more laughter into the house."

"I need to think about it. I love the caretaker's cottage. It's much more my style than this house, and it *would* solve a lot of logistical problems. But I'm not sure how I feel about strangers coming into my uncle's house."

"There's no reason to make decisions tonight. I just wanted to put the idea on the table."

"Thank you. I'll think it over." Thunder clapped outside, and she said, "I have a feeling your flight might be canceled tomorrow morning."

"I texted my assistant, Tia, when you were on FaceTime and I put off leaving for a day."

Her pulse quickened. "But you said you were on the cusp of closing a big deal."

"I am. I'm handling it. But you were a little overwhelmed at the thought of a tree hitting the amphitheater. What kind of a friend would I be if the theater got hit overnight and I left you to deal with the damage all alone?" He brushed her hair from her shoulder and slid his hand to the nape of her neck, looking at her like he'd never wanted to kiss anyone as badly as he wanted to kiss her right that second.

He'd changed his schedule for *her*? "The kind of friend who doesn't want more than what we've agreed to," she said softly, trying to play it cool and keep her hopeful heart under wraps.

"I'm not asking you to be *mine*, Tegs. I'm offering to stick around for another night and help deal with the aftermath of the storm. This weather is supposed to pass by tomorrow afternoon. I'll drive to New York then and take a flight from there to avoid any further delays."

His words stung because their connection felt real and deep, but she knew where they stood. She had never been a swoony, nonsensical person before, and she wasn't going to be one now.

She tried to push those feelings away, and when they continued pressing in on her, she tucked them into the things-not-to-overthink space inside her.

He dipped his head and kissed her neck, whispering, "That is, if you want me to stay."

"I do…"

He kissed her again, sending prickles of heat skating beneath her skin.

"How about you go grab some blankets." He kissed the edge of her jaw and said, "And I'll start a fire in the living room." He kissed a path across her cheek and brushed his lips over hers, light as a feather, causing her breathing to hitch. He kissed her softly, trailing kisses to her other ear and turning her to liquid heat with every touch. "We'll have an old-fashioned campout." He gazed into her eyes and said, "Clothing optional."

As his lips met hers, she selfishly hoped the storm might last a few more days.

IT WAS QUIET in the house except for the crackling of the fire and Tegan's appreciative sounds as she peeled a layer off another roasted marshmallow. The sweatshirt she'd changed into while he'd made the fire hung off one shoulder, and her barely there silk sleep shorts left every inch of her gorgeous legs on display.

"I'm telling you, you don't know what you're missing out on. This is the *best* way to eat them," she insisted. "Open up and taste it."

"I have never seen anyone eat roasted marshmallows in layers." He opened his mouth and she put the sugary treat on his tongue.

"See? Pure deliciousness." She held her stick over the fire again, roasting the rest of the marshmallow.

"It is good, but I can think of a *much* better way to eat them." He waggled his brows.

"You're *right*. Hold this." She handed him the stick, jumped to her feet, and ran out of the room.

He finished roasting the marshmallow, and he was eating it when she returned with her arms full.

She sat on the blanket and dropped a box of Teddy Grahams, a plate, and a bag of Hershey's Kisses between them. "S'mores."

"With Teddy Grahams and Hershey's Kisses?"

"I had to improvise." She pushed two marshmallows onto each of their sticks and said, "Can you roast those while I prepare?"

"Prepare?" He chuckled and held the sticks over the fire. "Who taught you to eat marshmallows in layers?"

"Nobody. I just like to savor things." She lined up several Teddy Grahams on the plate and began unwrapping chocolates. When she had a plateful, she took her stick from him and twirled it over the flames. "I think they're ready."

They put their tiny s'mores together, and as he popped one into his mouth, Tegan frowned.

"Jett Masters, tell me you did *not* just put the chocolate on top of the marshmallow and eat it."

"What's wrong with that?"

"Are you *kidding*? 'You're killin' me, Smalls!'" She picked up a Teddy Graham. "'First you take the graham. You stick the chocolate on the graham.'" She put the Hershey's Kiss on the cracker and said, "'Then you roast the 'mallow. When the 'mallow's flaming, you stick it on the chocolate.'" She put the marshmallow on top of the chocolate. "Then you cover it with the other end.'" She put another Teddy Graham on top and popped the whole thing in her mouth.

"Did you just quote *The Sandlot*?"

"Mm-hm," she said as she ate. "It's my favorite movie from when I was a kid. Right up there with *The Goonies*."

He couldn't believe his ears, much less take his eyes off the snarky little sexpot with marshmallow on her lip.

"What? Do I have something on my face?" She swiped at her cheeks.

"You're about to." He crawled to her on hands and knees and said, "I didn't think you could get any sexier, but I was wrong." He continued moving over her, taking her down on her back and earning that sweet laughter he wanted to bottle up and take with him when he left. "That was my favorite movie, too."

He dragged his tongue along her lower lip and sucked it into his mouth. She closed her eyes, bowing up beneath him with an alluring whimper.

"Let me show you *exactly* how I want to eat my marshmallows."

He stripped off their shirts, loving that she'd gone braless. She was the most beautiful creature, gazing up at him as he reached for the stick with the remaining roasted marshmallow on it. He peeled off the top layer, revealing the gooey center. "Open your mouth, baby."

"I like where this is going," she said playfully.

He fed her the warm layer of sugary goodness and covered her mouth with his, kissing her ravenously. The sugary treat melted against the force of their tongues, until there was nothing left but the taste of white-hot lust.

When he finally broke the kiss, she said, "Come back."

"Oh, baby, I'll be coming back for much more, but first…" He stripped off her shorts and dipped his finger into the gooey center of the warm marshmallow. "Don't worry, sunshine. I won't get anything inside you other than *me*." He painted the creamy deliciousness all around her clit and the outside of her swollen sex. He slicked his tongue along her center and took her swollen lips into his mouth, sucking them clean as she writhed and moaned. He dragged his tongue along her sex and teased her most sensitive nerves with the tip.

"Oh my *God*." She fisted her hands in the blankets beneath them as he sealed his mouth over those sweet nerves, and moments later her hips shot up and she cried out, "*Jett!* Oh God…need you…"

"Soon," he promised. He scooped warm chocolate from the plate and painted it around her nipples. Her eyes flamed as he brought that sugary finger to her mouth, gliding it over her lips. As he lowered his lips to her breast, he pushed his finger into her mouth and said, "Suck, baby."

And *holy hell*. She sucked his finger as if she were sucking his cock as he feasted on her breast. She swirled her tongue, and he pulsed his finger in and out of her mouth, grazing his teeth over her nipple, earning more sensual, needy sounds. He moved to her other breast, teasing and taunting. Their eyes locked and the little minx opened her mouth wider, letting him see her tongue working its magic.

"Fuck, baby. I need your mouth on me." He stripped and came down on his knees.

She dipped her fingers into the chocolate and wiped it all

over his hard length.

"You are my *every* fantasy come true. I want to watch you suck me, baby."

He sat with his back against the couch, and she went up on her hands and knees, playing with his cock perfectly. As she licked, sucked, and stroked, he dipped his fingers into her sex. She moaned around his shaft, drawing a groan from deep within him. She rocked on her hands and knees, fucking his fingers as she sucked him. The sight of her taking him in at both ends, the feel of her hot, wet mouth and equally hot, wet center, was too much to take.

"Suck it clean, baby, so I can bury myself deep inside you."

She made an appreciative sound, and then she released his cock and licked every inch of it. When she lowered her mouth over him again, she sucked so hard, he cursed. He tangled his hand in her hair, lifting her face, and crushed his mouth to hers, devouring her as she rode his fingers. Never in his life had he experienced anything so intense as getting dirty with the woman in his arms. He wanted to do everything to her, *with* her. He pulled her head back and growled, "Don't move."

He went up on his knees behind her, and she looked over her shoulder, her hair covering one eye. "Don't worry, sunshine. I won't take your ass without asking first." He pressed a kiss to the base of her spine, and then he aligned their bodies and thrust into her. Her head fell between her shoulders as he came down over her back. He kissed her shoulder and said, "Too hard?"

"No. The angle is so good."

"Kiss me while I fuck y—"

His words were lost in her insatiable mouth. Using one hand to balance, he reached between her legs with the other, wanting, *needing*, to feel her come. Her mouth fell away with a loud, hungry sound as he pounded into her.

"Don't stop," she pleaded.

He thrust faster, pressing his fingers harder against her slick, swollen nub. Her breathing quickened to frantic little gasps.

"That's it, baby. Let me feel you come around my cock."

She made a series of high-pitched, desperate sounds, and then her sex clenched tight as a vise and she cried out. She slammed forward and back, her ass slapping against him, taking him right over the edge with her in a blindingly intense explosion of lights and sounds. Fucking *fireworks*.

When he finally collapsed over her back, feeling her heart beating wildly, he lowered them to the blanket, still half buried inside her, and kissed her shoulder.

She covered his arms with hers, sinking back against him, and whispered, "I like your way of eating marshmallows best."

"Rest up, baby, because I can't wait to get *s'more* of you."

A LONG WHILE later, they lay talking by the fire, Tegan's head on his chest, their legs intertwined. Jett had never felt as relaxed as he did right then, listening to Tegan weigh the pros and cons of using the house for the productions.

"If I did it, do you think it would upset my uncle? He and Adele were married here. All his memories, the fabric of their lives, are all here in this house."

"I didn't know him, but from what you've said, it seems like he might have enjoyed having laughter under the roof instead of loneliness. You haven't said much about your aunt. What was she like?"

She tilted her face up to his, looking beautiful and sad at once. He pressed a kiss to her forehead, earning a small smile.

"Theirs was a tragic love story," she said. "My uncle was a Broadway actor before coming here. His father had also been an actor, but from what I'm told, his father was a real jerk and so much of a menace that eventually he wasn't able to find acting jobs. He's the one who built the amphitheater. I guess he wanted a place to perform. There's a lot of old money on that side of the family, and he took everything for granted, including Uncle Harvey, which was why he stayed in New York and had nothing to do with his father. After his father passed away, my uncle came here with the intention of selling the estate. But then he met Adele and he said he fell in love with her the second he saw her. She was a number of years younger than him, and he called her his *goddess of sweetness*. He said they were inseparable from that moment on, like they'd been a love story waiting to happen. But she lost both her legs in an accident on their seventh date."

"Christ, Tegs. That's horrible."

"I know, and from what my uncle said, Adele was so depressed after the accident, she tried to break up with him. She was so miserable, she couldn't stand being around herself and thought he deserved someone *whole*."

"I can't imagine what she must have gone through."

"What *they* went through. My uncle adored her. He said he stuck by her no matter how much she pushed him away. It was during her recovery that he learned how important laughter was. He used humor to break down her walls and get her to see that they belonged together and that he'd love her forever. He told me that he never pitied her. He just loved her so deeply, he couldn't imagine a life without her."

"Jesus…"

"I know," she said with a pained voice. "Can you imagine being loved that deeply?"

He couldn't imagine being loved by a woman at all, much less like that. Other than his mother and grandmother, who were pretty much obligated to love him, he'd never let a woman get close enough to chance getting hurt by him.

Tegan yawned, snuggling closer and moving her fingers through his chest hair. "I don't know if love like that is even possible for most people. I wonder if my uncle and Adele were just lucky and only so many people are destined for that type of happiness." She sighed and said, "Maybe that's it, because he made it his goal to help her see the humor in life, and it worked. I don't know if many men would have done that given her situation, but I'm glad he did. He deserved happiness, and she certainly made him happy. They were married two years after the accident. That's them in the picture on the table by the sofa."

He glanced at the picture of a tall, slim man wearing a dark suit, gazing into the eyes of a plump and kind-looking woman sitting in a wheelchair. Her white wedding gown covered her missing limbs. From the love in their eyes, Jett doubted she felt like she was missing a thing. "They look happy."

"They were. But remember how I said theirs was a tragic love story? He lost her to cancer eight years later."

Sadness welled his chest. "Oh, man. That's awful."

"I know. He spread her ashes in the garden, and he made it a point to laugh every day to keep her memory alive. They never had children of their own, but they had wanted them. Adele had told him that children saw life through untainted eyes, so after she passed, he surrounded himself with them and opened the theater to children's groups. He said children laughed the most, and in their laughter, he imagined Adele laughing, too. He said that was why he hosted buffets after every production, so children could be with their friends and enjoy life. But I think he wanted as much time around them as possible because of the memories of Adele they brought."

"He really does sound like he was one hell of a great man. Why don't you honor them both with the name of the theater? The Harvey and Adele Fine Amphitheater."

Her blue eyes shone brighter. "I like that. HAFA. It even has a cheery ring to it. That's perfect." She tapped his chest and said, "Good in the bedroom and in business. If you could bottle yourself up, you could make millions."

Already there, sweetheart.

Jett watched the shadows dancing around them as he listened to the storm battering the windows and the crackling of the fire. When he'd gone outside to check on the theater, he felt again that he'd been there before, and he still couldn't shake that feeling.

"I think I must have come to see a play here when I was younger," he said. "It feels familiar." The weird thing was, she felt familiar, too.

She yawned again and murmured, "I hope you did. I'd like to think he touched your life, too."

He did. He brought me you. He gritted his teeth against the strange thought, absently stroking her back as he wrestled with it.

He'd been thinking and doing weird shit all evening, like rescheduling his flight, not checking his phone while they were together, and getting annoyed when he'd received calls.

Although Tia had sounded equally annoyed with him when he'd asked her to reschedule his flight after she'd had to pull strings to get him on it in the first place. But he'd *wanted* to be here with Tegan, to help her with her business, with any damage the storm might cause, and fuck him sideways because he also wanted *this*. To be close with the woman who had made him happy for the first time in forever. But he wanted to understand *why* she had this hold on him. It wasn't just the sex, though their chemistry was off the charts. She was intellectually and emotionally stimulating, and she was *fun*. Her sense of humor and smart-ass comments made hours pass like minutes.

Why was such a beautiful, adventuresome woman still single? And why the hell had she agreed to this FWB thing with *him* of all people?

He opened his mouth to ask, but she was fast asleep.

On the floor beside them, her phone lit up, and a bubble appeared with the name *Jack Jock* and beneath it the message *How's my stubborn girl? Call me.*

Fuck.

He closed his eyes, telling himself to let it go.

But her words of wonder about love lingered in his mind.

She deserved to find a man who could give her the type of love her uncle had found.

Jett knew he *wasn't* that guy. Maybe *Jack Jock* was…

He gritted his teeth, holding her a little tighter.

Fuck it. It had been a hell of a couple days. He deserved a little *sunshine* before diving back into the work grind. He closed his eyes, but he wasn't fooling himself.

He knew he was just too damn selfish to walk away.

Chapter Eleven

TOASTY WARM IN her cocoon of blankets, Tegan awoke to the creak of the hardwood floors and the scent of Jett's cologne on the pillow. Delicious memories of last night rolled in. They'd laughed and lusted, satiating their every desire. She'd never laughed during sex before, but it was easy to be herself with Jett, and maybe that was because they didn't have those strings that often got too tangled and had to be cut free. Or maybe, *just maybe*, their connection went deeper than either of them realized.

She listened for the sounds of the storm, but it was Jett's hushed voice that caught her attention. He was pacing in the hall just outside the living room where she lay in front of the smoldering fire.

"I know I'm not around that much, but I'm here now. If you need anything, you can count on me."

Tegan rolled onto her stomach, peering around the sofa at Jett standing at the entrance to the living room with his back to her, wearing only his boxer briefs. And boy did he wear them well. She wondered if he was talking to Dean or his parents.

"Aw, come on," he said playfully. "You know you're my one and only."

Tegan's eyes widened. *So much for Dean or family.* She narrowed her eyes, sure she had smoke billowing out her ears. Being friends with benefits and seeing other people was one thing. Making sexy promises to some other woman while standing in *her* house after having a night of incredibly *hot* sex was another! And it was definitely *not* okay. She sat up, holding the blanket to her chest, and debated clearing her throat to let him know she was onto him.

He chuckled into the phone as he turned, catching her eavesdropping. He winked and lifted his chin, mouthing, *Good morning.* "I've got to run, Grandma. I love you, too. Try to behave yourself."

Grandma?

Relief and embarrassment intertwined. She warmed all over knowing he was up early checking on his grandmother. He ended the call and came to her side.

"Morning, gorgeous." He dropped to his knees, his clear blue eyes coasting over her face.

"You're so sweet, calling your grandma." She felt foolish for thinking he'd be sleazy enough to have been on the phone with another woman.

"She lives at LOCAL. I wanted to be sure she was okay, which she is."

"I'm glad to hear it. Chloe works there. Does she know her?"

"Yes. My grandmother knows everyone. She's feisty. You know those jokes about old ladies pushing their Life Alert necklaces just to get hot paramedics to come see them?"

"Yeah."

"Well, if my grandma Rose and her rowdy friends owned Life Alert necklaces, they'd not only push the buttons, but they'd probably bribe an electrician to rig up video cameras so they could catch the paramedics' asses on their way out the door."

"Oh my gosh. She sounds like a riot."

"She's pretty cool." He leaned down, kissing her softly. "It's raining out, but I think the worst of the storm has passed. The power is back on here, but thousands of people are still without, and there's a lot of storm damage up and down the Cape."

"Oh no." She reached for her phone and scrolled through texts from Jock, Chloe, and Harper, breathing a sigh of relief that Chloe and Harper were safe. "Have you talked to anyone? Chloe and Harper are fine. But what about Daphne and Hadley, and everyone at Bayside and Summer House?" Jett was looking at her phone with a serious expression. "Jett?"

He cleared his throat and shook his head, as if he were lost in thought. "Sorry. I spoke to Dean about an hour ago. Everyone there is safe. Daphne's apartment and the office have some water damage, but they're on top of it. She and Hadley are going to stay in one of the cottages, and the guys are helping her move. But we haven't been able to reach our parents. Dean and I both got fast busy signals when we called. I'm not too worried. It's probably issues with the lines. But I'm going to head down to Hyannis after we take a look outside to make sure there's no damage to your property."

She dropped the blanket and pulled on the shirt he'd worn last night. "I didn't hear any other crashes, so hopefully the theater's fine. Let's take a quick look and then we can get out of here and make sure your parents are okay."

"Tegs, you don't have to go with me."

"Are you *kidding*? What if you need an extra pair of hands? I'm not about to pretend that I didn't see you tense up when I mentioned your dad yesterday. Come on. We need to shower and we're wasting time." She tugged him up to his feet and headed for the stairs. "We should bring water bottles in case they need it."

"Tegan," he warned, stopping her midstride. "My father's not exactly easy to deal with."

"I didn't think it was going to be a picnic in the park. That's *why* I'm going, as a buffer." She strutted back to him and grabbed his hand, pulling him toward the stairs. "Geez, don't you know me by now? I love a good adventure."

"You have no idea what it'll be like," he said flatly. "I have no idea what he'll be like."

"And you have no idea how good I am at softening situations. Remember how uptight you were at the café, *Armani*? And look at us now. Trust me."

"Nobody disarms my father. He's a pediatric neurosurgeon with an ego to match his expertise."

"Wanna bet?" she said as they climbed the stairs. "Maybe all he needs is to lose the clothes that strangle him, too."

"You are not going to get my father out of his *clothes*." He smacked her ass, and she *yelped*, rushing up the stairs.

"I didn't mean it like that," she said through her laughter as he caught her around the waist and tackled her on the bed. She smiled up at him despite the tension riddling his body. "I don't want to sleep with him! Geez! I'm not a tag-team FWB *or* a homewrecker! I just think there are lots of ways to ease tension, and sometimes it's the little things that make the difference, like having a friend to distract him from that scowl on your face."

"How do you know I'll scowl at him?"

"Because the few times he's come up you've gone from sexy Robert Downey Jr. to Stone Cold Steve Austin. Now, get a move on. We have a lot to do!" She wiggled out from beneath him and strutted toward the bathroom, stripping off her shirt and tossing it over her shoulder. "And we *both* know how we are in the shower…"

THEY WERE QUICKER in the shower than they'd been yesterday, but they didn't pass up the chance to let their hands and mouths wander. When they finally left the house, the rain was trickling and the wind had diminished considerably. They hurried through the yard, stepping over branches and around puddles. Tegan was glad to see that the old stone amphitheater was unharmed. As they headed back to the SUV, her phone rang with a FaceTime call from her mother.

"My mother is addicted to FaceTime. Do you mind if I take it really quick?"

He opened the passenger door for her and said, "No. Want me to wait out here?"

"In the rain? No. Get in." She answered the call as Jett climbed into the driver's seat. "Hi, Mom. Hi, Dad. I can't talk too long. I'm on my way out."

"We just had to see your face, to be sure you were okay," her mother said. "The storm looked so horrible on the news, and the aftermath…"

"I'm fine. I promise. It's just raining now, and there's no damage to the property. But I'm going with my friend to check on his parents, so I have to run."

"Okay, princess," her father said. "Be careful, and we'll see you in a few weeks."

"I can't wait! Love you!" After she ended the call, she said, "Sorry. They worry."

Jett started the engine and said, "You're really close to them."

"Yeah. They're coming up for the opening of the children's program, Memorial Day weekend."

"Sorry I'll miss that," he said. "I'd like to come for the opening of the adult program, to see all of your hard work come to fruition."

She tried not to make too much of that and said, "Thanks. It's the first Monday in August. But if you can't make it, it's totally fine."

Jett drove down the long private road, maneuvering around the enormous pothole that had caused Tegan's car to land in the ditch, and said, "You need to get these potholes fixed."

"It's on my list. They aren't usually this bad."

"They should be nonexistent on a gravel driveway. We can talk to Justin's father, Rob Wicked, about fixing the foundation under the gravel to keep that from happening again."

"His father does roadwork? I thought he did home renovations."

"On the Cape, everyone does everything," he said as he pulled onto the main road, heading toward town.

Jett turned on the news reports, which told of downed trees, flash floods, and dune collapses on the oceanside. The roof had been ripped off a motel near Hyannis, and they thought it might be days before electricity was restored across the Cape.

"Check that out." Jett pointed up ahead to a tree blocking a driveway. An older couple stood under umbrellas, looking perplexed. Jett slowed the truck. "We should help."

"Definitely," she said as he pulled over. "But what about

getting to your parents?"

"We'll get there. If anything awful had happened, the hospital or the police would have gotten in touch with me or Dean." They pulled on their hoods and climbed from the truck. As they approached the couple, Jett said, "Looks like you could use some help."

The portly gray-haired man held up a trembling hand and said, "Can't manage my chain saw like I used to."

"I used to be pretty good with them. It's been a while, but I'm sure I'll be fine." Jett offered his hand and the man shook it. "I'm Jett, and this is Tegan."

"Jett?" the man said brusquely. "That your real name, son?"

"*Larry*," the tall woman chided him. She turned apologetic eyes to them and said, "I'm Greta. Please excuse my husband."

"It's okay. I get that a lot," Jett said. "I was named after my father's best friend, who was killed while serving our country. His real name was Jethro. He was a pilot, and everyone called him Jet, with one T. My mother didn't like the name Jethro, so they added a T and called me Jett. I think I lucked out."

"I'll say." Larry motioned toward the backyard and said, "Come on out back. We'll see if we can get the old chain saw up and running."

Tegan couldn't imagine Jett as a Jethro, but she wondered what had gone wrong between him and the man who had obviously named his son after someone he loved.

"Why don't you come inside where it's warmer, hon," Greta said.

"Thank you." Tegan followed her in.

"Do you live around here?" Greta asked.

"Yes. I recently inherited my great-uncle's property down the road, where the amphitheater is."

Greta pushed open the kitchen door and said, "Oh, you're *the* Tegan, Harvey's great-niece."

"Yes. How did you know?"

"Oh, honey, everyone around here knows that Harvey left you the property. We lost a special man when Harvey Fine left us. It was tragic when he lost Adele."

"Did you know her?" Tegan took off her coat and sat at the table, hoping she did. She hadn't ever met anyone who'd known Adele.

"Yes, even before she met your uncle. She was a doll, until the accident. I wasn't sure she'd ever get past that, but your uncle refused to let that tragedy steal her from him. I don't know how Harvey did it, but he got our sweet Adele back."

Greta told her stories about the great-aunt she'd never known. She told her what Adele was like as a young woman and how she'd fallen just as hard for Harvey as Harvey had fallen for her.

A little while later, Larry came through the kitchen door, his nose red from the cold. "The rain stopped. Tegan, that man of yours is doing a fine job out there."

Tegan had been so caught up in Greta's stories, she'd forgotten Jett was working outside. She glanced out the window. Jett was wielding the chain saw like a pro, cutting the tree into pieces. "I should help him move the wood out of the driveway," she said, putting on her coat. "Greta, thank you for telling me about Adele. I don't know anyone else who knew her."

"It was my pleasure. You're welcome to visit anytime." She wrote down her number on a piece of paper and gave it to Tegan.

Tegan went outside, and as she and Jett stacked the wood, she told Jett about their conversation.

"That's great, sunshine. I'm glad you met someone who lives close, too, in case you need anything."

"That's sweet, but I'm really fine out here."

Greta and Larry came outside as they finished stacking the wood and offered to pay them for helping.

"No need," Jett said.

"I'm a big believer in paying it forward," Tegan added. "Greta, thank you again for sharing your memories of Adele with me."

As they drove away, Jett said, "You're a pay-it-forward person, too?"

"What do you mean, *too?*"

"Don't tell me the guy at the gas station pocketed my money instead of paying for your gas."

"That was *you?*"

"Who'd you think it was?"

"No one," she said lightly.

He scowled. "The guy in the truck?"

She grinned, and he shook his head.

"*What?*" she said incredulously. "He could have been my soul mate."

"Women are so weird. How does paying it forward equate to a soul mate?"

"I don't know. Common interests and beliefs? Thank you, by the way. I appreciated the gesture."

"You can thank my grandmother. She used to say it wasn't how much money we had, but how we used it to help others that mattered."

"What does she say now? Something different?"

"Now she's too busy getting into trouble and trying to get me to start dating to worry about life lessons."

"You could try a dating app, like Chloe."

He gave her a deadpan look. "I don't need a girlfriend to disappoint."

"Why would you disappoint her?" she asked as he slowed to a stop behind a row of cars.

The muscles in his jaw bunched, and he nodded toward the policemen directing traffic up ahead. "Looks like it's going to take a while to get to the highway." He turned up the radio again, using the news to effectively end their conversation.

She mulled over his comment as they crawled through traffic. He was such a good guy, she couldn't imagine him disappointing anyone. She gazed out the window as he followed one detour after another. The radio announcer went on about extensive storm damage from Hyannis to Provincetown and listed the locations of emergency shelters.

"My fallen trees are nothing compared to the damage they're reporting. It sounds like we must have had a guardian angel watching over us."

"You're not kidding. Maybe your uncle was looking out for you."

She liked that thought.

A little while later they passed a small retail center where people were cleaning up debris and gathering branches, putting them through a wood chipper. Tegan saw Joni coming out of a food truck wearing a ladybug raincoat and purple rain boots, carrying a tray of food.

"That's Joni! Can we stop?"

Jett pulled over, and Tegan climbed from the truck, heading for Joni, who was handing out sandwiches to the people who were working.

"Jelly fish!" Joni exclaimed when she saw Tegan. She set

down the tray and barreled into Tegan's legs, giving her a big hug. "We're feeding the workers. Why are you here?" She looked up at Jett as he approached and said, "Hi, Diego!"

"Um, hi," Jett said, looking confused.

"Diego's a character in *Dora the Explorer*, a kid's show," Tegan explained.

Joni grabbed Jett's hand, tugging him toward the food truck. "Dad's making food for the workers. You can help if you're not grumpy. Dad says there's no time for grumpy today."

"I'm in a pretty good mood," Jett said. "I can help for a few minutes, but then I have to go check on my parents to make sure they're okay."

"Where are they? At the zoo with the monkeys?" Joni asked.

"Probably." Jett looked over his shoulder at Tegan, holding up one finger and mouthing, *I can't say no to her.*

That was a far cry from the stressed-out guy who had walked into the café with the phone pressed to his ear and had ignored Joni.

He climbed the steps of the food truck and was greeted by Rowan. Jett shook his hand, motioning toward Tegan. Rowan waved as Joni ran to her again.

Joni took Tegan's hand and said, "You can help me pass out food while the doodlybutts make more."

Tegan loved that her *doodlybutt* couldn't say no to Joni any more than she could.

IT TOOK FOREVER to reach Hyannis after they left Rowan and Joni, and Jett was inundated with phone calls on the way.

Tia was coordinating his business trips for the week and had rearranged his Chicago meeting to take place in his LA office instead, and he fielded a half-dozen calls regarding Carlisle Enterprises. A typical Monday.

"Sorry about that," he said gruffly, annoyed by his last conversation, as he exited the highway. He needed to get his ass to his LA office.

"It's okay. You put off your flight because of me. I don't expect you to let your business fall by the wayside."

He scoffed. "There's no chance of that happening. I might have one of the best financial teams in the industry, but nothing happens in my company without my approval. I've got my fingers on the pulse of every deal."

"Okay, then...Tell me what I need to know about your parents."

He thought about her FaceTime conversations with her parents. Her father was a world away from his. "My mother is great. She's warm, outgoing, and *steady*. My father runs one of the most prestigious neurosurgery practices on the East Coast. He's used to throwing money around and expecting the world to bend to his will."

"Sounds *challenging*."

"You could say that." He wondered how his brothers would describe their father. Would they describe only the man their father had recently become? Would Dean relay the truth—the good, the bad, and the horrid? Their father had moved out for a while when they were growing up. Doug had never carried the anger over their father's leaving that Jett and Dean had, and he'd lived overseas for so long, Jett wasn't sure how well he even knew their father anymore.

He was so used to pushing away thoughts of his father, it

took no effort to do it now, as they drove into Hyannis. When he came home to visit, he was usually on the phone on the way to and from the airport and in and out of town so quickly, he didn't notice his surroundings. But now the devastation of his hometown couldn't be ignored. His old stomping grounds looked like a scene out of a doomsday movie. Trees were snapped in half, taking down power lines and closing streets. Branches and debris littered sidewalks and yards. Store windows were broken or boarded up. Part of a roof was torn off a strip of retail shops, and people were carrying boxes out to the sidewalk.

"Holy cow. There's so much damage," Tegan said. "How far is it to your parents' house?"

"Not far." Jett navigated to the residential streets, circumventing a tree that had fallen across a road and crushed a parked car. Fences were down, streets were flooded, playsets were broken, and a trampoline lay sideways in a yard. He hoped he hadn't assumed wrong about his parents being okay.

He turned down the street on which he'd grown up. His massive childhood home came into view, and it looked intact. Even with that relief, his gut roiled in the way it had on visits home for as long as he could remember.

He stopped at the entrance to the long driveway. His father's black Lexus was parked in front of the house. Jett's muscles flexed, readying for a battle. It had been a long time since he and his father had verbally sparred, but old habits were hard to break. He wasn't proud of the fact that he couldn't just let the past go, but trust was Jett's most precious commodity— in business and in his personal life. Trust was to be respected. Once broken, well, that was a whole different ball game.

"Wow." Tegan's eyes widened. "This is where you grew up? It's gorgeous."

He knew she probably saw a stately three-story home perched atop the hill at the end of the long driveway, with a circular drive and three-tiered stone gardens. Even stark from winter the gardens gave the house an aura of elegance. But to Jett, his childhood home was a reflection of the man his father had been. It would always look like a bully—an ostentatious *ass* among a neighborhood of modest homes.

He started down the driveway, but Tegan said, "*Stop!*"

Jett slammed on the brakes. "What's wrong?"

"It's just..." She wrinkled her nose and unhooked her seat belt. She got up on her knees and leaned across the seat, putting her face right in front of his, and stared into his eyes.

"Tegan—"

She silenced him with the press of her lips. Then her hands were in his hair, her tongue delving deep and hungry in his mouth. She moaned, pressing her body against his, making him hard as steel. He pressed his foot harder on the brake pedal, his arms circling her, quickly becoming lost in her exquisite mouth and the sweet sounds she made. By the time their lips parted, they were both breathless.

She studied his face for a moment before saying, "That's much better. You no longer look like you want to kill someone."

As she settled into the passenger seat, he tried to get his foggy synapses to fire. He looked down at his erection, then met her amused gaze and said, "And you think looking like I want to fuck you is better?"

"*Much*," she said lightly, and motioned for him to drive. "Go on."

By the time he parked in front of the house, those old uncomfortable feelings settled back in. Only this time they weren't quite so all-consuming. But his parents came out the front door as he helped Tegan out of the vehicle, ratcheting up his discomfort once again. Jett straightened his spine, squaring his shoulders like a plebe readying for inspection. They were dressed in coats and boots, as if they were going somewhere. His mother's eyes widened as they descended the steps, a happy little gasp escaping her lips. His father's eyes narrowed, shifting from Jett to Tegan.

Jett's protective instincts surged. What the hell had he been thinking bringing her here? He stepped forward, creating a barrier between his father and Tegan.

"Jett! I thought you left town already! What a wonderful surprise." His mother pulled him into her arms and kissed his cheek. She smelled like almonds and summer, just as she always had. She was tall and slim, with silver hair that framed her face. She'd always been beautiful, and even now, with wrinkles and laugh lines, she was still radiant. She patted Jett's cheek as his father stepped beside her, and she said, "You look *good*, baby. Was your flight canceled? Or do we have your beautiful friend to thank?" She set a hopeful gaze on Tegan, who was beaming at his overzealous mother. Before Jett could respond, she said, "Hello, darling. I'm Sherry, Jett's mother."

"Hi. I'm Tegan." She stepped around Jett and hugged his mother like they were old friends. Then she turned her attention to his father and *whistled*. "Now I know where Jett gets his commanding presence from. Look at *you*, all *Pierce Brosnanish* with your sharp blue eyes and slicked-back hair." She patted his father's chest and said, "You make me want to go home and put on my best dress."

His father's gaze lowered to her hand on his chest, and his brows lifted. Jett moved swiftly, putting a hand on Tegan's shoulder and pulling her back to where he stood. He lowered his hand to her waist, keeping her close.

"*Tegan*, is it?" his father said, not unkindly.

"Yes, sir. Tegan Fine."

"Please, no *sir* necessary. Call me Douglas." His father offered his hand.

Douglas? His father had always gotten off on titles as a form of respect. He'd never once heard his father utter the words *no* sir *necessary*. As Tegan shook his hand, Jett tried to make sense of the man before him. Any minute now his father would start the inquisition, asking Tegan what she and her parents did for a living, where her family was from, and generally sizing her up.

"It's a pleasure to meet you," his father said. "And for the record, you look beautiful in your jeans and boots, so you can keep that best dress put away. Although with this weather, we might need *boats* instead of boots."

"I know, right?" Tegan said.

Jett's eyes darted to his mother, who nodded almost imperceptibly, as if she was confirming this new, lighter side of his father.

"Son," his father said, standing a little more rigidly. "To what do we owe this pleasure?"

And there it was. The discomfort and formalities they were still unable to move beyond. "Dean and I couldn't reach you, and we were concerned."

"Our phones have been down all day," his mother said. "But at least we have power. Janie came over a little while ago and said Mitchell might have to close the market for much of the season because of water damage."

"Oh man." Jett turned to Tegan and said, "Janie and Mitchell Myer live next door. They own the Corner Market. It's been in their family for generations."

"Jett worked there throughout high school," his father said. "To this day Mitchell says he was the hardest-working teenager he'd ever employed."

"He's always been a hard worker," his mother said. "Jett, I'm sure you've checked on Rosie?"

"I did, and she's fine."

"That's good," his mother said. "This storm was a doozy."

"We're heading into town to see how we can help," his father said. "Would you like to join us? Put those muscles to work?"

"You're going to *help*?" The words came out before Jett could think to stop them.

His father held his gaze, jaw tight. "Yes, Jett," he said evenly. "Mitchell's been our neighbor for decades. I operated on his daughter's brain tumor. He employed you at a time when you were ornery as a bugger, and—" His mother touched his father's arm, and in an instant, his father cleared his throat and lowered his eyes for a beat. When he lifted them, a humble expression appeared, and he said, "I'm grateful that Mitchell gave you a chance and provided an outlet for your drive and determination." He shifted his focus to Tegan and said, "Even when he was a kid, Jett wanted to be the best at everything. He joined every sports league and worked when other kids were out goofing around. I swear my son was gone more than he was home."

Avoiding you, Jett thought wryly, with a side of guilt. There was no end to the emotional battering.

"I bet the apple didn't fall far from the tree," Tegan said cheerily.

Jett sure as hell hoped it had.

"What do you say?" his mother said. "Do you have time to help?"

"Sure, we can help. We have all day," Tegan said excitedly.

Great. He'd imagined a quick hello and then getting the hell out of there. Now he was stuck. "We'll follow you over."

"Wonderful!" his mother said.

They climbed into their respective vehicles. The second Jett settled into his seat, Tegan said, "Did you bring a knife?"

"Why would I bring a knife?" He started the engine and followed his father's car.

"We need something to cut through the tension between you two."

He grinned, shaking his head. "I warned you."

"Yes, you did. Now spill, *Armani*. What am I dealing with here?"

"We're not going there," he said sternly.

"Oh, yes we are. Women talk, you know, and I'd rather hear it from you than from the girls."

"Seriously…?"

"Look, it is what it is," she said. "Not everyone has an easy upbringing. Was your dad physically abusive?"

"What? No." He glared at her.

"It's nothing to be ashamed of if he was."

"Tegan, he *wasn't*."

"What, then? Did he push you too hard to be the best? Because everyone says doctors are the worst when it comes to that."

"He pushed us all, but that's not what caused the issues."

"Then what was it? Was he mean to your mom?"

Jett swallowed hard, remembering the cutting tone his father had used toward his mother in the weeks before he'd moved out. And later, after their grandfather had passed away and the weight of the entire medical practice had landed on his father's shoulders. But if he was going to survive the next few hours, he couldn't afford to drown in dark memories. He needed to end this conversation.

"He left us when I was a kid," he said too sharply. "He took off for a few months, okay? Can we drop it now?"

"Oh, I'm sorry. Was there…someone else? Another woman?"

Jett gritted his teeth. "No. Can we drop it, please?"

"Sure, but you're so bottled up. I just want to help."

No one can help.

"He came back, right?" she asked carefully. "I'm just trying to understand. I mean, it's obvious that you tweak each other's nerves, but he seems to be *trying*. He said some really nice things about you."

"Yeah, *ornery bugger* is real sweet."

"In all fairness, I've known many teenage boys, and that seems spot-on for most of them."

"Thanks for the vote of confidence."

"You mean the dose of reality?" she countered. "They were raising three boys. There had to be trying times. Your mom is awesome, by the way. I bet she knew just how to handle three wild sons. Did you notice the way she touched your father's arm and how he immediately let his guard down? That speaks volumes about how much she loves him and the strength of their relationship. I can tell he really trusts her."

"There's no doubt she loves him. Always has."

He followed his father into town, once again struck by the post-storm chaos. The parking lot of the Corner Market and the neighboring stores was flooded and blocked off. Several branches on the trees along the street were dangling like loose teeth ready to be yanked free. Jett glanced down the street to the dental office, where crews were working on fallen power lines. He parked by the drugstore, watching people pushing water away from the entrance with brooms. These businesses were the hallmarks of his youth, and now their lives were completely upended. It was one thing to hear about storms on the Cape while he was busy spinning deals thousands of miles away. But seeing the impact like this brought his past rushing back. The Corner Market was where he'd first discovered his love of business, and the dental office was where Lacey McGuire had worked when he was a kid, a pretty hygienist who had stirred his first real crush. She'd been in her late twenties, and he knew now how ridiculous he must have appeared, ogling her and trying to act cool in his basketball shorts and high-tops. He'd bought his first box of condoms at that drugstore. Man, he'd been nervous, waiting until there was almost no one else in the store before sauntering up to the register like he was an old pro. He'd thought he'd gone under the radar. But when he'd asked to borrow the car for a date that weekend, he'd endured a thirty-minute lecture from his father on responsible dating and respecting women. He'd learned a valuable lesson that day.

Never buy condoms in town.

He'd also learned that his father had eyes and ears everywhere. That night Jett had vowed to be just as powerful as his father when he grew up. That promise had gone right beside the more important one that he'd made years earlier, when his father had moved out—that he'd never be as *weak* as his father was.

Now, as Jett turned to Tegan, the woman who barely knew him but had offered to be there *for him* without hesitation, he remembered those promises. It was a good thing he was leaving tomorrow. She didn't deserve to be caught up in his family drama.

He softened his tone and said, "I appreciate you coming along and wanting to help, but maybe some things are too broken to ever be fixed."

"He must have really hurt you," she said sweetly. "I'm sorry for whatever you went through. If you ever want to vent, I'm a pretty good listener."

"I appreciate that, but I think this is crossing an FWB line, Tegs."

She pushed open her door and said, "Maybe you're right. I'm sorry. I just suck at watching friends suffer."

As they climbed from the truck and his parents approached, a new layer of guilt suffocated him.

"Why don't Tegan and I go find the ladies to see where we can be of the most help, and leave you and your father to do the heavy lifting?" His mother sidled up to Tegan and said, "Come on, sweetheart. Let's get to know each other better, and you can tell me all about you and Jett."

"We're just *friends*, Mom."

His mother waved dismissively, and as she and Tegan walked away, Jett heard his mother say, "So, how did you come into my son's life?"

"Tegan's a spunky one, like Emery. I like her," his father said as they headed around to the front of the building. "In my day, I wouldn't have let a woman like that get away."

Jett stopped walking and turned on his father. "Look, I'm here, and I'm happy to help. But in my eyes, you have only ever been with Mom. So please don't try to turn today into something it's not. We're not buddies."

His father bristled. "I was referring to your mother." He lowered his voice to an icy tone and said, "There has only been your mother in my life since the day I met her. I understand you are determined to condemn me to hell for leaving all those years ago, and that's your right. But if you think for one second that I'm not going to keep trying to show you I'm a better man now than I have ever been, you're sorely mistaken."

Before he could respond, his father strode away, leaving Jett to curse himself for saying shit he didn't mean. He didn't think his workaholic father had ever cheated on his mother. That wasn't even a consideration.

And why he'd spewed such a hateful comment was a mystery to him.

His father turned around, and their gazes collided. Jett stood up taller, bracing for a verbal lashing.

"You coming, son?" his father asked casually. "There's a lot of work to be done."

Chapter Twelve

LIKE MANY SHOPS on the Cape, the Corner Market resembled an old two-story, cedar-sided house. The white fence surrounding the front patio had been broken during the storm. Debris had crashed through the window, and a large branch from the old tree out front had snapped and crushed the front of the roof. Jett and his father, along with friends and neighbors Jett hadn't seen in years, waded through ankle-high water, clearing shelves and salvaging goods. They got the water under control in a couple of hours, but it took several more to clean up the mud and empty the building. Jett fielded business calls, talking while he worked. His mother and Tegan had brought lunch from the deli down the street a few hours ago. The deli provided food at no cost to the volunteers. His mother and Tegan had been running between the market and several neighboring businesses, pitching in wherever they could.

Jett glanced out the front window, catching sight of Tegan holding the arm of an older woman as she walked with her toward the drugstore. They'd been in Hyannis all day, and Tegan hadn't taken a single break. When she'd brought bottles of water for him and his father a little while ago, she'd been flushed, and he'd wanted to haul her pretty ass into the stockroom and make her feel all kinds of good. But he'd quickly learned that she'd been fraught with worry because several of the shop owners were talking about needing to close for a good part of the season. He'd explained to her that most of the businesses on the Cape survived only because of the summer tourist traffic. Sadness had risen in her eyes. She'd said she felt selfish worrying about the amphitheater when so many families stood to lose so much.

He was thinking about that when his mother walked into his line of sight.

"You okay, Jett?" she said. "You look troubled."

"I'm fine," he said, stacking cans into a box. "Who's that with Tegan?"

"I'm not sure. Tegan saw her get off the bus on our way over, and she went to help her. She's a special girl, honey. Did you know she travels all over the world by herself? She's very adventurous and self-assured."

He heard the hope in his mother's voice and said, "Mom, you know I'm not in a position for a relationship."

"Oh yes, you've made that quite clear. Tegan was very forthright with me. She said she's too focused on running the amphitheater to get tied down in dating and such. The way she said it reminded me of you. I guess I don't understand kids these days."

"I'm in my midthirties, Mom."

"You know what I mean. You'll always be my *boy*. I just don't understand how dating could ever be a bad thing. You work so hard. I'd think you'd want someone to share your evenings with, to get your mind off work and relax."

He gave her a deadpan look. "Mom..."

"I know. I'm just *saying* that dating should be a happy

thought, not a pain in your rear end. Why didn't you tell me she was Harvey Fine's niece? He was such a wonderful man."

"I didn't have time to say much when we arrived. I have only known her for a couple of days, Mom. It's not like I know her family history."

Her eyes held a hint of motherly intuition, the kind that said she knew just what they'd been doing for those days. "She said you were helping her with a business plan for a new production arm to her uncle's business. That's a big undertaking for a single woman."

"It's a big undertaking for *anyone*," he corrected her. "She's experienced running her own businesses and claims she's doing fine. She can handle it."

"Yes, I believe she can. Oh, there's Bryson. I want to catch up with him." Bryson Myer was a year older than Jett. They'd played sports together in high school. "I'm really glad you're here." His mother gave him a quick peck on the cheek and said, "Tegan said you'd stay for dinner. Your father's going to be thrilled. I have chicken pot pie soup in the Crock-Pot."

Jesus, Tegs. Dinner...?

Despite not being thrilled about sticking around for dinner, his stomach churned excitedly at the thought of his mother's cooking.

As his mother went to see Bryson, Jett looked across the room at his father, pulling cans from a high shelf and stacking them in a box. His father had always been an aggressive leader, taking charge of every room he walked into, commanding and directing, even when he had no business doing so. It was something Jett both admired and disliked about him. Today his father had thrown him for a loop. *Another loop*, he corrected himself. He'd come into the building and found Bryson, who was coordinating the efforts of the volunteers. Instead of telling Bryson what he was *willing* to do, which Jett would have put money on his father doing, his father had surprised him and said, *I'm here to work. Where do you need me?* He'd been busting his ass ever since.

His father clipped his hand on the edge of the shelf as he hoisted the box into his arms, and grimaced.

"Dad! I'll get that." Jett hurried over and took the box from him. "You shouldn't lift anything this heavy."

"I might be old, but I'm not feeble."

"I didn't mean…" Jett's eyes caught on his father's hand. "You're bleeding." He set down the box.

"It's nothing."

He inspected the gash. "That doesn't look like nothing."

"It's fine. I'm a doctor, remember?"

"Yeah, and sick children need your hands to be in working order. Who's going to save their lives if you get hurt?" He motioned toward the restroom. "Let's go get that cleaned up."

"When did *you* start taking care of *me*?"

"Since you turned into a man I don't recognize and put your skilled hands on the back burner."

"Maybe you'll be around to help when I'm too old to take care of myself after all."

"There's a world of difference between making you clean out a wound and changing your old-man diapers."

His father put a hand on Jett's shoulder and said, "I'd never expect that of you, son. No need for you to get jealous over your old man's hardware."

THEY WERE STILL chuckling when they came out of the men's room. Jett didn't know how it happened, but they were actually getting along.

"Tell me about your girl," his father said.

"She's not my girl, Dad. We're just...good friends." *In and out of the bedroom.*

The truth in that thought threw him for a minute. He'd been thinking about Tegan all day. Not just about how much he wanted to kiss her or take her in his arms every damn time he saw her, but about her business and ways he could help her get things organized and off the ground. He thought about how selflessly she'd come with him today and how effortlessly she'd disarmed his stone-hearted father.

Correction.

My once-stone-hearted father.

His father had been anything but stone-hearted today, working tirelessly without complaint, checking in with the other volunteers to make sure they didn't need a break. Jett hadn't joked around with his father since he was just a boy, before his father had moved out. Before his life had taken a turn for the worse.

Who was he kidding? Before his life had been forever changed.

Mitchell Myer was heading their way. The robust man who had taken Jett's ornery ass under his wing looked like he'd aged ten years since Jett had seen him last Christmas. His shoulders were rounded forward, his gray hair looked thinner, and his cheeks were sunken. He looked devastated. *Broken.*

"Mitchell," his father said.

"Douglas. Jett." Mitchell shook their hands. "Thanks for coming out to help. Mother Nature sure threw us for a loop this time."

"I'm sorry you got hit so hard," Jett said.

"Me too." Mitchell exhaled wearily. "Did you hear about Ralph Stowe?"

Ralph Stowe owned the sporting goods shop down the road. When Jett was growing up, he'd donated cleats and other sporting supplies to some of the less fortunate families around town. Ralph and Beth Stowe had five grown children, one of whom was disabled and lived with them.

His father said, "Yes. I just heard. Sherry and I will swing by the hospital tomorrow and visit Beth to see if she needs anything."

"What happened to Mr. Stowe?" Jett asked.

"He was driving home from Boston last night and was one of five cars in a pileup on the highway," his father explained. "He suffered a head injury and several broken bones. Luckily, he should make a complete recovery, but it'll take some time."

"That's awful. Is anyone taking care of the store?" Jett asked.

"Yes. He has a very capable manager on site handling things," Mitchell said. "His oldest daughters are driving in from Boston today to help Beth care for Stacy, and his two boys are flying in tomorrow."

"If I can do anything, please let me know," Jett offered.

"Know anyone who can work a miracle?" Mitchell said jokingly, but Jett knew he wasn't joking.

"We'll get it all cleaned up and help out as much as we can," his father reassured him. "Bryson said you might have to close for a good bit of the season. That's a hard knock to take."

Mitchell scoffed. "A hard kick in the ass is what you mean. These storms don't just affect my family. Sure, Bry has his own son to feed now, and he relies on the income from the market, as we do, but I've got fifteen full-time employees whose families also rely on our success. We make eighty percent of our income over the summers. With half the stores on this block alone suffering damage, I don't expect they'll be able to find employment anytime soon to cover their income. Normally I'd try to help them out, but between the repairs from when those three nor'easters wreaked havoc with our house and business two winters ago, helping Jamie get back on her feet after losing everything in that hurricane a few years back, and helping Bryson cover his lawyer fees for his divorce, we're already mortgaged to the hilt."

No wonder the guy looked broken.

Outside of his brothers and his friends at Bayside, Jett hadn't kept up with many people he'd grown up with. He'd known Mitchell's daughter, Jamie, had moved to North Carolina and that Bryson had gotten married, but he'd never heard about the rest.

"I'm afraid it might be time to cut our losses and find something a little less dependent on the elements to put food on the table." Mitchell looked around the store and said, "We've had a good run of it. I can't complain."

"What you need is an angel investor," his father said.

"The whole damn town does," Mitchell said. "I'd better get over to the drugstore. I want to make sure Sally's doing okay." He shook their hands again and said, "Thanks again."

After he walked away, Jett said, "They need a whole lot more than an angel investor."

"No doubt," his father said.

"Someone to negotiate on their behalf to get discounts for repairs and teach them how to turn their mom and pop shops into more profitable businesses so times like these don't sink them. They need better contingency plans."

"You can't exactly plan for a tree through the roof."

"No, but they can learn from this. Do a risk assessment of the trees, hanging signs, and anything else that may cause damage in another storm and eliminate the risks as best they can. Have annual building inspections to ensure there are no leaks or other structural issues in general, not just for storms. These are old buildings and need to be treated as such."

"All that takes money and know-how."

"That's true. But you know as well as I do, it takes money to make money. If that branch had been cut back before the storm, we wouldn't be standing here right now."

"Well, son, then they need a miracle after all, because it would take a really special person to dedicate that type of time, energy, and resources to this town."

"Not to mention the emotional toll of dealing with all the bullshit. It would take a team, not just one person."

His father held his gaze and said, "Led by someone who cares enough about the town to make it happen. There are very few people who can make something of that magnitude come to fruition, and around here, I know of only one."

"Who?"

His father cocked his head, grinning.

"Oh, hell no. I'm leaving tomorrow. I'm working on acquiring Carlisle Enterprises. Their headquarters is in London, and once I take it over, it's going to suck up every second of my time for the next several months."

"It was worth a shot. Hopefully Mitchell and the others will find their way."

"You've got more money than you could ever spend. You can do it," Jett suggested.

"Son, I know a hell of a lot about one thing—*medicine*. And more specifically, neurology. It takes a far smarter man than me to understand the ins and outs of multiple businesses, much less how to come back from this type of devastation."

Jett was struck by the message his father was sending and the look of pride and something more in his eyes. Something Jett had rarely seen since he was a kid. It was the look that told him his father believed he could do anything he put his mind to. Jett was riveted by that look.

"I think Bryson has taken a shine to Tegan," his father said, jostling Jett from his thoughts.

He followed his father's gaze to Tegan and Bryson standing a few feet away. Tegan was gushing over something Bryson was showing her in his wallet. Jealousy clawed up Jett's spine.

"It looks like Bryson's trying to reel her in with pictures of his adorable towheaded little boy. But"—his father raised his brows, amusement dancing in his sharp blue eyes—"she's not your girl, so you probably won't give it another thought."

Like hell he wouldn't. She may not be *his* girl, but she sure as hell wasn't going to be *Bryson's*.

Chapter Thirteen

TEGAN COULD HARDLY keep a straight face as she and Jett climbed from the SUV at his parents' house that evening. Jett had swooped in like an eagle defending his nest while she was talking with Bryson. He'd draped an arm over her shoulder, acting like they were a couple. But he'd been tight-lipped ever since. She probably shouldn't enjoy the thrill his possessiveness incited in her, but how could she not? Ever since their first kiss, she had been trying not to let her feelings for Jett grow into something more than friendship, but it was proving to be an impossible task. He was so much more than the uptight suit-wearing guy she'd met at the café, the man who'd seemed *above* getting his hands dirty and had insisted that work was his *life*. He had not only pushed off work to help her, but he'd also helped their friends at Bayside, jumped right in to help the lovely couple earlier today, and spent the rest of the day doing things for others. She knew they were together only because of their FWB agreement and that if she let on about her feelings, he'd probably end things.

But keeping such *strict* emotional boundaries was killing her.

Did he even recognize how much happiness he'd exuded as

he'd greeted old friends with pats on the back? As he'd worked alongside his father, a man he clearly had trouble seeing for the man he was trying so hard to be? Or was he fooling her and everyone else?

As his father unlocked the door, she looked at the two of them. They were very much alike, serious minded and work oriented. Two peas in a pod in that regard. But she'd noticed that Jett was warmer toward the people he'd talked with today than his father was. Douglas hadn't been *cold*. He'd simply been more *poised*, caring with an air of dignity that said he was an important man. But what Jett's father lacked in warmth, his mother made up for in droves.

Jett put a hand on Tegan's back as they followed his parents into their house. After they removed their wet boots and jackets, Jett took her arm, walking toward a stairway to their left, and said, "I'll show Tegan where to wash up."

"Okay, sweetheart," his mother said. "There are fresh towels in the linen closet."

Jett dragged her up the stairs like he was on a mission.

"I don't think your mom bought our *just friends* label," she whispered.

He sort of grunted as he led her into a luxurious bathroom and closed the door behind them. He stalked toward her with a predatory look in his eyes. Her pulse quickened. He was so freaking *hot* he should be illegal.

"New FWB rule," he said gruffly. "No filling up your dating card when we're out together."

She couldn't stop the smile splitting her cheeks. Did that mean he felt their connection as deeply as she did? Did he want *more*? Hope fluttered inside her. Bryson was super-sexy, and he was as nice as could be, but she wasn't interested in him. He didn't have an edge like Jett, that certain something that made her light up inside every time their eyes connected. Bryson also had a little boy, and Tegan was nowhere near ready to settle down in that manner. She had a business to build and adventures to go on.

But she wasn't about to tell Jett that. Not when this was the perfect time to fish for his true feelings.

"But we said we could date other people," she said, wide-eyed and innocent.

His eyes narrowed. "When we're *not* together."

"It's not like I'd go out with him *tonight*, while you're here."

His chest expanded with a deep inhalation, and in the next second, he lifted her up and put her on the counter, wedging himself between her legs. He leaned in so close, his breath became hers. "So, you *did* set a date?"

"No *asking* for details, remember?" she said sassily.

"*Tegan...*" His warning was underscored by the heat of his stare.

Courage bubbled up inside her, and she said, "You're *jealous.*"

"I don't get *jealous,*" he said sharply. "I'm *annoyed,* and you would be, too, if I had made a date with some chick today."

She was about to deny it, but she couldn't lie. Instead, she ran her fingers over his chest and said, "Admit it. You're having as much fun being together as I am. We've *connected.*" She said *connected* low and sinisterly, like it was a bad word.

"And I can't wait to *connect* again." He hauled her to the edge of the counter, grinding against her as he kissed her neck, sending rivers of heat through her core. "We are so fucking *fun...*"

She pressed on his ass, and he grinded harder against her,

creating delicious friction. She closed her eyes as he kissed and nipped at her neck and jaw. He palmed her breast, causing her nipples to pebble and burn. She felt herself go damp against his hard heat, and her thoughts began to fracture. She struggled to hold on to them and panted out, "Admit it. You like me."

"You know I like you, Tegs," he said in a husky voice. "Or I wouldn't be here."

He continued his mind-numbing assault. He lifted her shirt and bra and began kissing her breasts. He brushed his scruff over her tender skin and demanded, "Agree to the rule."

"Convince me," she said breathlessly.

He guided her hands to the edges of the sink and lowered his mouth over one breast. He sucked and licked, kissed and taunted, until she was hanging on to her sanity by a thread. He slid his hand between her legs, rubbing her over the top of her jeans, taking her up, up, *up*. So close to heaven she could taste it.

"*Agree*," he said harshly.

"*Yes!* I agree. Just don't stop," she pleaded.

He brought his mouth to her breast again, and she held her breath, readying for one of the explosive orgasms she knew he was capable of giving her. She had a fleeting thought about his parents waiting for them, but when he placed a single kiss on her nipple, those thoughts skittered away.

"Again," she said dizzily.

But instead of his hot mouth on her skin, she felt him righting her bra and sweater. Her eyes flew open as he took a step back. "Why'd you stop?"

He flashed an arrogant and way-too-fucking-sexy grin. "You were so good to me in the driveway earlier, I thought I'd pay it forward." He reached for the door and said, "It's never a good idea to try to outnegotiate the master."

He walked out, leaving Tegan hot, bothered, and planning her revenge.

By the time she got herself cooled down and washed up, the table was set for dinner and Jett was nowhere to be seen.

"There she is," his father said. He'd changed into a pair of slacks and an expensive-looking sweater. "Jett's on the phone with Tia out on the porch. How she keeps up with his schedule seven days a week is beyond me." He picked up a bottle of wine and said, "Would you like a glass?"

"Sure. Thank you." As he poured the wine, she said, "I'm sorry I took so long. My sister called while I was washing up." She'd come up with the excuse while she was running her hands under cold water, trying to take the edge off her raging hormones. Douglas handed her a wineglass. "Thank you. Can I help with dinner?"

"Thanks, sweetie, but as soon as Jett comes in, we'll be ready to eat," Sherry said. "I'd love to hear about your family. How wonderful that your mother had two girls. I always wanted a little girl, but it wasn't to be. Instead, I've been blessed with two wonderful daughters-in-law. Do you have any brothers?"

"No, but if it makes you feel any better, my mom always wanted boys. My sister and I are really close, but when we were young, we argued a lot and we'd give each other the silent treatment. My mom used to say it would be easier to deal with shouting than silence."

"I think your mother and I should compare notes. Our boys were thick as thieves when they were young. Our house was always noisy and impossible to keep clean. Dean came inside every day with half the earth in his pockets, and he was always planting *something*. Doug, our oldest, used to bring home injured animals to heal and dead animals to bury." She held up her index finger and said, "But not before first cleaning them in the kitchen sink. I always thought he'd become a vet, but he followed in his father's footsteps instead."

"Remember the snake?" Douglas asked with a chuckle.

"How could I forget?" Sherry said. "It was lost in the house for days before Dean found it in the toy box and shrieked bloody murder."

"Oh my gosh," Tegan said. "How did you get rid of it?"

"Our fearless boy got to it before I was even down the stairs." She pointed out the patio doors at Jett, pacing with a serious expression as he talked on the phone. "He would have taken on Godzilla if it was threatening one of his brothers."

"Was he into animals or nature?"

"No. Jett was busy cataloging and organizing his baseball cards with his father. Oh, how he loved checking them off their lists and memorizing the stats on the back of the cards. Jett used to do anything he could to earn money just so he could go to Bud's Sports with his father and get a pack of baseball cards on the weekends."

"That must have been fun." Tegan tried to imagine Jett and his father being that close.

"It was," Douglas said in a way that made Tegan think he missed those days. "But things change. Bud's is long gone. They went under years ago."

She wondered if Jett missed those days, too. "Does Jett still collect cards?"

"No, he stopped when…" Sherry's voice trailed off as she opened a cabinet.

"When he was a boy," Douglas said, moving beside Sherry. He touched her hip and said, "I'll get that." He withdrew a stack of bowls and set them on the counter. His eyes lingered on Sherry's, and a silent message Tegan couldn't read passed between them, but the heaviness of regret seemed to remain. He squeezed her hand, then turned a lighter expression to Tegan and said, "While the house was loud and hard to keep clean when the boys were little, nothing compared to three testosterone-laden teenagers playing every sport known to man. Our house became a veritable locker room."

Sherry began filling the bowls with soup. "All of our boys were good at sports, but Jett was truly gifted. He was recruited by Boston College to play baseball."

Wow, that was news to her.

Jett came through the door and put a hand on Tegan's back, looking skeptically at his parents, and said, "Sorry I was on the phone so long. Tia got me a flight out of Hyannis tomorrow morning instead of leaving from New York."

Disappointment knotted in Tegan's chest. She'd forgotten he was leaving so soon.

"That sounds better than driving to the city," his mother said.

In an effort to quell the longing burrowing inside her, Tegan said, "I had no idea you played college baseball."

"Who told you that lie?"

"Oh, *Jett*," his mother said. "We were just telling Tegan that you were recruited. We hadn't gotten around to saying that you turned down the scholarship to study business."

"Do you regret not playing?" Tegan asked, and his parents' eyes moved to Jett.

Jett scoffed. "Not even a little. Nobody has any claim on me. I could buy a frigging baseball team if I wanted to." He picked up two bowls and said, "This smells great, Mom."

Tegan followed him to the dining room with the other two bowls. As they set them on the table, she said, "Why did you stop collecting baseball cards?"

"I outgrew it," he said curtly as his parents carried in Tegan's glass of wine, the wine bottle, and three more glasses. He shot a dark look at his father and said, "You didn't tell me the treehouse got damaged in the storm."

"Given your dislike of all things nostalgic, I actually thought you might be *pleased* that I've decided to have it taken down." His father handed Tegan her wineglass and said, "Would you like a glass of wine, son?"

Jett's eyes never left his father's, tension buzzing like flies between them. "I'll pour myself a glass of whiskey."

"I think I will, too," his father said, stalking after him toward the kitchen.

Tegan felt sucker punched. She had no idea what had gone wrong. She looked at Sherry and said, "I'm sorry. I didn't realize asking him about when he'd stopped collecting cards would put him in a bad mood."

"Oh, honey, it's not what you said. I can't remember the last time we spent an entire day with Jett, and I'm sure you're the one who deserves the credit for that."

"He wanted to come. I'm just here to support him."

"Mm-hm. So you two claim. It's hard to believe that once upon a time Jett was the apple of his father's eye and his father was his knight in shining armor. They're two of the hardest-working, deepest-*loving* men that I have ever known. Unfortunately, they're also two of the stubbornest." She sipped her wine. "They're at war with themselves, but they insist on taking it out on each other."

"I don't understand. Why would Jett be at war with himself?"

"He's spent so much time running from any ties that might slow him down, he's gotten himself all tangled up in knots."

Jett and Douglas came out of the kitchen, drinks in hand, faces mirror images of discomfort.

"Beneath those ruffled feathers are two incredibly good, *loyal* men," Sherry said in a hushed voice. She turned her back to them and added, "Jett will push you away like you're the enemy, but trust me, honey, he's worth holding on to." She gave Tegan's arm a supportive squeeze and sauntered around to her seat.

"Shall we eat?" his father said.

Jett pulled out a chair for Tegan, and as she sat down, he leaned closer and whispered, "Sorry you came yet?"

She met his gaze as he sat beside her. The regret in his eyes tugged at her heartstrings. He put his hand on hers beneath the table, squeezing it as his mother had squeezed her arm, and in that moment, she swore the regret turned to something more like longing or hope. *At war, indeed.* "Not even a little," she said honestly, wanting to understand him now more than ever.

Relief pushed away the regret she'd seen, and as they ate the delicious meal his mother had prepared, the tension hovering over them like a dark cloud eased. His parents told stories about Jett and his brothers, most of which Jett denied, all of which were touching and painted pictures of close-knit brothers.

Jett nudged Tegan's arm and said, "If you learned how to cook like this, I might hang out with you more often."

"Nah, I'm good," Tegan teased, earning a hearty laugh from his father.

Jett scowled.

"I'm sure a vivacious, smart woman like Tegan has plenty of

friends who are willing to cook *for* her," his mother said, which only intensified her son's scowl. "I had the best time getting to know you, Tegan. Thank you for helping so many people today."

"It was amazing to see the community working together," she said. "It reminded me of home."

"Where are you from?" his father asked.

"Peaceful Harbor, Maryland. It's a small coastal town, and the community is very supportive, like yours."

"That's quite a move for you," his father said. "Has it been a difficult transition?"

"I'm thinking of it as an adventure. It's not difficult, although the house is lonely without my uncle, and it's a little scary to try to fill my uncle's very big shoes. But I'm giving it my all. I'll be going back to Maryland in October, then returning in the spring. I met a lot of really nice people today, many of whom knew my uncle and had been to the theater. That helps, knowing I'm carrying on something people enjoy."

"Jett mentioned that you were Harvey Fine's niece and had inherited his amphitheater," his father said. "He was a remarkably kind man, and I'm sorry you lost him. He gave generously to the Pediatric Neurology Foundation and helped many families."

"Thank you. I don't know anything about the foundation, but my uncle chose his philanthropies very carefully, and I hope to carry on his legacy with the same spirit and generosity."

"That's very nice of you. Jett's grandfather was one of the first pediatric neurosurgeons. He started the foundation to—"

"Dad, please don't try to sell her on the foundation."

His father nodded. "Forgive me. There was a time when I believed I had to have my finger in every pot of my practice and in every aspect of the foundation simply because our family name was on it, and unfortunately, my family paid the price for that dedication." He met Jett's steely gaze and said, "But things have changed." He returned his attention to Tegan and said, "I wasn't trying to sell you on the foundation. I'm so used to educating people about the value of the programs, I don't realize how it must come across outside the medical community."

"It's okay." She looked at Jett and said, "I'm sure you've probably heard about the foundation a million times, but I know nothing about it. And now that I know it was founded by your grandfather, I'm interested in hearing more. Do you think you can sit through it one more time?"

"Sure," Jett said, sending another silent message to his father. This one felt a little less tense.

Tegan listened as his father described how the foundation served pediatric patients through advocacy, education, research, and support initiatives. The pride in his voice was palpable, and it quickly became clear how big a role he played in the foundation and how important it was to him.

"We have an annual fundraising event coming up in a few weeks. I know Jett is usually tied up with business when it takes place, but I'd be honored if you'd consider attending as our guest. You can meet the people who run the foundation and decide for yourself if it's the type of program you'd like to support."

"I would love that," Tegan said excitedly. "Thank you. Is it formal? Should I wear a little black dress, or...?"

"It's black tie, but don't worry about running out to buy a fancy dress. Just wear something comfortable. I'm so thrilled that you'll attend," his mother gushed. "You'll sit with us, and I'll introduce you to everyone."

"I make most of my dresses. I think I know exactly which one to wear," Tegan said.

"How wonderful. You really are multitalented."

"When is it this year?" Jett asked gruffly.

"The first Friday in June," his mother answered.

"I'll be there," Jett said. "I'll take you, Tegs."

Hope fluttered like a bird in her chest, and she didn't even try to calm it.

"Are you sure, Jett?" his father asked. "I know it's difficult for you to break way. Tegan will be in good hands with us and your brothers. I'm sure Susie and Emery will enjoy having her there, too."

"I'm *sure*," Jett said sternly. "I'll make it happen."

His mother put her hand to her chest and said, "This is so exciting. You haven't attended one of your father's events in so long, I feel like I might cry. With Doug and Susie flying in this year, it'll be a reunion." She held up her glass and said, "Here's to new beginnings *and* new friends."

They lifted their glasses, and though Jett appeared stressed again, his parents looked elated.

"Tegan, did you ever go with your uncle to the hospitals when he volunteered?" his mother asked.

"Yes, several times. He always took me and my sister at least once when we were in town. He said it was good for us to help others."

"I thought you looked familiar, and now it makes sense. I make rag dolls for children with terminal illnesses, and I think I met you and your sister one summer. You were just a little girl then, maybe seven or eight. Does your sister have brown hair?"

"Oh my gosh! That was you? I will never forget that day. You were in a patient's room when we walked in, and a boy was reading to her. You gave me a doll and told me a story about how each doll held a little bit of magic, and you said the story he was reading was about the doll you gave to the little girl. I still have my doll. You were the inspiration for my bald baby tribe."

"That little boy was Jett," his mother said softly. "He was twelve or thirteen, and broody as could be. I dragged him with me that day to give him a little perspective on life."

"No way." Tegan turned to Jett, who looked like he was caught between intrigue and holy-shit-what's-going-on. "Do you remember that?"

"I don't know. This is all very weird. What's a *bald baby tribe?*" Jett asked.

"That's what I call the baby dolls I make. I started making them for my niece, Melody, when she was really little, and then her friends wanted some. Now I make them for my friends when they have babies, and I bring them to kids at the hospital in Peaceful Harbor around the holidays."

"But why are they *bald?*" Jett asked.

"To avoid anything that could come loose and be a choking hazard. I draw the faces, too."

"It was meant to be," his mother said. "*Fate.*"

Fate...Tegan thought of her uncle, and she couldn't help but wonder if he'd been pulling strings again.

"Well, son," his father said with a nod. "I think this is a sign that you've chosen a very *special* friend."

Jett shifted in his seat, pressing his hands to his thighs, looking as uncomfortable as a lion caught in a trap. Tegan wondered if that past connection was too much for him, crossing too many lines of familiarity. Did he regret saying he'd attend the event with her?

Jett's phone rang, as if the powers that be knew he needed an *out*. He whipped it from his pocket, glanced quickly at the screen, and rose anxiously to his feet. "I have to take this. Excuse me." He escaped to the patio without so much as a backward glance.

Tegan fidgeted with her napkin, watching Jett pace like a caged animal. Sadness billowed inside her. For her, *yes*, but even more so for his parents, who probably thought they were being supportive with their comments about fate and Tegan being special, only to have their son turn his back on all three of them.

"He works so hard," his mother said.

"Sometimes I wish the apple *had* fallen farther from the tree," his father said solemnly.

Chapter Fourteen

HOURS LATER, JETT lay with Tegan snuggled against him naked and sated in her bed, wondering when his life had gotten so mixed up. From the moment he'd seen Tegan at the gas station, she'd invaded his thoughts, disrupting his ability to focus. But spending the day with his parents and helping the community that had been there for him as a kid had served as a crowbar, prying up the heavy iron lid he'd used to keep memories of his youth locked down tight. Now those memories and the guilt they stirred—for never looking back, for his botched relationship with his father, for taking that fucking phone call at dinner—assaulted him, and he had no idea how to turn them off.

"If you think any harder, smoke will start coming out your ears." Tegan rose onto her elbow, gazing at him thoughtfully.

He felt himself smiling despite the war raging inside him. *She* did that to him. He should thank her for putting up with him, for being so much more of a friend to him than he'd ever had before. How did she do it after just a few days? She complicated his feelings, his thoughts, his *life*, even more than they already were.

"I thought I'd worn you out," she said. "Want to talk about

whatever's got you staring up at the ceiling?"

How could someone so beautiful and full of life bring on so many conflicting emotions? Flashes of heat and bright lights competed with the darkness inside him. The darkness continued stacking up like bricks, only to be knocked down by something she said or did. He had no idea what to do with it all, and he felt like he was losing his mind.

"Was it because I brought up the baseball cards or said I'd go to the fundraiser with your parents?" she asked sweetly. "I wasn't trying to upset you or wheedle my way into your life."

"It wasn't that. Or maybe that was part of it." He sat up and raked a hand through his hair, agitation grating beneath his skin like sandpaper. "It was *everything*." He threw off the blanket and pushed to his feet. "From the second my father greeted you *without* an inquisition about what your parents did for a living and all the bullshit he used to care about to the way you disarmed him in the exact same way you disarmed me. Like he and I are the *same*." He paced, as powerless to stop his escalating voice as he was the vehemence spewing out like lava. "I don't recognize that man we were with for most of the day. I don't fucking *trust* him. And then seeing you and my mother looking as close as she is to Emery and Susie? What was that all about? You're not my *girl*, Tegan, and she treated you like you were. You *acted* like you were. And the worst part about it is that neither of you did anything *wrong*. Being nice and warm is who you two *are*. You look at life through rose-colored glasses, full of hope and faith. And that's a *good* thing," he said angrily. "I wouldn't wish my cynicism on *anyone*. But we're night and day, you and me. My glasses are *cracked* and *dark*. I know the shit real life brings, the lies people tell, the way everything you believed and thought you could count on can be torn apart, leaving you swamped in the ugly dredges of reality. And *today?*" He threw his hands up. "That was a fucking eye opener. All those people who helped me get through life as a kid, who made a difference in my life in the smallest fucking ways—knowing my name when I walked into a store, or giving me a ride home when I fell off my bike and broke my arm. Mitch Myer lit my world on fire, for fuck's sake. He gave me something to focus on at a time when I wanted nothing more than to fuck something up. *He's* the reason I found my niche, because he actually talked to me like I was worth talking to, not like I was the angry little shit I'd become back then."

He swallowed hard, every word reawakening the anger he'd been consumed by all those years ago. "Mitch, the guy who saved me from myself, has been through hell these last few years. Now he's *floundering*, and I'm out there earning more money than I can ever spend, and I had *no* idea his family was having such a hard time. He might lose his family's business and have to start all over. What the hell is that? Then there's the nightmare of the gallery. Desiree is expecting and Andre and Vi are supposed to take off. I know they're more Dean's friends than mine, but still. And dinner tonight? What a mind fuck that was, standing on the other side of that damn patio door, watching you with my family. For the first time in my entire life, I wanted to be on the inside looking out instead of the guy who's always on the outside looking in. I don't even understand where that came from or what to do with it. And tomorrow I'll be on a plane going back to my normal life, as if all this shit isn't taking place in what was once *my* community. You know the nail salon we passed near my parents' house? That used to be Bud's Sports, where I bought cards every weekend with my father. Those were the best days we ever had together. I've driven by that corner every time I visited my parents and was so focused on getting in and out as fast as I could, I never even realized it was gone until Dean mentioned it to me. What the hell does that say about me?"

He paused to catch his breath and realized Tegan's lips were pursed and her brow was knitted. "*Shit.* You don't want to hear this."

"Yes, I do," she insisted. "I hear what you're saying, and I want to talk about all of it. I *do*. But it's hard to focus when you're naked and your willy is bouncing around at eye level."

He looked down, and an incredulous laugh fell out. He felt the knots in his chest loosening. *How the hell...?* It was all so overwhelming, he dropped to the edge of the bed, lowering his face to his hands to try to get a grip on himself and all that he'd said.

"Come here." She lowered his hand and pulled him down to his back beside her. "It sounds to me like your mind is a pretty scary place." She laid half her body over him and folded her arms on his chest, resting her chin on them. "Like all your ghosts came rushing out of the closet at once."

"You think?" he said sarcastically. "Sorry for laying all that on you. That wasn't fair."

"I'm glad you opened up to me before you imploded." She leaned forward and touched her lips to his. "Friends talk, Jett. This is good."

It had been so long since he'd had a friend with whom he'd wanted to talk about anything real, he'd forgotten how good it felt to get things out of his system. But it wasn't fair to her. He tucked her hair behind her ear, telling himself to keep his mouth shut before he did any more damage, but she wasn't pushing him away or looking at him like he'd lost his mind, and

"What am I going to do with you?" slipped out.

"Continue letting me in," she said. "Let me try to help."

"Nobody can help, Tegs."

"Okay, then let me listen and say unhelpful things. You can't tell me that you don't feel better getting all of that off your chest."

He did, but that came with guilt.

"You said your father left for a while when you were young. Is that why you don't trust him?"

"Tegs, don't. You don't want to do this."

"I *do* and I *am*. Out of everything you said, that's what bothers me the most, because even from the little time I've spent with him, I can see that you're a lot alike. And he seems as weighed down and haunted as you do. If he can't be trusted, then I really misread him, and I might have to rethink our friendship because trust is the foundation of any type of relationship."

He felt a fissure tear through his chest. "You can trust me."

"Can I? How can I know that?"

"Because I don't make promises I can't keep. I don't lie."

"Is that what he did? Broke a promise? Lied?"

"What do you think?"

"I think I don't want to *assume*, because people are complicated, and we see what we want to see. It isn't always what's real."

"My point exactly."

She shifted beside him and propped herself up on her elbow. "So you don't trust him because he left when you were young?"

"It's more than that. Let me give you a quick recap of life with my father. When I was young, I was enthralled with sports.

I started watching games when I was four when I happened upon one on TV. My father wasn't into sports, but he taught me everything about baseball, football, hockey. My favorite was baseball, and when I was six, he taught me to collect baseball cards, how to catalog them, read the stats, even how to value the condition of the cards. He taught me the difference between the teams and leagues. There was nothing I didn't know. He'd make up jobs that he'd pay me to do, and then on the weekends he'd take me to buy packs of cards with the money I'd earned. We were tight, and life was good. It was a great childhood. My mother was always waiting for me when I got home from school, my brothers and I raced around like fools all the time, and my father collected cards and played ball with me after work until my arm felt like it might fall off."

"Sounds storybook perfect."

"I was lucky. But when I was eight or nine my father started changing. He worked until nine or ten at night; then he'd come home and shut himself in his home office. We rarely saw him, and when we did, he was in a foul mood, just unbearable. I remember lying awake at night waiting for the front door to open just to get ten minutes with him. But he'd shrug me off and disappear into that office. My parents, who had rarely argued, were suddenly fighting all the time."

"That's a drastic change. It sounds horrible," Tegan said empathetically.

"Yeah, well, it gets worse. I was a kid, so I don't know if it took months or years for things to get so bad. Kids' perspectives are skewed. But it felt like it happened fast. Then he moved out, and my mother said it was because they weren't getting along. It didn't make sense to me that the people who taught us about forgiveness were giving up."

"Is that when you stopped collecting cards?"

"That's when I threw the damn things out. His leaving made me feel like everything in my life was a lie. I was a *kid*. I had *no* idea how to separate what was real and what wasn't. In *one* evening, he negated everything he'd taught me to believe in. It didn't help that I wasn't buying his reason for leaving. I didn't know *what* had happened that caused the change or that caused him to move out, but I knew that my mother adored him despite their fights. I knew she'd never ask him to leave. So there I was, in my upside-down world, and none of it made sense."

"That's so sad. Did you tell them you were confused?"

"I think I told my mother, but I was pissed at both of them, so who knows what I really did. I was angry at my father for leaving and at my mother for letting him. And then my mom went on a few dates, or so we thought. At that point I was sure there was more going on, that maybe he was having an affair or had one and she'd found out. My mind went to some pretty dark places."

"That must have been difficult for you and your brothers, to see your mother with other men."

"It was for Dean. I don't know about Doug. He kept to himself after our father left. But I remember being so angry at my father that I was glad she was doing it. How's that for spiteful?"

"I don't hear spite. I hear *hurt*," she said, brushing her fingers along his chest. "I can't imagine seeing either of my parents going on a date with someone else."

"It turned out that they weren't really dates, but we didn't know that until about two and a half years ago, when Dean and Emery got together. My mother told me that my grandmother had sent those men over to make my dad jealous so he'd get his ass back home."

Surprise shone in her eyes. "Grandma Rose to the rescue. Did it work?"

"I don't know if it was the dates that brought him home or not. But if I had known then what I know now about why he left, things might have been different when he came back. But that still wouldn't change the past two decades."

"What do you mean?"

"When she told me the truth about the dates, she also told me why he really left when we were kids. He was in practice with my grandfather, who was mean as a snake to everyone including my grandmother. But he was a real charmer to his clients. He was a leader in his field, prominent and well respected, like my father. According to my mother, my father spent years trying *not* to become the type of man his father was, but he was under a tremendous amount of pressure with the growing practice and my grandfather's demands, and it finally broke him. That's why he changed, and in the end, that's why he left us. He was afraid if he didn't get himself and his work under control, he'd lose our family for good. While he was gone, he focused on becoming a better man. He was working, but he managed to see a therapist several times a week and to see us probably more than he did in those months before he left. I was too mad to appreciate any of it, and when he moved back home, my faith in him was broken. It took about a year before I even *started* to trust him again."

Pain rose in her eyes. "That's a long time for a young boy. Did your brothers forgive him right away?"

"They were much more forgiving than I was. Maybe not fully, but they weren't asses about it."

"Do you always hold grudges?"

It would be much easier for her to simply tell him that none of this was his fault, but instead, she poked the bear. He knew she was fishing to see if she should waste her time with him or not, and he also knew she was strong enough to walk away if he wasn't the type of person she respected or wanted in her life. Maybe that's why he felt comfortable enough to continue being honest with her, and said, "I haven't been in a situation where I cared enough about anyone to allow their actions to affect me."

"That sounds lonely."

The sadness in her eyes caused an ache inside him, and he realized how cold he'd sounded. But he didn't want to lie to the one person who made him want to understand himself better. "I'm too busy to be lonely."

"With *women*?" *Women* came out just above a whisper.

"No." He touched her cheek, wanting to soothe the worry in her eyes. "I'm not a man whore. I'm busy with work, babe. This—you, right now—this is the closest I've been to anyone. *Ever*. I've said more to you about that whole situation than I have to my brothers. Even more than I've said to my grandmother, and I tell her just about all my gripes."

"Thank you for trusting me. But can I ask you something else?"

"Does it matter if I say no?" he teased.

"Ah, you're learning. Your dad was really great today, and if you started to trust him again when you were a kid, then things must have gotten better, right? So, are you still holding that grudge?"

"I'm sure it seems that way, but *no*. He was great for a few years after he moved back home, and things eventually got better between us. But then the pressure of the job got to him

213

again, and he became even worse than he had been before he left. But this time he stuck around, and when I was a teenager, I wasn't afraid to stand up to him. We went head-to-head, yelling matches, accusations. I hated the way he acted better than everyone, the way he treated my mother. God only knows how she loved him through it. That's why I joined every sports team and worked all the time, to avoid him and all that our house represented. I put all of my energy into those things and focused on getting out of the house. When I went away to college, my sole focus was to become smart enough to take the business world by storm, so I would never need anything from him again. I worked my ass off as a grunt to a group of investors throughout college, learned a lot, and basically cut all ties with my father. Not that he noticed. When my grandfather died, which was around the time Dean was going away to school, I started investing my inheritance and got lucky. It was a good thing I didn't lose my ass, because my father took over the medical practice and became an even more self-righteous prick than ever."

Tegan winced.

"Sorry, babe, but it's true. You can ask anyone. Even my mother. You wanted to know why I don't trust him? It's because the man you met today isn't the person I've known since I was a teenager. You've heard how long his new attitude lasted after he moved back in. Having been through that, how can I trust who he'll be tomorrow? Or next year?"

"I don't understand how anyone can be that much of a Jekyll and Hyde."

"I think it's part of who he is. Bad genetics maybe."

"I'd ask what that says about you, but good people come from bad parents all the time. And it sounds like he started out as a great dad and *then* he got overwhelmed, which actually says a lot about him, to overcome that kind of upbringing. What snapped him out of that horrible place this last time?"

"Believe it or not, Emery chewed him out for the way he treated people."

"*Emery* did? Holy cow. She has guts."

"She's a spitfire. She ripped him a new one. I was there. I heard it all, and I have no idea how she got him to listen, because I've told him how much of an arrogant ass he was *many* times over the years, and it had no impact."

She tapped his chest and said, "Because you're too close to him."

"We're *not* close. We're trying, but we're still miles apart. You saw me when we got to the house today. There's so much water under the bridge, we're drowning in it. Just being on the Cape stresses me out."

"I didn't mean *close* as in your relationship. I meant you're two peas in a pod. Too alike." Her lips curved up, and she said, "When I first saw you at the gas station, I thought you were an arrogant ass, too."

He swept her beneath him, earning a giggle that felt like balm to his agitation. "You thought I was *hot*. I could tell by the way you gawked at me."

"Hot, *yes*, but you looked like you *knew* it. Luckily, you've since proven you are a lot more than just a handsome face."

She didn't look at him the way his family and some of his friends did, like he was the bad guy, and that helped ease his tension even more.

"After all you've been through with your father," she said softly, "I understand what you're saying about not trusting him. But if he started out as a good father, someone you admired and loved being with, then isn't there a chance he's finally come full circle? That who he is now is the man he'll always be? Or have you already condemned him to never being worthy of your trust again?"

She was so *good* a person, she reeked of hope, and that slayed him, because he didn't want to crush it. How was it possible that he felt lucky and guilty at once? "I don't know. All I know right now is that before you came along, I wouldn't have thought twice about any of this. I'd get on that plane tomorrow, and seven minutes later I'd be entrenched in work, my family and the devastation of the storm forgotten. I'm a fucking prick, Tegan, and I don't deserve your friendship."

JETT WAS SO tortured, there was no escaping his pain or his confusion. But beneath all that angst, Tegan saw the hurt he carried. She saw the lost and lonely boy whose world had been shattered, the angry teen who had forced himself into survival mode and plowed into manhood with a vengeance, and the serious, passionate man gazing into her eyes who believed he'd risen above it all. She also saw the hard truth bullying its way in. Jett was standing on the cusp of the volcano that he'd always jumped over with blinders on, and for the first time since that all-powerful teen had taken his future by the horns and stormed out of his father's life, those blinders had been torn off, and he was seeing the volcano for all that it was.

She wanted to take away his pain and the loneliness he so vehemently denied but wore with the weight of an anchor. She was pretty sure Jett was going to break her heart, but she already cared too deeply to walk away. She didn't want to save herself, and she knew she couldn't *save* him. He'd never allow that. He was too in control, too walled off, too intent on being a one-man army. God knew he'd needed that steel will to get past the pain he'd described and to climb the mountains he clearly had.

No. Nobody saved Jett Masters, and she was okay with that. She didn't want to save him. What she wanted, what she *ached* for, was to be the very thing he'd spent a lifetime running from. To be someone he could *trust*, someone who he *knew* wouldn't take that trust for granted, even by accident. Someone who saw the man he wanted to be, even if he didn't—and who believed if he truly wanted anything in life, he would find a way to get it.

She wanted to be his *friend*. It would be easier if that was *all* she wanted. But since she couldn't change her feelings, and she knew better than to try to change his, she did what her uncle had taught her to do. She threw caution to the wind and followed her heart.

She touched his cheek and said, "I'm here."

He leaned his face against her palm, a silent war lingering in his eyes despite his soft tone as he said, "I hate that I dragged you into this madness."

"I know you do," she said softly. "But whether you think you deserve my friendship or not, I'm here, and I *want* to be here *with* you as much as I want to be here *for* you."

"Tegs," he said, full of emotion. "I don't want to hurt you."

"Then don't." She rose up and pressed her lips to his, hoping to silence his demons.

He kissed her, but his body remained rigid. She knew he was holding back, trying to rebuild those walls that had cracked, trying to protect himself from what she knew he felt. Probably also trying to protect her from getting too close. His muscles were so tight, he was shaking. But there was no hiding the desire gusting off him, seeping beneath her skin and filling her up until *she* was trembling, too. They were both scared of the intensity of their connection, and maybe he was as worried as she was about how badly a fall from that type of passion could hurt. But it was inescapable, drawing them together like metal to magnet.

They *needed* this, and *he* deserved it.

She tore her mouth away and said, "You can trust me."

"I know," he panted out.

"Then let go and *show* me."

His mouth came ravenously down over hers. His heart thundered wildly as his arms snaked beneath her, crushing her to him. He gripped the back of her head, taking the kiss deeper, *rougher*, like he was chasing his demons away with every stroke of his tongue. She gave herself over to him, wanting that freedom for him, wanting him to know how much she trusted him. Adrenaline coursed through her veins as his hands moved over her skin, down her torso and hips. He clutched her ass, his scruff abrading her cheeks. He made a primal sound and tore his mouth away.

"*Fuck*," he said angrily.

"What's wrong?"

He looked down at her, his jaw clenching repeatedly, and then, like a sail that lost its wind, he said, "*Everything*," in a long, soft breath.

She didn't know what to say as his lips touched hers, kissing her so tenderly she thought it might be *goodbye*. She closed her eyes, wanting to savor every last second, to memorize the feel of his arms around her, the taste of his mouth, the beat of his heart against hers. She wanted to stop time, to live in this moment for as long as humanly possible. She pressed her hands to his back, feeling his muscles flex against them. She held her breath, expecting him to pull away. But he didn't retreat. He threaded his fingers into her hair, holding her face between his hands, and kissed her *longer, slower.*

This wasn't goodbye.

She didn't know what it was, but the longer they kissed, the more relaxed he became. He rocked his hips, brushing the crown of his hard length along her wetness. He wasn't rushing, wasn't thrusting into her. Everything felt *new,* the weight of him on her, the tenderness of his touches, the mingling of their breath. She was lost in a sea of sensations and wonder. He drew back and brushed his scruff over her cheek, kissing her there. His lips trailed lightly over her cheek, her chin, her jaw. His hands skimmed down her body, slowing to caress her waist, hips, and thighs. His hands lingered there, squeezing, kneading, as if it were the first time he'd really felt her. Lust and something much bigger grew inside her, seeping into every crack and crevice, until there was no more room to even think. She could only *feel, want,* and *crave.* Her fingers trailed along his back and into his hair, earning another primal sound, less urgent, more appreciative and sensual than the last. His visceral sounds did her in, making her tingle and burn. His mouth moved to her neck, sucking and licking, until she went boneless in his arms, her entire body hot and yielding. He rolled them onto their sides, keeping her close. His mouth found hers again, parting her lips with his tongue, claiming and possessing her like a tide claiming the shore. He slid one hand behind her knee, lifting her leg to his outer thigh. His cock pressed against her again. His tongue swept deeper, and he clutched her ass, holding her tight against him. She could barely breathe, for the want consuming her.

"Tegs," he whispered, his lips never fully leaving hers.

Their gazes held as he entered her ever so slowly, burying himself deep inside her. The hope she was trying to keep at bay reflected in his eyes, and her heart swelled with a dizzying surge of emotions. His brows slanted, confusion swimming in his eyes. He pressed firmly on her bottom, thrusting impossibly deeper. The bedroom blurred, and the air rushed from her lungs. Never in her life had she felt so wanted, so *connected*. As they found their rhythm, passion flowed like a river, swiftly building in intensity, burgeoning and expanding. They didn't kiss, didn't speak, could only cling to each other, consumed by their ecstasy as they soared up to the stars. They were fire and rain, desert and meadows, flying, crashing, sinking, *floating*. They were powerless and powerful at once, existing on a new plane.

As their shaking, sated bodies sank limp and tangled to the mattress, "*Jesus*," slipped from his lips like a secret.

She didn't dare speak, for fear of pulling them out of this incredible oneness.

"I've never..." he whispered, and then he kissed her, as if he didn't want to finish his thought.

He didn't need to, because she had *never*, either. Never felt like that, never been so lost and so found at the same time. Never known that she'd never be the same person again.

Chapter Fifteen

BY WEDNESDAY AFTERNOON, as Tegan drove to Harper's house, the sky was clear, the air was crisp, and the power had been restored across the Cape. While it would be months before all of the storm damage was rectified for some businesses and homeowners, cleanup crews had made great headway clearing away downed trees and other debris. Standing water dissipated, shutters and boards came down from storefronts and houses, and for many, the storm was nothing more than a blip in their busy lives. Tegan felt like she'd lived a year during those rainy days with Jett, which had made saying goodbye that much harder.

She'd been trying to keep busy to avoid thinking about, and *missing*, him. She'd spent yesterday cleaning up debris in her yard and had paid an impromptu visit to Greta and Larry, helping them clean up, too. She'd even stayed for a cup of tea and more stories about Harvey and Adele. She'd then thrown herself into business mode, determined to get through her to-do list to prepare for Harper's productions. But hours later, she still felt as though Jett had etched himself into her skin. She'd replayed their goodbye a hundred times, trying to figure out the dichotomy that was Jett Masters. The deeply emotional man who had shared pieces of himself she'd never expected Monday night had been gone by Tuesday morning. He had been wide-awake at five o'clock, showered and on the phone with Tia by six, and from that moment on he'd been practically *all* business, sending emails and making arrangements for his upcoming meetings. Tegan had gotten a brief glimpse into his work life: meetings from sunup to sundown on the West Coast for the next week and a half, and then he was off to Louisiana to assess some type of business venture before coming back the morning of the wedding. It seemed he'd carried the patterns he'd developed as a teenager to keep himself too busy to come home in adulthood.

Tegan was trying to accept the truth. No matter how deep their connection had felt, or how long and sensual the kiss goodbye he'd given her, it was obvious that Jett didn't have space for anything more in his life than work and an occasional rendezvous. His text last night, wishing her luck discussing a partnership agreement with Harper, had validated that thought. She'd hoped he'd say something more intimate, especially since she knew he was lonely even if he didn't want to admit it. But when no further texts rolled in, she'd kept her *I miss you* to herself and had played it cool, replying with wishes of good luck with his business deals. She resigned herself to the fact that she'd see him again in less than two weeks at Gavin and Harper's wedding and they'd have one night together. She had no idea how long it would be until she saw him again after that.

As she climbed the steps to Harper's front porch and knocked on the door, she was as ready to move forward as she could be.

The door swung open and Harper stood before her, looking like a seventies throwback in a colorful boho-chic dress. Her long blond hair lay loose over her shoulders with one fine braid down the middle of the left side.

"Wow, fancy car," Harper exclaimed.

"*Ugh*. I'm glad I have it, but I hate it. It was my uncle's, and it's like driving a bus compared to Berta. But Berta quit on me during the storm, and the mechanics haven't had a chance to look at her yet."

"Bummer. I know how much you love that car." Harper's bangles jangled as she waved Tegan in. She hung up Tegan's coat and said, "That storm was wicked. I feel bad for Des and Vi, but it sounds like Rick has everything under control and he's riding the insurance company to get things moving along. Did you have any damage?"

"I was lucky. I only lost a few trees, and there wasn't any damage to the theater. I texted Daphne yesterday to see how she and Hadley were getting along in the cottage. She said she feels guilty because she loves the cottage so much."

"I love that girl. She's forced out of her apartment *with* a baby and *she* feels guilty." Harper sat down and said, "She's the sweetest person. The guys are working on the repairs to her apartment and the office this week, and some of the girls are getting together to help paint Monday evening. Want to help?"

"Absolutely." Tegan sat beside Harper and pulled a notebook out of her messenger bag.

"Great. I was so excited when you called. I didn't think you'd be ready to nail down timelines until after my honeymoon, especially since Emery said you've been with Jett ever since the party."

"How did Emery know I was with Jett? I haven't spoken to anyone about him since he left, not even Chloe when she texted about the next book club meeting."

"Apparently Jett's mom called Dean to get the scoop on you two, and he asked Emery, who mentioned it to Serena and the girls over breakfast yesterday morning." Harper clapped her hands together and said, "So…? What *is* the scoop? We all thought Jett left the morning after my bachelorette party."

"There's no *scoop*." Tegan was afraid to say too much because it would just make her miss Jett even more and she'd done a great job of sidetracking herself, so she kept it brief and simple. "We had a good time the night of your party, and when he found out his flight was canceled, he came over…and *stayed*. The next day we went to check on his parents, and we ended up going into town with them to help clean up from the storm, and then we stayed for dinner. Jett helped me with the business plan. He's *so* good at it." *And many other things.* "But he's gone now, and here I am, ready to get the ball rolling."

"I can see that. But how did you and Jett leave things? Are you going to see him again?"

"Mm-hm, at your wedding." A smile tugged at her lips, and she said, "*After* your wedding."

"So there *is* a scoop! You guys are seeing each other?"

"Sort of, but not really. We're FWBs."

Harper's face scrunched in confusion.

"Sorry. Friends with benefits," Tegan explained.

"*Tegan*," she exclaimed. "That's pretty much seeing each other, right?"

"Not exactly. He's not my boyfriend or anything. I wouldn't call him to tell him about my day. We'll just get together when he's in town. I'm busy, he's busy, and neither of us has time for complications right now."

"Right now or *ever*?" Harper asked.

"I…um…I'd rather not dissect it, you know?"

"Boy, do I know that feeling. Did I ever tell you that Gavin and I first met at a music festival in Romance, Virginia? He was supposed to be my one and only *fling* with a stranger. I swear I fell in love with him that night. I didn't think that was even possible."

"Whoa, we're not talking *love* here, Harper."

"I know *you're* not." Harper rubbed her arms and said, "I have goose bumps just thinking about that night with Gavin. I spent a year telling myself I was crazy and believing I'd never see him again. I never even knew his last name. And then fate stepped in. Now we're getting married at the Silver House on Silver Island, where we spent a romantic weekend last summer. You never know what might happen between you and Jett."

"Actually, I do," she said regretfully. "He's been honest about not wanting any commitments, and I'm so busy..." Worried their conversation was about to go from *simple* to *complicated,* she tried to change the subject. "Speaking of which, let's get started. I have so many things to go over, like the new name of the theater. The Children's Amphitheater no longer makes sense since we'll be hosting adult shows. I decided to change it to the Harvey and Adele Fine Amphitheater, or HAFA."

"That's a great idea, and HAFA is really catchy, but that was the *worst* segue I've ever heard."

"I know. Just go with it," Tegan said with a soft laugh. "I can't think too much about Jett or I'll miss him. So...getting back to the business. Evan said the website will be ready for beta testing by next Friday, with purchasing portals for both the children and adult productions. He referred me to Brandon Owens, a graphic designer in Harborside, Massachusetts, to design the HAFA logo. I spent all morning FaceTiming with

Brandon, going over ideas and color schemes. He's amazing, and he hopes to have several concepts ready by Monday. Hopefully I'll have the final logo within a day or two after that, and I'd love your input on it."

"Of course. I'm happy to help in any way I can."

"Great. I'll email you once I have some options." Tegan readied herself for the more difficult conversation as her phone vibrated, and Jett's name flashed on the screen. "Sorry, let me just…" Her pulse quickened as she read the text. *The woman I'm meeting with must have gone to the Tegan School of Organization. She just pulled out a notebook covered in sticky notes.* Tegan bit her lower lip, trying to hide the joy rising inside her.

"Nothing to spill, *huh?*" Harper teased.

"He's just making fun of my organizational skills." Tegan typed, *Then she's probably awesome. You should def do business with her!* She put her phone on the coffee table, trying to ignore the flutter in her chest, and said, "Okay, where were we?"

"By the goofy grin on your face, I'd say it doesn't matter, because now you're daydreaming about Mr. Tall, Dark, and Handsome."

"*Nope.* I'm not going there." She tried not to think too hard about the fact that Jett was thinking about *her* and said, "Let's see. We've covered the amphitheater, but we need to figure out our partnership."

"We've brainstormed all winter. I thought we figured it out already."

"I know, and we're pretty much on the same page. The adult productions are going to be handled in the same manner as the children's programs. You'll take care of the productions and pay for the use of the theater, and I'll run the theater and continue doing local advertising to get the name out there, and network with the right community groups, that sort of thing."

"Yes, exactly. So what's left to figure out?"

"Well, with that scenario, I'm only doing local marketing, which is limited in and of itself. But also, Harvey never advertised the children's programs, only the availability of the theater. I don't mind advertising your specific shows locally. I want you to succeed. But when Jett brought up having an attorney draft a legal partnership agreement to avoid any potential conflicts in the future, it got me thinking of so many other things we can do. What if we tried to blow this out of the water and really make a name for ourselves?"

"I thought we agreed on a soft launch."

"We did, and I think we should still do exactly that. But we both hope that what we're starting will develop into a business as well-known as the children's productions, where we sell out a year in advance."

Harper sighed. "That's our pipe dream."

"It doesn't have to be," Tegan said eagerly. "When we first talked, I was nervous about jumping in and screwing up because I've never had formal training to run a business, and I worried about letting you down. But after working with Jett on the business plan, I realized my ideas are not only viable but really good and might be worth trying. Not that I want fame or fortune to be our goal, but I would love to earn fame and recognition for *you* as a screenwriter and producer. Jett had a lot of great ideas, including holding the productions in the big house if there's bad weather, and that got me thinking about your vision of one day hosting winter productions. And *that* made me wonder about other things, like what if you decide to make the productions interactive at some point?"

"Like mystery theater?"

"I haven't thought it through, but yeah, something like that."

"It's a cool idea, but nothing too dark—more like mystery with a romantic and humorous twist. *Cozy mystery/romance theater.* Now, *that* sounds awesome!"

"There are so many things we can do by bringing in the idea of using the house—"

"And it would feel even more intimate and special. We could do a special holiday production. I love this, but that's your *home*, Tegan. Where would you live?"

"In Jock's old cottage behind the house. I haven't made the decision to move there, but I've spent the last day and a half trying *not* to think about Jett, so I've had time to think about all the things we could do with the house. It would alleviate the issues of bad weather completely. No canceled or delayed shows or messing with tents. But if we did that, I'd have to renovate, and that takes money. The whole thing takes money, but I think I'd only renovate if we really wanted to make this happen on a bigger scale, which brings me to some of my other ideas, like advertising off the Cape—in Boston, Connecticut, New York, Rhode Island. I started thinking about *all* the possibilities. I know we're starting small with the soft launch at the end of the summer, but we could build buzz this year and get people excited for next year."

"That's a great idea," Harper exclaimed. "Since I've been writing for the newspaper, I've made lots of media contacts. I could reach out to them about doing a review of the launch show. I know it's dreaming big, but I would love it if our shows became the kind everyone hears about and wants to get in on. I don't care about the money we earn, but it's hard work writing the plays and putting them together."

"I agree. My friend Penny, back home, is a social media genius. She taught me all the ins and outs of it. I bet she'd have ideas about how to market the theater as *exclusive* so it stands apart from others."

"That's awesome. But, Tegan, how do *you* feel about all of this? It sounds like it would be a lot of money. I have some capital to kick in, as I mentioned before, although it's more expensive to put productions together than I thought it would be. I know you said you don't want to split the profits, but if we do this, you have to. There's no two ways about it."

"I know. That's the other thing Jett brought up. If we move in this direction, then this first year we're going to spend a lot more than we thought. But you have your wedding coming up, and I don't want to put pressure on you in any way. We can wait and see how things go this summer and next, and then maybe try to go bigger if we think it'll work. But if we do decide to try to move forward in a bigger way now, and work toward building a program the way we're talking about, then we should have a legal partnership agreement in place, because there are so many opportunities for conflict. Jett threw a few out there, like what if we succeed and we sell out a year in advance for the next few years, and then you decide to take your productions elsewhere?"

"I'd never do that."

"I don't think you would, but that's the type of situation Jett brought up that's probably smart for us to address in writing. What if I decide I don't want to run the amphitheater anymore? Or you get a better offer than Trey, but you get it because of all the marketing and outreach we've done? I'm not looking for money, or to own the rights to your productions, but at the same time—"

"We *both* have to be protected," Harper said emphatically. "Tegan, we're doing this *together*. I'd never cut you out of a deal, no matter how big or small, and I have no issue putting it all in writing. We're *both* taking huge risks. You're taking a risk on my writing and production skills, and you're talking about moving out of your home and renovating it to make this program work. I'm taking a risk by putting all my time and energy into the writing and production of the shows and relying on your ability to market, coordinate, and run the business. It's a *joint* venture. We're in this together, and we should share any deal that comes through. In my eyes, there's no alternative."

"Okay, but maybe you should think about it. I haven't decided about the house yet, but if we don't use it, there are the options we talked about for permanent tentlike structures."

"They could work, too. But hold on. You're leaving at the end of October. What happens then?"

"Hopefully by then most of what I'm doing can be handled remotely, but we'd probably have to hire someone to be on site for each show, especially if we do them *this* winter. I don't think we should start winter shows until next year, to give us a chance to really build buzz and work out all the kinks. I thought we could talk about all of our options and also about what happens if we decide to try and we fail."

"We are *not* going to fail," Harper insisted.

"I know, but Jett hammered the contingency thing into my head pretty hard."

Harper chuckled. "What else did he hammer *hard*?"

"We are *not* going there!" Tegan gave her a playful shove.

"Okay, fine. *Geez.*"

"Would you want me asking about how Gavin is in bed?" Tegan lifted her brows.

"Heck no. I can hardly believe that gorgeous stud muffin is going to be my husband in less than two weeks. We'd better get down to business or I'm going to start gushing about him."

Tegan laughed. "Okay, but are you sure you don't want more time to think about it?"

"*Yes.* I already know how well we work together from our *hours* of FaceTime. We're good together, Tegan. I'm *in.*"

Over the next few hours they hashed out all the details, from business to finances. They worked through each of the scenarios Jett had mentioned as potential conflicts, and a few more of their own ideas. Tegan took thorough notes, jotting down everything they could think of that should go into a legal agreement. They agreed that she should talk to the attorney Harvey had used for the business about drafting an agreement.

"I don't know about you, but I'm elated with this new direction," Harper exclaimed.

"Me too. I have a great feeling about this," Tegan said as she put her coat on.

"Wait. We didn't talk about names for our partnership."

"Oh, right. Any ideas? How about Wheeler Fine Productions?"

"That's so formal." Harper's eyes widened. "I've got it! How about Two Hot Babes Dreaming Big?"

They both laughed.

"More like Two Hot Babes *Making* It Big," Tegan said.

"I love that one. Who will see the name of the company?"

Tegan shrugged. "I'm not sure. But that's a good point. If we do succeed, media outlets might mention the company name. Maybe we should go with something simple, like Bayside Productions?"

"Oh my gosh. I've got it! We can pay homage to Jett for

sparking the idea and call it Fine Wheeler Bayside Productions. FWB Productions!"

They both burst in hysterics.

"He'd never even know if we called it by the whole name and not FWB!" Harper said. "Come on, we should do it! It's so fun!"

"*No way!* I can't do that. What if things end badly between me and him? Then I'd always have an *icky* feeling when I saw the name of the company."

"Okay, *fine*," Harper relented.

"Wheeler Fine Productions is a good name, don't you think?"

Harper bumped her with her shoulder and said, "How about Fine Wheeler?"

Tegan sighed, and then they both said, "Bayside Productions."

"See?" Harper said. "We're great business partners. I'm so glad you hooked up with Jett."

"I know why *I'm* glad we hooked up, but why are *you* glad?"

"Because if you guys hadn't gotten together and worked on the business plan, we might never have come to this decision." Harper hugged her and said, "I can't wait to hear what other ideas you come up with after your sexy wedding weekend!"

Tegan's pulse raced at the thought of another night with Jett. "He's flying in the morning of your wedding and leaving the next, so we'll only have one night together, not a whole weekend. And after two weeks apart, I'd imagine the only *talking* we'll be doing is hot-and-dirty pillow talk. Sorry, Harp, but there's no way I'll share *that* with you."

"Pillow Talk Productions has a nice ring to it," Harper teased.

"Oh my gosh. I'm leaving now."

Tegan laughed all the way to the car. She loved her and Jett's pillow talk, and now she missed being in his arms, kissing him and being kissed *by* him, even more. She wanted to see his face, to feel the way he made her giddy, dizzy, or just plain *hot*. As she fastened her seatbelt, she remembered how her heart had leapt when Jett had appeared at her window during the storm. God, she missed him. She reached for her phone, and debated texting to share her news. She wanted to *call*, to hear him laugh at Harper's FWB name suggestion, and to hear him make a snarky, sexy comment in response.

But calling crossed lines that might send him running for the hills.

He might not have the time or the desire for a relationship, but he *had* texted her when he was in a business meeting. Was he making space for a *real* friendship, or just keeping the lines open enough for their sexy trysts?

Ugh! Being friends with benefits was supposed to be *easy*.

She nixed the idea of calling but thumbed out a text. *Thanks for the business advice. Harper and I are moving forward in a new and exciting direction.* She set the phone down and started the car, surprised when her phone vibrated seconds later and Jett's name flashed on the screen. *I didn't know you swung both ways. You good?*

She sat in Harper's driveway staring at those last two words.

She typed, *Yes, just missing my friend. How about you?* A little voice in her head told her not to send the message, that it was too much too soon. But she pushed that little blue arrow anyway, gripping the phone like a lifeline and watching the screen for his response. Two minutes passed, four, five…

Anxiety swam in her belly as she put the car into gear, and

his response rolled in—*Missing my benefits.*

Swallowing hard against that cold reality slap, she shoved her phone in her bag and headed home.

Chapter Sixteen

JETT SAT AT the desk in the office of his luxurious LA penthouse suite Friday evening poring over the financial history of a company Jonas had brought to him as a potential investment, but no matter how hard he tried to concentrate, his thoughts circled back to Tegan. He missed talking to her, hearing the hope and happiness in her voice. She was a bright light in a world that had been gray for so long, he had no idea what to do with the plethora of things she made him feel or think about. He'd thought not texting for the last two days would help clear his head, but he'd still thought about her every damn minute. He couldn't stop wondering if she was seeing Bryson. Wasting her gorgeous smile on him. Or on fucking *Jack the jock*. Was he the one she'd been fielding texts from during the storm? As if that wasn't enough to sidetrack him, on the heels of all those thoughts came images of the devastation in the community in which he'd grown up.

He'd been so far off his game this week, when he'd spoken with Leslie Carlisle about selling Carlisle Enterprises, which she and her brother had taken over after their father had passed away, he kept hearing Tegan in Leslie's nostalgic reasons for not selling. Before getting to know Tegan, Jett would have had a dozen sharp rebuttals spilling from his lips without a second thought about Leslie's feelings. But he'd stumbled, remembering how important it was to Tegan to carry on her great-uncle's legacy.

His phone rang, and his grandmother's name flashed on the screen. He picked it up, glad for the distraction, and said, "How's the coolest grandmother at LOCAL?"

"She's wondering why the heck she had to hear about her grandson's girlfriend from his mother."

"Christ," he muttered under his breath. "Please disregard anything Mom said. Tegan's a good friend, not my girlfriend."

"Is that what you kids call it nowadays?" Rose teased.

He imagined his grandmother's blue-gray eyes dancing with amusement and said, "We're *not* having this conversation, Gram. How are you?"

"I'd be better if you had brought your blond beauty to meet me."

"I just told you—"

"Save your breath, Jetty. Even your father said he saw starry eyes."

"Wishful thinking on his part. Tegan wasn't *starry*-eyed. If anything, he saw reflections of the daggers he and I cast toward each other. Tegan was probably trying to figure out why she'd agreed to come with me."

"He wasn't talking about Tegan."

"Nice try, Gram. You can stop fishing for details, because I'm not taking the bait."

"I don't *fish*, honey. Emmie told me you spent a couple of days with your new *friend* when everyone else thought you'd left the Cape." Rose had been an active mother and grandmother and had loved gardening. But years of suffering from scoliosis and disc issues had left her wheelchair bound. And then she'd met Emery—Emmie. As a yoga-back-care specialist, Emery had been able to develop a program for Rose and worked with her several times a week to help her get on her feet again. It had been two and a half years since they'd begun working together, and Rose was able to once again enjoy gardening and even dancing, as long as she was careful.

"I think my personal life should be off-limits to the Bayside grapevine."

"I'll try to remember that," Rose said. "I want to know *all* about the woman who can compete with your business."

"There is no competition for business," he said far more casually than he felt.

"Says the man who wakes up thinking about his next big takeover. Speaking of which, what thoughts are you waking up to these days?"

He closed his eyes, laughing softly. His grandmother wasn't afraid to talk about sex, drugs, or anything else she had on her mind. "Please don't."

"There's my answer. You're thinking of Tegan," she said. "It's about time you got a little lovin' in your life. You're a smart, virile young man, and from what I hear, Tegan is quite a catch."

"She's great, Gram, but don't get your hopes up."

"*Great* is a useless word. Tell me what you really think of her, and then I promise not to ask you any more questions."

There was an unspoken agreement between them that anything they told each other went no further. Rose had been honest with him about falling out of love with his grandfather because of how bitter and mean he'd become and how she'd been disappointed in Jett's father for following in his father's footsteps. When Jett's father had started trying to change this last time, Rose had been just as mistrustful of his efforts as Jett was. She'd since embraced his father's changes, but she'd never once pushed Jett to come to the same decision. He trusted his grandmother, and as he thought about Tegan, he realized he trusted her, too.

"She's *different* from other women," he relented, but he had been trying so hard not to think about Tegan, he had a difficult time articulating all the things that made her different, so he said the first thing that came to mind. "She can't dance, but she dances like she's on a stage, proud to be seen."

"I like her already."

"She loves to eat, especially ice cream, and she isn't afraid to say *no*."

"I bet you're not used to that," she said teasingly.

"*Gram*," he said sternly. "Family means a lot to her. She doesn't go on and on about them the way some people do, but she gets this look on her face when she talks about them. You can *feel* her love for them. She inherited her uncle's theater business, and she's more interested in doing a good job to uphold *his* reputation than her own, and she would rather drive the beat-up car her uncle gave her forever ago than the newer, nicer one he left her." He felt himself smiling and said, "Her brain works in crazy ways, but she's so smart, Gram. Probably smarter than me in many ways. And there's this *goodness* about her that makes you want to be around her, to be more *like* her. She worked all day in the cold, damp weather after the storm and never once complained or acted like she'd rather be somewhere else. Her sense of humor is cute and snarky. She's not afraid to call me on my shit. I like that a lot. When she talks, I want to hear every word she says, and *man*, is she sexy.

Unforgettable, really."

"Oh, Jetty. She sounds wonderful."

He winced. He'd gotten so caught up in thinking about Tegan, he'd forgotten he was talking to his grandmother.

"And you're seeing her again at your friend's wedding?"

"Why are you asking? It's obvious Emery or someone else told you that I was."

"Just making sure you haven't already canceled because of work."

He was planning to be there, but there was always the possibility that something might keep him from showing up. "Like I said, don't get your hopes up. Now, you've used up your question quota, so what else would you like to talk about?"

They talked about his brothers, and Rose said she hoped they would start families soon. Jett told her not to get her hopes up with that, either. His brothers didn't seem in a hurry to have kids, and after what they'd experienced, he didn't blame them.

"I guess you've heard about the vultures swooping in again in Hyannis."

"Vultures?" he asked.

"The investors who tried to buy up the businesses in town after the last nor'easter. They're back, and this time it seems like folks are ready to sell."

"Wait a second. Slow down, Gram. Who, exactly? Which businesses?"

"Let's see, there's the Olsons' dry-cleaning business, and Bradleys' seasonal shop at the end of Main. You know the one with all the floats and yard ornaments they put out front in the summertime. We used to take you kids there."

"I know the one."

"I'm most upset about Mitchell thinking of selling. When

your grandfather was first courting me, there was a soda counter in the back of the store. He used to take me there and we'd talk for *hours*. Those are good memories, and when I think of them, they remind me why I fell in love with the old grump. I'll be sad when the store closes, but Mitchell's family has been through so much these last few years. From what I hear, the investors want to buy all the businesses on the block, tear them down, and put in a fancy office complex."

Jett's chest constricted at the thought of Mitchell and the other small businesses giving up, not to mention what an office complex would do to the already overcommercialized town. "Is anyone fighting it? Who's trying to buy them? They'd have to get approval from the town."

"I don't know any of that. But it's a shame. They call it progress, but if you ask me, people are spending so much energy *progressing* they forget what it feels like to breathe fresh air and enjoy life."

"Mm-hm," he said absently, thinking about his hometown being taken over by an investor who had probably never stepped foot on the Cape. "Gram, I've got to run."

"Okay, honey. I love you."

"I love you, too. I'll call you next week."

"I look forward to it."

After ending the call, he rang Tia on speakerphone and went to retrieve his laptop.

"Shouldn't you be nose deep in financials or getting laid?" Tia's best friend, Becca Nunnally, said when she answered Tia's phone. Becca lived in Port Hudson, New York, and worked for Aubrey Stewart, co-owner of LWW Enterprises and one of the most successful women Jett knew. She also shamelessly flirted with him every chance she got. He'd forgotten she was spending the weekend with Tia.

"How's it going, Bec?" He set his laptop on the desk and sat down.

"That depends on what you need from Tia." Music blared in the background. "We've got a weekend of clubbing planned. If you're going to steal her away, the least you can do is fly back to the city and keep me company while she works. I promise to keep your mind off work."

Becca was a gorgeous blond with an hourglass figure, a penchant for dressing like a pinup girl, and a chip on her shoulder bigger than Manhattan. *No, thank you.* "Put her on, please."

A few seconds later Tia said, "Hey, boss."

"Hi. I need you to get me everything you can on each of the businesses on the 600 block of Main Street in Hyannis."

"Okay, can you email that to me? I've had a few drinks."

"Doing it now." He pulled up his email program on the laptop. "Find out who's trying to buy the properties there, too."

"Sure. Why the sudden interest in the Cape?"

"I don't know yet."

"Does it have to do with the reason you canceled your flight Monday?"

"No," he snapped, and then corrected himself. "Sort of."

"You sound strange. Are you okay?"

No, I'm not fucking okay. I've got a chick who is fucking with my head, the man who helped me find my way out of hell is about to lose his family business, and the deal I've been working on for months is giving me heartburn. He bit back that response and said, "Fine. Can you get it done?"

"Of course. Is there anything else you need?"

"Yeah. A drink. I'll talk to you later." He ended the call,

grabbed his wallet, and headed downstairs to the hotel bar.

Jett spent a lot of time living in the penthouse suites of the hotels he owned and had spent too many evenings in hotel bars. Within seconds of walking in, he pegged the two women sitting at a table checking him out as easy prey, looking to hook up with just about anyone who would have them. *Good luck, ladies.* He sat at the bar and glanced at the guy two seats to his right, who was eyeing the redhead talking with the bartender at the other end of the bar, and immediately deemed him a dick-head—a married man who took off his wedding ring in order to score. Those types of men weren't smart enough to realize their rings left tan lines. The woman drowning her sorrows a few seats to his left was too upset to be looking for a date. She'd probably had a recent breakup. She glanced over, and a forced smile appeared. He had enough of his own shit to deal with. Jett nodded in greeting and turned his attention to the young male bartender heading his way.

He wiped the bar down in front of Jett and said, "What'll it be?"

"Whiskey, neat." Jett's mind shot back to Tegan. Was she out on a date with Bryson or some other guy? Was she sitting in a bar looking for a guy to pick up, or dancing, confident and hot as sin in a skintight dress?

The redhead was watching him. Jett turned away, thinking about texting Tegan.

He caught movement in his peripheral vision. The redhead was on the prowl, and he was her prey. She sauntered over and sat on the stool beside him, crossing her long legs. Her tight black dress barely covered her voluptuous curves.

"Hi there," she said, her eyes roaming over him seductively. "How's it going?"

"My night just got a *whole* lot better," she said. "Are you here on business?"

The bartender set Jett's drink in front of him and said, "Want to run a tab?"

Jett shook his head and paid for the drink. Then he turned to the redhead and said, "Yes, business. You?"

"I work in pharmaceutical sales. I'm here for two more nights for a conference..."

His phone vibrated with a text, and he had a fleeting hope that it might be Tegan and she hadn't made a date with Bryson or some other guy after all. It pissed him off that he cared. The redhead went on about the conference, and he pulled out his phone and read the text from Tia. *I forgot to tell you I was able to book the suite you wanted at the Silver House for the wedding.* He shoved his phone in his back pocket, annoyed that he was disappointed it wasn't Tegan, and turned his attention to the woman beside him.

The redhead leaned closer and said, "I hate small talk."

"Who doesn't?" He was thinking about Tegan loosening his tie at the café. Did she *ever* engage in small talk? She was so...*Tegan.*

"You're not a serial killer, are you?"

He sipped his drink thinking about the stupid question. What serial killer would answer honestly? He shrugged and said, "What do you think?"

She eyed his dress shirt and slacks. He'd ditched his tie and jacket in his room. The hungry look on her face probably sent many men to their knees, and she said, "If you are, I can think of no better way to die." She brushed her leg against his and said, just above a whisper, "Maybe I'm a serial killer?"

"You sound like a dangerous woman." *And clearly not a*

smart one. He took another drink, weighing his options for the night.

"Only the best kind of dangerous."

Maybe one night with the redhead would help him get his head on straight.

The thought left a sour taste in his mouth. He thought about Tegan on a date with some other guy and downed his drink.

The redhead put her hand on his leg and said, "We should get out of here."

"You're absolutely right." He pushed to his feet and tossed cash on the bar for a tip. He said, "Have a nice night," to the redhead and stalked out of the bar.

When he reached his room, he was more in need of a drink than when he'd left. He paced the floor, chest tight, nerves fried, and checked the time. It was still early in LA, but it was eleven thirty at the Cape. If Tegan had gone on a date and hooked up with another guy, she'd probably be in his arms right now.

"Fuck it," he ground out through gritted teeth. He wasn't about to let that happen.

TEGAN SAT ON the living room floor pinning pieces of fabric to Joni's costume, streaming *Friends*, and talking to her sister on the phone using her Bluetooth earbuds. She'd spoken to the auto shop earlier today, and they'd told her that Berta needed a new engine. She'd called Cici to grieve, and they'd relived all the great times they'd had with her, from their first road trip to the last time Tegan had driven to the city to see her, when Berta had gotten towed because Tegan hadn't realized she'd parked in a no-parking zone. Tegan knew it would take a while to get over Berta.

Cici finished filling her in on an upcoming photo shoot for a family who'd just had twins, and Tegan noted it in her calendar to do the edits. When her sister told her about how happy she and her husband, Cooper, were, Tegan began to feel a little better. Cici knew just how to cheer her up. She updated her about the adventures of her three-year-old nephew, Billy, who had recently decided he wanted to be a fisherman and was wearing rubber boots twenty-four-seven and refused to eat anything *but* fish, and her seven-year-old niece, Melody, who had told her father that she was never going to have a boyfriend because boys were stupid.

"Did Cooper celebrate?" Tegan asked. She adored Cooper. He was a loving father and an adoring husband. "We all know he'd like to lock her up when she turns thirteen and let her out when she's thirty."

"He made her say it again while he videotaped her so he can show it to her when she starts liking boys again."

"You mean like next week," Tegan teased, sitting up to look at the pieces of fur she'd pinned to the bodice of the costume.

"I know, right? She's so fickle. I swear she could be your child."

"I'm not *fickle*. I'm very stable. I don't quit jobs willy-nilly, or like someone one minute and hate them the next."

"You're right. *Fickle* isn't the right word for you, though I think it is for her. You make decisions on a dime, though, like within the first *five minutes* of a date."

"I did that *twice*. I just don't believe in wasting time." A couple of years ago Tegan had gone on a few blind dates. She'd decided within minutes of meeting the men that they were not right for her and had made excuses to leave. "And in my defense, I am really good at reading people."

"*Three* times. You dumped one guy at your front door, another on the way to dinner, and the third took you to the fair, where you pretended to get sick from cotton candy. You texted me on the way *to* the fair and said he was a dud but that Berta was broken down and you wanted funnel cake."

"Oh my gosh, you're right. I'm an awful person."

"No, you're not. You have strong instincts, and you're not afraid of anything. Melly's getting more and more like that. It worries me sometimes."

"I know it does. But she's a smart girl, and she's only in elementary school. It's not like she's going to do drugs or have sex. At least not yet."

"Please don't talk about my daughter and those things in the same sentence. She's growing up so fast. I hope she gets your ability to size people up, but I'd rather she was like me about making big decisions. I want her to think everything through to the minutest detail, so she's fully prepared."

Tegan moved to the bottom of the mermaid tail and began pinning in place the colorful scales she'd cut out. "Is that a *dig*?"

"Definitely not. You can go from one thing to the next without blinking an eye, and you always land on your feet. But she's my baby girl. What if she doesn't land on her feet? What if she follows some guy across the country and he hurts her?"

"Then you'll be there to help her find her way back, and I'll be there to kick the shit out of the asshole who hurt her."

"I'm holding you to that, you know." Cici sighed heavily and said, "Being a mom is scary. Let's talk about something else.

Has anything new happened since we texted Sunday night, when you were working on your business plan with some guy you met at a party?"

"Gosh, that seems like forever ago."

"He must have *worked* your brain into a tizzy. Who is he? What's he like? Are you being careful?"

"He definitely did a number on my brain, and I am always careful." She leaned down to pin on a scale and said, "His name is Jett Masters, and he's a complex guy."

"Jett Masters? Why does that name sound familiar?"

"He said Cooper and Jackson handled a photo shoot he was in for a feature in a magazine. Or maybe it was just one of them—I don't remember."

"What magazine?"

"I have no idea."

"Hold on." Cici called out, "Coop? Does the name *Jett Masters* ring a bell?"

Tegan heard Cooper's deep voice, but she couldn't make out what he was saying, so she continued pinning scales on the costume.

"Oh my gosh, Teg!" Cici said loudly, startling her. "He was featured in *Forbes* a few years ago as one of their self-made men who had made it big paying it forward. How can you *not* know this?"

"Why *would* I know that? It's not like I asked to see his résumé before I slept with him. I guess that explains his Armani suits and why he has no time for a life outside of work. I had no idea he paid it forward on that big a scale. I love that."

"Holy cow, Teg. He has to be really rich to have been in *Forbes*."

"Why do you sound awestruck? You and Cooper had more

money than you could ever spend *before* Uncle Harvey left us his millions. It's just money. It's not like it can buy anything that matters."

"You're right, but it feels like something you should know about the guy you're sleeping with."

Tegan sat back on her heels and said, with a pang of unease, "It's not like we're dating. He doesn't live around here, and he travels all the time. We're just hooking up when he's in town."

"*Oh.*" Cici sounded surprised. "I know you're great with change and you don't like to rely on anyone, but are you okay with that? It sounds very unlike you."

"It was my suggestion."

"Really? You talk a big game when it comes to men, but you're sensitive, Teg. I worry about you getting hurt."

"Oh, I'm *definitely* going to get hurt," she said, thinking about Jett's text. *Missing my benefits.* He could have meant it flirtatiously, but he could have also been reiterating the line between them. The fact that he hadn't texted since was a good indicator of his intent being the latter. "He's charismatic and charming, but he's also tough, as in he's got *thick* walls around his heart. But I've seen what he's like when he lets them down, and, Cici, I can't stop thinking about—" Another call rang through, and Jett's name flashed on the screen. "Holy shit. That's *him.*"

"I don't like this, Tegan. You're worth more than occasional hookups."

"I knew you wouldn't like it, and I love you for that," she said hurriedly. "But I'm not Melly, and I gotta go." She blew her sister a kiss, took a deep breath, and switched to Jett's call, trying her best to sound relaxed. "Hey there, Armani."

"Hey," he said angrily.

There was a long stretch of silence.

"Um…Are you okay?" she asked carefully.

"*Fine.* You *alone*? Can you talk?"

"Alone on a Friday night? What am I, a loser? Joey and Ross are keeping me company. Chandler's in the kitchen with Monica at the moment, but…*Oh!* Here they are," she said when they appeared on screen.

Jett ground out a curse. "Go back to your party."

"My par…? You mean the *television* show? Oh my gosh, Jett! Haven't you ever seen *Friends*?"

"I don't watch television."

"It's on Netflix now, but *really*? Like *never*?"

"Never. So…you're alone, then?"

"Yes. Why are you asking? What's going on? You sound angry."

A moment passed before he said, "I'm not angry," in a calmer voice. "I'm just…I don't fucking know. I thought you might be out."

"Like on a *date*?" She remembered how jealous he'd been of Bryson and couldn't resist needling him. "With Bryson?"

"*Fuck* Bryson," he growled.

He *was* jealous! "Let me get this straight. You thought I might be on a date, so you called to sabotage it? To *cockblock* me?"

"No. *Yes.* Damn it, Tegan, I don't know. I can't stop thinking about you, and *yeah*, the idea of you fucking Bryson pisses me off. I told you I'm a prick."

"Jealousy doesn't make you a prick. It makes you human."

"Then I'm used to being *superhuman*. This *blows*. I shouldn't have called, but you've totally messed with my head."

"Maybe that's not such a bad thing," she said carefully.

"It's bad, believe me. I haven't been worth shit all week at work. I just need to figure this out."

"What is *this*?" She sat back against the side of the couch.

"You. Me. Why you've invaded my thoughts."

"Well, I am *hot*," she teased, loving the laughing-groaning sound coming through the phone. "We have great chemistry, Jett, and we work well together. There's no mystery to why we can't stop thinking about each other."

"You've been thinking about me." He said it with relief, not as a question.

"What did you think would happen? You'd leave and I would fill up my dating card the second you left?"

"I don't want to think, Tegs. I just want to hear your voice."

"Okay," she said softly, feeling all kinds of wonderful. "Let's catch up. Tell me about your day."

"My days are booked with meetings and conference calls with analysts, lawyers, and clients. That's the last thing I want to talk about. Tell me about *your* day, Tegs. What have you been doing? What are you doing now?"

"I'm mourning Berta. They couldn't fix her."

"Oh no. I'm sorry."

"Thanks. Cici and I paid homage to her, reliving all our memories. It feels weird, and sad, like I've lost another piece of my uncle."

"Aw, babe."

She wasn't going to let her sadness ruin their call. "It's okay. She needed a new engine, and even the guy at the shop said it wasn't worth it. So for now I'll drive my uncle's car, and who knows, maybe I'll learn to love it. Moving on to happier news..." She told him about what she and Harper had decided for the direction and name of the production company, and how she'd been working with Brandon on the logo as well as ad designs.

"That's great. Do you feel good about everything?"

"I really do, and I wouldn't have had the guts to bring it up to Harper if not for you."

"Eventually you would have gotten there. Tell me more about your week. I like hearing your voice."

She moved to the couch and sank down to the cushions. "I FaceTimed with my parents yesterday. I swear they always act like they haven't seen me in years when we never go more than a week without talking."

"That's nice, Tegs. You're lucky."

"Yeah," she said, realizing too late that she might have accidentally made him feel bad about his relationship with his father. "I also talked to my best friend from back home, Leesa." She told him all about Leesa and her family. "I also talked to a few other friends from home who are in Chloe and Daphne's book club with me. We had a lot to catch up on. What about you? Do you have friends in LA? Do you catch up with friends in the areas where you travel?"

"No. Just business associates."

"*Oh.* What about on the weekends? Do you catch sporting events? Baseball games?"

"No, I don't."

"But you loved baseball. I think I need to find out when baseball season is and drag you to a game."

He chuckled, but then his voice turned quieter and he said, "We're so different, Tegs. You're a social butterfly, and I'm a workaholic whose closest friends are guys I grew up with but hardly ever see."

"You do have the power to fix that, you know. I'd be lost

without my friends. Just knowing they're around makes me happy. How often do you and your brothers talk?"

"Every few weeks or so. What about you and your sister?"

"We text all the time and talk once a week." She told him about her conversation with her sister, leaving out the part about *him*, and ended up rambling on about how adorable Melody and Billy were.

"I can hear how much you miss them," he said empathetically.

"Yeah. But it's probably good that I don't see them too much because Cici's worried that Melody will end up like me and make big decisions without giving them enough thought."

"I've seen your clock diagram, Tegs. I know just how thoroughly you think things through. Your niece would be lucky to turn out like you."

She liked hearing how much he believed in her. He asked if she'd had a hard time when Cici moved to New York and about where she'd traveled over the years and whether she had a favorite spot. She told him about each of her favorite places and realized she'd been talking for almost forty-five minutes.

"Am I totally boring you?" she asked.

"Not even a little. I could listen to your voice all night."

She swooned at that. "I bet you've seen some cool places with all the traveling you've done."

"I do business internationally, but I don't really have time to sightsee."

"What about vacations? Do you have a favorite vacation spot?"

"I can't remember the last time I took a real vacation."

"Jett Masters, when do you rejuvenate? Even superhumans need downtime."

"Have you forgotten Monday night?" he said seductively.

"Sex can't be your *only* source of rejuvenation. I mean, it's a great pick-me-up, but our bodies and minds need more than that. You need to get out and *experience* more than offices and hotel rooms. Breathe in fresh air, climb mountains, or explore a new town, learn the culture, soak in the history, and gorge on new foods. I love meeting people from around the world. Everyone's lives are so different, but on some levels we're all the same. I think about the people I meet and the places I've been all the time. It's like they're rooted inside me somewhere, and it's fun to revisit them in my head. I have a *long* bucket list, too, including trying out the best bakery in every place I visit. Don't you feel like you're missing out? Wouldn't you love to explore a rain forest or traipse across a desert? The world is a *huge* place. Don't you want to see it?"

"I want to *own* it," he said.

"Where's the fun in that? To each his own, I guess. You go right ahead and try, and once a year, when I go on my adventures, I'll send you pictures."

"Where are you right now?" he asked.

"In my living room. I was working on a mermaid costume for Joni with lion fur and wings. My place is a *mess*."

"I want to see it. I want to see *you*. Let's FaceTime."

A minute later his handsome face appeared on the screen. It happened so quickly, she didn't have a chance to fix her hair, which was pulled back in a headband, or put on something nicer than the old faded shirt she'd made in college. But none of that mattered as she gazed into his eyes, feeling a little light-headed at the way he was looking at her.

"*Tegs...*" he said softly. "God, you're beautiful."

"I'm a mess," she said, absently touching her hair.

"You're the best thing I've seen all year."

Butterflies took flight in her belly, and she said, "Let me show you Joni's costume." She flipped the camera and showed him the mess of fabric and supplies scattered around the room. "I'm making all the scales different patterns, and the wings will be glittery. I told you it was a mess." She flipped the camera again, and her heart skipped at the light in his eyes.

"I like your messy room, and the costume is incredible. She's going to love it. How did you learn to do that?"

"My mom taught me. She was always making clothes for us when we were growing up, and I used to bug her about making me these funky outfits. I think she taught me to sew so I'd stop bugging her. I've made my own clothes forever." She waved to her faded long-sleeved patchwork top. "I made this in college, and I made the jumper I wore to Harper's bachelorette party."

"It's a good thing I didn't tear it into shreds in my haste to get you naked."

Her pulse quickened at the thought. "I can make more…"

His laughter was like music to her ears. She loved this version of his smile. It was more carefree than she'd seen before.

"I'll remember that," he said. "Want to see my place?"

"Yes."

He showed her his luxurious hotel suite. His laptop sat on the desk beside a stack of folders and loose documents. The coffee table was also littered with papers. There was a living room, kitchen, and dining area. She imagined him coming back to the empty room, kicking off his shoes, and sitting right down to work until he was bleary eyed.

"Pretty boring room, huh?" he said, turning the camera back to him as he walked to the couch and sat down.

"It looks nice."

"It would be a hell of a lot nicer if you were here."

His comment was so unexpected, she wondered if he even realized he'd said it. "If I were there, you probably wouldn't get much work done."

"True." He leaned back and said, "What's on your schedule for the weekend?"

She noticed his quick subject change, but she didn't mind. She knew that in his head, he'd already crossed a lot of lines by calling. Tegan noticed her phone battery blinking red. She hurried upstairs to plug it in. They joked about Jett thinking the characters from *Friends* were real, and they talked about their favorite meals—his was steak and potatoes; hers was anything Mexican with lots of colorful foods, like red, yellow, and orange peppers—their biggest pet peeves—he hated wasting time, incorrect grammar, and head games, while she disliked (because *hate* was too strong a word) men who demeaned their girlfriends or wives, friends who took advantage of each other, and Boston cream doughnuts that weren't filled with enough custard—and their least favorite colors—they agreed dark brown was the *worst*. Jett told her about a crush he'd had on a dental hygienist and how he'd spent hours playing out scenarios between them in his head, and she told him that the first time she held hands with a boy she got sweaty and nervous, and she was afraid to do it again for weeks afterward. They talked about their first kisses, the prom she went to and the one he didn't.

Hours later, as the clock hit two a.m., they were still talking. Tegan lay on her bed feeling like she was talking with someone she'd known for years, happier than she could ever remember being.

"What are you thinking?" he asked softly.

"That I'm glad you called."

"Me too. Tell me something I don't know about you, Tegs."

"I like when you call me *Tegs*."

That earned a sexy grin. "Something else. Something no one else knows about you."

Her nerves tingled. *I'm falling for you and I know I shouldn't* was on the tip of her tongue. She didn't know what to say, so she said, "You first."

He was quiet for a long moment before saying, "I want to know everything there is to know about you."

"That's not a secret about *you*." She was sure he was giving her a pat answer to keep from having to expose a real secret.

"Isn't it, though?" His eyes drilled into hers.

Oh God. You meant it.

"Now that you know my biggest secret," he said, holding her gaze, "it's your turn."

"Um…" Her body prickled with the desire to confess her feelings, but she was scared to do it, remembering how he'd gone from being open and emotional Monday night to all business Tuesday morning.

"Come on, Tegs. Give me something."

"Okay. I probably should have told you this when you were here. I'm not interested in going out with Bryson. He seems nice, but I'm not ready to date a guy who has a child."

"No?"

She shook her head. "I want kids one day, but I helped raise Melly after she was born, and I know how much time and attention kids need. I have a lot I want to accomplish before giving up that much of myself."

"Such as?"

"Figuring out the theater business, traveling, falling in

love…" Her eyes widened when that last part slipped out. "I mean *one day*, not now."

His eyes narrowed, studying her, as if he were weighing the truth of her words. "You've never been in love?"

"I didn't mean to say that."

"The most honest things come out accidentally. You're such a big-hearted person. Have you really never been in love?"

She shook her head, seeing an opportunity to shift the focus off her, and went for it. "I'd ask if you have, but you already said you've never been closer to anyone than we were Monday night."

"I haven't; you're right. The strange thing is, we're fully dressed and thousands of miles apart right now, and I feel even closer to you than I did Monday night." He exhaled, like he'd been holding that in for a while, and said, "I shouldn't tell you things like that when we both know I can't be the guy you need."

But you can be the one that I want. "I've never *needed* a man in my life."

He sat up, jaw tight again, and said, "It's late. I should let you get some rest."

"Okay," she said softly.

"Good night, Tegs, and for what it's worth, I didn't just miss our benefits. I missed you."

Chapter Seventeen

"FEEDING TIME AT the zoo," Violet said as she walked into Daphne's apartment Monday evening carrying two pizza boxes. She wore a pair of tight leather pants and her ever-present motorcycle boots, looking like she was ready to go for a ride.

"Thank you," Daphne said as she set down her paintbrush and picked up a slice of pizza.

Harper reached for a slice. "This looks delicious."

"I'm starved. Thank you." Tegan set her paintbrush down on the paint tray.

"Me too," Chloe said, snagging a slice and handing one to Serena.

As Tegan bit into the delicious pizza, Emery peered around Serena and said, "There are so many toppings. What kind are they?"

"The kind *you* didn't have to make." Violet handed Emery a slice and said, "If you don't love it, pretend it's your husband and fake it."

Emery laughed, nearly spitting out the bite she'd taken.

"I doubt she has to fake anything with that man," Chloe said. "If a guy looked at me the way Dean visibly eats her up, I think I'd pass out."

Tegan's mind went straight to last night's sexy FaceTime session with Jett, and she felt her cheeks burning. She shoved more pizza into her mouth, eating as fast as she could, and picked up her paintbrush. She and Jett had been FaceTiming nightly, talking into the wee hours of the morning. He hadn't been kidding about wanting to know everything about her. He'd asked each night about the progress she was making on the theater and Joni's costume, but he also liked knowing what else she was up to, like going to the Sundial Café for breakfast. Each night he found his way back to her youth, asking about what she was like as a teenager and how she'd changed since then. He'd often interject with tidbits about his life back then, giving her insight into how his relationship with his friends had changed when he began putting all his energy into staying away from home. She loved their video chats and wanted to hold on to every second they shared, wishing the calls wouldn't end. Two nights ago they'd watched an episode of *Friends* together, after which Jett had said he could *take* Ross, Chandler, or Joey with his eyes closed. She secretly loved when he got jealous, even though he tossed out enough clarifiers to keep the lines in the sand drawn between friends with benefits and something more. But there was no denying that the more they learned about each other, the deeper and more intense their connection became. Last night, as she lay sleepily gazing into his eyes, she could *feel* his desire, and they'd ventured into sexier territory. What started as a few seductive innuendos had quickly turned into confessions of their dirtiest fantasies. Unable to hold back, they'd both gotten carried away and stripped naked, taking each other over the edge with whispers and moans as they'd touched themselves. Seeing his big hand wrapped around his erection, his sexy-as-sin blue eyes locked on her as he seduced her with dozens of filthy whispers was hotter than anything she'd ever experienced.

"You should join us," Harper said, jerking Tegan back to reality.

Everyone was on their second or third slice of pizza already. Holy cow, how long had she been daydreaming? Tegan set her paintbrush down as she scrambled to figure out who Harper was talking to. She hoped it wasn't *her*, because she had no idea what she was talking *about*.

"The last time I painted, Andre and I were naked and the paint was *edible*," Violet said.

Tegan breathed a sigh of relief, telling herself to stop thinking about Jett. Especially naked! She picked up another slice of pizza and took a bite.

Violet looked at Chloe and said, "I heard Justin got caught at your place in the storm. About time you gave him a ride."

"*What?*" Emery scowled. "You spent the night with Long Dong Naked Man and you didn't tell us?"

Chloe popped her last bite of pizza into her mouth and picked up her paintbrush. "You've *all* lost your minds. The only kind of *wet* I got that night was caused by running through the rain."

"Is *that* why you didn't return my call until hours later?" Tegan asked, glad for something to concentrate on besides her steamy video chat.

"No," Chloe insisted, but something in her eyes told Tegan there was more to the story.

"Then you're an idiot," Violet said, heading for the door. "Justin's a great guy, and you could use a man who knows what he's doing in bed to loosen you up a bit." Her eyes shifted to each of the girls and she said, "Don't forget, Desiree's making dessert for everyone tonight."

"I'm looking forward to it," Tegan said, finishing her pizza. Because of the time difference, she and Jett usually talked around eleven o'clock, which gave her all evening to have fun with the girls.

"I have to pick up Hadley from my mom as soon as we're done painting," Daphne said. "I'll try to make it. But if Hadley's cranky, I might have to skip dessert."

On her way out the door, Violet said, "Bring her along and let her nap in a playpen. Des is making enough to feed an army."

"We'll help with Hadley," Serena offered.

Daphne's shoulders sagged. "You know how much I adore my baby girl, but if she's cranky, it will ruin everyone's night. The only person who can make Hadley smile these days is *Uncle Jett*, and he's gone. I swear she's in love with the birdhouse and bird he bought her."

Tegan's ears perked up. "*Uncle* Jett?" She picked up her paintbrush and went back to painting the windowsill.

"He spoils Hadley rotten," Daphne explained. "When he comes into town, he brings her gifts, and he sends her presents *every* holiday. She was totally into monkeys last Thanksgiving, and he sent her an enormous stuffed monkey. I swear it's two feet tall. That man would make an amazing father if he ever wanted to be one."

Tegan was taking mental notes, incredibly curious about this new information. "Did you guys ever go out?"

"No, no, no," Daphne said, waving her hands like she was warding off a villain. "He's *way* too much man for a girl like me. He gets me all flustered. He's so well put together and *in charge*. But he brings out the best in my daughter, who isn't impressed by anyone. She acts like he's the cat's meow."

More like the lion's growl.

"I don't think he'll ever settle down or get married, much less have a family," Emery said as she painted. "At least not here. He can barely stand to be in the same state as his father. He's owned waterfront property here forever and has never done anything with it."

"Why would anyone buy property and not do anything with it?" Tegan asked.

"He *is* an investor," Serena pointed out as she dipped her paintbrush in the paint tray. "It makes sense if he wants to flip it one day. But, Em, people change. Rick came back for good when he met Desiree."

"What do you mean, *came back*?" Tegan asked.

Everyone looked at Serena. She set down her paintbrush and said, "Rick was living in DC when he met Desiree. When he was a teenager, he and his family were out on their boat, and they ran into a storm that hit fast. Rick and Drake were on deck with their father when their father went overboard. There was nothing they could do. They never found his body, and Rick blamed himself."

"Oh my gosh. That's awful," Tegan said.

"It is, and it took a toll on Rick and Drake's relationship," Serena said. "Drake held down the fort at home when Rick left the Cape."

"Like Dean," Emery interjected. "He always tries to make up for Jett's absence from events and family get-togethers. They're working on things, but I know Dean wishes Jett would get his butt back here and just make things better once and for all."

Tegan understood how missing family gatherings could be

difficult, but she wondered what steps his family had taken to try to mend that broken bridge. "Does anyone ever go see Jett?"

"I don't think so," Emery said. "He travels a lot, so maybe it's too hard to nail him down."

"Well, I think Jett is trying as best he can," Tegan said, feeling protective of him. "He put off work Monday and we spent the day with his parents helping in the community, and then we all had dinner together. There was tension between him and his father, but it wasn't oppressive. It kind of waxed and waned. And Jett is *going* to the fundraiser in June. He has a business to run, and his business requires a boatload of travel. He's in LA now, and he'll be in Louisiana Thursday. It's not like he can just give it all up and move here." She didn't tell them about their calls, or that with all that Jett had going on, he still found time to call Rob Wicked and arrange for him to fix the pothole that had swallowed Berta and the others on the private road, which Rob had completed yesterday.

"I didn't mean he wasn't trying," Emery said softly. "I just meant that it's been a couple of years, and everyone misses him. I know Dean wants his brother back as much as he wants things to be better between Jett and their dad."

"I think Jett would like that, too, but things are complicated between him and his father," Tegan said as her phone vibrated with a text. She set down her paintbrush and pulled her phone from her pocket, smiling at Jett's name in the text bubble.

"Is that from *the cat's meow*?" Serena asked as she went back to painting the trim by the door.

"Who else makes her smile like that?" Chloe chimed in.

Tegan opened the text, turning her back to the girls, and was surprised to see a picture of a plate of Mexican food, with the caption *Lunch, Tegan style*. Another text bubble popped up.

I have no idea why you put up with a prick friend like me, but thanks. You're expanding my horizons in many ways. I especially liked last night's eye-opening experience.

She thumbed out a response. *You're not a prick. You're like a porcupine, prickly on the outside. But for those of us who are lucky enough to be allowed to peek beneath that armor, you're as enticing and wonderful as hot apple pie on a cold winter's day.*

"Oh my God," Chloe said over Tegan's shoulder as she sent the text.

"Chloe!" Tegan shoved her phone in her back pocket.

Chloe pointed her paintbrush at Tegan and said, "Don't *Chloe* me. You're spouting poetry. You've *totally* fallen for him."

"I have *not* fallen for him! And it's *not* poetry."

Chloe scoffed. "It might as well be. It's all lovey-dovey and squishy. I warned you not to fall for him, Teg." Her expression softened. "You heard what Emery said. He's never moving back. He won't ever settle down."

"I said I don't *think* he will," Emery clarified.

"It's okay, Em," Tegan said. "I know where Jett stands, and I know where I stand. He's funny and sexy and I like getting to know him. It's not like I'm hoping he'll marry me."

Chloe set down her paintbrush and said, "Are you sure? Because I don't want you getting hurt."

"Do you think *I* want to get hurt? Harper is counting on me. *I'm* counting on me. I don't have time to be hurt. But I do have time to get to know a man I'm attracted to. Do you know how long it's been since I met a guy I *wanted* to get to know and who wanted to get to know the *real* me? Who I am and what made me the person I am today? A guy who asks about the places I've been and the places I want to go? Someone who respects the weird way I do things, and my business sense?

Someone who wants to know me beyond being a great fuck?"

The girls exchanged surprised glances.

"This *is* Jett Masters we're talking about, right?" Emery asked.

Tegan rolled her eyes.

"She didn't mean that how it sounded," Serena said. "It's just that Jett's not really like that. Chloe and I grew up with him. He's never been interested in anyone like that as far as I know."

Tegan sighed and sank down to the couch. The tarp crinkled beneath her. "Well, he is interested in all those things about me."

Daphne sat beside her and said, "He always takes the time to ask how I'm doing. I think there's a great guy beneath all that cold-shoulder stuff. I wouldn't blame you if you fell for him."

Tegan nudged Daphne and said, "Thanks. I haven't fallen for him. But I could. I really like him."

The girls gathered around her, kneeling and offering advice all at once.

"That's okay," Harper said. "Let fate play its hand."

Chloe looked at Harper like she was crazy. "You're setting yourself up to get hurt, Teg. I don't think it's a good idea. Guys like Jett don't care about the hurt they leave in their wake."

"I don't believe that," Tegan said. "He has a big heart, even if he doesn't show it all the time." She wanted to ask them if they would show their hearts if they'd been hurt like he had, if they'd witnessed two important men in their lives—their father and grandfather—turning mean and selfish. She sure wouldn't risk being hurt again.

"Some guys don't care," Serena said. "Jett's a great guy, and while I think Chloe might be right about you getting hurt, I think he *would* care if he hurt you. He's still mad at his father, and his dad has been trying to make things better for a *long* time. That says something about him."

"There's a lot of water under that bridge," Tegan said. "Stuff that you guys probably don't know and that I can't share, because it's not my story to tell. I'm glad you care about me, but I *know* the risks involved with being close to Jett. My entire life has been about taking risks. I've worked three jobs to stay afloat. I've traveled by myself to foreign countries. Moving here and taking over my uncle's business was a huge risk, and who knows how it'll end up. But I'm *here*. If the theater fails, it'll hurt me way worse than any man ever could. And saying all this is a big risk, too. I know that being honest with you guys about this and going against your advice could cost me our friendship."

"Teg, that's not true. You're our friend, but we don't judge your decisions. We just want to watch out for you," Chloe said earnestly.

"Maybe not, but it feels like a risk—and a freaking scary one because I love you like sisters already. But if I ran from everything that could potentially hurt me, I'd be going backward." Her gaze moved over the concerned faces of her friends, and she said, "I am so lucky to have friends like you. And you're right. I might get hurt, and I *don't* think Jett will ever move back here. But that doesn't really matter because I'm moving back to Maryland in October anyway." She drew in a deep breath and said, "I lost my favorite uncle, and he left this big gaping hole inside me. But he taught me to take life by the horns and enjoy the hell out of it. What matters is that I'm happy *now*. And I'm *going to* let fate stick her hand into my life and wave her magic wand, because being with Jett, talking to him, getting to know him feels better than anything has for a very long time."

"I'm going to cry," Daphne said as she threw her arms around Tegan. "Be happy, Tegan. Just be happy."

Before Tegan could catch her breath, the others converged on her with hugs, apologies, and emphatic encouragement.

"I want to be you when I grow up," Daphne said. "You're so confident."

"Not always," Tegan choked out. "I just hope you all will be here for me if it turns out that I'm making the biggest mistake of my life."

"We've got your back," Harper said.

Chloe touched Tegan's hand and said, "I'm sorry. Maybe it's the big sister in me. I just worry about you."

"I worry about me, too. But I meant what I said. I'm happy, and I'm not afraid of what happens next. Especially since I know you guys will be here to catch me if I fall."

Chapter Eighteen

JETT WAS FRONT and center in Tegan's mind as she drove to the Sundial Café Wednesday morning to deliver Joni's costume. She and Jett had stayed up far too late talking again last night, but a little fatigue was nothing compared to how close they'd become. She'd filled him in on the progress she'd made with the marketing plans for the theater and told him she'd been seriously thinking about moving into the cottage. He was glad she was considering it, and when she told him that she and Harper had received, and ratified, the partnership agreement from the attorney, he'd praised both of them for protecting their friendship. She'd shown him the logo she'd chosen for the amphitheater, and just as she and Harper had, he'd loved the logo Brandon had created for Bayside Productions. Her friends and family cheered her on, but Jett had really taken an interest, querying her process and decisions, guiding and looking out for her in ways others hadn't, and that felt better than anything. They'd also talked about her uncle, and she'd shed a few tears. Jett was so compassionate and easy to talk to, she'd confessed that she wasn't looking forward to going through his things. Jett had said he wished he could be there to help, and the look in his eyes had told her he'd meant it. She wished he could, too, but knew it was impossible. He'd said he couldn't stop thinking about Mitchell and the others who had been affected by the storm. He hadn't elaborated, but after everything he'd said to her the other night, she thought it was good that they were still on his mind. Right before they had ended their video chat at nearly three in the morning, Jett had said, *One of these days maybe we'll catch a sunrise.* Then his whole face had brightened, and he'd said, *The morning after the wedding, before I leave town, let's make a point of catching that sunrise.* In that moment, she'd realized several things all at once—he was making future plans for them, even if only for a sunrise, she didn't know where he was going the morning after the wedding, and most surprising of all, she realized it didn't matter where he went. It seemed like he would always be traveling.

What mattered was whether he made plans to come back.

Tegan parked her uncle's car in front of the café, still wishing she had Berta. She gathered her things and headed for the café. She'd been there a few times over the last two weeks for breakfast, and she still got a little thrill remembering that first encounter with Jett. That wasn't the only thing tugging at her as she walked into the nearly empty café. She still expected to be greeted by Joni's cheery voice, but the energetic little girl was back in school.

"Hey there, sugar," Rowan said from behind the counter.

"Hi. I finished Joni's costume." She handed him the gift bag and said, "I hope she likes it. I gift wrapped it and put a note inside with a little story about how the costume was made by animals in the park. I love her imagination."

"You're really something else. Thank you. Carlo would have loved you." He set the bag on the counter behind him and said,

"This costume is all Joni's been talking about. I know she'll love it."

"Let's hope so."

"What are you hungry for today?"

"No breakfast for me. I can't stay. I have to go through my uncle's things. I've been putting it off for long enough." She'd told Rowan all about inheriting the theater and her big plans over breakfast the other day.

He leaned his forearms on the counter, so they were eye to eye. His shaggy hair fell forward. He pushed a hand through it, bringing it all to one side, and said, "I know a thing or two about how difficult it can be to go through a loved one's belongings. Can I give you some advice?"

"Yes, *please*. Every time I try to go through them, it's too sad."

"Take your time with every little thing. I know you feel like once you sort through it or put it away, you'll feel better. But for me, the sorting was the part that made me feel the best. It was hard at first, and I cried a lot, but then I allowed myself to relive the memories one at a time. That really helped. Sometimes we have to give ourselves permission to cry in order to heal. For me, it was giving away and putting away Carlo's things that did me in. But once I had soaked up every good memory, and even some of the bad ones, it became easier."

"I have been trying to just push through it."

"I think most people do, but like I said, it was easier for me not to. Do you want me to come by and help? Having a friend with you might make it easier."

"No, but it's nice of you to offer." Cici had offered to help, as had several of the girls. But Cici had enough on her plate with her own family, and Tegan didn't want to burden her friends with something that might bring her to tears.

"Okay." He stood up to his full height and said, "If you change your mind, you know where to find me."

"Thank you." She looked at a couple sitting by the window holding hands across the table, and it made her miss Jett even more. It also made her think of her uncle and Adele. She knew her love of *love* had come from her uncle, and just seeing that couple made her want to do something to encourage it. "Have they paid for their meal yet?"

"Yeah, when they ordered. Why?"

She dug out two twenties from her wallet and put them on the counter. "They look so in love, they inspired me. This is to pay for a meal for the next couple that comes in."

"Paying it forward. I like it." He opened the cash register and put the money in. "Love is a wonderful thing."

"Can I ask you something personal?"

He shrugged. "Sure."

"You've brought up Carlo a couple of times, and when you do, you get the same look my uncle used to get when he talked about his wife, Adele, who he lost eight years after they were married. How did you know when you were first falling for Carlo?"

"I didn't. There was no *falling* involved. I'm convinced we fell in love in another life and found each other again in this one, because the second I met her, I was a goner."

"Wow, really?"

"Yes, and I know how it sounds. Most people fall for each other over time. But with Carlo, it was like a meteor crashed into me. *Bam!*" His face lit up. "I totally dug everything about her from the get-go. My friends thought I was crazy, but *man*, she was my world. She was stubborn as a mule, and she'd argue just for the sake of proving that nobody could make her do a damn thing. But I even dug that about her. Sometimes she'd take off, needing her own space for a day or two, but I knew she'd always come back." His brows knitted. "I guess the way I *knew* I was in love with her was that I would have done anything for her, no questions asked. Why? What's on your mind?"

"I don't know. Just curious, I guess."

"Does it have something to do with Inspector Gadget?"

Tegan felt herself blushing. "Maybe a little."

"He was definitely into you when we saw you the day after the storm and he helped me make sandwiches. He asked a lot of questions, came across as *protective*. He seemed like a nice guy, too."

"I know he's into me," she said, but it sure felt good hearing it from Rowan.

"You think you're falling for him, then?"

She shrugged noncommittally, but her quickening pulse was anything but noncommittal.

"I'm taking that as a waffling *yes*. There's one way to know for sure. Stop seeing him."

"What? *No!*"

"Yup, you're on the downhill slide."

She shook her head, laughing. "You are…"

"Right?"

"I don't know," she said. "I've got to go."

Tegan drove home *waffling* between happy thoughts of a downhill slide and dreading going through her uncle's things. By the time she got home, the dread overshadowed her happier thoughts. She was surprised to see an Edible Arrangements truck in her driveway and the driver heading for her door.

She flew out of the car and said, "Hi! Is that for me?"

The deliveryman turned with an enormous bouquet of chocolate-covered fruits in one hand and a red box in the other.

"If your name is Miss Fine, it is," he said.

Her heart leapt. Only Jett would call her *Miss Fine*! She thanked the deliveryman and hurried inside with her goodies, anxious to read the card. She set the vase and the box on the kitchen counter and opened the card as fast as she could.

Hope this helps you through the harder parts of today. Jett

She sighed dreamily at his thoughtful words. She opened the box, delighted to find a dozen chocolate-covered strawberries. She plucked one out, took a selfie biting into it, and sent the picture to Jett with the caption *You can't imagine how much I needed this! I'm dreading going through my uncle's things. Thank you!! It will definitely help ease the sadness.*

His reply vibrated a minute later. *If I were there, I'd enjoy eating those off your body with my hands tied behind my back.*

Holy cow…

Yes, please.

Another text rolled in from Jett. *Distracted from the dread yet?*

Oh, this man knew just how to get to her. She replied, *YES!*

She finished the strawberry, and as she reached for another, Jett's reply came through. *Good. We'll get room service the night of the wedding. I can't wait to see you. Maybe you should consider asking some of the girls to help you today. I'm sure they wouldn't mind.* She loved that he was trying to fix things for her from thousands of miles away. She replied, *Strawberries, a sunset, and you. Sounds perfect. Maybe I will call a friend. Or maybe I'll put it off for another few days and just enjoy this feast. Thank you!*

As she carried the box of strawberries into the living room, she received another text from Jett. *Heading into a meeting. Good luck.*

She set the box on the coffee table, looking over the looming piles of Harvey's things. She snagged another strawberry and sank down to the couch, trying to mentally prepare for a day of sadness. Her phone vibrated, and she hoped it was Jett. But when she pulled it from her pocket, she saw Jock's name on the screen. A wave of disappointment hit her, and she knew that was unfair, since Jock had talked with her for nearly an hour yesterday afternoon about the idea of her moving into the cottage and using the big house for the productions.

She opened and read his text. *I've been thinking about it and I think moving into the cottage is a great idea.* She was glad he thought it was a good idea, because the more she'd thought about it, the more excited she became.

Maybe this process *would* be easier with a friend, and it just might do Jock some good, too, to gain some closure. She called him.

"Hey, Teg. What's up?"

"I think I need you."

He chuckled. "I always knew one day it would come to this. I'm sorry, Teg, but you're like a little sister to me. I don't think we should go there."

"Very funny. I'm being *serious.*"

"So was I," he said, his smile coming through loud and clear.

"*Jock,*" she pleaded. "I'm going through Harvey's things, or rather, trying to go through them, and I just...I need help. Are you in the country? Is there any chance you can help me sometime in the next week? I can't look at all these piles for much longer."

"Aw, Teg, I'm sorry. I knew I should have stuck around to help you last summer."

"You were pretty much a mess, too. If it's too hard for you, it's okay. Maybe tequila will help me through."

"That's never a good idea. Remember the night we played Never Would I Ever? Never would I ever have thought I'd end up holding your hair while you barfed."

"Oh, *right*," she said, remembering that hilarious night. "I owe *you* one, not vice versa. Never mind."

"You probably owe me more like ten, but who's counting? I'm at my brother Levi's in Harborside, hanging out with him and my niece and visiting a couple of my cousins. They've probably had enough of me by now. I can be there in a couple of hours."

"*Wait*. You're with your family? You should definitely stay and visit."

"The rest of my family isn't here right now. I've been here for a week. Levi, Jesse, and Brent are working, and my niece, Joey, is at school. Give me a few minutes to wrap things up here and swing by the school to give Joey a hug; then I'll take off."

"Are you *sure*?"

"Absolutely. Besides, Harvey will probably strike me down if I don't."

JOCK ARRIVED JUST shy of three hours after Tegan had called, a welcome sight for her troubled eyes. Her clean-cut friend sported thick scruff, and his dark hair looked long overdue for a trim, giving an edge to his normally refined appearance. Tegan ran into his arms, and they hugged for what felt like forever.

"I missed you!" she said as he set her on her feet.

"I missed you, too, Teg. It's nice to be back."

"Do you want to move back to the cottage? Or you can move into the house if you'd rather."

"Thanks, but no thanks. It's time I moved on. But I'll probably hang around the Cape. Maybe rent a room somewhere by the water so I can try to write."

"Yes! At the resort! I have a great idea. You can take Daphne or Chloe to the wedding as your date."

He chuckled as he grabbed his bag, and they headed inside. "Trust me, I've got more baggage than American Airlines. The last thing I need is to date one of your friends." Jock had also met Harper's friends last summer when he, Tegan, and Cici and her family had been in town for the funeral. They'd stayed for the Fourth of July and had run into Harper and her friends in Provincetown.

"I'm not talking about dating. I'm just saying you could be friends with benefits, like me and Jett."

He dropped his bag by the front door and said, "How about you be my friend and feed me as a benefit? I'm starved."

They went into the kitchen, and he snagged a piece of fruit from the bouquet. "Jett?"

"Uh-huh."

"I don't want to know what you had to do for this," he teased.

They chatted about Jock's travels and about her and Jett as he ate, and Tegan admitted that she'd been avoiding certain parts of the house, like Harvey's bedroom. Which was why Jock suggested they start there. *Like ripping a bandage off.* By the time they made their way upstairs to start going through Harvey's things, she was already feeling better. It was much easier to face the chore with Jock telling stories and joking with her. They worked through the bedrooms, boxing clothes and items to donate and heirlooms to send to her parents, and then they moved downstairs. They chatted the whole time, which made the process much less difficult. Now, as the sun dipped from the sky, they sat on the floor of Harvey's office sorting through boxes of pictures.

They were separating pictures of Harvey's life before he'd come to the Cape from the pictures of his life after he'd moved there. Tegan was also keeping a small stash of pictures of her and Harvey to show Jett. Eventually she hoped to get them all digitalized.

"They're all mixed together without rhyme or reason. Why did he keep them like this instead of in photo albums?"

"Because he was a stubborn old bastard. I tried to get him to let me have them made into digital files dozens of times, but he wanted no part of it. He liked to look through them, hold them, *study* them."

She set a picture of Harvey and Adele on a pile. "Really?"

"Oh yeah. He enjoyed the memories they brought."

"Did he share them with you?"

"When he was in the mood, but most of the time when he snickered or appeared sad and I'd ask about it, he'd give me that look. You know the one, like you couldn't possibly understand whatever he was thinking, and he'd wave me off."

"He was such a pest to you. Why did you stay?"

Jock looked at the picture of Harvey he was holding, and a thoughtful expression came over him. "We clicked. We were good for each other."

"That makes me happy." She took out another picture, one of Jock when he was much younger and Harvey standing by the amphitheater with a group of children. "Jock, look how young you are in this. You were so cute. It doesn't even look like you needed to shave yet. And look how *skinny* you were." She scooted closer and showed him the picture.

Jock snagged the picture and said, "I'm still young and cute."

"I wasn't saying you were old. But I definitely would not call you *cute*. Cute is the twenty-year-old kid in the picture."

"Twenty-*two*," he corrected her, gazing down at the picture.

"Close enough. You were cute back then, but now you're a man, and strikingly handsome. I bet you couldn't have grown that little beard you have going on when you were that age. You were brooding back then, too, which is understandable after all you'd gone through. Lucky for you, you've worked that brooding into a mysterious aura, like a movie star people admire and wonder about."

"I'm nothing to admire or wonder about, Teg. I'm just a guy trying to figure out how to get through this life like everyone else." He held up the picture and said, "This was taken the first year I worked for Harvey."

"Wow." She studied the image of her uncle standing beside Jock. Harvey was a bit shorter than him. He stood straight, with his slim shoulders pulled back, handsome and *regal* in a gray cardigan and dark slacks. "He'd been in a wheelchair for so long, I didn't remember what he looked like without it."

"He fought that wheelchair like he could actually *win*."

"Of course he did. You know he fired every caretaker who worked for him before you within just a few months of their starting."

"I know. He told me that they treated him like a dying old man, and he had a lot of life left to live. But he lost his battle with that damn chair just about two years after I started working with him. By then I had studied everything I could about emphysema, and I'd brought a nurse in after he was in bed at night for a few weeks to prepare and learn about the realities of living with a man in his condition and the care he'd need. I was as ready as I could be, but when it happened, when he could no longer take more than a few steps without his legs giving out, I swear I wanted to tear apart that stupid chair *for* him. He was so full of life, he deserved better than to be confined to a wheelchair and strapped to an oxygen tank for years on end." Jock paused, as if he had to rein in his emotions, and a moment later he said, "Did I ever tell you how badly he scared me that first year?"

"No. You didn't talk to me much until you'd been here for a couple of years, remember?"

He leaned his shoulder against hers and said, "Sorry if I was a dick, Teg."

"You weren't. You were grieving, and all that brooding made you fascinating to me. I remember before you told me what you'd gone through, I was always trying to make you smile."

"You talked *endlessly*. Meanwhile, your uncle was torturing me in every way he could just so he could laugh."

"He always said that nothing was more valuable than laughter," she said as his voice tiptoed through her mind. "I loved his sense of humor."

"That's because he wasn't scaring the hell out of you. Do you have any idea what it was like to go check on him and see him sprawled out, half on the bed, half off, with his oxygen tube around his neck?"

Tegan's eyes widened with shock. "What?"

"The bastard would fake his own death every few weeks. I was a damn mess because of him. And when I made the mistake of telling him that my brothers and I always scared the crap out of each other for fun, he took it up a notch and actually hired a guy to pretend he was a burglar one night."

"Oh my God. Are you serious?" She could totally see her uncle doing something like that.

"We're talking about *Harvey*. Do you *think* I'm kidding? The guy he hired had a gun, which turned out to be a frigging play prop. So there I was, standing in front of Harvey with my arms out, protecting him from this guy and planning my attack, when the guy aimed the gun at my chest."

"Oh *no*..." She winced, knowing Jock would have done anything to protect Harvey. "What did you do?"

"I acted on instinct and grabbed his arm, twisted and flipped, and had him on the ground in seconds. Harvey was laughing his ass off, but the poor guy suffered a broken wrist. That was the last time Harvey did anything like *that*, but he still did all sorts of other shit."

She laughed and reached into the box. "That poor man. The fake burglar, of course."

"I felt horrible." Jock looked at the picture and shook his head. "I miss him, Teg. I miss Harvey every day."

"Me too," she said softly. She took out another picture, trying to keep the sadness at bay. In the picture, Harvey was in his wheelchair, dressed like a doctor, and Jock was dressed up like Frankenstein. "When was *this* taken?"

Happiness glimmered in Jock's eyes, and he set down the picture that he'd just pulled from another box, taking the other from Tegan. "That was our fourth Halloween together. We both loved Halloween, so we put the word out to the groups that came through for the amphitheater that we were giving out candy. We'd decorate the outside of the house like a graveyard with smoke and that sort of thing. Or rather, I decorated and Harvey directed, and then we'd sit on the front porch dressed in awesome costumes and give out a trunkful of candy. He loved it, and I have to tell you, I did, too. But the best part of the night was after trick or treating was done. Harvey and I would watch horror movies together."

"I didn't know he liked horror movies."

"That's because you were his happy girl. He never wanted anything scary or bad in your life. I think he considered you and Cici the daughters he never got to have."

"I'm sure he did. He would have made a great dad."

They worked through a few boxes, talking about how much they missed him and the fun times they'd all had together. When they finished going through the pictures, Jock went into the closet and came out with a large wooden box.

"What's that?"

"I don't know. It was inside a cardboard box with Adele's name on it." He set it down and sat beside her.

Tegan opened the wooden top, revealing what looked like an endless number of handwritten letters. She picked one up and looked over her uncle's shaky handwriting. "It's a love letter from Harvey to Adele, written after she died. Listen to this." She read the opening of the letter. "My sweet Adele, it's been four hundred and eighty-seven days, and the pain is no less than the day I lost you. I hear you whispering my name in the mornings, and I open my eyes expecting to see you..." Tears stung Tegan's eyes, and she lowered the letter to her lap. "I can't read these. We should bury them in the garden where Adele's ashes were spread."

"Okay, we'll do that." Jock took the letter and placed it in the box; then he put his arm around Tegan, drawing her against him, and held her. Her back rested against his side and he pressed a kiss to the top of her head. "You okay?"

She nodded. "He loved her so much. She was so lucky."

"I think they were both lucky."

"Do you think we'll ever find that kind of love?" She put her hands over his arm, which was belted around her, glad he was there and missing Jett fiercely.

"That would require dating first, and you know where I stand on that. But you…"

She closed her mouth to keep her thoughts about Jett from spilling out.

"The woman who never shuts up is being *awfully* quiet." He wiggled his arm. "Teg, has chocolate-covered fruit guy turned into more than an FWB? Is he your one and only?"

She turned and buried her face in Jock's chest. "I'm in so much trouble!" She banged her forehead on his chest but couldn't keep from gushing about Jett. She sat back, her legs folded beneath her, and said, "I thought our benefits were going to far outweigh our friendship, but we've been talking every night, FaceTiming—"

"Oh God. No naked details please," Jock said.

"No naked details, I promise, but it's not just the sexiness. We *talk* for *hours*, about *everything*. I know him better than I know you, and I've known you for more than a decade. He's complex, though, with baggage. Probably more than American Airlines, like you, but I don't care. I want to be with him all the time. I count down the minutes until our calls, and I don't want the calls to end."

"You're falling for your friend with benefits? Does he feel the same way?"

She fidgeted with the edge of her shirt, nervously admitting the truth. "I don't know. When we're talking, I feel like we're both on the same page. I see it in his eyes and in everything he says and does. Even the fruit he sent today shows how much he cares. But he'd never say it, and he's been very clear about not wanting more."

"Then don't make it into something it's not, Teg. This guy is probably going to hurt you, and then I'll have to hurt him. Why do women do this to themselves?"

"It's not *our* fault," she said vehemently. "It's not a one-way street, Jock. You might not have dated much, but the guy *always* plays a role in things. He tells me he misses me, and he says romantic things that make me melt inside. And when we are together? I can't even begin to describe what it's like. I want to get lost in *us* and never find my way out."

"I'm glad you found someone who makes you happy, but guys are pretty cut-and-dried. If he's drawing lines in the sand, I'd bet he means them."

"Maybe, but I think he's just scared, and I understand that because of everything he's been through. Plus, he travels *all* the time. He's going to Louisiana tomorrow and, after the wedding, overseas for like a month, so there are valid reasons we can't have more. But..." She lowered her eyes and said, "I can't help it. I'm crazy about him."

Jock lifted her chin and smiled reassuringly. "Crazy enough to not lose your mind when he's gone for a month?"

"I think so."

"Well, that says something. Do you think he can ever give

you what Harvey and Adele had?"

She swallowed hard, trying to push past the painful nugget of truth lodged in her throat. She thought about what Rowan had said about knowing he loved Carlo because nothing could have kept him away, and she knew that for Jett, it wouldn't matter if he fell in love with her. Work would always come first.

"Teg?" Jock nudged her knee.

She met his gaze and shook her head. "But I don't know if anyone can give me that." Agitated, she pushed to her feet, determined not to wallow in the reality of her and Jett's future, when their present was so wonderful. "Let's get started on the den. We have a lot to do and can't afford to be sidetracked."

IT HAD BEEN a hell of a day. Jett had woken up worrying about Tegan, and that worry had been his constant companion throughout the entire day of grueling meetings. Thankfully, the Carlisle information was coming together well. The kid had emailed today, just to needle him. He was heading to London this week to meet with the Carlisles. Jett wasn't worried. Zack was a lot of things, but richer and savvier than him weren't among them. If things continued progressing without any hitches, Jett and his team would be in London the week after next, meeting with the owners and evaluating their current staff and procedures. Unfortunately, what they'd discovered about Mitchell's company, and several of the other Hyannis businesses Jett was considering helping, wasn't as promising. Most were barely keeping their heads above water. They were anything but solid investments. Jett didn't know what to do about that, because for some fucked-up reason, he couldn't stop seeing the defeated look in Mitchell's eyes, or the challenge in his father's when he'd brought up the idea of Jett's helping them. He had no idea how he'd live with himself if Mitchell had to sell out because he had no other option, much less if those hallmark stores of his youth were wiped out by big business.

He pulled out his phone, and the sight of Tegan's beautiful face on his lock screen loosened the knots in his chest. He still couldn't wrap his head around the power she had over him. When they talked at night, he ached to hold her, to feel her breath on his chest as she slept safely in the confines of his arms. She'd sent him several pictures from the other night when she'd had dessert with their friends at Summer House. The one on his lock screen was his favorite. She was holding a gigantic piece of cake, speckles of paint dotting the bridge of her nose, and she was grinning from ear to ear. He was pretty sure that grin was meant for the cake, not for him, but he didn't care, because seeing her joy made him happy.

He swiped to unlock his phone, revealing his second favorite picture, taken later that night in the dim evening light of her bedroom. She was lying on her belly, gazing into the camera, giving off a gently sexy vibe, like a warm breeze he couldn't help but get caught up in.

Damn, he missed her.

He thumbed through the pictures of her and the girls making silly faces. Tegan had taken pictures with everyone that evening, including Dean. His brother's muscular arm was around Tegan's shoulder, and he was giving Jett the finger, despite his smiling eyes. When she'd shared the details of her evening with him and told him how much fun she'd had with Drake, Rick, and Dean, he'd been jealous as hell that he'd missed out on the time with her. He knew he was different from the guys he'd grown up with. They knew how to be boyfriends and husbands, how to put down roots so deep they'd never break free. Even his brothers, who had grown up in the same house with him, knew how to be the kind of men Tegan deserved. They knew how to settle down, to spend evenings chilling by a bonfire, or under the moon in a hut, not thinking about work or the ghosts of their pasts. So why the fuck did Jett see his father and all that he didn't want to be every time he looked in the damn mirror?

He glanced at Tegan's picture again. *Why do you make me question everything?*

It didn't matter *why.*

Despite his private vow to never be in a position to disappoint a woman or a family as his father had, Tegan had gotten under his skin, and he didn't want to tear her out. But he couldn't silence the voice in his head reminding him of the truth. Didn't the fact that he was in LA while she was at the Cape working through her grief alone prove that he couldn't be the man she needed?

His hand fisted around the phone, and he pushed to his feet, pacing, fighting that voice. He *wasn't* his father. He'd made damn sure of that, hadn't he? He'd sent chocolate-covered fruit. He'd texted. He'd done what he could. His father wouldn't have even *noticed* his mother's pain, much less tried to ease it.

The gnarly feeling in his gut told him he might be wrong.

Fuck...

He could fix this. He called Tia.

"What's up, boss?" she said when she answered.

"I need you to change my flight to Silver Island from Saturday to Friday morning, and I want to fly into Hyannis, not the island. *Early*. Crack of dawn."

"You're meeting with the directors of EBC Friday."

Jett had purchased EBC, a healthcare management company, six months earlier and had done major restructuring. The six-month reviews of his acquisitions consisted of looking at the company from the top down. Jett met with and reevaluated management, operational processes, and employee morale, to get a general feel for how his new endeavors were shaping up on their turf, not just on paper. He prided himself on that personal commitment, but what the hell good was that if he let Tegan down?

"I don't care. Rearrange it. I'll stay late Wednesday and Thursday, whatever it takes."

"I'll try. What's going on? Is this about the Hyannis properties?"

"No, but I might have a meeting about them while I'm there."

"Okay, let me know what you need for that. But why the rush to get to the Cape?"

"I have to take care of a few things."

"Anything I can help with? Should I call Daphne and book you a cottage?"

"No. I'll stay with Tegan." He closed his eyes. *Shit.*

"*Whoa*, hold on a second," she said. "*Tegan?* Does Tegan have a last name?"

"Fine," he relented.

"Your *booty call?*"

"*T, stop*. She is *not* a booty call."

"She *was*," she reminded him. "Remember when you asked me to track her down for you?"

He ground out a curse. "Yes, and you refused, which means you lost the right to be annoying."

"We both know my annoyingness has no limits. Is she the reason you canceled your flight *last* week?"

"Yes. Now can you please stop the inquisition?"

"In a sec. You've never once mentioned a woman other than the girls at your brother's resort or your mother or grandmother, much less put off work for one, which means this is a bigger deal than Carlisle Enterprises."

"*No*, it's not."

"You might be excellent in business, boss. You can spot weakness from a mile away and negotiate the hell out of a deal, but I'm not so sure you know how to decipher women, or your feelings toward them. Have you done your due diligence?"

"I'm not doing due diligence on Tegan."

"See? You just proved my point. You're lost when it comes to dating."

"We're not dating."

She sighed. "*Again*, you're out of touch. Pretend you're me and I'm taking off work to be with a guy. You'd call Reggie Steele and know everything about the guy two hours later."

"It's different. You're a woman. Guys take advantage of women."

"And women take advantage of men. Are you *certain* she's not after you for your money?"

He scoffed. "She couldn't be less interested in my money."

"Does she know about your schedule? That you're going to London for almost a month? Possibly longer if you close the deal? That you change your plans on a dime and zip out of the country to nail a deal?"

"She knows work comes first."

"Well, she won't after Friday, will she? You have to think of the message you're sending."

He thought about that for a minute before responding. "I've got it under control. Anything else?"

"Yes. It's about time you let a little sunshine into your life. Can you tell me something about her?"

"No."

"You know I can find out anything I want about her. You taught me how. Just give me something *small*. Anything at all."

He chuckled. "Okay. She's as smart as she is beautiful."

"Come on, boss. That's not news. You're gorgeous, so of course she's attractive, and you don't have patience for stupid people, so smart is a no-brainer. Stop playing games and cough up a nugget to satisfy my curiosity."

"God, you're a pain. She makes me think in ways I haven't in years."

"She's *kinky*. Gotcha!"

"*TI*" he snapped.

"I'm *kidding*. That's good, Jett, and I'm proud of you. I feel like my baby boy is going to the prom."

"Goodbye, Tia…"

Jett was in a great mood when he ended the call, and he knew he'd done the right thing. He checked the time. It was still too early to call Tegan, so he called Mitchell.

"Hello?"

"Mitchell, it's Jett Masters."

"Hi, Jett. How are you doing?"

"Great, thanks. The reason I'm calling is that I heard you and some others have been approached by an investor."

"We have, and quite frankly, they're talking numbers that would be hard to turn down for folks around here. The insurance companies have been slow, and people are getting antsy. It's been a rough few years."

"I understand. Do me a favor. Don't sign anything yet, and ask the other business owners on your block to do the same. I'm flying into town Friday morning, and I'd like to talk with you and the other business owners later in the day to toss some ideas around."

"What type of ideas?" Mitchell asked.

"I'm not sure yet, but I'm working on a few things. Think you can pull people together between now and then?"

"I can do that. Where do you want to meet?"

"I have no idea. I haven't thought that far ahead."

"Why don't we meet at my house?" Mitchell suggested. "What time are you thinking?"

Jett quickly thought through Friday. He had seen the piles of Tegan's uncle's things stacked around the house, and he didn't want to rush her through the process of going through them. He assumed they'd work all day, grab some dinner, and then he could meet Mitchell.

"How's seven thirty?" Jett suggested. "Is that too late?"

"That's great. I don't know what you have up your sleeve, but whatever it is, I sure do appreciate you keeping us in your thoughts."

"You're never far from them." *Anymore.*

After talking to Mitchell, Jett was too psyched about his plans to see Tegan to wait until eight o'clock to give her the news. He went to the window, looking out over the lights of the city as he called her.

"Jett, hi!" She sounded out of breath.

"Hey, babe. How are you doing?"

"*Good.* My friend Jock has been here for *hours* helping me go through my uncle's things. We might have to pull an all-nighter to get through it all, but we're making progress. I'm so sorry, but would it be okay if I called you tomorrow?" She lowered her voice and said, "Or I could try later, but he's sitting right here, and I don't want to blow him off since he came into town just to help me."

He ground his teeth together, silently cursing himself, and forced the most casual tone he could muster to say, "No worries. We'll catch up tomorrow."

"Okay," she said happily. "Thanks for understanding. Jock has been an amazing help. I'm really lucky to have a friend like him. Have a great night."

She ended the call before Jett even said goodbye.

He felt blindsided. Sucker punched.

He paced angrily. Was Jock a friend like *he* was her friend? *He's there, asshole. You're not.*

Chapter Nineteen

"WHERE *ARE* YOU?" Tia's angry voice blared through the speaker of Jett's phone. "The driver has been waiting for you for thirty minutes. You're going to miss your flight."

"Cancel it." Jett turned into Tegan's driveway and said, "I'll go to Louisiana next week." An unfamiliar car came into view, and he ground out a curse, reminding himself he was the idiot who had left her to deal with her uncle's things alone. But he sure as hell didn't expect her to shack up with a dude for a night.

"What do you mean, *cancel it*? What is going on?"

"I'm on the Cape."

"*What?* You said *Friday!* We could have sent Jonas to deal with EBC. He knows that company inside and out. Did something happen? This isn't like you. I can probably still get Jonas to do it."

Jonas Cross was a fast learner, and he'd been managing several projects. But he wasn't *Jett*. He threw his car into park and said, "Get off my case, Tia. It's *my* company, *my* reputation. I'll take care of it *next week*."

"You're supposed to be in LA next week *and* the week after to go over the final docs with legal before you leave for

London."

He threw open his door and climbed from the car. "I'll fly to Louisiana Sunday morning and LA next Friday morning. We'll cram the meetings into a week. Tell the staff to plan on early mornings and late nights. We'll get it done."

"Jett, you're worrying me. Just give EBC to Jonas. You know he can do the work. I know you *think* you're unstoppable, but at some point you're going to get worn out."

"Not in this lifetime. I gotta go. I'll fly out Sunday morning, as planned. Just change the destination."

He ended the call and stalked past the asshole's car, his hands curling into fists. He'd worked out hard last night, trying to rein in the guilt and anger that had consumed him, but it hadn't even taken the edge off. He'd finally chartered a private plane for the trip to Boston, and then he'd driven like a bat out of hell to get to Tegan. Nothing would stop him now.

He ascended the stairs and pounded on the front door. He heard a man's voice, turning his guilt to blinding anger.

The door opened, and music blared. A tall and too-fucking-fit dude stood before him wearing nothing but a towel, his hair damp from a shower Jett did *not* want to think about. If Tegan showered with this guy, he'd lose his fucking mind.

The guy made no bones about sizing up Jett. "Can I help you?"

Jett instinctively squared his shoulders and thrust out his chest. "I'm here to see Tegan," he said sternly, fighting the urge to blow past him.

The guy glanced at Jett's rental car; then he lifted his chin and said, "And you are?"

Her fucking boyfriend was on the tip of Jett's tongue, but it wasn't true, and for all he knew, this guy had convinced her to forgo their FWB arrangement for a monogamous relationship with his pretty-boy ass. "Jett Masters. She around?"

The man stared at him for a long moment, jaw tight, eyes narrowed, before finally stepping aside and nodding. "She's in the kitchen."

Jett brushed past him, shooting a look into the living room on his way to the kitchen. His chest constricted at the sight of blankets and pillows on the floor. Hurt and anger warred inside him as he stormed into the kitchen, and his heart stumbled, rooting him in place in the entryway. Tegan was dancing to the blaring music, arms flailing, hips jerking in front of pancakes on a griddle. Her baggy sweatshirt nearly covered her tiny flannel shorts, and her pink slipper booties banged and slid on the floor as she sang about holding her girl at the top of her lungs. Her hair was a mass of tangles, and even knowing she might have been with the asshole standing behind him, she was still the best fucking thing he'd seen all year.

Holy hell. He was screwed.

"Tegan!" the other guy called out over the music.

Tegan startled. "Geez, Jo—" She turned, and her eyes caught Jett's. She dropped the spatula she was holding and yelled, "*Jett!*"

She ran toward him, stumbled, and he caught her in his arms. She climbed him like a tree, wrapping her arms around his neck and her legs around his waist, grinning like he'd given her the world—and fuck him, because he wanted to do just that.

"What are you doing here?" she hollered, and then she pressed her lips to his, tearing them away too fast. "I can't believe you're here!" she said before he could respond. She looked at the other guy and said, "Jock! This is Jett!" She kissed

Jett again and said, "I thought you were going to Louisiana? Why are you here?"

As she slid down his body, Jett kept his arm around her, trying to make sense of her reaction while the half-naked dude she'd spent the night with was standing right there. *Fuck it.* If she didn't care, neither did he. "Because I screwed up, Tegs. I should have come yesterday to help you with your uncle's stuff. I know you've got this guy, but, Tegs, he's not *me*. The two of you aren't *us*." He glanced at Jock and said, "No offense, man."

The guy looked too shocked to move.

"I didn't expect you to drop everything and come here," Tegan exclaimed. "I understand about your work."

"I know you do, but you shouldn't have to. Not when your heart is breaking from losing a man who meant everything to you. I want to be the guy you lean on when you're sad. I want to be the one who wipes your tears and hears the stories that go along with the time you spent in this house. I want that, Tegan. I don't fucking know how I'll do it, and I'm sure I'll mess it up a hundred times. But I want to *try* because you deserve that, and I hope you'll give me a chance."

She leapt into his arms again and crashed her sweet lips to his, giving him the answer he needed and unraveling all the angst that had been eating him alive since they'd talked last night.

"I'll just...*uh*...go get dressed," Jock said.

Tegan shooed him away as they kissed, and Jett poured all his relief and all the emotions he'd been holding back into their kiss, turning her smile into the sensual sounds he'd so missed.

She pulled back, breathless, and waved into the kitchen. "The pancakes! Turn off the griddle and take me upstairs."

He'd never turned off an appliance and ascended steps so

fast.

"Where'd you find that guy?" he asked between kisses in the bedroom as he pulled off her sweatshirt.

"Jock was my uncle's caregiver for years." She tugged open the button on his jeans.

His heart ached as she tugged off her slippers. He didn't want to know what had happened between her and Jock, but at the same time, he *did*. "I saw blankets on the living room floor."

"We fell asleep watching a home movie." She pushed up his shirt, and as he took it off, she said, "He's like a brother to me."

Relief stole his breath, and he wondered if that relief made him an asshole. "Fuck, Tegs" came out almost as apologetically as he felt. He drew her into his arms and said, "I'm so sorry. I thought..." He gazed into her beautiful, trusting eyes, and his truth poured out. "It shouldn't have taken another guy for me to see what was right in front of me, to listen to the scary-ass things going on in my head and in my heart. I *can't* change my life on a dime, Tegs. I won't make promises I can't keep. But when you told me Jock was here, that he'd come from out of town to help you, I realized how badly I'd failed you."

"But we're just friends with benefits. I knew you couldn't come, and I didn't ask you—"

He silenced her with a kiss, and said, "You shouldn't have to ask, not when every night we were becoming so much more than we thought we'd be. I can't go a day without thinking about you, wondering how you are, what you're doing, wanting to hold you. I want to be here when you need me, and I don't know if I can even make that happen, or if it's enough for you to end our nonexclusive arrangement and make it exclusive."

"It's enough," she said quickly. "You're enough, Jett. I don't know what will happen a month or six months from now, if I'll want more or you'll want less. But I know I want this now. I want to be with *you* exclusively."

"Thank Christ." He crushed his lips to hers, and they made out as they stripped naked and tumbled to the bed.

He laced their fingers together as he lowered his lips to hers, and she shifted beneath him, welcoming him into the sweet haven of her body. Their lips parted on their moans, and he felt the same rush of emotions that had overtaken him almost two weeks ago. It was *still* here, only now it was stronger, bigger, *bone deep*, too substantial to be severed by time or distance. Neither one spoke, or moved, and he wondered if she felt it, too.

She touched his lips and said, "I can't believe this is real, that you're here."

"I'm here, baby, and I've missed us so much."

His mouth covered hers, kissing her deeply as their bodies moved in perfect harmony. She held him tighter, their intensity building with every thrust of their hips, every grind of their bodies, every stroke of their tongues. They both went a little wild, clutching, scratching, groping, biting, and pleading indiscernibly, holding on to each other like they needed their connection to survive. The room around them blurred. Jett was lost in a sea of magnificent sensations, consumed by the woman in his arms as she cried out his name like a demand, "*Jett—*" giving in to the sensual beast within her. Fire and ice rushed down his spine. He fought to stave off his orgasm, dipping his head beside hers. He gripped her ass, lifting her hips and driving deeper, working her up to a moaning, whimpering frenzy.

"Come again for me, baby," he growled against her cheek.

He sealed his mouth over her neck, sucking the way he knew she loved. Her head fell back with another pleasure-filled sound, her body squeezing tight and perfect around his cock. "*Tegan*—" broke free in a gust of passion and lust, and so much more.

Chapter Twenty

"I STILL CAN'T believe you're here," Tegan said after they showered and dressed later that Thursday morning.

"I can't believe I'm here, either. You bewitched me over video chat, cast some sort of spell on me and drew me into your web." Jett gathered her in his arms and kissed her.

"Well, you won't hear any apologies from me. Are you exhausted, staying up all night to get here?"

"Rejuvenated."

"You're amazing." She went up on her toes and kissed him. Then she took his hand and said, "Come on. You should formally meet Jock. You'll like him."

"Even more so since you didn't sleep with him," he said as they started down the stairs.

"We did *sleep* together," she teased.

Jett smacked her ass, earning a melodic laugh.

"You said you didn't get jealous, but I guess you were wrong." She stopped suddenly and said, "Shoot. I forgot my phone. Go grab some coffee. I'll be right down." She headed back up the stairs.

Jett went into the kitchen and found Jock making pancakes.

"Hey," Jock said. "You hungry?"

"No thanks. I'll just grab some coffee." As Jett made coffee, he said, "Listen, Jock, I'm sorry for coming in here guns cocked. I thought you and Tegan were more than friends and got a little hot under the collar."

"She's a special girl, definitely worth getting worked up over." He transferred three pancakes to a plate and said, "Is Tegan coming down? Should I make her pancakes? She can't cook worth shit, but the girl can eat."

Jett chuckled. "Yeah. She just went back up to get her phone, and"—*after a round of mattress wrestling and damn hot shower sex*—"I'm sure she'll want to eat."

Jock poured batter onto the griddle, then turned and crossed his arms, facing Jett head-on with a serious expression. "Tegan told me about your *arrangement*. I know she comes across as confident and strong, which she is, but that doesn't mean she's immune to being hurt."

"That's why I'm here. I don't plan on hurting her. Our *arrangement* has changed to an exclusive relationship," he said proudly.

Jock nodded and flipped the pancakes. "I did a bit of research while you were upstairs. You see, I knew of you as a kid. I think everyone around here did."

"You're from the Cape?"

Jock shook his head and said, "Silver Island. You've got a couple years on me, but I watched you play ball against our high school. You were a legend for a while. Rumor had it that you'd gotten a full scholarship to play baseball at Boston College."

"I turned it down." Jett sat at the table and said, "I went into business instead."

"I wondered what happened when we didn't see your name on the rosters." Jock transferred Tegan's pancakes to a plate. He grabbed a bottle of syrup and sat at the table across from Jett. "From what I've read about you, you're a man who has it all, probably used to women who are very different from Tegan."

Jett knew where their conversation was headed, and he was impressed with Jock's tactics, bringing up their youthful connection, gaining his confidence before going in for what he was sure would be a threat if he did wrong by Tegan.

"I'm not *used to* women of any kind," Jett said. "Tegan is the only woman I've ever let get close to me."

Jock's eyes narrowed. "A rich guy like you who travels all the time? Hobnobbing with the rich and famous? You want me to believe that you haven't used that power to gain certain *favors?*"

"I'm not saying I'm a saint. I've been with plenty of women, but none that I wanted to get to know like Tegan. And honestly? I don't give a damn what you believe." He paused, holding Jock's gaze. "But I'm sure Tegan does, which is the *only* reason I'll explain myself to you. *Once.*" He let that sink in before saying, "I had a great father who turned into a raving asshole. When something like that happens, you question what you're capable of, who you'll end up being, and what kind of damage you'll leave behind. Rather than become the dick he was, I avoided personal connections and created an untouchable empire. *That's* where my focus has been since I went away to college. So, yes, Tegan is the *first* and *only* woman to get under my skin." He splayed his hands, his gaze remaining trained on the man across the table. "Believe it or choose not to. As I said, my only concern is that the woman upstairs knows I'm trying to learn how to be a better man for *her*. And if I fuck that up, whatever you think you can do to me is nothing compared to what I'll do to myself."

Jock studied him with a discerning expression.

"My two favorite men eating breakfast together?" Tegan said as she breezed into the room a minute later. "Are we friends yet?"

Jett cocked a brow, giving Jock the opportunity to respond.

"We're getting there," Jock said with a friendlier expression. "Jett and I appear to have a lot more in common than I thought."

WHEN TEGAN, JETT, and Jock first began organizing the boxes that were going to the Salvation Army, Jett and Jock weren't talking much, which made for an uncomfortable start to their time together. But over the course of an hour or two, they began working together, making decisions as a team instead of bumping chests like Neanderthals. By late afternoon, as they packed Tegan's belongings and carried them into the cottage, Tegan realized the tension had dissipated, and the two men were bantering like buddies.

She followed Jett into the cozy cottage living room, enjoying the view as he bent to set down the box he was carrying.

"You going to stare at his ass all day?" Jock asked, setting down another box.

"Probably." She would probably stare at him all day and night, because his showing up, and everything he'd said, was so completely unexpected, she kept reliving it in her head.

Jett turned with a lustful look in his eyes. "Let me get that." He took the box from Tegan's arms.

"I had it," she said.

"I know you did." He kissed her softly, and said, "But I'm here to be used, so *use me, baby*."

Jock grumbled something indiscernible and said, "Are you two going to need a hankie to tie on the cottage door?"

Jett pulled Tegan into his arms and said, "Nah. Just text before you walk down from the big house. If we don't answer, wait an hour before trying again." He gave her a chaste kiss and chuckled as he went to unpack a box of books.

"What are we, sixteen?" She opened the box of pictures and knickknacks she'd brought from home and said, "From now on, that subject is *off*-limits between you two."

Jock chuckled and said, "Where do you want this box of photography stuff?"

Tegan pointed to the guest room. "Can you put it in there?"

"You read horror, Tegs?" Jett asked.

She looked over and he held up *It Lies*, the book Jock had written. "That's my copy of Jock's book. He wrote it."

Jett looked at the cover. "It says Jack Steele. Is that a pen name?"

"That's my real name," Jock said as he walked into the room.

"My uncle coined the nickname *Jock* because of how athletic Jock looks."

"Don't believe her," Jock said. "Harvey loved to give me hell. When I first started working with him, he jokingly called me Jock one afternoon, and I told him to never do it again. *Big* mistake. All it did was fuel his fire. From that moment on, he not only called me Jock, but he also introduced me as Jock to everyone. After a while it stuck."

"He's gone now. You could go back to Jack," Jett suggested.

"I could," Jock said. "But Harvey taught me more about life

than you could ever imagine. Sticking with the stupid name is the least I can do."

"Cool," Jett said. "It's not a bad name. Any relation to Reggie or Shea Steele?"

"They're my cousins. You know them?" Jock asked.

"Yeah." Jett nodded. "I've used Reggie's PI services many times, and Shea does PR for my company."

"Small world," Jock said. "Reggie's a trip, and Shea's a bulldog in business, but man, she can talk your ear off in a social setting."

"They're both great. Tegs, mind if I borrow this?" Jett asked. "I'd like to read it."

"No. But it's really creepy."

"I can handle creepy." Jett turned the book over and scanned the back cover. "Number one *New York Times* bestseller for sixteen weeks in a row. Impressive, Steele. What else have you written?"

Tegan and Jock shared a knowing look. She knew how private he was, so she said, "He started caring for Harvey and lost his muse."

Jett looked at Jock, and she could tell he knew there was more to the story.

Jock rubbed the back of his neck with a pinched expression and said, "Actually, I stopped writing before I met Harvey. I lost my girlfriend...and our baby. Harvey's the reason I'm six feet upright instead of six feet under."

"Oh man, I'm sorry." Jett put the book down on the coffee table and said, "I can't imagine what that must have been like."

"You don't want to, believe me." Jock headed for the cottage door and said, "I'm going up to get some of your clothes from the closet, Teg. I'll be back."

After Jock left, Jett said, "I'm sorry. I didn't mean to upset him."

"That's okay. I'm surprised he told you the truth. He didn't tell me until we'd known each other for a couple of years. I've never heard him talk about it any other time, until now. I get the impression it's one of the reasons he doesn't like to go home to Silver Island."

"Maybe she was from the island and he feels guilty. It sort of explains why he trusted me this morning after we talked."

"What do you mean?"

"He's protective of you. He wanted to be sure I knew he was watching out for you. You know, warning me not to hurt you."

"He did?"

"Mm-hm. Don't look so surprised. You said he's like a brother. That's what brothers do. I gave him a very brief glimpse into my past, and I guess he felt a kinship. Sounds like we've each gone through our own form of hell, his being much worse than mine. If you're right about why he doesn't go home, then we have the commonality of trouble with family, too. Poor guy. I'm glad he has you in his life."

They unpacked the boxes and retrieved Tegan's sewing machine and all of her sewing paraphernalia from the house, along with the rest of her clothes. As she unpacked pictures of her family and friends, Jock and Jett checked the locks on the windows and the back door, as if they could have broken in the time since Jock had moved out. *So silly.*

She heard Jett say, "Hey, man, if you're still having trouble finding your muse, I've got investment properties all over the world. You're welcome to stay in any of them."

"Thanks, but I've been traveling, and it doesn't help. I think I'm going to stick around for a while after the wedding."

Tegan peered into the bedroom and said, "On the island?"

Jock shook his head. "That's going to be a short trip, Teg. After the wedding I'll stop in to see my parents, because you know my mother would kill me if I didn't."

"I *love* Shelley!" Tegan exclaimed.

"You've met her?" Jett asked.

"Yes. I've met most of Jock's family, when they'd stop by to visit him over the summers. His mother is the friendliest, warmest, most exuberant person I've ever met. She *loves* to feed people, so you know she and I get along great. And his father is a total silver fox who adores his wife. They're so cute together."

"That pretty much sums them up," Jock agreed.

Jett looked at him curiously and said, "Why not stay there?"

"It's complicated. If I'm ever going to write again, it won't be on the island, that's for sure," Jock explained. "I'm coming back to the Cape after the wedding."

"Great. Can you watch out for Tegs when I'm gone?" Jett asked. "Make sure no one bothers her or shows up when they shouldn't?"

Even though it was flattering to hear how much Jett cared, she said, "I don't need a babysitter."

"That's not what I meant," Jett said as they came into the living room. "This is a big property, and you're out here all alone."

She pulled a picture from the box and set it on the bookcase. "I was in the big house all alone, too. I'm *fine*."

"Sorry, man, but I'm not staying in the house beyond tonight," Jock said. "I'm going to the resort tomorrow to see if I can rent one of the cottages for the summer. But don't worry. There's never been any trouble on the grounds, and there's a state-of-the-art security system in the cottage and the house."

"There is?" Tegan asked.

Jock frowned. "I showed you how to use it. The control panel is behind the painting in the foyer."

"Oh shoot! I forgot all about it. See, Jett? I'll be fine. If there was something to worry about, Jock would know, because nobody knows this house and property like he does." As she said it, she realized how true that was. "*Jock,*" she said in a singsong voice.

"Uh-oh. Here it comes," Jock said. "That's her I-need-a-favor voice."

Jett chuckled.

"I don't *need* it, but I would sure appreciate it. I know you didn't really want to stay here, but since you haven't found your muse yet, if you *could* see your way clear to stick around just until after the opening in August, you could go with me to meet the people who run the children's productions. You know them all, and you know the process for setups and lighting and what could go wrong. In fact, you know *everything* I need to understand, and it would help me earn the trust of those people if you were there. I can't believe I didn't think of that before, but it really would." Her voice escalated excitedly. "Oh, Jock, *please*? If you do this one thing for me, I'll do anything you want! I'll cook your meals, wash your clothes, whatever you want."

"She's right about building trust," Jett said. "That makes smart business sense."

Jock's brows knitted, but a smile curved his lips. "Why do I feel like I'm being railroaded?"

"I don't mean to railroad you, and you can totally say no and I won't be upset. But while I *know* I can handle taking over this business, having you by my side would make it so much less stressful and put the people who have worked with Uncle Harvey for so long much more at ease."

Jock sighed. "*Fine.*"

She threw her arms around his neck. "Thank you!"

"But there are a few caveats," he said firmly.

"Anything. Anything at all!" Tegan promised.

"I've seen you cook, and the thought of you touching my skivvies feels *wrong* on too many levels. So *no* cooking and *no* doing my laundry."

"Fine. *Deal!*"

Jett chuckled.

"And when we're not working, we respect each other's space," Jock added. "I've gotten used to being alone, and as much as I love you, I like my alone time, Teg."

"Deal. No problem. You just made me so happy!" She hugged him again and said, "I'll even try to help you find your muse."

Jock scowled. "*Space*, Tegan. Remember?"

"Space. Got it. Yes. Absolutely," she said, walking backward. "There will be no muse seeking going on." She was so elated, she struggled not to hug him again. In an effort to distract herself, she grabbed the picture and set it on the bookshelf. "See? Back to work, as usual."

Jock shook his head.

Jett leaned in for a kiss. "You're a smart woman, babe." He picked up the frame she'd just put on the shelf and said, "I know this isn't Cici because of the blond hair. Is this Leesa Braden? The one who runs a Girl Power group?"

"I can't believe you remember that," she said.

"I remember everything you've said to me. She has a daughter, Ava. *No.*" Jett shook his head. "Avery! That's what it is. She's married to Cole, a doctor, and she met him when she sweet-talked the last cranberry-walnut muffin out of his hands for you, and then she won Cole in a bachelor auction." He reached into the box and picked up a picture of Tegan, Cici, and Melody. "And this has to be Melly and Cici. You have a cast on your ankle. Is this when Cici reconnected with Cooper?"

Tegan closed her gaping jaw, as shocked as she was touched, and said, "Did you take notes?" He had truly listened to everything while she'd rambled on about family and friends. She'd thought he had, but she couldn't be sure if it was hopeful thinking or the real thing.

Jock patted her on the shoulder and said, "Better watch out, Tegan. You won't be able to slip anything by elephant brain over here."

"No kidding," she said softly.

"I'm going to grab that box of love letters and a shovel. Meet you guys by the garden?" Jock asked.

Tegan had told Jett about the letters they'd found and that she wanted to bury them by Adele's ashes. She was glad that he was there. She had a feeling she and Jock might both need a little extra support tonight.

"Sure. We'll be right there," Jett said.

Jett set the picture on the shelf and took Tegan's hand in his, drawing her into his arms, and said, "I might be slow on the uptake with regard to understanding and acting on everything that's happening between us, but from the moment I met you, I have listened to every word you've said. I've thought about your stories, the look in your eyes as you shared them, and the way each one has helped mold you into the woman that you are. Don't ever doubt that. It's why I'm here, Tegs. I can't shake you off, and I don't want to."

He touched his lips to hers, and she held on tight, sure she'd melt into a puddle of goo if she didn't.

Chapter Twenty-One

USUALLY JETT WAS wide-eyed at five thirty in the morning, but wakefulness crept in one sensation at a time Friday morning. He became aware of Tegan's warm body draped along his, her arm resting on his chest. Her summery scent floated around them, and her sweet breath warmed his skin. He didn't want to move a muscle as last night played out in his head like a movie. Tegan and Jock had said their goodbyes to Harvey and then they'd buried the wooden box of letters in the garden beside a rosebush Jock told them Harvey had loved, and they'd marked the location with several large stones, which Tegan set out in the shape of a heart. She'd said she wished she could have buried Berta there, too. Jett had never felt anything when he'd upgraded vehicles, but the pain in her voice was so real, he'd wanted to get her car and let her do just that. Hell, he'd wanted to have a freaking eulogy and ceremony for the damn car. They'd had dinner with Jock at the big house, and they'd had a great time washing away all her sadness with good conversation and laughter. He'd forgotten what it was like to spend time with friends just for the fun of it and realized how much he'd missed it.

He pressed a kiss to Tegan's head and rested his cheek there, thinking about when they'd come back to the cottage alone and had finished going through her boxes. She'd told him stories about every single item, from pictures to trinkets. She seemed to love each one of them. She continued telling him tales as they set up her photography and sewing rooms, hanging tapestries she'd made, pictures of her niece and nephew dancing in the rain with her, and three strings of colorful flags with letters on them that spelled LAUGH, SHARE, and INSPIRE. Finally, they'd set up her bedroom.

He opened his eyes, blinking several times at the slice of sunlight streaming in from the sliver of space between the curtains. What time was it? Panic flared in his chest. He needed to check his email. He'd checked it a few times yesterday, and again last night, but he knew what waited for him every morning. Details of possible investments, updates on current projects, client issues, and a hundred other items that would require immediate attention. He also needed to make sure he hadn't fucked things up too badly with EBC by rescheduling his meetings to next week.

But as his gaze trailed over the tiny colorful lights they'd strung around the ceiling, he didn't move. His anxiety about work was nudged to the side by a pang of desire to wake up with Tegan in his arms and see *that* bedroom more often, to make love to her *there*, and fall asleep naked and sated, as they had last night. He wanted to see her life in Maryland, to walk on the beaches she'd told him about, visit her favorite places, meet her family, Leesa, and her other friends. He wanted to take her to New York and spend the day with her sister's family and see her with her niece and nephew. He wanted to see her spreading her light around those she loved in the same way she'd done in every room of the cozy cottage, when she'd made the cottage *hers.*

Just like you spread your light on me...

He ran his hand down her hip, kissing her head again as he glanced into her closet. She'd hung her clothing haphazardly, mixing shirts in with dresses, pants, and jackets. There was no rhyme or reason, so different from his own organized closet, with suits and dress shirts arranged by color. He shifted his gaze to the dresser, where a basket overflowed with brushes, scarves, an ereader, and Lord only knew what else. He liked all of her quirks and the way her clever, creative mind worked in uniquely *Tegan* ways. Beside the basket was the wooden box Harvey had given her when she was sixteen. Jett imagined her as a nervous teen leaving her uncle's house with a set of car keys and returning after her adventure to the gallery confident and ready to take on the world. He wished he'd had a chance to get to know the man who'd had such an impact on his girl.

My girl.

Man, he liked the sound of that. He'd never imagined how good it could feel to care about a woman like he was growing to care about Tegan, much less that he'd ever want a relationship. Even the thought used to bring forth not-in-this-lifetime comments. But now his right arm was numb beneath Tegan's head and she'd drooled on his chest, and there was no place on earth he'd rather be than exactly where he was. He kissed her again, surprised by how many times he'd done it since he'd woken up. It took no thought to show Tegan affection, because for the first time ever, he was letting his heart lead him instead of his head. It was as terrifying as it was complicated and wonderful, and he hoped like hell that he could pull it off better than his father had.

He reached for his phone, careful not to jostle her as he

unlocked the screen. Holy shit, it was *nine thirty*. He thumbed through emails one-handed, fighting the urge to get on his feet and down to business.

Tegan snuggled closer, making a sleepy sound.

Fucking hell.

He sifted through emails again, looking more closely at the specific issues, his mind chasing every one of them. He should get up and work for the next few hours, *then* spend time with Tegan. He knew he should do it, but no part of him wanted to. He thumbed out a text to Tia. *Can you handle my emails today? Review, respond to buy me time, and text urgent matters.*

His arm dropped to the mattress, and the phone lit up a minute later with Tia's response. *Are you with Tegan?*

He typed *Yes.*

She responded immediately with a celebration emoji and then a meme of the cast of *Seinfeld* doing a happy dance, and finally, *I'll do it for a selfie of the two of you.*

He thumbed out, *Don't fuck with me.* She responded with, *That's Tegan's job* followed by a winking emoji and then, *SELFIE or the answer is NO.* He replied, *SHE'S SLEEPING! I'll send it later.* She sent back two lines of emojis with heart eyes and a thumbs-up.

She was as pesky as he imagined a younger sister would be, but he was lucky to have her. He set his phone down and wrapped his other hand around Tegan, feeling knotted up and relieved at once.

Tegan stretched, pressing her breasts and thighs against him and turning her beautiful, sleepy eyes up to his. "You're still here."

"Did you think I'd take off?" Christ, he must really suck at this relationship stuff.

"No. I had a nightmare that I woke up to a note that said you had to get to Louisiana and you'd *see me around*."

He rolled her onto her back, moving over her, and said, "I'm here, babe, and I'm all yours. I asked Tia to handle things today. I know you're gaining access to the new website today for beta testing, and I'm sure you have other things you need to take care of, so if you want me out of your hair, I'll knock out a few emails. But I'd like to check out the website with you."

"I think you need to send Tia an Edible Arrangement."

"I pay her well, and besides, she bribed me. I have to send her a selfie of us."

"So fun! I officially *love* her!" A stunning smile spread across Tegan's face. "Did you really put off work for the whole day?"

"Almost. After I decided to come see you, I called Mitchell and asked him to set up a meeting with some of the other business owners in Hyannis. I'm meeting them tonight at seven thirty."

Her eyes widened. "You're going to help them? Oh, Jett, I'm so happy! I was worrying about Mitchell and the other business owners having to delay their openings and lose all that money from the season. Your mom told me how devastating that would be for not only the owners, but their employees, too."

"Don't get your hopes too high, sunshine. I'm not sure how much I have time for or what I can do. This is a preliminary meeting. I'm gathering information and thinking about options."

"I get it, but it's a start. Remember how you were stressed over leaving after the storm? That big heart of yours couldn't let it all go."

"It couldn't let *you* go, that's for sure," he said, kissing her chin.

"Or *them*." She wound her arms around his neck and said, "I think we should celebrate. Unless you're too tired. Did you sleep okay, or have you been up half the night?"

After they'd finished unpacking last night, Tegan had noticed how tired he was from traveling overnight, and she'd suggested they cuddle on the couch and watch a movie. Jett wasn't a cuddler, but he'd loved cuddling with Tegan. Hell, he'd loved *unpacking boxes* with her; of course he was into lying on the couch spooning her as they watched a movie. At least they'd started the evening that way, but as usual, their tender kisses and caresses had turned to unstoppable desire. They'd ended up naked, sweaty, and satisfied and were fast asleep in each other's arms by eleven o'clock.

"That spell you cast is still hanging on. I slept late." He trailed kisses down her neck. "But even if I'd stayed up all night, I'd still have energy for *you*." He dragged his tongue over her nipple, earning a sexy sigh.

She bowed beneath him, rocking against his arousal. He covered her nipple with his mouth, sucking gently. She writhed and mewled as he kissed his way to her other breast, savoring her hungry sounds. He worked his way down her body, loving every dip and curve from breasts to thighs.

"You're so fucking beautiful," he murmured against her inner thigh as he spread her legs.

He licked and kissed all around the very heart of her, using his fingers to tease her wetness. She whimpered and pleaded for more. He slipped two fingers inside her slick heat and pressed his tongue to the cleft of her sex.

"Oh *God*," she panted out, digging her heels into the mattress. "This is *so* much better than video chat."

He chuckled and lifted his face to see her laughing. He nipped at the tender skin of her inner thigh, earning a giggling *yelp*. When he lowered his mouth, he turned those adorable giggles into moans of pleasure. He licked and loved her fast and deep, then slow and torturously, repeating the pattern until she was at the verge of release, her entire body trembling. He held her on the cusp of climax, savoring her needy sounds, her sweet taste, and her body reaching, wanting, *begging* for release. He intensified his efforts, bringing his fingers into play where she needed them most, giving her everything she wanted. A string of erotic sounds flew from her lungs as she came apart, clawing at his shoulders. *Marking* him.

When she finally came down from the peak, she panted out, "More, more, *more!*"

He dragged his fingers and palm along her glistening sex, getting his hand nice and wet. She opened her eyes, watching as he rose onto his knees and stroked his throbbing cock. She bit her lower lip, her lustful gaze never leaving his hand as he worked himself tight and slow. She reached between her legs, touching herself. Holy hell, she was a fucking *goddess*.

"I need your mouth on me, baby."

She pushed up to her elbows, and he shook his head.

"Stay down, sunshine. I want to go *deep*, and I'm nowhere *near* done feasting on you."

He straddled her shoulders and came down over her, pressing a single kiss to her sex.

"Yes," she whispered as she fisted his cock, guiding it to her mouth.

"Stroke me tight as you suck me. I want to *feel* like I'm inside you as I devour you."

She gripped his cock like a vise, sucking and stroking as he used teeth, hands, and tongue to drive her wild. Her moans vibrated around his shaft, sending mind-numbing sensations racing through his core. She grabbed his hip with one hand, pulling him in deeper. His cock hit the back of her throat, and he withdrew to keep from hurting her, but she slammed his hips down, taking him to the root and holding him there. *Message received, loud and clear.* His girl wanted control, and he was happy to give it to her. He pushed two fingers inside her, and she worked him faster, squeezed him tighter. He returned the favor with fervor, pumping his fingers in and out of her. She rode his hand as she sucked harder, but stroked slower, creating a dizzying rhythm that made it difficult for him to think straight. But he was determined to make her come again. He slid his other hand beneath her and lifted her hips, focusing on the bundle of nerves that made her toes curl. She spread her legs wider, grinding against his mouth.

Oh yeah, his girl liked that.

Her muscles flexed and her hips shot up. Bullets of lust bolted down his spine as she cried out around his cock. Her sex pulsed tight and hot around his fingers, and she gripped his cock even tighter, sending him crashing into his release. His hips pistoned fast and hard. But she didn't turn away, didn't slow her efforts, swallowing everything he had to give while in the clutches of her own intense climax.

Fucking. Perfect.

When the last aftershock shuddered through them, he fell onto the bed beside her and wiped his mouth. Then he gathered her limp body in his arms as the world slowly filtered back in.

"You destroy me, sunshine…"

She made a sweet sound and yawned sleepily.

"Did I hurt you?" He caressed her jaw, hoping he hadn't

been too rough.

She shook her head and whispered, "So good."

She snuggled into the curve of his body, and he kissed her shoulder, her neck, and stroked her hair. He lay holding her for a long time, caressing her back, hips, and face. He was filled with a deep desire to take care of her, to bring her pleasure in ways that weren't sexual. Because *this*—holding her, being trusted by her—was *everything*.

He kissed her cheek and said, "How about I run a hot bath?"

"Only if you're getting in with me."

"I wouldn't have it any other way."

JETT MASTERS KNEW how to spoil a woman in *and* out of bed.

The most luxurious bath Tegan had ever experienced had turned into the most hilarious one. She and Jett had taken their time bathing each other, and Jett had said the sweetest things, making her feel all sorts of good and special. Then they'd washed each other's hair, which hadn't gone quite as smoothly. After making horns and mohawks with their hair, Tegan got soap in Jett's eyes, and her efforts to rinse it out led to soap in *her* eyes. They ended up in fits of hysterics and had to get into the shower to finally get clean. Now they were sitting at the kitchen table, and Jett was studying her new website, taking notes, and making suggestions. It felt incredible to see months of her and Harper's dreams and plans coming to fruition. She couldn't wait to start placing ads and getting their name out there.

As great as that felt, it was equally wonderful to see Jett solely focused on the site, as if *she* were his most important client.

"What do you think?" he asked.

"About what? Sorry. I must have been daydreaming."

He leaned closer and kissed her. "Daydreaming? Now, there's something I've never done. What's it like?"

She climbed from her chair onto his lap. Her arms circled his neck and she said, "Well, first you need to be emotionally and physically too blissed out to think straight."

"My girl did that to me already."

"*My girl,*" she whispered. "I can't believe you just said that. I never thought I'd have this with you."

"Me either. But it's not like I have a choice in the matter. I'm going to start calling you Tabitha because of your bewitching powers." He kissed the tip of her nose. "Now, tell me about daydreaming. I seriously do not get it."

"Oh, come on. Surely you've daydreamed. What were you thinking when you were blissed out?"

"*Damn, that was awesome.*"

"You're such a *guy*. Maybe you can't daydream, because that's when you would have probably done it. I was lying in your arms listening to your heartbeat, reveling in the feel of your arms around me and the warmth of our bodies. I wondered if you felt as close to me as I felt to you, or if you were just thinking about the sex. Well...you've answered that question, haven't you?"

She started to get off his lap, and he tugged her back down. She rolled her eyes and said, "It's okay, Jett. I get it. It was hot, and girls and guys aren't on the same wavelength. It's not a big deal. I'm not mad or anything."

"It *is* a big deal, but it was a lot to wrestle with. I'm still wrestling with it."

"What? Hot sex?"

"No, Tegs. How much being that lost in you changed me. How ever since the night I told you about my father, we've connected on a different level."

"If you make a smart-ass remark about my mouth, I *will* slap you."

"We should patent your mouth," he said, and quickly leaned away, preemptively dodging a slap. Then his eyes turned serious, and he said, "When we're close like that, it's a little overwhelming. My mind goes places with us that I wouldn't even know *how* to get to."

"Sexual places?"

"With you? Always, but that's not what I mean. Other places, emotional places."

"I like the sound of that, but are you just saying it to make me feel like I wasn't alone in my mushiness?"

"I'm a lot of things, but I'm not a liar, especially not with you."

"Then you *did* daydream." She touched his face, and he leaned into her hand the way she loved. "And you daydreamed about *us*, which is a bonus. Does that mean I can call you my *boyfriend*?"

He flashed a cocky grin and said, "Babe, after what you did to me this morning, you can call me anything you want."

"I swear you're about ten people all wrapped up in one: an arrogant businessman, a filthy-talking lover, a cocky boy-friend—and *yes*, I'm staking claim—a confused and angry son, a thoughtful friend…"

"That's only five."

"I'm sure there are more. I'm banking those empty spots until I figure them out." Her stomach growled, and she covered it with her hand. "We forgot to eat!"

"Funny, I remember a feast."

She swatted his arm and popped to her feet, pulling him up beside her. "You've done enough helping me for today. The website can wait until Sunday when you're gone. I'll need to keep busy so I don't lose my mind anyway."

"I told you last night that I'm coming back next Friday before I go to London. I'll need my Tegan fix."

"I know, but it'll still seem like forever when we're apart. With the time difference and your work schedule, we won't be able to have our nightly video chats."

"We'll figure it out."

"I'm counting on it," she said, tugging him toward the door. "Let's go on an adventure."

"What kind of adventure? It's pretty gray outside."

"Scared of a little gray sky, Mr. Masters? It seems like gray skies, clear or cloudy, are about all we're going to get on the Cape this time of year. But I don't think even a gray sky could dampen the first ever Jett and Tegan adventure. We'll take turns choosing where to go. You start." She pulled on knee-high leather boots over her leggings, and her stomach growled again.

"Sundial Café," he said as he grabbed her coat and helped her put it on. "Where we first met."

"*That* would be the gas station. We could stop for some beef jerky."

"I've got your beef jerky right here." He hauled her against him and kissed her.

"I just figured out number six," she said as they left the

cottage. "*Fuckable flirt.* Maybe you can borrow my mask from the bachelorette party."

"*You're* wearing that mask tonight, darlin'."

"Well see," she said sassily. "I kind of like the idea of you masked and on your knees."

The sinful look in his eyes stopped her in her tracks. He closed the gap between them and grabbed her ass, holding her against him. His eyes drilled into her, and in a husky, sexy voice, he said, "I want you to think about me on my knees, masked and naked, doing everything you ask. Think about it *all day*, so by the time we get back, you're good and ready to be taken every way you can think of."

Holy moly...

He sauntered away to open the car door as if he hadn't left her frozen in place, salivating over images of him masked and on his knees...

Chapter Twenty-Two

"COME ON, BEFORE we miss our chance!" Tegan pulled Jett toward the go-karts at Skull Island Adventure Golf and Sports World in South Yarmouth.

They handed their tickets to the bearded man running the go-karts, and Tegan said, "Hi. I'm Tegan and this is Jett. This looks so fun! How long have you worked here?"

The guy eyed Jett, and Jett just grinned. After their visit to the Sundial Café this morning, he knew there was nothing he could say to stop her curiosity, and he wouldn't want to. She'd talked to the other couple who was having breakfast at the café for more than half an hour, and when Rowan had brought their food, he'd joined their conversation, too. He had raved about how much Joni loved her costume, and said she'd even worn it to school. He'd sat with them for a few minutes, and Jett had enjoyed getting to know him. Rowan was an insightful guy, and Jett had learned that he was also from Silver Island. His family ran one of the marinas and most of his family still lived there. Jett and Rowan had exchanged numbers, and Jett was looking forward to talking with him again.

"Couple years," the guy answered.

"Do you like it? I bet it's fun seeing all the different people."

She asked him for tips and tricks to driving the go-karts and about how busy they got in the summer, and then she hiked a thumb at Jett and said, "Thanks. Now you can watch me beat this hotshot."

"You're a trip. You talk to everyone," he said as they headed for the go-karts.

"We're on an *adventure*! Adventures are about exploring our surroundings, investing in them, and experiencing everything they have to offer. Including beating you in this race." She went up on her toes and kissed him. She waved at a red go-kart and said, "Get ready to lose, Masters. Berta 2.0 is about to leave you in the dust."

"Dream on, sunshine." He blew her a kiss and climbed into the black go-kart parked next to hers.

Jett hadn't realized how competitive Tegan was. He beat her by a nose their first round, and she insisted on trying a second one. When they'd tied, she'd demanded a third. He thought about letting her win, but he had a feeling she'd know if he did. He gave it his all, but his girl had learned the track, and she beat him by about three seconds.

"Woo-hoo!" she hollered as she climbed from her kart, beaming brighter than the sun. "Told you I'd beat you."

Jett swept her into his arms and kissed her smiling lips.

His phone rang with Tia's ringtone. He reached for it, then remembered what Tegan had said about answering calls when he had a woman on his arm. "Sorry, babe, but this is Tia. I should get it."

"Oh! Can I say hi?"

She looked so excited, he couldn't say no. He handed her the phone.

She answered the call and said, "Hi, Tia? This is Tegan.

Thank you *so* much for helping Jett today!"

Only Tegan would answer the call as if they were old friends, and for some strange reason, that made him even more crazy about her.

"Uh-huh," Tegan said, her eyes dancing with mischief. "Okay. I totally understand." She paused, listening. "I know, *right?* Well, you'll be happy to know I just creamed his butt on go-karts." She flashed a cheesy smile at Jett, listening again. "Yes, *go-karts*. We're at an adventure park."

By the look on Tegan's face, he was sure Tia was wondering what drugs Tegan had given him.

"Okay, I'll let him know. Thanks, Tia. I hope I can meet you someday."

Jett held his hand out for the phone, and Tegan mouthed, *One sec.*

"That sounds great! I'd love it. Thanks again. I'll do it right now, promise!" She ended the call.

"You *ended* the call?"

"Uh-huh. She said your flight is set for Sunday, and she booked you to come back here next Friday evening. She also said you probably forgot your suit for the wedding and to text her if you want her to FedEx it. She's amazing. Come here; we have to take a picture." She sidled up to him and took a selfie. She handed him the phone and said, "Can you send that to Tia and give her my number? And can you send me a copy of the picture and her number?"

"Why do you need her number?"

"She and her friend Becca might come up this summer and we're going to try to get together. You don't mind, do you?"

"Um..." *Did he?* Hell, he didn't know, but the idea of his work and personal lives colliding felt strange. Tegan was looking at him with those trusting, happy eyes, and *strange* no longer felt like such a bad thing. "No, it's fine."

"Are you sure? I should have asked. I'm sorry. I wanted to thank her for helping you out today, and then we just clicked. But if it bothers you, I totally get it. I'll back off. *Promise.* I have a tendency to act first and ask questions later."

She wrinkled her nose, and damn if his chest didn't squeeze.

"It's fine. Come here." He pulled her into a hug. "I'm glad you two talked. You probably just saved me an inquisition."

"You'd better send the selfie. She said if she didn't have it in ten minutes, she was canceling next Friday's flight. I like her. She's ballsy."

"Reminds me of someone else I know," he said as he sent the text to Tia. "Is that why she called? The selfie and the flights?"

"I think so. Oh, she said to tell you that she had everything else under control and that you should take time off more often."

He texted the selfie and Tia's number to Tegan's phone and said, "Yeah, that can't really happen."

"I know," she said softly.

There was no disappointment in her voice, but she couldn't hide it from showing in her eyes. "Sorry, babe. I'm heading into a crucial time with the London deal."

As if a light switch had been flicked, her eyes brightened and she said, "I know. Don't worry about it. Come on. I'd like to show you the real reason I wanted to bring you here."

She dragged him across the lot and said, "I know how much you loved baseball, and it sounded like it had been a while, so…" They walked around a building, and batting cages came into view. "I thought I could watch my boyfriend do his thing."

His heart swelled, and he felt a little choked up. "People I've known my whole life haven't tried to get me to pick up a bat since high school." He pulled her into his arms and said, "You've known me for *ten minutes*, and you brought me *here*. You are unlike anyone I've ever known."

"That makes two of us. See? You're my perfect partner." Her eyes widened and she said, "I'm feeling lucky today. That's number seven on my list of what you are. My perfect partner."

He knew he wasn't perfect, much less partner material in business or in his personal life. He was too controlling in business and too broken personally. He had no idea how he'd gone from wanting exclusivity with Tegan to being deemed her *perfect partner*. But when she looked at him with those faith-filled baby blues, he wanted to figure it the fuck out.

"Come on, hotshot," she said. "Show your girl what you can do with a baseball bat. I'll try not to drool while I imagine you in tight baseball pants."

God she was amazing. "Remind me never to take you to a game." He gave her a quick kiss and headed into the batting cage, ready to blow his girl away.

Tegan cheered for him like he was on the field, and her energy made him feel like a superstar. Jett hadn't felt that good about himself since he was a little kid, before his father had left. After hitting dozens of balls, he brought Tegan in for a turn. She was about as coordinated with a bat as she was at dancing, but that made it even more fun. He stood behind her, positioned her hands on the bat, and tried to teach her to hit the ball, but she kept wiggling her ass against him, making him hard. They laughed and kissed, and she finally hit a few balls before they made their way around the rest of the park. They played the best of three rounds of mini golf and spent enough money to buy the entire arcade just to win two teddy bears, because after Jett had won one, Tegan said the bear would be lonely unless it had a friend. He had a feeling she just liked to watch him get frustrated every time he failed to win and then tease him out of it with kisses and cuteness. It wasn't a hardship. They'd eaten enough corn dogs, funnel cakes, and popcorn to last a lifetime, and as they climbed into the car, it felt like they'd spent a weekend at the park. A gloriously happy and romantic weekend.

Tegan rested her head back against the seat and said, "That was so fun. It's your turn to choose our next adventure."

He leaned across the console and said, "I choose you." He threaded his hand into her hair, drawing her closer, and kissed her breathless.

"Wow," she said softly. "The man can *kiss*."

"The *woman* can kiss, too. I've never laughed as much as I do with you, Tegs, and I can't remember the last time I didn't think about work all day."

"I know. Tia texted me about an hour ago to ask if I was really a murderer who had done away with you, because she'd never gone this long without hearing from you."

"I don't know if the two of you being friends is a good thing or if it'll make my life hell."

She wrinkled her nose again—*so fucking cute*—and said, "Probably both. You'd better choose our next destination so you're not late for your meeting. I'm not done adventuring."

He shifted back to the driver's seat, his old haunt suddenly appearing in his mind. He hadn't thought about that place for years, and now, as he tried to figure out where to take her, he could think of nothing else. "Buckle up, baby."

As Jett drove to Wellfleet and down streets he hadn't been

on for almost a decade, anxiety prickled his limbs. He glanced at Tegan, gazing out the window like just *being* made her happy, and that anxiety slipped away. He didn't understand how seeing her, or being with her, helped calm his demons, but maybe there were some things he didn't have to understand to accept.

He reached for her hand, holding it as he drove down the secluded road, shielded from the rest of the world by woods and brush. He parked at the dead end, in front of the dune, and got out to open Tegan's door, taking in the wild rose, beach plum, and other bushes and foliage that had grown immensely since he'd last been there several years ago. In a few weeks there would be splashes of pink flowers and red berries. Dune grasses would fill out and birds would nest. *Tegan would love that.* Hell, she'd probably make a birdhouse for them.

"Where are we?" she asked as she stepped from the car.

"An old haunt of mine. Come on." He took her hand, leading her toward a narrow space between two waist-high bushes.

"Are we allowed to be here? There's a no-trespassing sign. We could get in trouble."

"Scared of a little trouble, Adventure Girl?" he asked as he helped her up the dune, holding back prickly bushes to clear the way.

"I don't know. Do you know the owner? I think you can get in big trouble for trespassing."

"I know who owns this place. Sometimes he can be a bit of a prick, but I have a feeling you'll know what to do if he gets upset."

When they reached the clearing at the top of the dune, Tegan gazed out at the expansive view of Cape Cod Bay and said, "Jett," full of wonder. "Is that the bay or the ocean?"

"It's the bay." He placed one hand on her hip and pointed

across the water to their right. "Out that way is Provincetown." He pointed in the other direction and said, "The resort is over there, and your property is down the coast, past Eastham and Orleans and inland a bit."

"This is amazing. It's so private. How'd you find this place?"

"I happened upon it when I was a teenager. I didn't want to go home after a baseball game, so I drove around and ended up on the road that leads here. It felt like it led to someplace no one would ever go, like forgotten land, the perfect place to escape. That's what kept me coming back. This place was a godsend."

"Your secret hiding place." She slid her arm around his waist and rested her head against him. "I wish I'd known you then. We could have gone on adventures together instead."

"You wouldn't have liked me, Tegs. *I* didn't like myself back then. I didn't like *anyone*."

"Not even your mom? Your brothers?"

"I don't know," he said. "I didn't *dislike* them. I was pissed at my parents and angry at my brothers for not holding our father's back against a wall."

"What about Drake and Rick?"

"Before they lost their dad, I think I was probably a little jealous of all of my friends for not having to deal with the same shit I did. But when they lost their dad...we were all a mess."

"That's understandable."

"I don't know if it's understandable or not, but I pulled away from everyone except my grandmother."

"Why not your grandmother? What made her different?"

She gazed up at him without judgment, and he could have thanked her for that. He'd felt judged for so long, he was sick of it even though he knew he deserved it. "My grandmother didn't gloss over what my father had done. She acknowledged the anger and pain he'd caused. She eventually forgave him, but she never pushed me to do the same."

"Maybe she thought if she did, she'd lose you, too."

No one had ever suggested that before, and as he thought about it, the idea felt raw and sharp. It felt *wrong*. But he wasn't a stupid man, and even though he didn't want to believe it, he knew she might be right.

"Grandparents see everything from a different perspective," Tegan said sweetly. "It must have been hard to have such a special connection with your father, learning baseball, collecting cards together, and then to feel like you were left behind. I never had that type of special bond with my parents. I love them, and we're *close*, but if my uncle had suddenly stopped seeing me over the summers, I would have been heartbroken."

Jett had always known what he'd felt when his father had left was bigger than anger, but he hadn't been able to define it. *Heartbroken* was the emotion he'd never been able to name. Tegan embraced him, and she didn't say anything more. She didn't have to. She'd already given him the missing piece of his fucked-up puzzle of a life he'd never realized he was missing.

She looked up at him and said, "I bet on some level your grandmother wanted to make up for all that your father had done because it was her son who had done it, even if he left for good reasons. But also, she's your *grandmother*. She loves you, and she knows how amazing you are apart from whatever trouble you're having moving forward with your dad. You guys are obviously trying, and I'm sure she's proud of you both for that."

But was he proud of himself? He knew he could try harder. "I've spent a lifetime avoiding personal connections, but you make me want to be a better man, Tegs. You make me want to live a fuller life, a *better* life, beyond the world I've created for myself."

"For a guy who tries not to make personal connections, you're pretty good at the boyfriend thing. I know how little time you have, and you've already done more than I ever thought you would for us. We're on an *adventure*, and you haven't been tied to your phone or stressing over work like everyone warned me you would be. And soon you're going to be in a room with people you grew up with, people you *didn't* turn your back on when you got on that plane after the storm. They're probably scared and confused about where to turn next, and you've pushed business meetings aside, you're pushing *us* aside tonight, to make time for *them*. I know you said not to get my hopes up about you helping them, but even meeting with those people could give them hope or direction. All those things say so much about who you are and the connections you hold dear. You are a hell of a man, Jett, and I'm sure if you and your father want it bad enough, you'll find your way back to solid ground. It might never be what it was, or what your family wishes you had with him, but that's okay. All that matters is that you and your father are happy with wherever you end up."

He was too mystified by her insight to respond.

"So, tell me," she said, looking around. "Is this hiding place *yours*? Are you the owner? Because Emery mentioned that you owned property on the Cape."

"Yeah, babe. It's mine."

"What do you plan to do with it?"

"Nothing. I just wanted to own it. I haven't even been back here since I purchased it several years ago."

"Do you want to know what I think?" she asked, walking

along the edge of the dune grass.

"Always."

"I think you never found the answers you were searching for when you were a kid, so you used all that anger and heartbreak to fuel your success, and from what I've heard, you succeeded beyond everyone's expectations, maybe even your own." She walked toward him, the wind lifting the ends of her hair. "You've proved to your father and everyone else that nothing can hold you down. But you never figured out all that crap between you and your dad, and this gorgeous property, your hiding place, holds all those emotions and questions that you struggled with as a teenager. You got them out of your *head* enough to carry on, but they never sailed away. They're buried in the very ground we're standing on." She grabbed both sides of his jacket collar and spoke in a hushed, conspiratorial tone as she said, "Maybe, just *maybe*, you thought that one day you'd come back and find those answers *here*."

"You think you're pretty clever, don't you? That planting all that stuff in my head will make me think about it and work harder to figure things out."

She bounced on her toes and said, "A girl can hope."

He had to laugh, because his beautiful pixie knew just how to get to him.

"But I guess there's always the chance that you just wanted to *own* this property like everything else you've bought. Because if there's a mountain, Jett Masters wants to climb it!" She patted his chest and said, "Whatever the reason, I'm really glad that you took me here. I like getting to know *teenage Jett*. I still wish I had known that brooding kid who kicked ass in baseball. I bet we would have had fun together despite all the stuff you were dealing with."

"You make everything sound so easy."

"Not *easy*, just *possible*. After I lost my uncle, I realized we had all those weeks together over the summers, and they were amazing, but I still wish we had more time together. It wasn't *enough*." Sadness rose in her eyes. "I miss him."

Jett reached for her hand and said, "I know you do. I'm sorry, babe."

"It's fine," she said with the smile that always seemed at the ready—for herself and for others. "I'm *supposed* to miss him. I *loved* him. I don't want to push you in one direction or another where your family or your father are concerned. Whatever you do or don't do has to be your choice. But if I learned one thing from my uncle's death, it's that once a person is gone, *that's it*. All we have are memories, good or bad. You've been wrestling with this for a long time with no answers in sight. Maybe you should ask yourself a really awful question. If you found out today that your father was going to die tomorrow and you'd *never* see him again, that you'd run out of time to figure out what *you* wanted or how to get back into each other's good graces, would all that water under the bridge that you've been drowning in still be enough to keep you away? Or would you swim with everything you had and risk going under just for a chance to salvage whatever you could with the father you once adored?"

Before he could wrap his head around the images she'd painted, she spun on her heel and said, "Do we have time for one last adventure before your meeting? Because I could sure use some fried clams and ice cream."

And just like that, she shared her light, leading him out of the darkness.

WITH A BELLY full of clams and ice cream and a heart full of *Jett*, Tegan raced him to the car in the parking lot of Arnold's Lobster and Clam Bar. They'd lost track of time and were running late. She flew into her seat and tugged on her seat belt, saying, "Go, go, go!" but Jett was one step ahead, already turning onto Route 6 and speeding toward the highway. As he put on his seat belt, she rested her head back and said, "Will we make it?"

"If traffic isn't bad, we should get there right on time." He reached for her hand. "Today was incredible."

"So fun," she agreed, thanking the stars above that he didn't hate her after her thoughts about him and his father had tumbled out. He'd been quiet on the way to Arnold's, and she'd wondered if she'd just cut their relationship off at the knees. But when they were waiting in line, he'd put his arms around her from behind and kissed her cheek. From that moment on, he'd been his charming self.

"I'm sorry that I don't have time to drop you at home, but you can take the car and I'll take an Uber back to your place when I'm done."

"How long do you think you'll be?"

"I don't know. It could take an hour, or it might take two or three. It depends on how things go and what direction I decide to move in."

"I think I'll go into town and explore. I've really only seen the one block where Mitchell's store is. Chloe told me about a few shops at the mall I'd like to check out. Maybe I'll drive around and find your old school so I can try to spot the tree under which Katie Garland stole your first kiss in elementary school."

He squeezed her hand again and said, "When you and I kissed, it was like there was never anyone before you."

"You are such a charmer."

He waggled his brows.

They arrived at Mitchell's house at seven thirty on the dot. "Good luck!" Tegan said as he handed her the car keys.

"I don't need luck, babe. This is business. If I want it to happen, it will." He kissed her and said, "I need to figure out if the people running the businesses are smart enough and eager enough to carry out what's needed to turn bigger profits and how much time I can spare to teach them."

"*Oh.* I thought it was about helping them save their stores. But I guess they go hand in hand. You're not in the business of losing money."

"That's right." He winked, and she watched him walk up to the door. He embraced a woman who she assumed was Mitchell's wife and went inside.

She was debating where to go first when Jett's father's car came down the street, stopping beside her.

Sherry rolled down her window and said, "Tegan, what a nice surprise. What are you doing here?"

Tegan bent down to see Jett's father, and she noticed an elderly, white-haired woman in the back seat watching her with interest. "Jett has a meeting with Mitchell and some of the other business owners whose properties were damaged in the storm."

"Does he?" his father said.

"We didn't even know he was in town," Sherry said.

"It was spur of the moment. I'm sure he was planning to call you," she said, even though she had no idea whether he was planning to call them or not. "But we've been out all day, and we were running late from dinner, which is why I'm here. We didn't have time for him to drop me off, so I was just going to head into town and keep myself busy until he was done."

The woman in the back seat leaned forward and said, "You won't find anything more interesting in town than the three of us. I'm Jett's grandmother Rose, and I'd *love* a chance to get to know you. Why don't you join us?"

Tegan glanced at Mitchell's house, conflicted. She didn't want to upset Jett by spending time with his family, and she definitely didn't want to get into a situation where she was expected to talk about *him*. But at the same time, she liked his parents and she was curious about his grandmother.

"Rose made cherry pie," Sherry said.

"That sounds delicious." Tegan put a hand on her stomach. "But I just ate fried clams and ice cream. I couldn't eat another bite, but I'll come in for a few minutes."

"Climb in, honey," Rose said, and Tegan sat beside her on the way up to the house.

Jett's father helped Rose inside, though she moved quite spryly. She was petite and funny, teasing him about treating her like an old woman. Inside, they hung up their coats and went into the living room. Jett's father offered them drinks, which Tegan and Sherry declined.

"I'd love a glass of wine." Rose looked at Tegan and said, "Good for the heart, you know." She sat on the couch and patted the cushion beside her. "Sit here, honey. Emmie told me about what you're doing with the amphitheater. I think it's wonderful. I want to hear all about you and those spicy romantic comedies you're going to be hosting. But first, *where* did you get those sexy boots? My friend Mags would kill for them. Sherry would look nice in them, too. Wouldn't she, Douglas? Remember how cute she was in those white go-go boots when she was younger?"

Jett's father gave his wife a heated look and said, "How could I forget? Sherry still has the nicest legs around."

Sherry blushed. "Where did you say you got them, Tegan?"

"I think I got them back home at Chelsea's Boutique, where I do seamstress work."

"Did you hear that, Sherry? She *sews*." Rose lowered her voice a little and said, "That means you're good with your hands. No wonder Jetty came back into town."

"*Rose*," Sherry warned with a shake of her head, but her smile told Tegan that she loved her mother-in-law's feistiness as much as Jett did.

Tegan told them about the seamstress work she'd done, and the costumes she made for Princess for a Day, a children's boutique. She also described the costume she'd made for Joni. Rose asked her a lot of questions, eventually asking about her family and then circling back to the amphitheater.

"Will you be offering senior citizen discounts for the romantic comedies?" Rose asked. "Many of my friends are on fixed incomes, but they won't want to miss out on seeing those hot young actors."

"Mother, *please*," Jett's father said from his perch on the love seat beside his wife.

Rose sipped her wine and said, "We might be old, Douglas, but we're not dead yet." She turned to Tegan and said, "We all need a little light in our lives, don't we? How can we order tickets for the shows?"

"We're testing a new website right now, but it should be ready soon. I'll make sure Jett gives you the address once it's up and running."

"Did I hear you say that you and Jett had been out all day?" his father asked. "Does that mean he's not here just for the business meeting?"

She felt guilty that Jett had come to see her and hadn't even called his parents to let them know he was in town. She debated saying he'd come just for the meeting, but she was *not* a good liar. "No. He was supposed to be traveling, but I was having a hard time going through my uncle's things, and he came to help. I'm really sorry he didn't call to let you know he was in town."

"If I had a pretty woman like you by my side, calling my family would be the *last* thing on my mind," Rose said.

His father raised his drink as if he agreed and took a sip.

"Did you enjoy your day together?" his mother asked.

"We went on a magnificent adventure." Tegan told them all about their day and how fun it was to see Jett at the batting cages. "I wish I could have seen him play ball when he was a teenager."

"He was a handsome boy," his mother said.

"Tough as nails and smart as a whip," his father said. "There was nothing Jett couldn't accomplish."

"Sherry and I went to almost every one of his games," Rose said. "Douglas had to work, of course, but we took loads of pictures and Sherry filled him in on all the details. Jett loved baseball so much. Douglas, do you remember how he used to rattle off all those statistics?"

"He was something else." His father looked at Tegan and said, "He still is. I can't get over that you got Jett to play mini golf and arcade games. He needs more of that in his life. I was old and gray before I learned what *quality time* really meant. I'm glad he's not following so closely in my footsteps after all."

"You raised an amazing man," Tegan said. "I know Jett works a lot, but even when we're apart he makes time for me. We have a lot of fun together, and we're both competitive so we always end up laughing." *Or having sex*, but she wasn't about to say *that*.

"That makes me so happy," Sherry said. "When our boys were little, they laughed all the time. Sometimes I'd just stop what I was doing to listen to them playing. They'd always end up in the treehouse. It could be dead silent, and I'd wonder what they were up to, and then laughter would float out from behind the treehouse walls, or there would be a flurry of commands and discussions, and their toy guns, or whatever they had that day—for Jett it was usually a baseball bat—would suddenly poke out over the walls aimed at invisible villains."

"They were crafty," his father said. "It seemed like they were always planning things, scheming. Jett couldn't have been more than five or six when they made a pulley using about three dozen nails and some rope with one of my wife's baskets tied to it."

"I used to send lunch or snacks up to them in that basket," Sherry said with a faraway look in her eyes, as if she were reliving the memories.

Rose shared more stories about when the boys were little, how they'd try to trick her into giving them extra treats or letting them stay up late when she had them overnight. Every memory stirred another story, painting a picture of a happy family when Jett was young, and a very different family when he was a teenager, just as he'd described. But the more Tegan heard, the clearer it became that even in the not-so-good times, his parents' love was always there.

When Tegan's phone vibrated with a text from Jett asking where she was, she got a little nervous and thumbed out, *At your parents' house. They saw me getting into the car and invited me over. I'm sorry!*

"Oh, goodness, look at the time," Sherry said. "Rose, I'm so sorry. You wanted to be home by nine, and it's already nine thirty. Honey, we need to go."

As they rose to their feet, the front door flew open and Jett strode in like a man on a mission. His eyes moved swiftly over them as he strode to his grandmother and kissed her cheek, a cautious, "Hi, Gram," coming out. Tension billowed off him as he slid an arm around Tegan's waist and said, "What's going on?"

"Relax, Jetty," Rose said. "We're just getting to know your lovely friend."

Tegan put her arm around him, sinking into his side, and felt some of that tension dissipate.

"We heard you had quite a fun day together," his mother said.

"And that Tegan blew you away on the go-kart track," his father said teasingly. "Seems like you might have met your match."

"She's badass in business, too," Jett said, as if he had something to prove to his father.

"So I've heard," his father said casually. "You met with Mitchell? I'm glad you found the time."

"Me too." Jett inhaled deeply and blew it out slowly, releasing more of the lingering tension. "It was strange being at the head of the room with the men and women who watched out for me when I was a kid."

His father's lips tipped up, and he said, "Yes, I remember

that feeling."

"I don't know what they were expecting, and I went in there not having a clue as to what I could possibly offer with my limited time. But I wanted to at least hear them out, maybe offer suggestions or throw some money at them and put one of my guys on it. But when I walked in, they acted as if I hadn't been gone all these years, welcoming me with open arms, saying how proud they were of me and that they always knew I'd do well."

"They're good people," Sherry said. "Everyone asks about you and your brothers. Just because you're living somewhere else doesn't mean you're forgotten."

"Yes, but I was not a very *kind* teenager." His eyes shot to his father, and Tegan felt him tense up again.

"That's putting it mildly," Rose said under her breath.

"Thanks, Gram," Jett said sarcastically, tightening his hold on Tegan. "It's true. I was a jerk."

His father lowered his chin, looking at Jett with the seriousness of a businessman and the eagle eye of a father, as he said, "All teenagers are a bit headstrong, but not all of them carry that determination into manhood, as you have. Have you decided to help Mitchell and the others?"

"Don't know yet," Jett said sharply.

"Well, I'll be interested in hearing what you decide to do, if anything," his father said.

"Oh goodness, look at the time," Rose said in an obvious attempt to lighten the mood. "Jetty, can you and Tegan drive me home?"

Jett shifted his eyes away from his father, and said, "Sure."

Jett helped Tegan with her coat as his father assisted Rose with hers. Jett hugged his mother and then he shook his father's hand and said, "I saw the treehouse hasn't been torn down yet."

"I called Rob Wicked, but he and his boys are tied up several weeks out."

Jett's gaze darted toward the backyard, and then he said, "I'm coming back into town a week from Friday evening to see Tegan. I have to leave at six the next evening for London, but if you want, I can swing by for a few hours and we can fix it for Doug and Dean's future kids. You know they'll talk you into putting up another one anyway."

His father kept a stiff upper lip, but the emotion in his eyes brought a lump to Tegan's throat. Sherry and Rose both looked as though they might cry, too.

His father nodded and said, "Sounds good. I'll order the wood."

"That's wonderful," Sherry exclaimed, blinking rapidly. "Tegan, can you make it, too?"

"Absolutely. I'd love to. Rose, will you be here?"

"I wouldn't miss it for the world," she said coyly.

After another round of hugs and warmer goodbyes, they left. The second the door closed, Rose said, "What have you decided about helping Mitchell and the others?"

Tegan wondered why Rose thought he'd made a decision already.

"There's no way I'll hand them over to someone else. This is *my* town, and those people were there for me dozens of times. I want to be the one to help them get back on their feet and make their businesses even stronger."

"The man who said he'd never go back to his roots is doing just that," Rose said.

Jett gave her an annoyed look.

"That's how you grew your business, honey, teaching others

how to grow theirs," Rose said.

Confused, Tegan said, "Why didn't you tell your father what you'd decided?"

"I don't know," he grumbled.

Rose turned her wise gray-blue eyes on Tegan and said, "It's tug-of-war, honey, as typical of men as their need to mark their territory."

"But wasn't the treehouse an olive branch?" Tegan asked.

As they made their way down the driveway, Rose said, "It was a branch from a very thorny bush."

Jett gave a confirmatory nod, keeping one arm tightly around his grandmother, and said, "You okay, Gram? Am I going too fast?"

"No, sweetheart. You're finally moving at the perfect pace."

LATER THAT NIGHT, Tegan gazed out the bathroom window at the moonlight kissing the tops of the trees as she dried off from a shower, thinking about her life. She'd come to the Cape expecting an adventure, and when she'd first suggested she and Jett try being friends with benefits, she'd expected it to be relatively easy to remain unattached. She'd been wrong on both counts. Carrying on her uncle's legacy might have begun as an adventure, but the theater had become a part of her. Or maybe it always had been, and she simply hadn't realized it. And Jett? She clutched the towel to her chest. Her heart had felt like it might explode when she'd seen him standing beside Jock in her hallway yesterday morning. It had been like a dream, working with him and Jock to move her things, making a *home*

out of the cottage. She loved the cozy space, and she loved that Jett and Jock had become friends. She thought about the amazing day they'd had, and goose bumps rose on her flesh. She could still feel the joy and determination vibrating in the air as Jett had swung the bat, and his laughter and the cocky comments that followed. She could still see his eyes turning dark and seductive with every furtive touch they'd shared. She loved how their competitive natures pushed them to win and also drew them together in celebration. And she was proud of him for trying to bridge the gap with his father. Thorny branch or not, he was making an effort, and that filled her with happiness. She felt like she was walking across that rocky bridge with him, and that made her happy, too. She sighed. She loved everything about their coupledom.

She loved everything about *him*.

"You coming, babe?" Jett called from the other side of the bathroom door as she hung up her towel.

Her pulse quickened. "Just a sec."

She slipped on her silk cami and matching panties and opened the door, melting at the candlelit bedroom. Her eyes found Jett kneeling naked and masked beside the bed, and her body ignited. She swallowed hard, her nerves tingling.

"I always keep my promises," he said seductively.

She'd been so swept away with everything else, she'd forgotten about *this* promise. A sly grin spread across his lips as she went to him, hoping her weak knees wouldn't give out. She wanted to look at all of him at once, his delicious lips, broad chest, thick thighs, and the sinful shaft waiting to bring her pleasure.

"Good evening, Miss Fine. I'm here to fulfill your every desire."

A whimper slipped out before she could stop it. He was gazing up at her through the sexy mask that said FUCKABLE FLIRT on it. *Oh God. This man...* Her emotions were too big, whipping around inside her like a storm trying to break free. She was breathing too hard, falling too fast, but she didn't want to stop.

Jett ran his fingertips along her legs, sending shivers of heat racing through her. "Where shall I start, beautiful?"

How was she supposed to *think*, much less speak? She scrambled for her voice, for a command to give him, and whispered, "Take my panties off."

His hands trailed up her outer thighs, light as feathers, and he drew them down. Then those piercing eyes found hers, making her heart pound even harder. God, he was really doing this! She was so nervous, her voice trembled as she said, "Kiss your way up to my mouth."

He started at her ankles, caressing her legs as he slowly and meticulously kissed a path up one leg, lingering on the tender skin behind her knee, sending titillating pleasures darting through her. He loved every inch of her hamstrings and thighs, teasing so close to her sex, she grabbed his shoulders to keep her knees from giving out. Her desires rushed out in a heated demand. "Lick me."

He thrust his tongue between her thighs, slicking along her wetness. Her sex clenched, and she didn't even try to hold back. "Use your hands, grab my ass, suck my clit. Make me *come*." She might be the one in control, but he was the master, taking her right up to the clouds. Lights exploded behind her closed lids, and still he was *relentless*. She forced her eyes open, wanting to see him as he pleasured her. Their eyes collided with the force of an earthquake, making everything that much more intense.

He clutched her bottom tighter, forced her legs open wider, and used his wicked mouth to send her soaring again. The world careened around them as she tried to pull him to his feet. But he pushed his hands beneath her top, playing her like a symphony once again, leaving her boneless and shaky.

"*Up*," she panted out. He rose and his arms circled her, holding her to him like she was precious. "Take the mask off." He pulled it off, and the emotions in his eyes stole her breath once again. "Jett," came out like a plea.

"I know, Tegs. I feel it, too."

He guided her to the bed, coming down over her. As their bodies came together, he dipped his head beside hers and whispered, "You said I'm seven people, but I only want to be one." He lifted his face and gazed into her eyes. "I want to be yours, Tegs. Just *yours*."

Chapter Twenty-Three

JETT COULDN'T REMEMBER a time when the thought of attending a wedding didn't spur a feeling of dread. The lengthy ceremony, the tears, and even the toasts that followed had always felt fake and unnecessary. He'd always thought it was much ado about an antiquated union that could, in his eyes, end only one way. But Saturday evening, as he sat with his arm around Tegan while Gavin and Harper recited their vows in a flower-filled room at the Silver House on Silver Island, *everything* changed. He was no longer the odd man out, making excuses to leave early and checking his phone fifteen times an hour. He'd asked Tia to screen his messages and delegate what she could to Jonas and other staff members for the next twenty-four hours, allowing him to focus on the woman who was opening his eyes to things he'd never realized he was missing out on.

While everyone else was captivated by the bride and groom, Jett couldn't take his eyes off Tegan, sitting pin-straight on the edge of her seat with tears streaming down her cheeks. It didn't matter how adventurous she claimed to be, he knew that she was a put-down-roots kind of woman. The type of person who loved traditions like family gatherings at holidays, spending weeks with her favorite uncle every summer, and taking annual trips without having much of a plan. She liked weekly talks with her sister and catch-up calls with her parents, and she deserved to have all those things and so much more.

An outburst of cheers and clapping as the bride and groom shared their first kiss as a married couple jerked Jett from his thoughts. Tegan turned teary, elated eyes on him. He felt his chest crack wide open as she leaned into his arms, sniffling against his shoulder.

"That was so beautiful," she said through her tears.

He held her and said, "Not nearly as beautiful as you are." When she'd come out of the bedroom wearing the blousy-sleeved, low-cut, pale pink dress with white polka dots she'd made over the winter for the wedding, he'd been speechless.

She drew back and said, "I'm a mess. Is my eyeliner smear-ing?"

He brushed away her tears. "No smears, babe. And you're not a mess; you're happy for them, which makes you even more attractive."

Everyone stood up, clapping as Gavin and Harper made their way down the aisle. The people standing at the ends of the rows threw rose petals from baskets lining the aisle.

Tegan leaned into Jett's side with a dreamy expression as she clapped and said, "They look so happy!"

He wanted to say that she'd get that one day, too, but some things were too big to even think about. He kept her close as they made their way to the banquet room with the other guests.

Jock fell into step beside Jett and said, "That was really something."

"Great wedding," Jett agreed. "How are you holding up?" On the ferry ride to the island, Jock had confided in him about having a rocky relationship with his twin brother.

"Good. A few more hours and I'll be back on the ferry, doing even better."

"We're here if you need us," Jett said as they joined their friends gathered near the open bar.

"That was *so* romantic. Look at the lovebirds." Serena lifted her and Drake's joined hands, motioning across the room to Gavin and Harper, surrounded by their families and talking with the young blond photographer.

"They look almost as in love as we are," Drake said as he drew her into his arms.

"I love weddings." Desiree leaned into Rick and said, "Remember ours?"

"I'll never forget that day." Rick kissed her.

Andre pulled Violet closer and said, "Neither will we. It's the day we came back into each other's lives."

"You were lucky Violet didn't kill you that day," Serena reminded him.

Andre had shown up as Violet's mother's *plus one* for Desiree and Rick's wedding, and from what Jett had heard, sparks had flown.

"Seriously, though," Serena said, "don't you think Gavin and Harper's first married kiss was *hot*?"

"Their vows are what got me," Tegan said. "They were poetic and heartfelt."

"Gavin's vows made me cry," Daphne said, struggling to hold on to Hadley's hand.

Hadley clutched one of the birds Jett had given her as she tried to escape her mother's grasp, chanting, "*Dock! Dock!*" Her hand slipped free and she toddled over to Jock as fast as she could in her pretty pink dress and white shoes and hugged his legs, smiling like she'd found her happy place.

"Hey, I gave you that bird and *he* gets the attention?" Jett teased, but Hadley was totally focused on the man whose legs she clung to. Discomfort riddled Jock's face. Knowing that Jock had lost a child, Jett swooped Hadley into his arms and said, "Come here, pretty girl. Let's talk about your bird."

Jock's shoulders visibly sank with relief, and he said, "I'm going to grab a drink."

"*Dock!*" Hadley cried, reaching for him as he walked away.

Daphne took her crying daughter from Jett's arms and said, "Sorry, Jett." She smoothed Hadley's hair, trying to quiet her. "Shh, honey. He'll be back. Let's play with your bird."

Jett and Tegan exchanged worried glances. Jett thought about going after Jock, but just then the photographer joined them and said, "Hi. I'm Tara. Harper and Gavin asked me to take pictures of your group. We can wait until your little one is in a better mood. I'll be taking candid shots, too, throughout the reception. Harper's planning a bonfire on the patio with anyone who's staying the night. I'll be sure to get pictures then, too."

"That sounds fun," Tegan said. "Thank you."

Hadley scowled at Tara. Her cries had subsided, but tears still dripped down her cheeks.

"I don't blame you, sweetness. My niece, Joey, thinks her Uncle Jack is the icing on the cake, too." Tara turned to look over her shoulder at Jock, who was ordering a drink, and said, "Jack is one of the kindest men I know."

"Are you his sister?" Serena asked.

"Oh no, sorry. I didn't mean to confuse you," Tara said. "My sister is Joey's mother, and Jack's brother Levi is her father. They're not together. Levi is raising Joey, and she just adores

Jack. I think I'll go say hello."

As Tara walked away, Daphne said, "It's weird to hear her call him Jack since we know him by his nickname."

Tara embraced Jock, and Serena said, "I wonder if *she* thinks he's the icing on the cake, too."

"I don't know, but Jock grew up here, and Harper said her photographer was from the island, too. I'm sure they're close," Tegan explained.

"I wonder how close," Daphne said under her breath as Hadley tried to wriggle out of her arms.

"Are you interested in Jock, Daph?" Desiree asked.

"What? *No*," Daphne said as she set Hadley down, and Hadley toddled off in Jock's direction. "Of course she'd make a beeline for him."

As Daphne went after Hadley, Tegan turned to Jett and said, "Do you think he's okay?"

Jock had a drink in his hand, and he was talking with Tara. "He seems fine now."

Emery burst into the group and said, "This place is *gorgeous*. No wonder Harper didn't want to settle for any other location. Did you see the view?"

The Silver House was built on a bluff overlooking Sunset Beach and Silver Harbor. It was one of the most sought-after wedding destinations on the East Coast, despite its limited capacity. The banquet room they were in had views of an expansive patio, gardens, arbors, and the harbor.

"Can you imagine how gorgeous this place is in the summer with all the flowers in bloom?" Dean said.

"No more gorgeous than Bayside," Serena said, snuggling up to her man, and everyone agreed.

Jett slid his arms around Tegan's waist from behind. She

glanced over her shoulder, and he whispered, "You were too far away." He kissed her neck, and she leaned back against him, making a contented sound, as Chloe and Justin joined them.

"*What* is going on here?" Chloe asked, eyeing Jett and Tegan.

Justin put his arm around her and said, "Jealous? Because I'll happily stand in as your FWB."

"Wait. Where have you two been this whole time?" Emery asked.

"*Around*," Chloe said lightly. Then she turned a sterner voice on Justin. "I'm not in the market for an FWB, thank you very much." She scooted out of his grasp. "Although, Beckett is looking awfully delicious in that suit, isn't he? Maybe I *will* rethink my FWB stance."

"Like I've told you before," Justin said with an edge to his voice, "when you're done with the Ken dolls and ready to ride a real man, I'm your guy."

Chloe scoffed.

"For the record, Tegs and I are no longer just friends with benefits," Jett explained. "We're exclusive now."

"You *are*?" Emery exclaimed. "That's awesome!"

Dean didn't share his wife's excitement. His eyes were locked on Jett, as skeptical as ever.

"I'm so happy for you guys," Desiree said. "You're great together!"

"We're happy for you, too," Drake said.

"Wait? When did this happen?" Chloe asked.

"A few days ago," Tegan said. "Jett surprised me Thursday morning. We had the best day yesterday, and he's coming back in two weeks before he goes to London."

"That's right, babe." As Jett lowered his lips to her cheek,

Dean scoffed and stalked toward the patio doors.

"What's wrong with him?" Serena asked.

"I don't know," Emery said. "Maybe I should go after him."

"I'll go," Jett said. "I'll be right back, Tegs."

When Jett pushed through the doors, the brisk evening air stinging his cheeks, Dean was already down the patio steps and stalking across the lawn below.

"Dean! Wait up." Wind swept over the bluff as Jett jogged over to him. "What's going on? You okay?"

Dean spun around, his hands curling into fists, and seethed, "No, I'm not fucking okay."

"Whoa." Jett took a step back. "What's got you all pissed off?"

Dean glowered at him. "How many years have I picked up the pieces after you?"

"I don't kn—"

"*Seventeen*, Jett. That's how long ago I lost my brother. That's how long Mom and I have *tried* to get you to come back to us. Do you know how many times during those years you've used work as an excuse not to see us?"

"Dean, let—"

Dean closed the distance between them, bumping Jett with his chest, and said, "How do you think Mom's going to feel when she hears you put off work for a piece of tail?"

Jett grabbed Dean by the collar with both hands, driving him backward. "Don't you *ever* call her that again or I promise you it will be the *last* thing you ever say."

Dean charged forward, taking Jett to the ground. They wrestled and punched, grunted and cursed, battling for dominance. Fists connected with bone as years of repressed hurt and anger raged between them. Jett knew he deserved every fucking punch he took, but he wasn't about to let Dean say shit about his woman. Jett used all his strength to push his brother over and straddled his torso. Dean grunted, teeth clenched, the veins in his neck and arms bulging.

"Don't say *shit* about my girl!" Jett cocked an arm, but Dean was too big, too strong, and too fucking angry. He threw Jett off, and Jett landed with a *thud*, but he was on his feet in seconds, barreling into Dean. They were shoulder to shoulder, two linebackers battling for the win.

"We both know you won't honor her," Dean fumed through gritted teeth.

In the next second Jett was on his back, pinned beneath his brother. Dean thrust his knees onto Jett's biceps and cocked his fist, his massive chest heaving.

"I *love* her, man," Jett hollered, shocked by his own admission. "You can fuck me up. God knows I deserve it, but not because of how I'll treat Tegan."

Confusion narrowed his brother's eyes.

"I love her, Dean," Jett huffed out. "I'm not going to hurt her."

Dean's anger didn't waver. "You don't know what love is. You're a control freak like Dad. You'll never put her ahead of anything else."

"Don't you think I see you and Emery? Drake and Serena? Our other friends?" He paused, trying to catch his breath beneath two hundred thirty pounds of muscle. "I know what it looks like, even if I don't know how to do all the right things. But if Violet could figure out how to love someone after all the shit she's gone through, I sure as hell can. I know I'm not you, and I fucking *envy* your ability to forgive and move on, to open yourself up to all the good shit in life. But I'm *trying*, man. I'm trying to learn for *her*. She makes me want to be a better person. She *believes* in me."

"Dean Masters! *What* has gotten into you?"

Their heads snapped in Emery's direction, and Jett's heart sank at the fear on Tegan's face as she and Emery ran toward them.

"Aw, shit," Dean said, crawling off Jett.

Jett pushed to his feet and offered his hand to Dean. Dean grimaced, but as the girls approached, he slapped his hand into Jett's, allowing Jett to haul him to his feet. Their suit coats were torn at the shoulders, they were covered in grass and dirt, and Dean had a bloody gash over his eye. Jett's cheek felt like it had been hit by a sledgehammer.

"It's *my* fault," Jett said. "We were just messing around and got carried away."

Dean gave him a *she'll never buy* it look. "Sorry, doll." He reached for Emery, who was busy swatting dirt from his suit.

"Your suit is rui—" Emery looked up at him and gasped. "You're *bleeding*." She lifted her hand toward the gash above Dean's eye.

"Are you okay?" Tegan ran to Jett. "Your *face*." She touched his face where he'd taken a punch. "You need ice for that."

He put his hand over hers and said, "I'm fine, babe."

"Are you sure? What can I do?" She plucked grass from his hair, then reached for his hand, holding it tight.

Guilt ate away at him. He felt horrible at having scared her. "Nothing. I'm sorry I embarrassed you."

"Do you know how lucky you are that no one else saw you?" Emery snapped. "You could have ruined Harper's wedding!"

He and Dean said, "Sorry," at the same time.

"You'd better be sorry." Emery glared at Jett. "What were *you* thinking, wrestling with Dean? He is *way* bigger than you."

Dean rubbed his chest, eyeing Jett, and said, "He got a few good ones in."

Emery rolled her eyes, as if she knew, as Jett did, that Dean could have killed him if he'd wanted to.

He walked Tegan a few feet away from Dean and Emery and said, "I'm fine, and I'm sorry to ask this, but would you mind giving me a few minutes alone with Dean?"

Fear rose in her eyes. "Are you going to fight again?"

"*No*, babe. I promise."

She stepped closer and said, "What's *really* going on?"

"Something that should have been dealt with years ago. We just have some stuff to work out."

After promising Tegan and Emery that they would *not* end up on the ground again, the girls went back to the resort.

Dean crossed his arms over his chest and said, "She really cares about you."

"And I care about her. Listen, Dean. Mom knows I'm here. I saw them last night, but you're right. I'm sure she was hurt that I didn't call to let them know I was in town. Some shit went down and I…" He didn't want to admit the truth, but this was the end of the line for them. He had nothing to lose. "I thought I was going to lose Tegan, and man, she's the best thing that has ever happened to me. You and everyone else pretty much gave up on me a long time ago—"

"Bullshit."

"Come on, Dean. Don't do this. You made the calls, you asked me to come back, but you also *knew*, just as I did, what my answer would be. I deserved it. Hell, I created the situation. But we both know you'd given up on me the same way I'd given up on Dad." He shrugged and said, "I don't know how to trust that the man he's been these last two years is here to stay. I wish I did. I want to. Tegan centers me. She makes me see things in ways I never have. She helps me to accept that I *want* to see those things. I know it's fucked up, but it's hard for me to look at Dad without seeing the man I was sure I was destined to become. Don't you think that scares the shit out of me? I don't want to be him, and I've spent my life keeping people at a distance because of that. But I *can't* keep my distance from Tegan."

Dean's expression didn't soften. "How many times have I told you that just because you look like him doesn't mean you have to act like him?"

"Whatever, man. It's deeper than that."

"It is deeper because you've been doing the exact same shit he did."

"I get that now, but I didn't before Tegan came into my life."

Dean's brows knitted, as if he was finally understanding what Jett was trying to say. "Does this mean you'll finally stop using work as an excuse? That you'll show up for more than a night or two over the holidays? That when you say you'll be here, you will actually show up?"

"It means I'm *trying*, and I'm sorry for hurting Mom—and *you*. You're the best man I know, and I owe you a whole hell of a lot more than gratitude for soothing over the hurt my absence caused. I owe you—I owe *us*—years we'll never get back. I can't fix that, Dean. I can't wave a magic wand and erase everything I've done, and I'm not asking for your forgiveness. I know I was a prick, but somewhere in your head you must know that I did what I felt I had to in order to survive with some modicum of sanity. But I promise you this: If you give me a chance, I will try my damnedest not to let you down again."

"You were a real dick."

"No shit. Trust me, you were a dick at times, too. Are you willing to try with me?" Jett stepped closer and said, "Fair warning—if you say no, I *will* throw you down and do you in."

Dean snarled. "You're an asshole."

"Yeah, but I'm an asshole with the hottest girlfriend around." He swung an arm over Dean's shoulder and gave him a quick hug against his side. "I am sorry."

"Me too, for calling Tegan a piece of tail."

"Yeah, what the fuck, man? Don't say that shit again." He stepped back and held out his hand. "Truce?"

Dean eyed his hand, and his lips curved up in a knowing smile. "I'm sure I'll regret this. *Truce.*"

He slapped Jett's palm, and then they slapped the backs of their hands, made fists and bumped them together, and they both made a blowing-up sound, splaying their fingers and drawing them up slowly. They both laughed as they made their way up to the patio, where Emery and the most beautiful blonde in the world were waiting.

TEGAN HAD BEEN worried about leaving Jett and Dean alone after seeing the marks on their faces and their torn clothing, but now she was glad she and Emery had walked away and left them to work out whatever was going on. They'd both been a little tense during dinner, but as the night wore on, the tension between them had eased. They had done shots with some of the other guys, and that had helped break the ice even more. And now, as Harper and Gavin danced their first dance as husband and wife, the tension had been replaced with brotherly banter. Tegan might never understand the way men worked things out with harsh words and rampant fists, but as Jett pulled her closer and they watched Harper and Gavin dancing, she didn't care. Whatever he and Dean had said, however many punches it had taken, had given her a new man to love. His laughter came easier, and his smiles were even more genuine, which made them even more devastating. He gave off a lighter vibe, and she knew that a burden had been lifted—not from his shoulders, but from his heart.

She watched Harper and Gavin whispering and kissing as they danced. They'd never looked happier. Tegan had never dreamed of a white wedding, or even seen herself as a bride. She had too much she wanted to do, too many adventures she wanted to have. But she was so happy with Jett, she could imagine having all those things with him—the adventures, the freedom to build the business with Harper without being held back, and maybe even a future she'd never known she wanted.

Jett pressed his warm lips just beside her ear and whispered, "What are you thinking right this second?"

Even his voice sounded more carefree. Her pulse quickened as she turned to look at him. The bruise on his cheek was darker now, and maybe it was the drinks she'd had, but she swore the way he was looking at her was different, too. It was as intense as ever, but there was more there, as if the fight had also freed a deeper, more emotional part of him.

"That men work in mysterious ways," she answered.

"Should I be worried that you're thinking about other men while you're here with me?"

The confidence in his eyes told her he knew exactly who owned her heart. She decided to tease him right back. "What do you think?"

"I don't think. I *know*." He lifted her hand and pressed a kiss to the back of it.

"What exactly do you know?" she asked softly.

He held her gaze, and her hand, turning the music and the din of their friends to white noise as he said, "That with you in my life, there's no room for anyone else in *my* head, or in my heart."

Everyone around the table pushed to their feet and headed to the dance floor, breaking into their private bubble. One of Tegan's favorite songs was playing, "Use Somebody."

"They're playing our song." Jett stood, bringing her up to her feet beside him.

As he led her to the dance floor, she said, "We have a *song*?"

"We have a few." He swept her into his arms, and as he guided their hips to the beat, he said, "I never noticed music or lyrics, sunsets or sunrises, or a hundred other things, until you came into my life." He touched his cheek to hers and whispered in her ear, "Now I hear and see *us* in everything."

She closed her eyes, soaking in his words, knowing he would lead their dance in the same careful way he was leading their hearts.

Chapter Twenty-Four

FLAMES FROM THE fire danced beneath the domed screen in the cool evening breeze, warming Tegan's cheeks as she snuggled under a blanket on Jett's lap on the patio of the resort. As promised, Tara had taken pictures of Harper and Gavin and all their friends and family as they'd sat around the bonfire chatting and drinking champagne. Against the backdrop of the moonlit sky, Tegan was sure they were going to be some of the most gorgeous pictures from the evening. Jock, Daphne, and several of their other friends, along with most of the wedding guests, left the island shortly after the pictures were taken. Harper's and Gavin's parents had long since turned in for the night, as had most of their coupled-off friends, leaving only Harper and Gavin, Dean and Emery, Chloe, Justin, and Beckett. Other than Dean and Jett ruining their suits and giving each other a few cuts and bruises, it had been a wonderful evening, Tegan didn't want it to end.

"Hey, Jett," Harper called from across the firepit, where she and Gavin were sharing a lounge chair.

Jett lifted his chin in acknowledgment.

"I'm really glad that you and Tegan are together, but please don't sweep her off her feet and steal her away from the Cape,"

Harper pleaded. "I need her here."

"I don't think you have to worry about that. It would take a hell of a lot to get Tegan to give up her uncle's legacy." Jett ran his fingers through Tegan's hair and said, "Right, babe?"

"Definitely," Tegan agreed. "Besides, I'd never do that to you, Harper. You know that."

"I do, but I also know how the right man can change everything." Harper rested her head on Gavin's shoulder.

Chloe and Justin were bickering about the validity of dating apps. Emery, who was sitting on Dean's lap, interrupted and said, "Chloe, I thought you were bringing a date tonight. What happened?"

"Her Ken doll had to get a facial," Justin said with a snicker.

Chloe glowered at him, and then she turned a flirtatious look on Beckett and said, "I remembered Beckett was going to be here, so..."

Beckett flashed a cocky grin. "I hear the bar stays open for another hour. What do you say we go check it out?"

"Oh shit, here we go," Dean said under his breath.

"That sounds great." Chloe pushed to her feet, looking elegant in a long-sleeved pale gray dress, and set the blanket that had been wrapped around her shoulders on the chair.

"I agree," Justin said, coming to her side and ignoring the disbelieving look she was giving him. "A drink sounds perfect."

Beckett shook his head.

Gavin chuckled. "He's my best buddy, Beck. He knows how you are."

"Dashing? Smart?" Beckett loosened his tie and said, "Good in bed?"

"I got no shame in my cockblocking game." Justin slung an arm over Chloe's shoulder and said, "Let's go, blondie."

"If you have visions of threesomes dancing in your head, think again," Chloe said as they walked into the resort.

"They are so funny." Tegan loved listening to the three of them.

"I wouldn't share you for all the money in the world," Jett said.

"Oh darn," she teased. "I was so looking forward to a little threesome action."

Jett nipped at her jaw with a low *growl*.

Dean chuckled and said, "Looks like you fell for the right woman. She's not afraid to push your buttons."

Jett hugged her closer and said, "Every last one of them."

"I wish tonight could last forever," Tegan said.

"I do, too," Gavin said as he rose to his feet. "But since that can't happen, if you'll excuse us, I'd like to take my gorgeous wife upstairs." He took Harper's hand, drawing her to her feet beside him, and wrapped his arm around her.

"Aw," Emery said sweetly. "Wedding-night lovemaking is the *best*."

"I'm counting on it," Harper said. "I hope we'll see you all at breakfast. We're leaving for our honeymoon at ten, so if you stay out too late and we don't see you, thank you so much for sharing in our special day."

A knot formed in Tegan's stomach as reality drifted in. Jett was leaving on the ten o'clock flight to Boston, and she and the others were taking the ten thirty ferry back home. She wasn't ready to be apart from him again.

"We love you," Emery called after Harper and Gavin, but they were already inside the resort, kissing on the other side of the glass doors.

"Are you up for a walk on the beach?" Jett asked. "I'm sure

the Silvers won't mind if we take the blankets down with us."
Alexander and Margot Silver, the distinguished couple who ran
the resort, had come out earlier to congratulate Harper and
Gavin personally. They'd brought champagne and a basketful of
blankets for everyone to use. It was a really special personal
touch, and it had left Tegan with the type of warm and
welcome feeling she hoped people would experience when they
visited her theater.

"Yes!" Emery hopped off Dean's lap.

"I think he was talking to Tegan," Dean said as he stood up,
towering over her.

Jett glanced at Tegan, his silent question, *Do you mind if
they join us?* as clear as his sexy blue eyes. She shook her head as
she climbed off his lap, happy that he wanted more time with
his brother.

Jett wrapped the blanket around her shoulders and said,
"It's cool, Dean. Join us. We've never been on a double date."

"Yay!" Emery cheered.

They made their way down the stone steps to the beach.
Cold air whipped off the water, stinging Tegan's cheeks.

"I guess we should have thought about the wind and the
drop in temperature by the water." He held her close, keeping
the blanket tight around her.

"No, this is wonderful." Tegan kicked off her heels, glad she
hadn't worn nylons. "We don't have *time* to be picky about
temperatures. All we have is tonight. Our first moonlight
adventure. Take your shoes off and we'll put our toes in the
freezing water."

"You're *nuts*. I think you might be my spirit animal!" Emery
took off her heels and said, "Come on, Dean. Let's put our feet
in the water."

Dean raised his brows at Jett, who was busy taking off his shoes and socks.

Jett rolled up his slacks and said, "Do what you want. I'm going on an adventure with my girlfriend."

Dean relented and crouched to take off his shoes.

Tegan dropped the blanket in the sand, took Jett's hand, and said, "Let's go!"

They ran down to the water with Dean and Emery, shouting to each other about how crazy they were. When Tegan's feet hit the wet sand, she shrieked and tugged Jett backward.

Jett burst into laughter and pulled her into his arms. "Change your mind, sunshine?"

"No!" she said through chattering teeth. "I just have to prepare."

"Come on, you guys!" Emery hollered from the water's edge. "Your feet will numb up quickly!"

Tegan gripped Jett's hand tighter and said, "Let's get numb!"

They ran across the wet sand and into ankle-deep water. She shrieked again and turned to run up the beach, but Jett caught her around the waist, lifting her off her feet. She wrapped her arms around his neck, holding on tight, and he pressed his lips to hers.

"I've got you," he said.

"Aren't *your* feet frozen?"

His smile turned wolfish. "Not when you're in my arms. You get me hot all over."

She wrapped her legs around his waist and said, "Then kiss me again."

She didn't have to ask twice. He kissed her deeply and sensually, heating her up from the inside out. Just as the world started to disappear, Emery kicked water at them and ran away laughing.

Tegan wiggled out of Jett's arms and shouted, "*Get her!*"

Emery ran behind Dean, then peeked around his shoulders. Dean splayed his hands with a challenging look in his eyes.

"*Christ*, here we go." Jett lowered his voice and turned to Tegan as he said, "You go right. I'll go left."

Thrills raced through her as Jett ran to Dean's left and she ran to his right. Dean lunged for him, and they both went down laughing on the wet sand. Tegan chased Emery, kicking water up and making her shriek. They ran until they were out of breath, clinging to each other giggling, both wet from the knees down.

Tegan turned just as Jett barreled into her and Dean barreled into Emery, and they hoisted them over their shoulders. The girls shrieked and kicked their feet, pleading to be put down as the men faced the open sea.

"What do you think, Dean?" Jett shouted. "Shark bait?"

"No! *Please*, don't!" Tegan pleaded.

"If you do, you won't get any lovin' for a month!" Emery warned.

"As if you could *ever* turn me away." Dean snickered and walked into knee-deep water. Emery pounded on his back, pleading for him not to do it.

"What about you, sunshine?" Jett asked as he followed Dean into the water.

The *last* thing she wanted was *less* naked time with him, so she said, "If you don't do it, we'll spend the *entire* day in bed the next time you come see me!"

Jett stopped walking.

"Me too! Me too!" Emery shrieked.

"Thanks for the offer, Em," Jett said. "But I don't think Dean would approve of you spending the day in my bed."

Dean spun on his heels and stalked back toward them, feigning an angry glower at his brother. Dean chased Jett down the beach, each slowed down by the weight of the giggling woman hanging over his shoulder like a sack of potatoes. They all ended up in hysterics, bundled up in the blankets, shivering as they retrieved their shoes.

"Hey, Jett," Dean said. "Sorry about what I said earlier. I can see how wrong I was."

"About what?" Emery asked.

"Nothing," Dean said, holding Jett's gaze. "We cool?"

"Yeah." Jett nodded as they headed up the stone steps toward the resort. "I'm coming back in two weeks to see Tegan, flying in Friday night and leaving Saturday evening for London. I told Dad I'd help fix the treehouse while I'm here. Feel like pounding nails?"

"What's wrong with the treehouse?" Dean asked.

"It got damaged in the storm and he was going to tear it down," Jett explained. "I figured you'd want them to hang on to it for when you and Em have kids."

The look of disbelief on Dean's face both pleased and bothered Tegan. It seemed everyone saw Jett as one-dimensional, work oriented and nothing more. She understood why they would see him that way, but it still irked her. She wanted to stand up for him, to make sure Dean understood how much of an effort Jett was making and how wonderful a man he was all around.

But Dean spoke before she had a chance. "I'm so glad to hear that. Just give me the time and I'll be there."

"Great. Bring Em," Jett said when they reached the grassy

knoll at the top of the steps. "Tegs is coming, and Gram should be there, too."

"Rose is coming?" Emery exclaimed. "That should be an *interesting* afternoon. Wait until you meet her, Tegan. She's hilarious."

"I met her last night when Jett was meeting with Mitchell Myer and some of the other business owners from Hyannis, and I loved her," Tegan said as they stepped onto the patio and headed for the firepit.

Dean shot a look at Jett. "What's *that* all about?"

"They need some guidance and financial help. Nothing major," Jett said modestly.

"Sounds major to me," Dean said, holding Jett's gaze.

"Can he tell you about it another time?" Emery pleaded. "I'm *freezing*!"

"Sure, doll." Dean draped an arm around her. "Jett, I'll catch up with you in the morning. This was fun. Thanks for sharing him, Tegan."

As Dean and Emery went inside, Tegan warmed herself by the embers of the fire. Jett grabbed a second blanket and wrapped it around her.

"What was Dean apologizing for earlier?"

He gathered her in his arms, holding the blankets around her, and said, "He was being protective of you when we were fighting and said some things he shouldn't have."

"Please tell me your fight was *not* about me."

"You were just an excuse, a gateway to trouble that had been brewing since we were teens. Before you, that fight would have ended very differently. Very *badly*."

"What do you mean?"

"I wouldn't have had a reason to stop, and Dean probably

would have been so blinded by rage…" He sighed. "Let's not talk about what could have happened. The fight needed to happen, and it led me and Dean back to each other. That's a good thing, and I'd really like to focus on that." He touched his forehead to hers and said, "You make every aspect of my life better. Is there anything else you'd like to know?"

"Just one tiny thing. I'd love to know how it feels to be naked and in your arms in that big Jacuzzi in our suite."

"Aw, babe." He kissed her lips. "By the time tonight's over, you'll know how it feels to be naked in my arms in the Jacuzzi, on the sofa…" He kissed her nose. "And everywhere else your beautiful heart desires."

HOURS LATER, AFTER fulfilling Tegan's every sexual curiosity, Jett lay in bed absently running his fingers along her back. It was nearing sunrise, which felt like a sucker punch, because after sunrise came breakfast, and then he was off to Boston to catch his flight to Louisiana, where he'd be tied up in endless meetings. How was he going to make it for two weeks without her? And in two weeks, after their one night together, how would he manage a month or longer without her? Their situation sucked, and it was all his doing. He was a self-fulfilled prophecy. He wanted a life that allowed no time to connect with anyone on a personal level, a life in which he was wealthier and more widely recognized than his father. He'd achieved *exactly* what he'd wanted.

Now he wanted Tegan.

But at what cost? This back-and-forth bullshit definitely was not the answer. The problem was, he didn't think there was an answer. But he knew one thing for sure. His sweet, patient, full-of-life Tegan needed to know how he felt.

He kissed her head and whispered, "Still up?"

"Mm-hm. Barely," she whispered.

"It's almost sunrise; don't doze off yet." He'd promised her they'd watch the sunrise, and there was no way in hell he'd break that promise.

She groaned. "I don't want to move from your arms."

"I know, babe. I don't want to move, either. I've been lying here wondering how I was going to leave you again." His throat thickened. "I hope you know that I *want* to be with you. I want to make love to you, to hold you when the emotions are so thick we don't have to speak to know what the other is feeling. I want to laugh with you, to watch your uncle's home movies and hold you when you cry. I want all those things, baby, but I can't give them to you right now."

"I know." Her fingers moved over his chest.

The intimate touch had become so familiar to him, he knew he'd feel it when they were apart.

"I haven't asked you to change your schedule. *Have I?*" she asked. "I know we've been up all night, but unless I was babbling deliriously, I'm pretty sure I'd remember saying that. I know how hard you work, and I respect your schedule."

"Thank you," he whispered. "You completely undo me, sunshine."

She moved on top of him and rested her chin on her hands, her smiling eyes holding his. "You undid me all night long. It's only fair that I undo you, too."

He ran his hands down her body, and she pressed on his erection.

"If you keep lying on top of me, we're going to miss the sunrise."

She wiggled her butt and said, "But you'll get to see a *full moon*."

"As much as I love your ass, I promised you a sunrise, and we're going to watch it." He wrapped his arms around her and rolled them onto their sides. "It's a damn good thing the last place we made love was in the shower, because if I had to shower with you now, we'd miss the sunrise and breakfast, and I'd probably also miss my flight."

"That sounds promising," she whispered coyly. Her gaze drifted to the bruise on his cheek. She reached up, touching it lightly, and said, "You do everything with so much passion. Is it any wonder that I'm falling so hard for you?"

Now it was his pulse quickening as her words soaked in, filling him so completely it took a moment before he found his voice. He brushed his lips over hers and said, "I'm so far past *falling*, I can no longer see the top of the mountain."

Their mouths came together in a penetrating kiss. Jett ached to make love to her one more time, to hear her cry out his name in the throes of passion and to feel her cling to him like he was the very air she breathed. But he knew her well enough to realize she'd regret it if they missed their chance to watch the sunrise together. Those types of experiences weren't coming nearly often enough.

He forced himself to pull away, gave her ass a loving tap, and said, "Get dressed, beautiful. Our morning adventure awaits."

Chapter Twenty-Five

BUNDLED UP IN jackets and sweaters, Tegan and Jett headed outside. They were greeted by crisp, cold air, dewy grass, and ribbons of dusky grays and soft purples above the inky water.

Tegan pointed to a white tent at the edge of the bluff. "I wonder what's going on over there."

"It's an adventure. I say we check it out." He took her hand and headed in that direction.

"What if we're interrupting something?" she asked, but excitement lingered in her eyes.

"Then we'll apologize and move on."

"It's so beautiful here. Harper said she fell in love with this island when she and Gavin were here last summer. Even though there's water around the Cape, I can definitely see the intrigue of an island. It's like a different world, where everything feels special," she said as they approached the tent. She held her finger in front of her lips and let go of his hand, tiptoeing to peek into the open front. "You have to see this!" She waved him over as she walked in.

He chuckled. He already knew about the twinkling lights lining the seams and the luxurious daybed layered with warm blankets on which they could lie comfortably and watch the sunrise. He'd chosen the scented candles, orchids, and red and pink roses that decorated the tops of elegant iron-and-glass tables himself, and he'd arranged for the cranberry-walnut muffins, croissants, and the array of crackers, cheeses, and sliced meats that he knew were under the lids of the silver serving platters, awaiting his hungry girl.

"Jett! There's a heater. Do you think Gavin did this for Harper? He thought of everything. I've never seen anything so beautiful."

"Neither have I," he said, unable to take his eyes off her.

"We should go. Someone went to a lot of trouble, and we might ruin it for them."

"It's for you, babe." He drew her into his arms and said, "You opened my eyes to a whole new world, and then you became it."

"You did this? For *us*?"

"For *you*, sunshine. I wanted to give you a morning to remember on all the mornings we're going to be apart."

"Oh, *Jett*." She wound her arms around his neck and kissed him. "You didn't have to do this. I mean, it's incredible, but *you're* enough for me. I hope you know that."

"I know." He also knew she deserved a boyfriend who was present more often, but he'd never once wondered if *he*, as a *man*, was enough for her, and *that* was a reflection of her beautiful heart and how she accepted him even with *all* his faults. She had embraced his heartache and was helping him to deal with it, and hopefully move past it. She not only made him want to be a better man, but she helped him to become one.

"I wanted to do this for you," he said. "You deserve to have adventures that you haven't even dreamed of yet. The sun is going to rise anytime now, so get comfortable and let me spoil you, baby."

As she settled onto the daybed, she said, "I can't get over this. How did you arrange it? We've been together the whole time."

"A gentleman never tells." He'd been planning it since the night they'd talked about watching the sunrise together when they were on FaceTime. "Hungry?" He lifted the top off the silver platter.

"Are those cranberry-walnut muffins?" she asked, reaching for one.

"Your favorite."

She snuggled closer and said, "You remembered," in that dreamy voice he loved.

"Every word you've said, since day one."

LONG AFTER THE sun had breached the sky and the noises from the resort filtered into the tent, Jett and Tegan lay in each other's arms, fully dressed, their bodies intertwined. Tegan hadn't wanted to join everyone for breakfast, and he was glad, because he wanted as much time alone with her as possible. But he knew he had to get a move on or he'd miss his plane.

He touched his lips to hers, and though it pained him to do it, he whispered, "I need to pack, babe."

"Okay," she said so softly he almost missed it.

They made their way into the resort and up to the room, where they packed their things in silence. Jett zipped his bag, trying to shift his thoughts from leaving Tegan to the busy workweek he had ahead of him, but there was no escaping the sadness hanging in the air between them.

He lifted his bag and turned to ask, "Did you get everything?" The tears in her eyes nearly took him to his knees. He steeled himself and gathered her in his arms. "I know two weeks seems like forever right now, but we're going to talk every day. I promise."

"How did this happen so fast?"

"I don't know, babe." He wiped her tears, his heart breaking, and said, "I'm sorry."

She shook her head. "I'm *not* sorry. I've never been happier than when we're together. I'll be fine. I'm just being silly. I have plenty of work to keep me busy while you're gone."

"You're not silly. I'm sad, too. *So* fucking sad. I'm going to miss the hell out of you, out of *us*." He kissed her softly and said, "But while I'm in Louisiana we'll only be an hour apart. You can call and text as often as you'd like. I'll be on the plane to LA Friday morning, but I should arrive by two your time. We'll see each other every night on FaceTime at eight o'clock your time, just like we have been."

She nodded, sniffling and blinking to dry her eyes. "I have my book club meeting at seven on Thursday. I won't be home until around ten."

"Do you want to talk before or after?"

"After. I like your voice to be the last thing I hear before I go to sleep."

"Then after it is. We'll only miss one weekend together, and then the following Friday night you'll be back in my arms." He hugged her tight, trying not to think about the fact that she'd be in his arms for only that one night before he'd be gone for several weeks. He cradled her face in his hands and kissed her.

"Your car is going to be here soon," she said.

"I know. I think I have just enough time to say goodbye to everyone if we go now."

She breathed deeply and stepped out of his arms, wiping her eyes. With an admirable stiff upper lip that slayed him anew, she said, "Okay. I'm ready."

He carried their bags down to the lobby, where their friends were milling about, talking excitedly and wishing Gavin and Harper a great trip.

"There you are!" Chloe exclaimed. "Did you lose your phone? I've been texting you."

"I turned it off last night, and we got up early to see the sunrise. I must have forgotten to turn it back on." Tegan pulled her phone from her back pocket and turned it on.

Chloe looked approvingly at Jett and said, "The *sunrise?* Who knew you were so romantic?"

He sure as hell hadn't. He didn't know if Tegan had opened his eyes to who he was always supposed to be, or if he was becoming this person who thought about sunrises and bubble baths solely for her. But his guess was a little of both. He squeezed Tegan's hand and said, "I'm going to say goodbye. I'll be right back." He didn't want to get caught up in time-consuming goodbyes, so he made a beeline for Dean.

"You taking off?" Dean asked.

"Yeah. I'll see you in two weeks." He pulled his brother into an embrace, holding him a little longer than usual. He was going to miss him. It had always been easy to put people out of his mind when he said a cursory *until next time* the night before he took off and then spent hours working. This was anything but easy. "Love you, man."

Jett added this new pang of missing his brother to the long list of things Tegan had opened his eyes to, only he wasn't sure how much he liked it.

As he released Dean, his brother looked at him like he'd lost his mind. "Love you, too. You okay?"

"He's probably hurting from that bruise you gave him," Emery said as she wrapped her arms around Jett and hugged him. "Love you, Jett. That was really fun last night. I'm so happy for you and Tegan. See you in two weeks."

"See you then, spitfire." He looked around at their friends, and that pang hit him again. He'd miss them all. He gave a cursory wave to the group and said, "See you next time."

Everyone waved and called out their goodbyes, but Jett was already on his way to Tegan, who was still talking with Chloe, and he was focused on only one thing—making sure she was okay.

Chloe looked up with a woeful expression as he approached. Tegan looked over her shoulder, and the strong woman who'd captured his heart put on her best fake smile, gutting him anew.

"See you in a couple weeks, Chloe," Jett said.

"I'll take good care of Tegan for you."

"I'll be *fine*," Tegan said with enviable conviction.

"I know you will." Jett laced their hands together, holding on tight. "Walk me outside?"

He grabbed his bag on the way out the door and gave it to the driver. Then he led Tegan a few feet away and embraced her. "I'll FaceTime you tonight. Eight o'clock."

"Great," she said too cheerily, staring at his chest.

He slipped his finger under her chin and lifted it so he could see her face. He saw right through her strong facade to the sadness swimming just beneath the surface, but he'd never call her on it. "I'm going to miss waking up with you in my arms and seeing your beautiful face first thing in the morning. But those are the things that will carry me through while we're apart. What can I do to make this goodbye easier for you?"

"I'm *fine*," she insisted. "I'm going to be swamped while you're gone. I'm giving the website a final once-over when I get back home today, and that should be up and running by the middle of the week. I have ads that start Friday, and I'm sure there will be questions from customers once that gets going. I have to schedule meetings with the lighting and setup crews. I was telling Desiree and Rick about remodeling the house so I can use it as a playhouse. Did you know Rick is an architect? I'm meeting with him Tuesday; then I'll call Rob Wicked for an estimate to do the work. I've got my big-girl panties on, and I'm ready to dive in feetfirst…"

As she rambled on about work, Jett saw through that, too. He crushed her to him, silencing her with a long, slow kiss, waiting for that moment she melted against him. When he felt the tension leave her body and she sank into him, he continued kissing her, because two weeks was a long damn time.

When their lips finally parted, he kept it light to avoid causing more tears, and said, "I look forward to seeing you strip off those big-girl panties on FaceTime tonight."

A genuine smile lifted her lips, and she nodded.

He gave her one last kiss and said, "Until tonight, sunshine."

He climbed into the car, looking out the window just as Dean appeared beside Tegan. Tears spilled from her eyes. Every muscle in Jett's body went rigid. He'd never before had to see the heartache he'd left behind. He thought he was done relying on Dean to pick up his slack, but as the driver pulled away from the curb and Tegan buried her face in his brother's chest, he wondered if it would ever really end.

Chapter Twenty-Six

TEGAN PILED HER laptop and notebooks into her bag Monday morning, shoved her feet into her favorite pair of fuzzy boots, threw on her jacket, and headed up to the big house. Jett had called half an hour early last night. He'd said he couldn't wait another second to hear her voice and see her face. He'd told her about his trip and had given her a tour of his hotel suite, telling her how much he wished she were there. But she'd decided after he left yesterday that she was not going to act sad or do anything else that might make him feel bad for taking care of business, and she was proud of herself for sticking to her guns. Rather than telling him that she missed him so much it had taken her all day to review the website and get her notes over to Evan, she'd said it was a good thing they had the time apart, because if he were there, she'd probably be doing *him* instead of the work that needed her attention.

It was *hell*.

Flying through the front door, she shouted, "Jock?" She hung up her jacket and hollered upstairs, "Are you up?"

"In the kitchen," he called out.

She went into the kitchen and found him leaning against the counter, a coffee mug in one hand, his phone in the other.

On the counter behind him was a plate of bacon, eggs, and toast.

"Hi." She dropped her bag on the table and took the mug from his hands, sipping his coffee. "I've got everything organized and ready to go. I hope you're ready to work." She handed him back his mug and snagged a piece of bacon. "I figured we'd start with contacting the production managers, then the lighting and setup crews." She took a bite of bacon, and as she circled back to the table, she said, "I think we should make flyers to put out at places like the Sundial Café. I know the ads start Friday, but customers can take flyers, and lots of people who are on vacation probably don't look at newspapers or local news online."

Jock turned his phone, showing her the local news he was reading.

"You're not on vacation, and I think it's a good idea. We should do it." She pulled her laptop, notebooks, and sticky notes from her bag and bent over the table, spreading them out as she said, "Then I thought we'd brainstorm about where twenty-five to forty-year-olds are hanging out, because when I talked with my parents yesterday, my mom came up with a great idea. We were talking about the book club I'm in, and she said she would assume that women who read romance are more likely to want to see live romantic comedies. I think she hit the nail on the head. We should connect with book clubs, bookstores, and maybe even talk to the local grocery stores about featuring a sign for the theater near their books and magazines."

Jock set down his mug and walked over to her. He put his hands on her shoulders, staring into her eyes.

"What are you doing? Do I have something on my face?"

She swiped at her cheeks.

"Looking for signs of drugs."

"What? I would *never*!"

"If you're not on uppers, then what's going on? Did you get *any* sleep last night?"

"Not really, but I've had plenty of coffee. Is there more bacon? You know what? I can make it." She headed for the stove.

Jock grabbed her hand and led her back to the table, shoving her into a chair. "Don't move." He retrieved the plate and his coffee and set the plate in front of her. "You really miss Jett, don't you?"

Waving her hand, she said, "I'll see him in two weeks. It's not a big deal." Then she shoved a piece of bacon in her mouth.

He arched a brow in disbelief.

"What?" she asked, mouth full.

"Do you remember what you did right after Harvey died?"

She finished eating and said, "I cried, and I called you."

"And you spent more than an hour doing exactly what you're doing now, rattling on about nonsense that was going on in your hometown."

"I did *not*." She shifted her eyes away.

"Tegan," he said sternly.

She could feel his disbelieving eyes on her, and she threw her hands up in surrender. "Okay, *fine*. I miss him. But it's not a big deal. I'm going to keep myself busy and these two weeks will fly by."

"Uh-huh." He sat back, casually sipping his coffee. "Do you want to talk about it?"

"No, I don't want to talk about it. I want to *work*. Do I have a sign on my head that says I'm weak and spineless and need support? *Geez.* Chloe called last night offering to come over and watch movies, and Emery texted asking if I wanted to have breakfast with the girls at Summer House this morning."

"Sounds fun. You should have gone."

She'd been afraid that if she went, they would have gotten the truth out of her, and then she'd be a weepy mess. "I really wanted to get started on this list."

The doorbell chimed and she said, "Are you expecting someone?"

"No. I'll be right back. You eat."

As she plucked another piece of bacon from the pile on his plate, she heard a female voice and thunderous footsteps heading down the hall. Tegan pushed to her feet as Chloe, Emery, Daphne, and Serena flew into the kitchen carrying bags and boxes.

"Absentee Boyfriend Damage Control at your service!" Chloe said as she held out a box and lifted the lid, revealing a dozen delicious-looking doughnuts.

Absentee...?

Emery dumped a grocery bag full of various types of chips on the table. Daphne tossed two gigantic bags of M&M's beside them and said, "Sweet and salty, which is what every woman needs when she's sad."

A wave of gratitude pushed through Tegan, but she was afraid to embrace it. Once she opened those floodgates, there was no telling what would come out.

"We've got you covered, Tegan." Serena set two laptops on the counter and said, "You don't have to go through this alone."

"I'm *fine.*" Tegan plucked a chocolate doughnut from the box and bit into it. "Seriously. I'm not the type of girl who needs to have my hand held just because my boyfriend is out of

town. Jett's *working*. He's not abandoning me. I'm totally fine."
She took another bite, filling her cheeks like a chipmunk.

The girls exchanged worried glances.

"She's worse off than we thought." Emery frowned. "She's in denial."

Serena touched Tegan's hand and said, "I've been there, girlfriend, and let me tell you, it's *not* a good place to be."

"I'm not in denial," Tegan mumbled. They were looking at her like it was a load of crap, and guilt ate away at her. "Okay, *fine*. I miss him like *crazy*, but I can handle it. So what if I printed out the picture of us that Daphne texted to me from the wedding and put it up next to my bed?"

"You did?" Daphne asked. "Wasn't it *so* special? The way he was looking at you was like he was mesmerized."

"I love it," Tegan admitted. She glanced at Chloe and the others and said, "But when we were painting, I got the impression that some of you thought it wasn't such a good idea for me to get serious with Jett. Why are you guys doing this?"

Chloe set the box of doughnuts on the counter and said, "That was before we saw you two together as a couple. Now we've seen how Jett looks at you, how he holds you and dances with you."

"And watches you across the room like you're his everything," Serena added.

Chloe stepped closer and said, "He made you a frigging *love nest* just to watch the sunrise. We were wrong, Teg."

The girls nodded in agreement.

"*I* was wrong," Chloe clarified. "I'm sorry for being overprotective. I assumed the worst. I should have trusted your instincts."

"You think what she said to you was tough?" Serena rolled

her eyes and said, "Try being her younger sister. But she only does it because she loves us."

Tegan's throat thickened with emotions, but she didn't want to cry, not in front of her friends and Jock. "I get it, and I appreciate it. But I'm really doing okay. I mean, sure, we talked until two in the morning, and it was as wonderful as it was torturous to see him and not be able to touch him. But that's what long-distance relationships are. I know what I signed up for and I'm fine with it."

"Maybe you are, but I know how it feels to be miles apart from your boyfriend. I moved to Boston right when Drake and I got together," Serena explained. "I know Boston is a lot closer than where Jett is right now, but how it feels to miss them is the same."

Chloe touched a laptop and said, "And you're building a business while you're missing him, which has got to be hard."

"And you lost Berta," Daphne added. "We know how much you loved her."

Tegan's chest constricted. She missed Berta, but she'd thought everyone would think she was silly if she told them.

"We should have been there for you after you got that news," Chloe said. "We were caught up in the damage from the storm, and then work, and the excitement of Harper's wedding. We never slowed down enough to properly welcome you into our sisterhood. But we're here now. And if you'll let us, we want to help you in every way we can. With the business, personally, whatever you need or want."

"Even if it's just watching movies and eating junk food," Emery said. "You're one of us, and from now on you can count on us to bother you every chance we get."

"Don't you have to go to your *real* jobs today?"

"*Sisterhood*, sweetheart," Chloe said. "Today you *are* our real jobs."

Tears burned Tegan's eyes, and she stuffed the last piece of the doughnut into her mouth, hoping to keep them at bay. But when the girls converged on her for a group hug, the tears broke free, tumbling down her cheeks.

"Looks like I'd better make more breakfast. Who likes bacon and eggs?" Jock asked.

All the girls cheered, giving Tegan a chance to try to pull herself together.

"Bacon goes straight to my hips," Daphne said sheepishly. "I think I'd better skip it."

"With a figure like yours, I wouldn't worry about it," Jock said as he went to the stove.

Daphne's cheeks pinked up, and Tegan had never seen her look so happy.

Emery clapped her hands and said, "Okay, Damage-Control Girls, *coats off.* We have work to do!"

Chatter and laughter filled the kitchen as the girls stripped off their coats, bringing Uncle Harvey's house back to life. Jock made a joke about not making this a habit because he liked to *ease* into his days, and Chloe declared, "Once-a-week breakfasts it is!"

Tegan stood back, basking in her new reality, knowing that with friends like these, she'd never be lonely again.

Chapter Twenty-Seven

JETT SAT IN the conference room of EBC Enterprises Wednesday evening trying to concentrate on the discussion at hand, but it was seven thirty and they'd been at it for twelve hours. Normally that wouldn't be a problem, but while he was mentally ticking off boxes, evaluating the progress EBC had made, he was also strategizing and making plans for the Hyannis projects, wondering if he should bring Jonas in to handle them while he was in London. And then there was Tegan…

He looked at his watch for the hundredth time, counting down the minutes until their call. He knew that once he heard her voice and saw her beautiful face, the chaos in his head would calm, but it wouldn't quell the emptiness leaving her had left behind. He hated that she was so far away, plowing through her projects without him there to lend support or to hold her at the end of the day. He was glad that Jock and the girls had stepped in to help, but that had also added to his guilt.

"I think that wraps it up for tonight." Ken Wallace, a senior director, looked across the table at Jett and said, "Unless there's something else you'd like to cover?"

"No, thank you. I think we've covered enough for now. I'm

impressed with the progress you've made in your department, and I look forward to seeing next month's reports. I think the implementation of the procedures we spoke of will go a long way now that the waves of the takeover have calmed."

As Ken and the others gathered their things, Ken said, "Thank you for putting your trust in my team. Your guidance has been priceless."

"My guidance is only as good as the team that carries it out." Jett shook his hand and said, "Keep up the good work."

After they left the conference room, Jett began putting away his things and called Tia. "Hi. I need you to set up a teleconference with Jonas while I'm in LA."

"Finally realizing you're spreading yourself too thin? That it's time to let him do those types of reviews?"

"No," he said, even though he no longer enjoyed the review meetings the way he once had. He spent enough time with the key players with the companies he acquired and restructured during the due diligence and acquisition processes to know how they'd manage. If he wasn't certain of their success, they would not be in key positions. Maybe the information he gained in these review meetings could be handled by Jonas or one of his other team members. But this review would be over in twenty-four hours and then he'd be on a plane to LA and on to the next project. The next review meeting wasn't for another three months. He'd worry about that sixty days from now. He had more pressing issues at hand.

"I'm thinking about bringing him in to manage the Hyannis projects," Jett explained. "Did you get the ratified contracts back from Mitchell and the other business owners yet?" The thought of handing Mitchell and the others off to Jonas added even more guilt to the already untenable amount weighing him down, but there was nothing he could do about it. He grabbed his briefcase and headed out of the conference room.

"Yes. The last one came in earlier today. But I thought you wanted to manage those projects yourself."

"I did. I *do*. But the Carlisle deal is twenty times the magnitude of all those shops put together. That's where my expertise is needed."

"Now, that sounds like the boss I'm used to. Throw some money at the little people and move on to the big guns."

Tia's words grated on his nerves like sandpaper. "I'm not throwing money at them, and they're *not* little people," he snapped as he pushed through the office doors and stepped onto the sidewalk. "Jonas can handle those projects with his eyes closed."

"I was *joking*. What's up with you? You've been so cranky since you got there. I'm thinking you're having Tegan withdrawals."

No shit. "I have a lot on my plate right now."

"No more than usual, except for that pretty little dessert waiting for you at the Cape."

"Maybe you're right about those withdrawals," he admitted. "Sorry. I didn't mean for you to take the brunt of my bad mood."

"It's okay. Now that you're in a little better mood, it seems like a good time to ask if you've approved my vacation request."

"I haven't seen it. When are you going?"

"August fifth through the ninth."

"Are you kidding? The week of Tegan's soft opening? I'm in no mood for jokes tonight, T. You know I can't be there for the opening of her children's program. There's no way I'm missing the opening of her adult program. I need you to handle things in my absence."

"You don't have to miss it. I promise. Tegan and I have been talking, and we've become friends. Becca and I want to go to support her. But don't worry. I talked to Lauren, and she's going to handle things while I'm gone." Lauren Day was Tia's right hand. She'd covered for Tia in the past and had done an excellent job.

"Tia, talking with Tegan is one thing, but if you do go out there and get to be great friends, I just worry—"

"Before you tell me that you don't think it's a good idea for me and Tegan to get to know each other like that, my loyalty is to *you*. I would never talk about you as her boyfriend, or anything like that. She and I have already talked about lines we cannot cross. We can be good friends without sharing all the sexy details of your relationship. But I *like* her, Jett. She's got such a positive outlook, and she's *real*. Do you know how hard it is to meet women who aren't fake or only out for themselves?"

"You know *I* think she's one of a kind." He didn't need Tia's approval of Tegan, but he trusted Tia and he liked knowing she thought so highly of Tegan.

"Well, so do I, and there is no stipulation in my contract about not being friends with women you go out with."

He pictured Tia's chin tipped up in defiance. "*Fine,*" he relented. "Anything else?"

"Nope! All good. Try not to bite anyone's head off before next Friday night. *Ta-ta*, boss."

Jett ended the call and looked for his driver before realizing he'd forgotten to text him. *Damn it.* He breathed deeply, filling his lungs with fresh Louisiana air, and Tegan's voice sailed through his mind. *You need to get out and experience more than just office walls and hotel rooms. Breathe in fresh air, climb mountains, or explore a new town, learn the culture, soak in the history, and gorge on new foods.*

He rang Tegan on FaceTime. Her beautiful face appeared on the screen, spreading her light like Novocaine to his angst, causing a rush of longing and shutting out the rest of the world.

"Hi, sunshine. How are you?"

"Hi. I'm good. I've gotten so much done already. The site is up and I'm starting the ads tomorrow instead of Friday. Rick has great ideas for remodeling the house and he's working on plans, and Rob Wicked said he'd put it on his schedule for the fall. He's coming out tomorrow before my book club meeting to get a feel for the house."

"That's great, Tegs. He does good work."

"That's what Rick said. Did I tell you that Jock and I have several meetings scheduled with my uncle's associates and the lighting and setup crews? I can't believe the first children's show is only a month away. How was your day?"

This had become her MO, talking about everything except how much she missed him. She was getting good at presenting a strong front, and he'd played along at first because he'd known she needed it and he hadn't wanted to cause her any more tears. But he couldn't take it anymore. He needed to tell her how he felt.

"My day was fine, but I don't want to talk about work. I miss you, baby. I miss you so damn much."

Her gaze softened, and she said, "I miss you, too, *so* much." She pressed her lips together, and he knew she was holding back.

"Tell me, sunshine. I need to hear it."

"I wake up in the morning and I forget you're not here because I dream about you every night," she said in a pained voice. "It takes a minute for me to get my bearings." She tilted her head back and closed her eyes for a beat before looking at him again with that stiff upper lip in place. "I promised myself I wasn't going to tell you that. I'm fine, Jett. I miss you, but we're *good*."

God, she was incredible. "I want to hear it, Tegs, because I see you in my dreams, too, and I hear your voice in my head. Let's go on our first Baton Rouge adventure and take a walk, explore the park."

Her face lit up. "I would *love* that! I have my walking shoes on. Do I need anything else? An umbrella? A coat?"

He didn't think it was possible for her to shine any brighter than he'd already seen, but her effervescence gave him goose bumps. "No. It's about sixty degrees with clear skies. All you need is my hand in yours. Can you feel our fingers lacing together? Our palms touching?"

"Yes," she said softly.

"Let me know if I walk too fast. This is my first FaceTime date, and I don't want to mess it up."

"You can't mess this up. It's the start of our best adventure yet, only to be outdone by our *next*."

She *destroyed* him in the very best way. He strolled down the block describing the surroundings, turning the phone to show her buildings and people on the sidewalk, then turning it back so he could see her. When he reached the pub on the corner, he said, "Are you hungry?"

"*Starved.* Always."

He chuckled. "That's my girl. How do you feel about a burger?"

"Sounds perfect. With fries!"

"You've got it." He went into the pub and sat at a table. He turned to the phone so Tegan could meet their waiter, and then he ordered their meal and a beer. He walked around the pub to show her the bar and she said hello to customers, waving and excitedly explaining that she and Jett were on a FaceTime date. By the time they got their food, she'd met almost everyone in the place. They laughed through dinner, and when he got up to leave, she insisted he hold the phone up so she could say goodbye to everyone. Jett never imagined himself doing any of those things, but he held that phone up proudly and announced, "Tegan Fine would like your attention."

"I had so much fun meeting you all!" Tegan shouted. "Enjoy your dinners, and remember to get out and enjoy the fresh air, too." She waved and the people at the bar cheered and waved back.

As Jett walked outside, he said, "Hand, please."

"*Oops.* Sorry. I had to cop a feel of your butt first," she said sassily.

"You'd better hold my hand, or I might have far dirtier wandering hands when we get to the park."

She giggled. "I love holding your hand, even virtually."

"I feel the same, which means your bewitching powers are still in full swing." He walked around the park, showing her the courtyard and the grassy areas where couples walked hand in hand.

"It looks romantic. Have you been through there before?"

"I've never been anywhere except the hotel and offices. The riverfront is just a few blocks away, but I've never been there, either."

"Let's go! I want to see the water."

Her excitement was contagious. He walked the few blocks to the waterfront, and she said, "Let's sit on the grass. What's it like there?"

Jett lowered himself to the grass without a care about his suit or anything else for that matter. He set down his briefcase and described the scents and sounds of the river and traffic. Tegan asked one question after the next, commenting on his every answer. He could see that she was soaking it all in, which made him want to do more adventuring with her.

"I wish I could touch you right now," she said, touching the screen.

A cool breeze swept off the river, and he swore he felt her fingers on his face and the warm press of her palm against his skin as he said, "It won't be long now…"

Chapter Twenty-Eight

THE NUMBER ONE rule of the book club stated that all in-person meetings *must* take place at a beach. Tegan and the other members had met at a beach in Harwich—and they'd frozen their asses off. It had been a cold, gray day, and they'd come prepared with hats, gloves, and blankets, but the wind had cut like ice. They'd stayed long enough to talk about Harper's wedding, but their teeth were chattering too much to enjoy their conversation. Gabe Appleton, the voluptuous redhead whose turn it had been to choose the book and the location of the meeting, had suggested they go to Common Grounds, the coffeehouse she owned not far from the beach. They'd been there for an hour and Tegan was finally warming up.

The unassuming café was hidden down a secluded road, and the atmosphere was lovely. A handful of guys played pool on the far side of the room, and a couple was having coffee at a table in the corner. Gabe's older brother, Rod, was playing guitar on a small stage, and her younger brother, Elliott, a gracious host and supposedly very talented baker, had disappeared into the kitchen with promises of fresh-baked treats.

"Did anyone else ugly cry when you read chapter twenty-one? When she sent him away?" Mia Stone, an outgoing brunette who worked as an assistant to world-renowned fashion designers Josh and Riley Braden, asked. "Because I cried like a baby."

The book club had members all over the country, and though most of their discussions took place in the online forums, they also met once a month at different locations. Each month a member was chosen at random to select the book they would read and to choose the location of their meeting. Those who could not attend were invited to chime in via video chat, as Mia Stone and Amber Montgomery were doing tonight.

"Yes!" they all said at once.

"Charlotte definitely ratcheted up the emotions in this book," Amber said. "She said it's because she got married and—"

"You *know* Charlotte Sterling?" Gabe asked.

"I thought I mentioned that in the forums when Gabe chose the book," Amber said sweetly. It was easy to imagine her running the bookstore she owned in Oak Falls, Virginia. She was kind and patient, and didn't seem like anything could rattle her. "Maybe I meant to and got busy with a customer or something. Char and I are LWW sorority sisters, the Ladies Who Write."

"Is that part of LWW Enterprises, the multimedia company? And does that mean you're a writer, too?" Mia asked.

"I'm not a writer. But the sorority house is part of LWW," Amber explained.

"That's so cool that you know Char," Steph said. "I wonder if she is as wild as the heroines in her books."

"Forget that. I wonder if that sex club is real," Mia chimed in. "I'm going to have to do some digging."

Daphne's eyes nearly popped out of her head. "You would go to a sex club?"

"Not to *do* anything," Mia said. "I'm not even sure I could muster up the courage to go in, but I know my sister Jennifer would. Wouldn't it be fun to be a fly on the wall?"

"I couldn't," Daphne said, blushing a red streak.

"No way," Amber agreed. "I can read about it, but only because nobody *knows* I'm reading about it."

"I'd go," Steph said with a shrug. "I'm sure Gabe would go with me, right?"

Gabe gave her a thumbs-up and said, "Heck yeah, baby girl. You know it."

"Me too," Chloe agreed. "Like Mia said, you don't have to do anything, but just being there would be thrilling."

"I don't think I could do that." Tegan would be too embarrassed to watch other people having sex, much less be a part of it. "But I'd totally want you guys to take notes, maybe a few cell pics, and give me all the details afterward."

They all laughed, and Daphne and Amber said they'd want notes and pictures, too.

"The other thing I loved about this book was that the heroine took control. She was feminine but badass," Mia said.

"That she was," Steph agreed.

Amber leaned closer to the screen and said, "Can you imagine doing all the things she did? Making your man get down on his knees, blindfolded, and telling him what to do to you?"

Tegan choked on her hot chocolate, spilling it all over the front of her sweater and the table. Chloe and Steph grabbed handfuls of napkins and started dabbing at her sweater and the table.

"Are you okay?" Steph asked.

Tegan's eyes were watering from coughing, and to make matters worse, now all she could see was Jett on his knees, naked and aroused, with her FUCKABLE FLIRT mask on his handsome face. "I'm okay." She cleared her throat and said, "Sorry. I must have taken in too much."

"That's what she said," Mia teased, making them all laugh.

"*Man alert.* Hush your sexy talk," Elliott said as he came out of the kitchen carrying a tray. He set it on their table, and steam rose from mini loaves of corn bread and chocolate chip cookies, filling the air with their enticing aroma. There was a cute ceramic honeypot in the middle of the tray, and a plate with pats of flower-shaped butter.

"Wow, this looks delicious," Daphne said.

"Thank you," Elliott said, handing each of them a plate.

Elliott had Down syndrome, and although he looked nothing like his tall redheaded sister and dark-haired brother, with his longish sandy-blond hair and short, stout stature, he shared Gabe's vibrant personality. He pushed his wire-framed glasses to the bridge of his nose and said, "Rod says 'Give a woman chocolate and she'll be yours forever.' I say give her corn bread and chocolate and double your chances."

Everyone laughed.

"You are a godsend, El. I needed this tonight." Steph reached for a cookie and said, "I should marry you."

Elliott said, "Get in line, Steph," earning more chuckles.

The café door opened, and Justin walked in, followed by a mountain of a man, both wearing black leather jackets. The big guy had tattoos on his neck, pitch-black hair, and haunted eyes.

"Dark Knights!" Elliott cheered as he headed over to greet them.

Justin lifted his chin and said, "El, my man. You hanging with the ladies tonight?"

"Are you freaking kidding me?" Chloe huffed out a breath.

"Who is the scary guy with Justin?" Tegan asked.

"That's his cousin Tank," Steph explained. "Dwayne's brother. He's a volunteer firefighter and he owns a tattoo parlor. He looks scary, and he is to those who warrant it, but he's a great guy."

"Are they Hells Angels?" Amber asked nervously.

"No," Steph said. "They're Dark Knights. They're not with a gang. They're in a motorcycle club, and they do good things for the community."

Justin high-fived Elliott and made a beeline toward the girls. Tank hung back, talking with Elliott.

"They're talking dirty about books," Elliott called after Justin.

Justin's eyes were trained on Chloe. His lips tipped up in a sexy smirk as he said, "Dirty talkers. Just the way I like them." He pulled out a chair from a nearby table and set it down backward next to Chloe. He straddled it, crossed his arms over the back of the chair, and said, "Talk dirty to me, baby."

"Oh, I *like* him," Mia said, earning a wink from Justin.

With a completely straight face, her eyes locked on Justin, Chloe said, "I'd better call Dwayne and tell him one of his mad dogs got loose."

"I'm here for the book club." Justin pulled a copy of the book they were reading out of his pocket and tossed it on the table. "I looked up the rules on the forum, and there's nothing that says a guy can't join."

"You must have overlooked the part that said the club founders have to approve all requests to join." Chloe crossed her arms and called out, "Tank," without turning away from Justin.

Tank approached, eyes black as night, expression cold as steel. A thick silver chain peeked out from beneath his beard, and his ears and nose were pierced. Tegan didn't care what Steph had said; the man made her nervous.

Tank grabbed the back of Justin's leather jacket with one massive, tattooed hand and lifted him to his feet. "Let's go, nimrod. You said you wanted to play pool, not track down a chick."

"That's not a *chick*," Justin said as Tank dragged him toward the door. "It's *Chloe*."

Tank scoffed and hauled him out of the café.

"*Whoa*," Amber said. "Where I live, we have *cowboys*. I'm not used to bikers. They scare me."

Mia said, "I *love* bikers almost as much as I love PIs."

Tegan wasn't into either. She was perfectly happy with her suit-wearing, sweet-talking, sexily arrogant investor.

"Are you sure that you and Justin aren't messing around?" Daphne asked Chloe. "He's really into you."

"He'd be into a loaf of bread if it had breasts and a vagina." Chloe snagged a cookie and bit it in half, inciting a long discussion about men.

Eventually the conversation circled back to the hero in the book they'd read.

"The poor guy didn't sleep for eight days after she sent him away." Steph finished the corn bread she was eating and said, "I wanted to climb into the book and give him some of my calming sleep spray. One spray on his pillow and he'd sleep like a baby."

Tegan finished her third cookie and said, "I need some of that."

"Are you having trouble sleeping?" Steph asked.

Tegan's phone vibrated with a text. "Lately I have been," she said as she pulled out her phone and saw Jett's name on the screen. It was only nine thirty. She wondered if he'd forgotten about her meeting.

"She and Jett are an item now," Chloe explained. "And he's traveling."

Tegan read his text. *Sorry to bother you. When you're done, check your email.*

"It must be hard to be apart," Steph said as Tegan opened her email and found Jett's message. "I'll definitely hook you up with sleep spray."

She read the message. *Tegs, our very first West Coast adventure is waiting for you.* She scanned the rest of the email, and said, "Thanks, Steph, but I may not need it just yet. Jett sent me a *ticket* to LA!"

There was an uproar of cheers, and everyone talked at once, but Tegan was in shock as she reread the email and ticket details. "I'm supposed to leave tomorrow afternoon for our very first West Coast adventure together and return Sunday!"

"That's so romantic!" Amber said. "You're lucky! You should go!"

"I was so *wrong* about that man," Chloe said.

"I wasn't," Daphne said with a giggle and a blush.

As the girls gushed, Tegan's heart sank, and she said, "I can't go."

"What? Why?" Mia snapped. "I don't even know the guy and *I'd* go!"

"No, I mean, I want to, but I just scheduled meetings for the theater this weekend. Jock and I are meeting with the setup and lighting crews, and we're having lunch with one of the children's show producers Saturday and meeting another one on Sunday. I can't just cancel everything."

"Yes, you *can*," Chloe said. "Or let Jock handle it. He won't mind."

"I can't just hand it off to him. My uncle left the theater to *me*. Jock is only helping, not taking over." Her heart was breaking. "Jett has changed his schedule for me several times already, and he's leaving for a month soon. I want to show him that I'll do the same. That he's worth the risk. But I don't want to get off on the wrong foot with the producers or anyone else that I need to work with for the theater to succeed. What should I do?"

"*Go!*" they all said at once.

"Don't freak out." Chloe took Tegan's hand and said, "Ask Jock if it would be a problem to reschedule. He knows the people you're supposed to meet with, and you know he'll give it to you straight."

"Call this Jock guy," Mia said. "I *need* to know if you're going."

"Okay." Tegan took a deep breath and called Jock. She told him her quandary and said, "What should I do? I want to go, but not at the risk of making a mistake with the theater."

"Teg, you *know* what Harvey would say. Nothing was more important to him than your happiness. Life is short. Go see Jett."

Happiness bubbled up inside her. "You're sure?"

"Absolutely. I can rearrange these meetings. The guy went all out for you. That's Harvey-and-Adele love, Tegan."

When she ended the call, the girls said, "Well?"

"Looks like I'm going to LA!"

Chapter Twenty-Nine

TEGAN HAD BEEN a solo world traveler for years, and never had she been as nervous as she was while she made her way to the escalator at LAX to meet Jett by the baggage claim. She'd changed her clothes four times that morning, wanting to look sexy for Jett, but also craving comfort for the long flight since it didn't touch down until eight thirty p.m. She'd finally settled on her softest cardigan and cami and paired them with her favorite skinny jeans and boots. She wasn't sure if she looked casual and chic or boring, but when she'd tried to dress sexier, she'd felt overdone, and she was far too nervous for *overdone*.

She stepped onto the escalator and peered around the man in front of her. Her heart skipped when Jett came into view standing by three men in suits holding signs with passenger names on them. Jett looked devilishly handsome in a dark sweater and jeans. Their eyes connected with the heat of summer lightning. His lips curved into the cocky grin she adored as he lifted a sign that read STICKY-NOTE GIRL.

She couldn't stop grinning.

He flipped the sign over, and it said I'VE MISSED YOU in big red letters.

She was shaking, dying to be in his arms, but as she neared

the bottom of the escalator, she reminded herself not to make a scene. Jett was a professional with a reputation to uphold. She didn't want to come across as an overeager, lovesick fool.

But when her feet hit the floor, she and Jett both rushed forward and he swept her into his arms, twirling her around as they kissed. How could she have debated missing this for a work meeting? She would never, ever make that mistake again.

When their lips finally parted, her feet still dangling off the floor, Jett gazed into her eyes as if he had all day just to look at her. Eventually he said, "God, I've missed you," and lowered his lips to hers again, kissing her breathless.

When her feet finally touched the floor, her hopeful, happy heart was fuller than it had ever been.

"Do you want to take a walk? Are you hungry? What do you feel like doing?" he asked, but the emotions in his eyes told her that he was hoping for the exact response she was ready to give.

"*You…*"

JETT HAD WARNED Tegan about the long drive from the airport to his hotel, but while the driver navigated traffic, they were too caught up in each other in the back seat for her to notice the time it took. She was still in a state of hazy lustfulness as they made their way through the luxurious hotel lobby. She was vaguely aware of people greeting Jett as *Mr. Masters* as they passed the registration desk. They stepped onto the elevator with a handful of other people. Jett held her from behind, his hard heat pressing temptingly against her, his tantalizing mouth trailing kisses along the back of her neck.

The second they were alone in the elevator, he spun her around, boxing her in against the wall with a fierce look in eyes, and said, "It can't have been only *days*. I swear we've been apart for *months*." His mouth crashed over hers, taking and giving in equal measure. Their hands moved hungrily, their hips ground lustfully, and when he tangled his fingers in her hair, pinpricks of pleasure darted over her flesh.

They stumbled into the penthouse, tearing their mouths apart long enough only to strip off their shoes, socks, and clothes on their way to the bedroom, where they tumbled to the mattress in a flurry of ravenous kisses and greedy gropes. Their bodies came together urgently, drawing a cry of pleasure from Tegan and a curse of raw passion from Jett. Tegan felt out of control and wild. She felt *primal*, clawing at his back, meeting every thrust of his hips with a tilt of her own as he pounded into her. Her breaths came in fast, stilted spurts. Their bodies slickened with sweat.

Jett's entire body corded tight, and he gripped her hair with both hands, gritting out, "*Come with me.*"

The thrilling mix of command and need in his voice shredded her last bit of control. She shattered into a million tingling pieces, clinging to him and crying out as Jett gave in to his own powerful release. Her name flew from his lips with the ferocity of a curse and the intensity of a prayer as they rode the waves of their passion.

They lay clinging to each other as aftershocks spasmed through their bodies. Jett pressed his lips to her cheeks and mouth, murmuring sweetness against her skin. As their breathing calmed, Tegan's vision started to clear. Moonlight spilled in through the windows, illuminating their entangled bodies.

"Thank you," Jett whispered into her ear.

She giggled and said, "For *sex?*"

He drew back just far enough for her to see pools of emotion brimming in his eyes so strongly, she could have felt them even if she were blind. Her heart turned over in her chest. He was the most passionate man she'd ever known. It drove him to succeed in business, and it was inescapable between them.

"For rearranging your schedule and flying all this way. For seeing something in me that I didn't even know existed."

"I think you must have known it existed," she teased, "because you sure knew how to use it. Or did you forget the *wow* factor? You scored an FWB by having great sex that first night. If not for that, well…Heaven knows who would have ended up in my bed next."

"You *know* what I'm talking about, you seductive little vixen."

He grabbed her butt, and she laughed.

"I didn't have to look very hard to see who you really were," she said more seriously. "All I did was show up for the adventure. You opened the door."

"But you took my hand and showed me the way," he said, shifting them toward the pillows.

Tegan caught sight of a framed picture of them on the nightstand, and another wave of happiness swept through her. They were dancing at the wedding, her cheek resting on Jett's chest, and Jett was kissing the top of her head. Their eyes were closed, and they were both smiling. Tegan got goose bumps all over at the emotion resonating from the picture. Her sister took hundreds of pictures of couples striving for one perfect shot just like that.

"Where did you get that picture?"

He pulled her closer, his leg hairs tickling her thighs, and said, "Dean texted it to me after I left Sunday. I missed you, so I printed it out and bought a frame in the shop downstairs."

"I think we share a brain. I did the same thing with a picture Daphne took, only in mine, we were gazing into each other's eyes like lovesick teenagers."

"How about lovesick adults?" he said.

Her stomach growled, and Jett chuckled.

"You've worked up my appetite, Mr. Masters. Does this fancy hotel have room service?"

"I've got your room service right here."

He moved over her, grinning like a man who couldn't get enough...and neither could she.

Chapter Thirty

"IF I WEREN'T here right now, what would you be doing?" Tegan asked as they walked down the busy sidewalk hand in hand Saturday afternoon. They'd spent the morning in bed, talking and just being together, and it had been wonderful. Now they were on another adventure, exploring LA together. Tegan had never been there.

"Thinking of you," Jett answered.

She turned around, still holding his hand as she walked backward, and said, "Nice try, *Charming Charlie*, but you just spent half the day doing dirty things to every inch of my body. You owe me the truth."

"Do I? You mean all those orgasms and the pastries from the bakery weren't enough?" He pulled her against him, stealing the millionth kiss since they'd begun exploring a little after lunchtime. "I *would* be thinking of you, as I said, but I'd *also* be working out in the hotel gym, reviewing contracts, researching, or taking care of whatever else needed my attention. That said, whatever I was trying to accomplish would be twice as difficult with thoughts of you running around my head."

"Does that mean I'm not good for you, professionally speaking?" she asked with a furrowed brow and stepped beside him once again.

He put his arm around her, needing her closer. "You are without a doubt the best thing that has *ever* happened to me."

She gazed up at him like he'd taken her breath away, and man, he hoped he had, because it was the truth.

They continued their walking tour, and Tegan was adorable, noticing and commenting on everything from the crisp blue sky to the colorful store awnings and brick pavers beneath their feet. She talked about the theater and how excited she was to be meeting the key people she'd be hosting. She told him about how helpful Jock had been, and Jett turned his thoughts inward, wondering if he'd feel any sense of jealousy. But the only thing he felt was happy for her to have such a good friend. It had been forever since Jett had been a good friend to anyone, and the worst part about that was that he hadn't even realized it. Tegan had changed that, and he didn't think she'd even tried. Just her presence, her acceptance of who he was, and her confidence to point out in the gentlest ways the things he'd done to perpetuate his own bad feelings toward his father.

"I can't believe you only go from your office to your hotel room when all of *this* is just down the block," she said, drawing him back to the moment.

"Nothing's ever been more interesting than work until you came along." He lifted her hand to his lips and kissed it.

"How did you keep that big heart of yours under wraps for so long?"

Before he could respond, she yelled, "Look!" and dragged him across the street toward a sports memorabilia shop. "Have you been in here before?" she asked as they entered the store.

"I had no idea it was here." He hadn't been in a shop like that since he threw out his cards. Even if he had known about it, he never would have considered going in.

His gaze swept over the store, and adrenaline pushed through him like a gust of wind as he took in glass displays of sports cards and framed autographed pictures of sports figures lining the walls. Shelves held helmets and bats signed by entire teams. Gloves and game-worn jerseys called out to him from the far end of the store, along with dozens of other types of sports paraphernalia, sparking a rush of memories. Jett remembered pointing at pictures of Ty Cobb and Babe Ruth when he was just a kid, exclaiming, *One day I'll get that one! And that one!* and then gazing into the display cases, his heartrate kicking up when he spotted a card he owned, and he'd proudly beam up at his father and say, *Look, Dad! I have that one!* The image of his father, as tall and solid as a towering oak to his little-boy self, his large hand engulfing Jett's smaller one, slammed into him as his father's deep voice broke out in his head. *With your arm, son, one day you'll own the field.* Memories of the deep-seated hurt that had come when his father had left pummeled him, the torturous feeling of being abandoned returned, and the nightmares that had followed him like ghosts crowded in.

Tegan touched his stomach, jarring him from the past to the present he so desperately wanted. She peered at him with wide, worried eyes, and he fought back against those ghosts with everything he had. There was no way he was going to let them ruin this adventure for his beautiful, big-hearted girl.

"You okay?" Tegan asked. "We don't have to look around if you don't want to."

He draped an arm over her shoulder, feeling her light block out the darkness, and said, "Not only do I want to look around, but has anyone ever taught you about baseball stats?"

"No, but I'm quite adept at checking out tight buns in

baseball pants," she said with a waggle of her brows.

He feigned a growl and said, "Baby, *why* do you poke the bear?"

"In hopes he might rear up and *poke* me back…"

JETT ENJOYED THE hell out of exploring the sports store, but what he loved most was sharing with Tegan the hobby that had once brought him so much joy. Teaching her about sports cards and how to understand the statistics inspired dozens of insightful questions. Her enthusiasm renewed his love of collecting. Before they left, she insisted on buying him a bobblehead figurine of his favorite player—seven-time Cy Young Award winner, pitcher Roger Clemens. When they finally left the store, they rode the trolley to the farmers' market, where they bought berries for breakfast tomorrow, and spent the rest of the day exploring on foot, eventually having dinner at an Italian restaurant. They shared their dinners and kissed more than they ate.

"LA isn't that different from New York," Tegan said as the sun descended from the sky and they made their way back to the hotel. "It's prettier here, though—greener, cleaner, and the buildings are shorter. Actually, it smells better, too. I take it back. LA is very different from the Big Apple. Thank you for bringing me here." She rested her head against him. "I love adventuring with you. I'm never going to forget a second of this weekend."

For the hundredth time that day, Jett had visions of future weekends like this, walking hand in hand, exploring cool places, and learning more about Tegan *and* about himself. He wanted to hear all the stories about her youth, college years, and the years in between college and when they'd met, until he knew all there was to know about her. Although he was sure that just when he thought he'd learned all there was to know about her, she'd surprise him with more stories she'd forgotten to share. He could spin deals until he was too old to think straight, but he knew none of them would measure up to her.

"You ain't seen nothing yet, sunshine. I have a little surprise for you."

She smiled up at him as they walked into the hotel. "There's *more?*"

"There's always more." He led her through the lobby, saying hello to the employees who greeted him as they walked past the reception desk toward the freight elevator.

"Everyone knows you," she said. "How many times have you stayed here?"

"Every time I've been in LA since I bought the hotel chain seven years ago." He took out his key chain, dangling the elevator key, and said, "Otherwise, how would I get this?"

"You *own* the hotel chain? Like, all of them?"

He unlocked the freight elevator and guided her inside.

"All of them," he said as they made their ascent. "I told you I was an investor."

"Yes, but I thought you meant a few businesses and properties. Not an entire hotel chain."

"Then you underestimated your boyfriend, babe."

"I guess that explains the Armani suits."

"That's just good taste and dressing the part." He gathered her in his arms and said, "Would you like a copy of my investment portfolio?"

"No. Everything I want is standing right in front of me, and it wouldn't matter if you owned a dozen hotel chains or you worked in a grocery store as long as you looked at me like you are now."

"God, I love you." The words felt as if they'd been torn straight from his soul. He felt stronger, freer, like his lungs were filled to capacity for the very first time. Her surprised, loving eyes teared up, and he said, "I do, Tegs. I *love* you. I love everything about you, from your sticky notes to your wild dancing and the way you stumble over your own feet sometimes. I love the way you say my name, and everything feels better when you're by my side."

Happy tears slipped down her cheeks. "I love you, too," she said shakily. "I didn't want to tell you because I thought it might scare you off."

"Nothing could scare me off from the only person who makes me feel whole. I wanted to tell you at the wedding, and every day after, but I didn't know how to go from FWBs to…"

"ILYs?"

"Exactly…" He kissed her, feeling like the luckiest man on the planet.

The elevator came to an abrupt halt, and the doors opened. Cool air swept in from the rooftop, and the lights of the city glimmered below. Tegan wiped her eyes, and Jett fought the urge to shout *She loves me!* as he took her hand and led her out of the elevator.

She stopped cold at the sight of a shiny dark helicopter and turned those gorgeous baby blues on him. "Jett Masters, *what* have you done?"

He shrugged one shoulder and said, "I fell in love." It was the most honest answer he'd ever given.

"Jett…?"

He took her hand in his and said, "I want to give you every-thing, Tegs, and that starts with showing you all that LA has to offer, even if I only have one day."

Chapter Thirty-One

JETT DIDN'T THINK there was anything more beautiful than Tegan Fine padding barefoot around his living room with her pink panties peeking out from beneath one of his T-shirts. It was Sunday morning, and she was talking with her parents. *Gushing*, actually, about Jett *and* their day together. She'd just finished describing the helicopter ride as *insanely romantic* and all the sites they'd seen as *overwhelmingly awesome*. Last night, as they'd flown over beaches and mountains, celebrity homes, and tourist sites like the Getty Center, Dodger Stadium, Universal Studios, and dozens of other places, she'd been like a kid at Christmas, elated at every single one.

"I've been thoroughly spoiled." Tegan turned and blew him a kiss.

He winked, still high from their *I love yous*. He was even more in love with her today, and he knew he'd love her more tomorrow and every day thereafter.

"I know!" Tegan exclaimed. "I'm getting there. I have a lot of meetings to take care of when I get back, and we're keeping our fingers crossed that the marketing will pay off. I can't believe the children's program opens in less than a month. I'm so excited that you're coming. I can't wait to see you. No, Jett can't come. He'll be in London."

He hated that he was going to miss the opening, but he was glad her family would be there. She'd texted Cici last night and had sent her pictures while they were in the helicopter. Jett wondered if one day he and Dean would find their way back to that close a relationship.

Tegan sauntered toward him as she said, "Yes, Dad. I promise not to forget to text when I land in Boston so you know I'm still alive." She paused, then said, "*And* when I get home." She paused again. "I'll tell him. I'll talk to you next Sunday. I love you."

She ended the call and picked a blueberry out of the bowl of fruit on the table, popping it into her mouth as she set down her phone.

"Everything good?" he asked.

"Yes. My dad said he's looking forward to meeting the man who makes me sound like I'm floating on air. His words, not mine."

Jett pulled her down to his lap. Her flight was at one o'clock, and he was already thinking about the next time he could see her. "I'm looking forward to meeting your family. I was thinking that you should fly out to London while I'm there."

"I would *love* that. But we're starting rehearsals with the children's theater groups and all the crews this week to make sure there are no unexpected issues. Rehearsals will run right up until two days before the first show opens, the last week you're away. I have to be there for them. I also have a ton of loose ends to tie up. Will your travel schedule lighten up after you get back from London?"

"At some point, but possibly not right away. Once the deal

is made, I'll have to spend a lot more time there. It sounds like it's going to be hard for us through the summer. You said you have more flexibility to travel when you're in Maryland. Does that mean after you go back home you can travel with me more often?"

She was quiet for a second. "Actually, I've decided to stay at the Cape. I've been thinking about it a lot, and it doesn't make sense to go back to Peaceful Harbor when I'm working so hard to get this new program off the ground. When we were helping in Hyannis after the storm, I realized that during the summer the people I need to connect with will have enough on their plates keeping up with their own businesses. After tourist season is over is a much better time to reach out to business owners who can help cross promote the new program."

"That makes good business sense." He knew she was right, but he still felt a stab of disappointment. "Are you sure you want to live there in the winters? It's pretty desolate, and colder than you can imagine. That storm was nothing compared to the nor'easters they get."

"I'm *happy* there, and I love my cottage and our friends. I'm not psyched about the possibility of worse storms, but as I've been working on the program and fleshing out my upcoming meetings and polishing my spiel, I realized something important. There's a big difference between running a business that the community takes part in and working behind the scenes. I don't want to *just* run my uncle's business. I want to be the person kids are excited to come see, like they were with him. And if Harper and I want to make the adult events something people look forward to coming to each year, that means putting myself out there, shaking hands, making friends, and remembering names. I know it sounds old-school, but that's how my uncle built his business, and I want to do the same. I love people, so hopefully they'll like me, too. I've also been coming up with new ideas to talk to Harper about. I know it'll be hard for you and me to be apart when you're traveling, but if we're meant to be, we'll find a way to make it work, right?"

"There you go spreading your bright light on us again. Of course we'll figure it out. I don't know why I expected that you'd really go back to Maryland. You're not a half-ass person in anything you do. It's one of the things I love about you. But what about your place in Maryland and your nip-and-tuck job?"

She laughed. "I can't believe you remembered my job at the boutique. You really do have a memory like an elephant."

"Hung like one, too." He nuzzled against her neck, taking a little bite and earning a sweet sound.

"Yes, you are. I talked to Chelsea the other day, and she's going to offer the job to the person who's filling in for me. My lease on the house renews in December, so I can just let that go. I was thinking about going back a week or two before Thanksgiving to get the rest of my stuff."

"And you're going to be okay living so far away from your parents? You're so close to them."

"Of course I will. I'll miss them, but you've seen how we are. It doesn't matter if I'm living in Kalamazoo or down the street; we'll still talk every week. They'll come visit, and I'll go see them. They have really full lives, and so do I." She put a few more berries in her mouth and said, "I'm officially extending my adventure, and I think Uncle Harvey would approve. What do you think?"

"I think you're brave and smart, and so damn cute, you make every decision look easy."

"Most of them *are* easy, even when they're big." She fed him a strawberry and said, "Let's take decorating, for example. You've obviously made a decision not to do it. I can't believe you've had this place for seven years and you have no personal effects in it. I'm not judging you or anything, but I seriously thought this was a hotel suite you had rented."

He ran his fingers along her arm and said, "I told you that before you I didn't *do* personal connections."

"I thought you meant with *people*."

"People, places, pretty much everything. But that's changing. I have our picture on the nightstand." He glanced at the figurine on the mantel and said, "And my thoughtful girlfriend gave me a bobblehead of my favorite player."

"Maybe one day Roger Clemens will have some friends with him."

"Does it bother you that I had no ties to anyone before you?"

"No, but it makes me sad for you and your family. I'm glad you and Dean are on more solid ground and that you're trying to work things out with your father. I'm curious, do you consider the Cape home?"

"I don't really think of any physical place as home, and I haven't for a long time. This is going to sound weird, but you feel like home to me, Tegs. It doesn't matter where we are, just having you with me makes me feel like I'm right where I'm supposed to be."

"That's the sweetest thing I've ever heard."

"Then how I feel makes sense, because you're the sweetest woman I've ever met." He ran his hand up her leg and said, "I don't think these berries are going to be enough to satiate me."

He brushed his fingers along her inner thigh and the center of her panties. "Luckily, my favorite meal is right here."

He dipped his head, taking a love bite out her neck. A breathy "*Ah*" fell from her lips as he lifted her onto the table. He continued touching and tasting, earning more of his favorite sounds. When he stopped, she opened her eyes, and he said, "How do you want me, baby? My mouth on your sweetness or my cock buried deep inside you?"

"Both," she said in one long breath.

TEGAN WAS STILL flying high when they arrived at the airport, but as her flight time neared, grief stepped in. She told herself that the weekend had been an unexpected gift too wonderful to let their goodbye turn tearful. When they reached the security checkpoint, Jett set down her bag and embraced her. Leaving should have been *easier* given the new step they'd taken in their relationship, but it was even more difficult.

He kissed the top of her head, and she tilted her face up, struck by the longing in his eyes.

"It seems like we're always saying goodbye," she said softly.

His lips tipped up. "But think of how mind-blowing our hellos are." He pressed his lips to hers and said, "I love you, Tegs."

He'd said it a dozen times since the first, and each and every one brought fresh chills. "I love you, too. Can we *not* say goodbye? It seems so final, and you'll be back home in five days."

"*Home.* I like the sound of that." He kissed her tenderly. "How about if we say *until next time* or *peace, baby*, or we could just go with the truth, *I'll be dreaming of you.*"

"I like that last one." She searched for the perfect words to replace goodbye, and the answer appeared. "*I'll be waiting.*"

"Perfect."

The warm press of his lips stole the sadness, replacing it with the joy of knowing that in five days she'd be in his arms again.

When their lips parted, he said, "I'll be dreaming of you," with a heated look in his eyes.

She was wrong. *I'll be waiting* wasn't quite right, even if it was true. She picked up her bag and said, "Better make them dirty," and winked.

His carefree laughter followed her into the security line. She thought about Jett's dirty dreams, and his teenage fantasy about a bikini-clad model tied to a bed came rushing back. She felt his eyes on her and glanced over her shoulder. He was eating her up with a wicked grin and an even more sinful look in his gorgeous eyes.

Oh yeah, baby. I'll be ready and waiting just for you...

She pulled out her phone and texted Chloe. *I need to buy a white bikini.*

Chapter Thirty-Two

"THERE ARE SOME things *every* woman should own." Chloe held up a hanger with what looked like two long strips of bright green string that joined into one in the back.

Tegan and Daphne burst into hysterics. It was Friday afternoon, and they were at the Hyannis mall shopping for Tegan's bikini.

Chloe struggled to keep a straight face as she said, "What? You don't think I can pull off Borat's thong bathing suit? It's clearly tailored just for me. The top part is only about an inch wide, which is perfect to cover my tiny boobs."

"You have perfect boobs," Daphne said, taking the hanger from Chloe. "But you are not wearing *butt floss*. You're too classy for that. You need something more elegant, like a black bikini and a wide-brimmed hat."

"Sounds about right," Tegan agreed, looking over a display of bikinis.

Chloe rolled her eyes. "You guys are so weird. I'm not any classier than either of you."

Daphne fished through a rack of cover-ups and said, "It was a compliment. You're very well put together. I *admire* you. You always look like you walked off the pages of a fashion magazine."

"Oh my God. I do not." Chloe put her hand on her hip and said, "I wear jeans and shorts *all* the time, just not to work."

"And you still look like a fashionista," Tegan said. "It's a good thing, Chloe. You don't act like a snob or anything, but you have mile-long legs and a sleek figure that sets you apart, in the same way Daphne is voluptuous and turns every man's head wherever we go."

Daphne spun around with her mouth hanging open. "You are *crazy*. I was curvy before I had Hadley, but I swear my sweet little girl must have been secretly injecting fat cells all over my body, because I'm carrying an extra twenty pounds on top of the pudge I had before I was pregnant. It's been so long since a man paid me any attention, I had to get out the lawn mower to shave my legs this morning because I've just plain given up."

"Daph, are you blind? Didn't you see the way Jock was drooling over you at breakfast last week?" Chloe asked.

"You mean when he gave me *bacon*?" Daphne asked. "He was probably thinking that I wouldn't notice another pound or two."

"I'm pretty sure *this* is what Jock was picturing when he was looking at you." Chloe dangled a hanger with a string bikini that had a sunny-side-up egg covering each breast and a bottom made of bacon-imprinted fabric.

"Ohmygosh!" Daphne's cheeks burned red. "He was *not*!"

Tegan laughed.

"Mark my words, that man wants to eat your bacon." Chloe made a dramatic biting motion toward the bikini bottom.

"Stop!" Daphne took the hanger from her and buried it in a rack. "He was just being nice, probably because he knows that everyone sees how much he dislikes Hadley."

The sadness in Daphne's voice brought Tegan to her side. She didn't want to breach Jock's confidence by telling Daphne about his past, but she also didn't want her friend to think the wrong thing about him. "Daph, he doesn't *dislike* Hadley. He's uncomfortable around her, that's all. Not all men are good with little ones."

"Are you sure? Because he cringes whenever she's near him." Daphne sighed. "Poor Hadley is going to spend her teenage years chasing all the wrong guys. I just know it."

"I'm *sure* about Jock," Tegan reassured her.

"He was only one of many guys looking at you at the wedding," Chloe added.

"You definitely piqued Jock's interest, but he's had a rough go of things. Don't take his reaction to Hadley personally."

"That's good to know." Daphne sounded relieved. "I didn't want to say anything about it, but he's rented a cottage at Bayside for the fall. I was kind of worried that it would be weird if he really didn't like her."

"Don't worry about that. Besides, Jock keeps to himself. I doubt you'll see much of him," Tegan reassured her. She and Jock had been working together for the past two weeks, and it was wonderful, but she never saw him in the evenings.

"And if you *do* see him, or any other gorgeous man, open your eyes to how fantastic you are," Chloe said. "Those fashion magazines you talked about me walking out of feature too-skinny women who are nothing more than *white noise*. Girls like me blur into the background: plain hair, lanky bodies, and angular faces. There's nothing special about how I look, and you know what? Maybe that's why I don't dress in typical beachy outfits like everyone else, because I have to use *clothes* to be noticed. But *you*? You look amazing in everything you wear.

You have the type of cleavage men want to bury their face in, an ass a man can hold on to, and I bet half the single men at the wedding were dreaming about your legs wrapped around them."

Daphne's cheeks flamed. "You're really good friends. I'm lucky to have you."

"We're all lucky," Tegan said, choosing a third white bikini to try on. "That's a big part of why I decided to move here for good in the fall."

"You *are*?" Chloe and Daphne said in unison.

"Yup! This is officially home to me now." Jett's voice whispered through her mind. *You feel like home to me...* Last night he'd said he couldn't wait to get *home* to see her. At first she wasn't sure if he realized he'd said *home*, but the look in his eyes had told her he had.

"And how does Mr. I Love You feel about you moving here?" Chloe asked.

She'd met the girls Monday night for dinner and had told them about their weekend and their confessions of love. They'd been as floored and elated as she was. Those three perfect words came so easily when they talked now. Jett even put *ILY* at the end of some of his texts, which made her giddy every time.

"He's supportive of the idea. Why?"

"Because he flew you to LA, spent a fortune on romancing you in a *helicopter*, told you he *loves* you, and we all know how he feels about the Cape," Chloe explained. "I know he's changing, and that's a huge deal. But knowing you'll be here year-round might worry him a little. He's spent so long avoiding coming back to this place."

"And what about Jett and Dean's fight at the wedding?" Daphne said carefully. "They seemed more at ease with each other afterward, but what was all that about?"

"I'm kind of pissed that I missed it," Chloe said. "The thought of seeing those two delicious men fighting is a total turn-on."

Daphne looked at Chloe like she was crazy. "You hate bad boys, and I don't understand why *fighting* would turn anyone on."

"You also think your bootylicious body isn't hot as hell, so I'm not surprised." Chloe smacked Daphne's butt, making her blush again. "You're hot as *eff*, Daph. One day I'll school you in the difference between a bad boy, like Justin, Dwayne, or Zander, and a gentleman who is rugged and stands up for his convictions and battles it out, like Jett and Dean."

Tegan pointed at Chloe and said, "Don't drool over mine and Emery's men. There are plenty of single fish in the sea."

"Isn't she cute when she's jealous?" Chloe teased as she put a pink bathing suit over her arm and continued fishing through the rack. "I was kidding. They are hot, but you *know* I don't want either of them."

"I know, but it was fun warning you off. I'm a *girlfriend* now. I have all sorts of new attitudes." She wiggled her shoulders, making the girls chuckle. "But in all seriousness, Jett's okay with me being here, and he's obviously trying to make things right with his family, since we're spending the day with them tomorrow. He told me last night that he's a little anxious about it. But he's a confident man who succeeds at whatever he puts his mind to, so I'm hoping for the best." She held up three white bikinis and said, "I'm also hoping one of these might help ease that anxiety."

"Does this mean you're *finally* going to tell us why you needed a virginal white bikini by *tonight*?" Chloe asked.

Tegan tried to stifle her smile, but it was a lost cause. She'd thought of nothing else but her sexy surprise since she decided to do it. "It's kind of embarrassing, but Jett had this teenage fantasy that involves a hot chick in a white bikini and a little tying-up action in the bedroom. I want to surprise him when he gets in tonight and make it come true. I've got it all planned with silk rose petals and scented candles. He should get in around eight, and I'm going to answer the door wearing a white bikini and high heels." Her belly fluttered, and she said, "*If* I don't chicken out."

"Holy crap, Teg. *I* want to be your boyfriend," Chloe said. "There's no way Jett will be anxious with all that naughtiness going on."

"That's it. I need a boyfriend." Daphne lowered her voice and said, "Everyone has an adventurous sex life except me. I have been married and divorced, and I have a little girl, but I've never had *that*. Don't chicken out, Tegan. He's going to be so happy."

"I hope so. I love him so much, you guys. I want this to be really special and intimate. Ever since that first night we were together, we just *clicked*, in and out of the bedroom, and it's only gotten better and...I'm rambling. I'm sorry." She laughed nervously, but she couldn't keep it all in. "But when we text, my heart races, and when I see him on FaceTime, I fall in love all over again. I know I sound ridiculous, but I've never felt like this before, and I've definitely never done anything like what I'm planning. What if he's tired when he gets there? Or too stressed? What if he thinks I'm trying too hard and that I look ridiculous?"

"If he's half as in love with you as you are with him, you could wear baggy sweats and shave your head and he'd still want to love you all night long," Daphne said.

"Seriously, Teg? I would not worry about that. One look at you and he is going to be sporting an iron rod." Chloe pointed to the bikinis Tegan was holding and said, "Now we need to get your head out of the clouds and your body into those bikinis so we can pick out the perfect one for your night of seduction. And while we're at it, Daph, what size do you wear?"

"I don't know," Daphne said. "I hate bathing suits."

"Rough guess?" Chloe urged as she picked through a rack of swimsuits.

"Fourteen? Sixteen? Maybe bigger after all the crap I've been eating."

Chloe grabbed a black one-piece in three sizes, and they headed into the dressing area. She handed Daphne the black suits and said, "Try these on."

"I just said I *hate* bathing suits," Daphne complained. "I look awful in them."

"Our previous conversations have taught me not to trust your judgment." Chloe gave Daphne a nudge toward a dressing-room curtain. "Get in there and change. We'll tell you if they look horrible."

Daphne swatted the curtain open and said, "I'm only doing this because I know you'll bug me until I do."

"Whatever it takes," Chloe said as she and Tegan slipped into their own dressing rooms. "Meet you at the three-way."

"That's what he said," Tegan said, making them all cackle.

A few minutes later, Tegan was standing in front of the three-way mirror admiring herself in a simple white string bikini that tied on her hips when Chloe came out of her dressing room wearing a pink one-piece with high-cut hips and a plunging neckline.

"Wow, Chloe. That's a great color on you."

"Thanks. You look gorgeous." Chloe touched the ties on Tegan's hips and said, "These are nice for easy access."

"Good point. I think I'm going to buy this one."

Chloe turned around, looking at her own butt in the mirror. "My butt is so blah. I would kill for some of Daphne's curves. Maybe I need to eat more bacon. I need to find one of those cover-up skirts."

"You have a great butt, and if you don't believe me, ask Justin. He's always looking at it." Tegan looked toward Daphne's dressing room and said, "Come on. I think she's hiding."

They went to Daphne's dressing room and Tegan said, "Daph? How does it look?"

"I look all dimply, like Hadley with cleavage."

Tegan and Chloe exchanged a disbelieving glance, and they peeked behind the curtain. She looked sexy and beautiful, and it saddened Tegan that her friend could see anything but what she saw. The solid bottom flattered her full hips, setting off the natural dip of her waist, and the laced-up bodice showed just enough skin to draw the eye.

Daphne covered her stomach and said, "See? *Hadley*, right?"

Tegan and Chloe stepped into her dressing room, and Tegan said, "If Hadley grows up to look like you, I'd lock her up. That suit is absolutely perfect on you. I promise you, if I thought you didn't look your best in it, I'd tell you, because I'm that big-mouth friend who always tells it like it is."

"What don't you like about it?" Chloe asked.

"I love the suit. It's beautiful, and it's really comfortable. But I feel a little self-conscious in any bathing suit. My ex always encouraged me to wear shorts over them."

"Is that why you do that?" Chloe asked. "Guess what, gorgeous? Your ex was an asshole who never deserved you in the first place."

"*True*, but there is a lot of me." She ran her hand over her thigh, looking embarrassed.

"So?" Chloe said. "There's not enough of me."

Tegan looked at the three of them in the mirror and said, "You think you're heavy, Chloe thinks she's too skinny. I could use bigger boobs and a more pronounced waist, but I'm not getting implants or removing a rib. My mom always told me that if I had those things, I'd want something else to be different. I'm sure she's right. I've never met a girl who loved everything about herself. At this point, I just figure I am who I am, and try to embrace myself, flaws and all. I wish you would, too, because all I see are three beautiful women who have better things to worry about than if we're eating too much or our butts are too big or too small."

"You know what? You're right. Forget the butt cover-up," Chloe said. "My scrawny ass will be on full display this summer."

Daphne ran her hand over her butt and said, "I agree with the idea, but it's still going to be hard to ditch my shorts."

"That's okay. You need to be *you* any which way you're comfortable," Tegan said. "But just remember, *we* think you look like a million bucks."

"Thank you." Daphne's eyes drifted down Tegan's body. "And *you* look like Jett's teenage fantasy come true."

Chloe scoffed. "Forget his teenage fantasy. She looks like his next meal."

AT SIX THIRTY that evening, Tegan was dancing to music as she set scented candles out in the bedroom. She put a few in the living room, too, and lit them all so the cottage would smell nice when Jett arrived. Then she set to work creating a trail of silk rose petals from the front door to the bedroom, getting more nervous with every step toward her grand seduction scheme. She knew Daphne was right when she'd said that she could wear baggy sweats and shave her head and Jett would still want to love her all night long. She had no doubts about his feelings for her. That was just one of the reasons she wanted tonight to be special for him. She'd had an incredible time in LA, but she'd paid the price. She'd been flat-out exhausted Monday, and she'd been hustling all week to make up for the work she'd put off. That had given her a better appreciation for the time Jett spent with her and with his family. His work was far busier than hers, with much higher stakes, and the constant travel these last few weeks had to take a toll on him. She wondered if his family ever thought about that, since it seemed like they never made the effort to go see him.

She spread rose petals over the comforter and placed the silk ties she'd bought on the pillow. Then she set out her white bikini and heels and stepped back to take it all in, trying to imagine how it would look to Jett. Would he see the romance she'd tried to inspire, or would he be too focused on sex? She shivered just thinking about his eyes darkening with desire, and she knew the answer to her own question. Jett would definitely be focused on sex, but even when he was animalistic, there was no escaping the love between them, and that in and of itself created romance.

The roses and candles just made it even more perfect.

It was almost seven o'clock. How would she survive being

this nervous for the next hour? She headed into the kitchen to have one of the Mike's Hard Lemonades she'd bought on the way home. She hoped Jett would remember that it was what they'd had the night of the storm. Her phone rang as she was opening the bottle. She hurried into the living room and snagged it from the coffee table. She was surprised to see Jett's name on the screen and hoped maybe he'd caught an earlier flight.

"Hi."

"Hey, sunshine. We've run into some legal issues with Carlisle. I'm really sorry, but I need to stay until we get this worked out."

"You haven't left LA?" She instantly regretting the shock in her voice. She knew he didn't need more pressure, especially after all he'd done to accommodate their relationship, but she'd been on a high all week anticipating the surprise, waiting to be in his arms again. She closed her eyes against the sadness welling inside her and reminded herself how important that deal was to him.

"No. I'm sorry, babe. I would have called earlier, but I've been tied up in meetings and lost track of time." His voice was laced with regret and frustration. "It could take a few more hours. I'm going to have to catch a flight out in the morning."

She looked around the room at the flickering candles, feeling sad for them both, but she vowed *not* to make him feel worse for having to work. "That's okay. At least you'll still be here in time to see your parents. Are you flying into Hyannis? Should I just meet you at their place tomorrow?"

"Yes, that's probably best. I'm sorry. I'll try to leave at the crack of dawn. We won't have much time. My flight leaves Hyannis at six tomorrow evening, and I catch a connecting flight at eight thirty for London."

She swallowed hard. *London.* Three more weeks apart.

His voice softened and he said, "Baby, I miss you so much. I'll make this up to you. After London we'll take a few days just for us."

"It's okay. I understand. But I won't be able to leave town, remember? I've got to run the children's program."

"I know. You won't have to. We'll stay there. I just want to be with you."

He didn't know about the surprise she had waiting for him, and he was already trying to make up for a few hours of missed time together. She fell a little deeper in love with him right then. She thought of her uncle and his love for Adele. Life was full of ups and downs, tragedies and celebrations, and she knew the love she and Jett shared could weather all of them.

She heard a male voice in the background, and then Jett said, "I've got to go. I love you, Tegs."

"I love you, too. But, Jett?"

"Yeah?"

"I just want you to know that even though it sucks that we'll miss out on tonight, I'm really proud of you for what you're doing. I know how important this deal is to you, so don't worry about me, okay?"

"God, Tegs. You're amazing. Thank you for understanding."

After they ended the call, she sank down to the couch, feeling like a golf ball was lodged in her throat. Tears streamed down her cheeks as she stared absently into space, missing him.

She sat there until her tears stopped falling and her cheeks dried. She was a little surprised she wasn't angry or resentful about her spoiled plans. But how could she be either of those things when she knew Jett felt just as bad as she did? No, those weren't the emotions pushing her to her feet to blow out all the candles or carrying her into the kitchen to retrieve the rest of the six-pack. There was no room for anger or resentment when the heart-crushing sadness of missing a man who was thousands of miles away had already consumed her.

Chapter Thirty-Three

JETT WAS DEAD on his feet as he climbed the porch steps to Tegan's cottage Saturday morning. It had killed him to call her last night, and as the meeting wore on and it had become clear that he would need to remain in London longer than he'd originally anticipated, he'd gotten even more agitated. He didn't want to waste another minute waiting to see Tegan. He'd chartered a plane, bringing the key team members with him to finish the meeting in the air. The team was now on their way back to LA.

He knocked on Tegan's door and rolled his shoulders back, stretching his neck from side to side. It was only five in the morning, and with the news he had to deliver, it was already the shittiest day of his life.

The curtains on the window next to the door shifted, and Tegan's sleepy face appeared. He heard the rapid click of the lock and the slide of a chain, and then his sunshine was in his arms, putting the cracked pieces of him back together.

"God, I missed you." As he kissed her, he realized she was fully dressed in jeans and a sweater. Her cheek was pink and imprinted with the upholstery design of her couch.

"What time is it? I thought you were coming later." Her

words ran together, and she wrapped her arms around his waist, sinking into him as if she'd used up all her energy. "Did you sleep on the plane?"

"No. I couldn't wait to see you."

"Bed." She took his hand, leading him into the cottage.

In the space of a few quick seconds, his shitty day got even worse. There were rose petals scattered on the floor, candles on every surface, and six empty bottles of Mike's Hard Lemonade on the coffee table. A blanket was balled up on the couch. His gut twisted. Had she done all that for him?

Tegan led him into the bedroom, where more pretty petals decorated the bed. Black silk ties were lined up on one pillow, and a tiny white bikini lay on the bedside table.

A white fucking bikini.

Christ.

What had he done?

"Baby? You did all this for us?" he asked as she climbed onto the bed, lying on top of the rose petals.

"Mm-hm. Hold me." She reached for him.

He toed off his shoes and climbed beside her, gathering her in his arms, his heart breaking. "I'm sorry, sunshine. I'm so fucking sorry."

"It's okay."

"No, it's *not*. I'm not just sorry for last night. I'm sorry because I'm going to have to extend my stay in London. I'll probably be there six to eight weeks, not three. There's no way—"

She pressed her lips to his, silencing him. Her sleepy eyes implored him to listen to her groggy voice. "You're here now. We'll figure it out."

"I feel so fucking guilty, baby," he confessed.

"It's work, not an affair." She snugged closer and whispered, "Hold me, close your eyes, *rest*. We've got a big day planned with your family."

He held her, and eventually he even closed his eyes. But there was no rest for a man whose whole world was right there in his arms, when in less than twenty-four hours he'd be thousands of miles away again.

WHEN THEY ARRIVED at his parents' house later that morning, Jett braced himself against the tightening in his chest. He waited for the anger to stir and the need to flee to grip him. But as he parked the rental car behind Dean's truck, he realized that for the first time ever, the discomfort in his chest didn't stem from the ghosts of his past pushing him to *leave*. It was born from the urge to *fight* those ghosts, to stick around and try to make things better. And the person who helped make that possible was sitting beside him, reaching for his hand.

"You okay?" Tegan asked.

She looked radiant in a long-sleeved pink lace shirt, and he hoped to hell things went well today, because he didn't want to disappoint her any more than he already had. He'd apologized a million times for last night, and she'd been just as forgiving as always, which made him even more determined to try to stop creating situations that called for apologies and forgiveness.

"Yeah." He leaned across the console to kiss her. "Thank you for sharing what little time we have with my family."

"I think I should thank them. You were theirs first."

As he touched his lips to hers, he saw Emery running toward the car from the side yard and Dean traipsing behind her. He gave Tegan a chaste kiss and said, "Here we go."

They stepped from the car, and his eyes met Dean's, which were a little less serious than normal. Their bruises and cuts had healed, but he knew their relationship would take much longer.

Emery hugged Tegan and exclaimed, "This is going to be so fun! Rose is out back with Sherry and Doug. We're going to make pies for after lunch." She looked at Jett and said, "I'm stealing your girlfriend!"

Tegan turned, her blond hair swinging around her smiling face.

"Go for it," Jett said, winking at Tegan. As they walked away, Jett tried to wrap his head around how good it felt to see Tegan with Emery walking into his parents' backyard like this was a weekly gathering.

Dean pulled him into a manly embrace and said, "I've got to admit, I half expected you to cancel."

"I'm here. Got in at five this morning."

"You sure you're ready to face Dad with a hammer in your hand?"

Dean didn't smile, and he probably hadn't meant it as a joke, which stung. Not that Jett would ever lay a hand, much less a hammer, on his father. But worrying about what would come from the two of them being in the same place for any length of time had been their reality for so long, Jett wondered if it could ever *really* change.

"I think I can handle it," he said, though as they headed into the backyard, every step brought trepidation.

His father was standing at the other end of the yard with his back to them. A tool belt hung around his waist, looking ridiculously out of place on a man who lived in expensive dress clothes, despite the jeans and denim shirt he wore today. His hands were on his hips as he stared up at the damaged treehouse. It was a simplistic design, four walls that had come up to Jett's chest when he was young, a deck with railings on one side and a tarp draped over a rope for a roof. The tarp was long gone, but the frayed and dirty rope remained stretched between two trees upon which the treehouse was built. Pieces of wood were nailed to one of the trees and served as a ladder that led to a hole in the floor. A branch had fallen and taken with it most of one of the walls and the deck.

Jett's gaze went to a mass of nails they had pounded into one of the trees when they were kids. They'd slung a rope over them and used it as a pulley. At the time, it had been one of their greatest inventions. They'd used it to lift toys and food and just about anything else that they were strong enough to pull up. They'd spent so many years playing in that treehouse, staying out from sunup until sundown. He could practically hear their voices now. Jett smiled with the memory. It was hard to believe he'd ever been that carefree.

"It seemed bigger when we were kids," he said to Dean.

Dean nodded. "It was the answer to our dreams."

Jett's gaze shifted to Tegan, who was talking with his mother, grandmother, and Emery on the patio. Man, how his dreams had changed. "Let me say hi to Gram and Mom, and then we'll get started."

"That'd be the path of least resistance."

Jett shook his head. "Are you going to ride me the whole day?"

"Probably." Dean folded his arms over his chest, his beard lifting with his grin. "Old habits and all that."

Jett muttered, "Ass," as he walked away, and heard Dean

chuckle.

Rose reached for him as he approached. Her hand was soft as butter and as frail as a bird, but she was still emotionally as strong as an ox. He kissed her cheek. "Hi, Gram."

"You must be exhausted," Rose said. "Tegan told us you had an overnight meeting *in* the airplane?"

"Just making the best use of my time," Jett said as he kissed his mother's cheek.

His mother said, "I'm glad you made it, sweetheart."

"Oh, I'm glad, too," Rose added. "But I'm not so sure the people who work with you feel the same."

"I pay them well," Jett reminded her. "We needed to hash out a few things for an acquisition I'm working on, and I needed to be here. I think it worked out well." He draped an arm over Tegan's shoulder and said, "Need anything before I get started on the treehouse?"

"She's fine," Emery said before Tegan could reply.

Jett held Tegan's gaze and said, "She's always *fine*." Tegan blushed and he kissed her, making her cheeks a little pinker.

She gave him a nudge and said, "Go do your thing. Your father is waiting, and nobody wants to hear you flirt with me."

"I do, honey," Rose said. "I'm an old woman. I need to get my thrills living vicariously through others, and my grandson is due some flirting."

"Enough, Gram," Jett warned. "And don't fill her head with made-up stories about when I was a kid."

"Like how you and Dean once measured your penises and had a big argument about whose was bigger over dinner?" Rose asked. "Oh, honey, I would *never* do that."

All the women laughed.

Jett scowled. "Lies, all *lies*. She's bordering on dementia, too. You can't trust a word she says."

He went to join Dean and their father by the shed. His father looked as uneasy as Jett felt, and Dean wasn't far behind, watching the two of them like a hawk.

"Ready to get to work?" their father asked.

Jett was relieved he hadn't gone for small talk. "Absolutely. What's the plan?"

Their father's eyes moved between Jett and Dean. "You mean you boys didn't make a plan?"

"Don't look at me," Dean said. "This was Jett's idea."

"It's cool. I've got this under control." Jett looked at the treehouse and quickly devised a plan. "We should probably start with the wall, then fix the deck."

"Why don't I work on the deck while you two work on the wall?" Dean suggested.

Nothing like being thrown feetfirst into the fire.

"Sure. Sounds good. Let's get our tools and ladders and get started. I've got to catch a plane at six." Jett headed into the shed.

His father followed him in and said, "I've got my tools. I'll get the ladder."

"I've got it, Dad," Jett said. "You don't want to mess up your hands."

"I'm not afraid to get my hands dirty. I'll do whatever it takes to put this thing back together," his father said.

Jett wondered if he was talking about their relationship or the treehouse. "Who's going to operate if you break a finger?"

His father picked up the ladder and said, "The next best surgeon."

Jett watched him walk out of the shed, feeling shell-shocked. He turned back to the tools wondering when work had fallen off the top of his father's list of priorities.

He snagged a pair of work gloves to give to his father and reached for a hammer.

Dean thrust a plastic toolbox in front of him and said, "I've got your tools right here."

"And I've got your black eye right here." Jett lifted a fist. He looked over the toolbox and recognized it from when they were kids. "Where'd you get that thing?"

"Mom was going through our old toys." Dean leaned against the workbench and said, "I told her our baby needed gardening tools instead, but you know…"

Jett froze. "*Baby?*"

Dean nodded, the pride in his eyes hitting Jett right in the center of his chest.

"That's great, man, congratulations." Jett embraced him. "Does everyone else know?"

"No. It's really early. We just found out and we figured we'd tell Mom and Dad first."

"They must be thrilled. Gram, too." Jett looked across the lawn at Tegan as she and Emery followed his mother and grandmother into the house. A ripple of longing moved through him. Would he and Tegan ever have that together? A family of their own? What would his kid have? A calculator? He gritted his teeth, knowing he couldn't look that far into the future when he was still chained down by his past.

"Everyone's excited," Dean said. "I still can't believe I'm going to be a father. The baby's due in January."

"Emery's feeling okay? She seemed like her normal peppy self at the wedding."

"She got lucky. She's only had a few days of morning sickness."

"Oh man, Dean. You threw her over your shoulder. You could have hurt her."

"You think I'd chance that? I was careful; trust me. Nothing is more important than my doll and that little baby inside her." Dean grabbed a ladder and said, "It'd be nice if at least one of our baby's uncles were around more often."

"I hear ya," Jett said as they went to join their father by the treehouse.

"I hope so," Dean said. "Because I don't think Doug's ever planning on living in the States again, and Emery's brothers are great, but they're not you."

Jett got a little choked up about Dean wanting him around his baby after all they'd been through.

"Ready, boys?" their father asked.

"Yeah. Did you get wood?" Jett asked.

His father looked down at his crotch and said, "Not yet. You?"

Dean burst into laughter, kicking Jett out of his momentary silence from the idea that their proper father would make such a joke.

Jett hiked a thumb at their father and said, "Who *is* this guy?"

Their father held out his hand and said, "Douglas Masters, reformed father *first*, selfish prick *last*. Nice to meet you."

Jett didn't know what to say to that, either, so he tossed the gloves to his father and shook his head, thankful his father had found a way to break the ice.

He and his father didn't talk much as they carried wood, set up ladders, and got themselves organized. They worked side by side, tearing off the old weather-beaten boards, and as time passed, they fell into sync working as a team and the tension between them eased. Dean worked alone rebuilding the deck, but his attention never left Jett and their father for too long.

The girls brought out lunch, and Jett said, "Ready for a break, old man?"

"I am. This is hard work." His father sat on the treehouse floor, red faced from his efforts. He took off his gloves, set them on the floor, and said, "We never did anything like this together when you were young. That's on *me*, along with a whole lot of other trouble. I'm sorry, Jett, for everything. For leaving when you were so little, for the time we've lost, and the way it's left a rightful chip on your shoulder and mine. I just want you to know that I don't blame you for the rift between us. I took a happy, confident little boy and turned his world upside down. I lived that nightmare with my own father, and I take full responsibility. I just hope that one day you can find it in your heart to forgive me enough that we can do more things like this."

Jett cleared his throat, trying to push past the emotions clogging it. He wasn't prepared for anything his father had said, and for the third time that day, he didn't know how to respond. He went with humor. It wasn't the best way to handle it, but at the moment it was all he could manage. "You sure you can handle more physical labor?"

"Like I said, I'll do whatever it takes to put this thing back together."

As his father descended the ladder, Jett saw that little boy whose world had been turned upside down even more clearly. He saw him turning into an angry, unforgiving teenager, and the truth slammed into him. His father might have broken his trust, but it was Jett who had worn the broken bones of their relationship like armor, causing them to lose the three years in between when his father had come home and when he'd become intolerable again. The lost years that followed were on his father, until the last two and half years, when he'd tried to change. Those lost years were on Jett. Had he been out for vengeance? Trying to hurt his father as his father had devastated him? He didn't want to believe he was capable of such a thing, but he knew the hard, ugly truth. Wounds had to be cared for in order to heal, and Jett had been merciless in his ire.

His father had *never* stood a chance.

As the burden of truth lifted, the chains of the past broke free, revealing a future Jett never expected—one that included seeing his father through new eyes.

"Jett?" Tegan called up to him. "Are you coming down?"

Her sweet voice tugged him from his thoughts. "Yeah, babe. Be right there." If not for Tegan, today might never have happened.

He looked around the beat-up treehouse knowing that the ghosts that had been his constant companion since he was a kid, that had ridden up the ladder like a gorilla on his back, wouldn't be making the trip down.

Thank God there was no roof to trap them in.

Fly, fuckers. Fly fast and far away.

"Everything okay?" Tegan asked softly as he climbed down to the ground.

He kissed her, and even *that* felt better than ever before. "Perfect, babe. Just perfect."

Chapter Thirty-Four

LUNCH INCLUDED A cacophony of excitement over Dean and Emery's baby news and a plethora of delicious food. After they finished eating, the men went back to work. They measured and cut, leveled and hammered, joking the whole time with each other. The girls were on the patio talking about the Wellfleet Flea Market and making something called jam pizza with Luscious Leanna's Sweet Treat jams made by their friend Leanna Bray-Remington. Her husband, Kurt, was a thriller writer. Jett wondered if Jock knew him, and now that he was thinking of friends, it dawned on him that Rowan's last name was Remington, too, and he wondered if he and Kurt were related. His mind continued wandering, thinking of how cool it would be to go with Tegan to check out the flea market, which he hadn't done in years, and to the drive-in movie theater. He'd almost forgotten about how his mother used to make popcorn sprinkled with sugar and cinnamon for them to eat while they watched movies from their car. His hungry girl would *love* that sugary popcorn. He caught Tegan sneaking another glance at him, as she'd been doing all afternoon, and he blew her a kiss. She pretended to catch it. He wanted more weekends like this, spending time with the family he felt like he barely knew and the woman he adored.

When they finally pounded the last board into place, Jett felt as revitalized as the treehouse.

Their father put a hand on his and Dean's shoulders and said, "We make a hell of a team, boys."

Those were words Jett never thought he'd hear, and they felt damn good.

He checked the time, and that good feeling soured. With the weight of lead in his gut, he pulled Tegan into his arms, and as everyone else talked about how great the treehouse looked, he whispered in her ear, "I've got to get washed up. It's almost time for me to leave."

Her eyes saddened, but she managed a sweet, "*Okay.*"

He went inside and washed up, and when he came out of the bathroom his father was walking out of the kitchen. He said, "Jett, do you have a minute? I want to show you something."

"Sure." Jett followed his father down the hall and into his office. He couldn't remember the last time he'd been in it, but he remembered all too clearly how many nights his father had locked himself in there. The bookshelves were packed tight with medical texts. A neat stack of files sat atop his mahogany desk, and family pictures lined the walls. Had they always been there? He couldn't remember, but then he realized it didn't matter. They were there *now*.

"Thanks for asking me not to tear the treehouse down," his father said as he unlocked the file drawer in his desk. "It was a labor of love when I built it, and I'm glad our grandchildren will be able to enjoy it."

"I didn't know you built it. I thought you hired someone to do it and they worked on it while we were in school."

"I probably should have." He set the key on top of the desk and said, "I never wanted you boys to feel like I did as a kid. My father never spent any time with me. He cared only about grades and the impressions we made on others. When you boys were born, I had every intention of being the type of father I'd always hoped for. I wanted you boys to grow up knowing how much I loved you and how important you were to me. I wanted to support your dreams, no matter how viable or silly. I know I screwed that up when you were a teenager and for what feels like forever after that, but we don't need to beat that dead horse. You boys were very convincing about needing that treehouse. Doug reasoned with me about you three needing privacy, but you were more visceral." He spoke in a kidlike voice and said, "'Come on, Dad. Don't you remember being a kid? We need a *fort*, a *headquarters* to plan our adventures.'"

"I remember that," Jett said, trying to keep his emotions in check.

"You were pretty damn cute. And Dean? He just wanted you and Doug to have whatever made you happy, so he'd turn those serious little eyes up at me and say, 'Please, Daddy?'"

"Always the peacemaker," Jett said.

"Yes, he has always sought peace. I didn't know a damn thing about building a treehouse, but you boys used to look at me like I could do anything back then. Let me tell you something, son. There is no greater joy and no heavier pressure than trying to live up to your children's expectations. I wanted to build that treehouse more than I had ever wanted anything in my life. But I had never even held a hammer, and I sucked at it."

Jett chuckled. "You must have been a quick study, because you handled the hammer like a pro today."

"I should thank Mitch for that. He and I built the treehouse together at night, after you boys were in bed. It took us two whole weeks, and I was exhausted. But I felt like I'd finally done something right."

"You did a lot of things right back then, Dad," Jett admitted, and it felt good to say it, to get out from under the hurt. "You did a lot of things right after that, too, and I'm sorry I never gave you a chance. I'm trying to change that now."

Emotions welled in his father's eyes. "Thank you, son."

"Knowing you went to all that effort after working all day and dealing with us in the evenings means a lot. This probably sounds lame, but thank you for caring enough to do that."

"I'd say that's what dads do, but we both know it wouldn't be true of all fathers. So I'll say, that's what dads *should* do. Now I want to show you something, and I hope you're not going to get pissed off, but I'm not getting any younger, and I don't want to miss an opportunity to give these to you." He pulled Jett's old blue baseball card binder out of the drawer.

Jett sank down to one of the chairs in front of his father's desk, unable to do anything more than stare at the sticker-covered binder. Then his father pulled out the sticker-covered wooden box containing the rest of his collection, stealing the air from Jett's lungs.

He came around the desk, set them before Jett, and said, "When your mother told me you'd thrown them out, my heart broke." His eyes teared up, and he swallowed hard, turning away to try to regain control of his emotions.

Jett did the same, sure the pain in his chest would be the death of him.

When their eyes met again, his father's were glassy as he said, "I couldn't let them go. I knew you were throwing *us* away, and I just couldn't…"

"I didn't…" Jett's voice was drowned out by his emotions. He cleared his throat and sat up straighter, but he still struggled for his voice. "I didn't think…I was a stupid kid, Dad."

"No, you weren't. That's why you've been angry at me for so long, because you're smart, Jett. I know you don't trust that I won't go back to being a self-absorbed jerk. Some days I don't trust myself, either, but I'm trying."

Jett heard himself saying those exact words to Dean, to Tegan. He gripped the arms of the chair, steeling himself against the emotions trampling through him, knocking him off-kilter, nodded toward the box, and said, "They all still there?"

His father nodded. "Yes."

Jett put his hand on the binder and cocked his head, meeting his father's gaze as he said, "Feel like checking them out?"

"What do you think?"

Jett flipped open the binder, engulfed by a rush of nostalgia. Each plastic page displayed nine baseball cards he and his father had bought and cataloged together. They began looking through the cards one at a time, testing each other on stats and reliving the moments when they'd found certain cards. Jett felt like he'd stepped back in time, like all those horrible years had never happened. As they neared the end of the binder and his father reached for the box, Jett realized it was never the cards that mattered. It was their connection, the bond they'd shared. And man, had he missed that.

"I found them," Emery hollered as she peered into the office. "Jett, you have to leave or you'll miss your flight!"

Jett uttered a curse and closed the binder, pushing to his feet. "Sorry, Dad. Can you take care of those for me?"

"You know I will," his father said. "I'm proud of you. Go

nail that acquisition; show that starry-eyed kid why you're king."

Jett nodded and gave him a quick hug. He gritted his teeth as he headed out of the office and said, "Thanks, Emery," as he strode past. Tegan appeared down the hall with his mother and the others. Frustration tangled up inside him. He didn't want to leave her, and now he didn't want to leave his family, either.

"What can we do to help?" his mother asked.

Jett looked at his watch. *Fuck.* He had to get out of there. "Dean, you're still okay taking Tegs home?"

"We've got her," Dean said.

Tegan ushered him toward the front door and said, "I'll get home, but you have to *go*."

"Not without a kiss for me, Jetty," his grandmother said. "My days could be numbered, you know."

"Gram, it's hard enough to say goodbye." He leaned down and kissed her cheek. "I'll be back in...*Damn it.* I forgot to tell you guys that I've got to stay in London longer, probably six to eight weeks. We've run into some issues, and it's...I've got no choice."

His mother counted on her fingers. "Oh no, you'll miss the foundation dinner. You'll miss seeing Doug and Susie, too."

Guilt sliced through him. "Sorry, Mom. I'll call Doug and let him know." He turned to his father and said, "I'm sorry, Dad. I wanted to be there. I meant it when I said it."

"Here we go again," Dean said.

Jett glowered at him. "Really, Dean? I just spent the entire day here, and you're giving me shit?"

"*Language*, Jett," his mother said.

"Let it go, Dean," his father said. "Jett, we understand. This isn't like before. We know this isn't an excuse to stay away."

But Jett's eyes were locked on Dean, and Dean looked like he was ready to explode. "If you've got something to say, get it out *now*, Dean, because I have a deal to close."

"Of course you do," Dean seethed. "You say you don't trust Dad's changes? Look in the mirror, Jett. His changes outlasted yours by a mile." He turned and stormed out the back door.

Emery ran after him.

"Oh boy. Here we go…" Rose said.

Jett started to go after Dean, but his father grabbed his arm and said, "Let it go. He didn't mean it. He'll cool off."

Tegan was looking at Jett like she was torn between crying and shouting, which gutted him. She probably wanted to slug him for missing the foundation dinner, too. It was all too much, and he couldn't fix a damn thing without missing his flight.

"I've got to go." He said a quick goodbye to his parents and grandmother, and he and Tegan headed out the front door.

"Are you okay?" she asked as he pulled her into his arms.

"Yeah." The word tasted bitter. "I hate leaving you, and *them*, and now Dean's pissed. It sucks. I'm sorry, baby. Do you want me to have a car take you home?"

She gazed up at him and said, "I'm fine. I promise. You had a great day. We *all* did. Enjoy that. Think about it as you prepare to conquer your next big deal."

"I'm going to miss you so fucking much." He kissed her, holding her tight.

"Me too." Her voice cracked. "I promised myself I wasn't going to cry. You need to go before I fall apart."

Christ. He felt like a monster. "I'll call you once I get to Boston if there's time between flights." He took her face in his hands and kissed her again. "You are my home, baby. Think of that. Don't cry."

"Go," she said shakily, nudging him toward the car.

He fucking hated this. "I'll dream about you," he said as he climbed into the car.

"Make 'em dirty." Tears slipped down her cheeks.

He gritted his teeth and forced himself to drive away.

TEGAN WATCHED JETT'S car disappear around the corner. She was so angry at Dean she could spit. She wiped her eyes, telling herself she should take a walk and blow off some steam, but she was *livid*. There was no calming her rage as she strode into the backyard with tunnel vision. Her eyes landed on Dean, who was pacing by the shed with Emery.

Tegan cut across the yard, vaguely aware of her name being called as she stepped in front of Dean and said, "What the *hell* was that?"

His eyes narrowed.

"Hey, that's my man you're talking to," Emery said. "Watch it."

"I'm sorry, Emery. But no one else seems to be able to see what's so obvious to me." She turned her attention back to Dean and said, "Your brother just flew *all night* to get here. I don't think he even slept a wink this morning, and he worked *all day*. He was kind, he was funny, and he was *present*. He didn't take phone calls or check his emails. How *dare* you give him a hard time for having to leave for work. I like you, Dean, but *who* do you think you are? You stand there high and mighty, telling Jett everything *you* think he does wrong, and I can't imagine why you think you're any better. I know he's stayed away, and he's buried himself in work in the past, but *he's* making every effort to change for your family. What are *you* doing to help your family come back together?"

Dean's nostrils were flaring like a bull ready to charge. She knew she was yelling, and that his parents and Rose were watching them, but she was unable to stop everything she'd been holding back from spewing out.

"Have you ever *once* gone to see *him*? All I hear about is how *Jett doesn't come back enough* and *Jett works too much*. Why is it *his* job to make the effort? Your resort isn't at full capacity over the winters. What are you doing during those months? Why aren't *you* jumping on planes to see him? Do you have any idea how exhausting it is for him to race home?" Tears flooded her cheeks, and she was shaking all over, but she had to get it out. "That man does *so* much and he gets zero recognition from you. It doesn't matter if it's less than you think you and your family deserve. He's making an effort, and he deserves credit for it. Love is not a competition, Dean. It's not all or nothing, family or work, or work or me, for that matter. There's room for all of us in Jett's life, but he has to figure out how to balance it after spending a lifetime not wanting to, and you should give him support and love so he *wants* to do that. Nobody wins when one person loses, and the more you push him away, the harder it will be for him to find his way back. *Please* think about how hard he's been trying. *Please* cut him some slack."

"I'm done needing anyone to cut me slack. Most of all you, Tegs."

Tegan spun around, shocked to see Jett standing there. *Oh God*, how much had he heard? "Did you miss your flight?"

He stepped beside her, his eyes trained on Dean as he said, "I'm not going."

"But the Carlisle deal?" Her head was spinning, confused.

He finally looked at her, his stormy eyes softening as he said, "I'm giving it to *the kid*, a guy I mentored a while back."

"But—"

"No buts, baby. I'm paying it forward, going back to my roots. No deal in the world could make me a richer man than being with you will. I don't know how I got lucky enough to walk into that party and walk out with you, but I thank God every day. You appeared out of nowhere, and like a shooting star, you lit up my life and showed me how much I was missing. I love you, Tegs. You're my *home*, and I don't want to miss another white bikini moment or be away from you for *days*, much less *weeks*."

"White bikini moment?" Emery whispered.

Tegan felt her cheeks burn and said, "What about work? You can't change your world for me."

"You are my world, sunshine. I'm not giving up all that I've built, but I've spent years reworking other people's businesses. It's time I focused on reworking my own life. I don't know exactly how everything will pan out yet, but I know I want to be here with you. I want to focus on rebuilding my community here and teaching the people who were there for me when I was growing up how to succeed. I want to spend more time mentoring and less time taking over." He looked at his parents and Rose, all of whom had tears in their eyes. "I want to spend time getting to know my family again." He took Tegan's hands in his and gazed into her eyes as he said, "I don't know if you'll get sick of me after I'm around for a few months, but, baby, I'm ready for this adventure if you are. I don't want to miss your openings or my father's foundation events." He looked at Dean and said, "Or the birth of my niece or nephew."

"You're giving up a multimillion-dollar deal?" Dean asked with a biting tone.

"Yes," Jett said with a challenging stare. "Do you have something to say about that, too? Because I'm *here*, Dean, and I'm not going anywhere."

"Yeah, I've got something to say." Dean's jaw clenched.

"*Dean,*" Emery pleaded, touching his arm.

The staggering ability to stare without blinking must run in the Masters genes, because neither man moved a muscle for what felt like forever.

"They're harder to crack than a couple of safes," Rose said.

Dean stepped forward, and Jett squared his shoulders, putting one hand in front of Tegan, nudging her a few steps back.

As Dean's hand rose between them, everyone spoke at once—"*Jett!*" "*Dean!*" "*Boys!*" At the same time, Dean said, "Welcome home, a-hole."

Jett took Dean's hand and hauled him against him, slapping him *hard* on the back as he said, "Careful what you wish for, dickhead."

Chapter Thirty-Five

TEGAN PULLED ON her cutoffs and ran into the closet to look for her sandals. A little thrill still ran through her when she saw Jett's clothes and shoes among her own. It had been three magical, adventurous months since Jett had decided to change his life and really make a go of things between them and with his family. He'd moved into the cottage, and they'd never been happier. Their schedules were complicated at times with the theater and his work, but Tegan wouldn't change a thing. Not even on mornings like today, when they'd gotten overly frisky in the shower and were running more than a little late for breakfast with Jock and their families. Tonight was the opening of *Pillow Talk*, Bayside Productions' first live episode. Tegan's family had come into town to see it, and they were staying at the big house with Jock, who had become such good friends with Jett, he'd stayed for the summer and was moving to the resort next weekend. Jock was making a big celebratory breakfast, and Jett's family was meeting them at the house.

Tegan was already a nervous wreck about the show, and now she was sure their families would figure out exactly why they were late for breakfast. *Ugh. Embarrassing.*

But so worth it!

She dropped to her hands and knees, quickly finding one sandal. Where the heck was the other one? She lowered herself to her elbows, peering under her dresses.

"Move your pretty little ass, sunshine, or all the bacon will be go—" Jett made an appreciative noise as he came into the closet and groped her ass. "*Forget* the bacon."

She glared at him over her shoulder, and butterflies took flight in her stomach. His hair was still wet from their sexy shower, and he was looking at her like he was ready for *seconds*.

"Hands *off* my bottom, Masters. That's what got us into trouble in the first place."

Jett was more hands-on than ever, in their personal life and in his business. Just as he'd done with Tegan's business plan, he'd meticulously worked through a strategy for reclaiming his life and shifting his focus to getting back to his roots. He'd rented office space in Hyannis, and he was knee-deep in helping Mitchell and the other business owners get back on their feet and learn valuable business practices. Sometimes Jett even worked out of Harvey's office in the big house instead of driving to Hyannis, but he and Tegan were insatiable and he didn't get much work done on those days. Unfortunately, Jock had caught them in a compromising position more than once. Now when Tegan visited Jett in the home office, they hung a scarf on the doorknob, *just in case.*

"You were taunting me with your nakedness." Jett sat on the floor and pulled her into his lap with a lascivious grin.

She wound her arms around his neck and said, "I was *showering*, and you had already showered, remember?" He'd gotten up early to go with Dean to pick something up in Eastham. "Stop looking at me like that. I can't find my sandal, and everyone is waiting for us."

He kissed her softly and said, "Today's your big day, sunshine. They expect us to celebrate."

The show had already sold out for the entire month, and tonight's episode was being reviewed by several media sources. It was already going better than she or Harper could have hoped.

"Oh, *right*. My conservative parents think celebrating means a nice dinner and a fancy cake, not feasting on each other and coming three times."

His eyes darkened. "You know hearing you talk dirty turns me on."

"If you can find my other sandal," she said in her most seductive voice, "I'll make *all* your naughty fantasies come true tonight after the opening, when nobody's waiting for us and we have *hours* to play."

They'd more than made up for the missed bikini fantasy and had enjoyed it so much, they'd begun leaving each other hidden notes spelling out their other fantasies. They were having fun living them out, but the bikini fantasy was still one of Jett's favorites. Tegan had found notes from Jett in a pint of ice cream in the freezer, taped to the visor in her uncle's car, and even in her wallet wrapped around her debit card, which was embarrassing when she'd pulled it out at the grocery store to pay. Her man was very sneaky, and very creative, and she *loved* it!

She whispered, "I'll even wear the white bikini," and felt him get hard beneath her.

He made a growling noise.

"Good luck!" she said, and pushed to her feet with a little giggle.

He smacked her butt, and then he scrambled on the floor in

search of her sandal, finding it before she even got out of the closet. He grabbed her around her waist, hauling her back against him, making her squeal as he smothered her neck in kisses.

"Come on, sunshine. We're *late*," he teased through his own chuckles, still holding her hostage with one arm belted around her belly, refusing to let her take a step forward and taunting her with dozens more kisses.

Not a day had gone by that they hadn't laughed. Even at first, when Jett had been working through new schedules with Tia—who Tegan had finally met and *loved*—and his staff, they'd still managed to find light on the darker, more stressful days. When one of the children's shows had run into snags and Tegan had worried the disappointed customers might never come back, Jett had talked her off the ledge and helped her make contingency plans in case it ever happened again. They made a great team, and every hurdle they jumped made them that much stronger.

Jett gave her a love bite on her shoulder and finally released her. She quickly put on her sandals. "We're *so* late!"

"Come on, beautiful." He snagged her hand and led her out of the bedroom. "We have to explain to your sister's family and our parents how you couldn't keep your hands off me."

"*What?* You better not!"

He flashed a cocky grin.

"Paybacks are hell, you know," she said as they went out the front door of the cottage. "You'd better think long and hard about opening that mouth of yours."

It was a warm, slightly cloudy morning, and Tegan had made arrangements for a tent, just in case. But she'd tossed a silent prayer up to her uncle, hoping he could pull a few more strings and convince the sun to come out. The house renovations would be done by the end of the year, and then tents would no longer be necessary.

"I'd rather think about something long and hard in *your* mouth." He tugged her into his arms, kissing her again.

"What has gotten into you today?" she asked, though she already knew the answer. He had gotten home from a business trip two days ago, and he was always insatiable after they were apart.

"Just you, baby." He draped an arm over her shoulder as they walked through the yard and along the side of the big house. "I hate being away from you."

He still traveled, but never for more than a day or two here and there now that he'd realized the value of virtual meetings. He was also delegating more, which allowed him additional time for mentoring *and* for Tegan. While she loved that extra time together, she was even happier that he and his family had made enormous strides, and they were getting closer every week. They'd attended the foundation dinner and had a wonderful time. She'd enjoyed getting to know his brother Doug and Doug's wife, Susie. Doug and Susie had stayed with his parents while they were in town, and Tegan and Jett had visited them every day. They'd even been spending more time with their friends. Tegan had discovered that Jett was some kind of baby whisperer. Not only did Hadley love him, but he had a magical touch with Desiree and Rick's new baby boy, Aaron, too.

Jett stopped walking to glance at the amphitheater and gardens, which were in full bloom and bursting with color. "Soon the setup crews and caterers will be here, and my girl will be on that stage with her business partner and introducing their very first show. This is your special day, Tegs, and I'm so *proud* of you."

"Thank you. I'm proud of myself, too. It's hard to believe my uncle's been gone for a year. In that time, my entire life has changed."

Jett drew her in his arms and said, "Jock told me that Harvey always believed you'd find happiness here. After everything you and Jock have said about your uncle, I think he brought you here to help *me* find happiness, too."

"I love how you think."

"And I love *everything* about you." As he lowered his lips to hers, her nephew, Billy, ran around the corner of the house giggling up a storm.

"I didn't do it!" Billy hollered as he ran toward them with his arms outstretched, clutching something in his fists. The fishing hat Jett had given him in May when her family had come for the opening of the children's program flew off his head. His shirt and shorts were covered with sticky notes.

"Billy, *don't!*" Melody yelled, chasing after her little brother. Her long dark hair flew out behind her. She was a skinny little thing, all legs and arms, and much to Cici's dismay, she had very little fear. "You're in so much trouble!"

"Uh-oh." Jett ran toward Billy as Cici and Cooper sprinted into the side yard around Melody. Billy was laughing so hard he had drool dripping down his chin.

"William Wild, stop right now!" Cici hollered, making Billy laugh even harder as he dodged Jett's attempt to grab him.

"*What* is going on?" Tegan yelled as Billy led them on some kind of mad-goose chase.

Cooper caught Billy seconds before he reached Tegan and lifted him over his head. "You little rascal! What did we tell you?"

"You are in big trouble, Mister!" Cici said, grabbing her side and trying to catch her breath. "I'm sorry, Jett."

"Sorry for *what*?" Tegan asked.

"*Tegan! Tegan!*" Billy yelled, shaking his hands at her.

Tegan headed for him and said, "I'm right here, buddy."

Billy's fists shot out, and everyone else yelled, "No!" as he opened his fingers, sending sticky notes flying through the air.

Tegan had no idea what everyone was so panicked about. She didn't care if he'd gotten into her office supplies. She tried to catch the sticky notes, but Cici and Jett knocked her out of the way, scrambling to pluck them from the air and the grass.

Tegan threw her hands up and exclaimed, "You're *all* crazy! I'm going inside."

"Bills!" Cooper settled Billy on his hip and said, "*Why* would you do that?"

"I told him not to, Daddy! I tried to stop him!" Melody shouted as Tegan walked by.

She spotted sticky notes scattered on the ground up ahead, and as she bent over to pick them up, Jett dove past her. His big body hit the ground with a *thud*, sprawled out over the sticky notes. Now she *had* to figure out what was going on. She spotted another one a little farther away and snagged it. Her eyes connected with Jett's for half a second before he ran after her. She shrieked and sprinted toward the front of the house, clutching the note and laughing hysterically. Cici and her family were running after them. Melody and Billy hollered her name, but she wasn't about to slow down. Jett snagged the back of her shirt, but she broke free and ran around the corner of the house and into the front yard as Jock and the rest of their families came out the front door. Tegan stopped cold at the sight of a car in the driveway covered with sticky notes, and her world went silent. Everything went silent save for her thundering heart. She'd know that car anywhere, but she couldn't believe her eyes.

Berta?

She looked down and opened her fisted hand, trying to make sense of what was going on. She uncrumpled the note, surprised to see Jett's blocky handwriting spelling out, *Your fancy foods.* She was confused and moving on autopilot as she stepped onto the driveway toward Berta. When she got closer, she realized he had written on every single one of the sticky notes. Goose bumps prickled her limbs as she stood beside Berta—*Berta!*—reading them.

The way your smile lights up the room.
Your sighs.
Your adventurous spirit.
Your love for me.
The way you see the good in everyone.
Your laugh.
The sounds you make when we make love.

She felt her cheeks burn, and her eyes sailed over what had to be hundreds of notes covering the car. Her heart felt like it was going to crawl out of her chest. She turned and said, "Jett? What's all thi—"

Her words were lost in the shock of seeing him down on one knee, looking at her like she was his sun, his moon, and his stars.

JETT HAD NEVER been more nervous in all his life as he

knelt before Tegan holding the ring he'd had made for her and saw their future in her loving eyes. Melody and Billy stood with their parents a few feet away, looking like they were going to burst. Cici looked like she might cry. Jock and the rest of their families were watching them from the porch.

Jett drew in a deep breath, and his mind went blank. Shit. He'd practiced this speech for the last two months, and now he couldn't remember a word of it. *Fuck*, fuck, fuck. "This wasn't exactly the way I saw today playing out," he admitted, silently praying he wouldn't screw this up and earning chuckles from their families. "But you taught me to trust my heart, so I'm going for it."

Tegan touched his face with a trembling hand. He covered it with his own, and her touch brought his words back to him.

"I watched my brothers and my friends fall in love, and I never wanted that for myself," he said, lowering her hand so he could hold it. "I didn't trust that I could be a good boyfriend, much less a husband. Then you showed up at the gas station like a ray of sunshine on the wickedest of days, and again at the café, like the world was guiding me to you. And then you took one look at me, and you knew I was hiding. You saw what no one else ever had, and you loosened my tie, trying to strip off everything I hid behind so you could see the *real* me. Then you saw me, the real me, the good, the bad, and the *lost*. I thought for sure that was it, but instead of turning away, you looked *deeper*. You were insightful, funny, confident, and so damn beautiful and smart, I thought I'd dreamed you up with your circle drawings and pepperoni, cheese, and olive cracker sandwiches. Baby, when you loosened my tie, you untangled the strings to a heart I didn't even know was capable of opening, much less loving someone like I love you. You spread your light over me and suddenly you were *all* I saw, all I *wanted* to see."

He rose to his feet, brushing the tears from her cheeks as his own eyes dampened, and said, "You showed me it was okay to trust and to love, and you showed me a world so vast and wonderful, I never want to leave it. This love we've created is bigger and truer than anything I've ever known. I don't want to imagine living a day without you by my side. I love you, Tegs, and I want a *forever adventure* with you. I want to make your tomorrow better than today, and every day thereafter I promise we'll shine brighter, love harder, and laugh louder than we've ever imagined possible. Will you marry me, sunshine? Let me be the man your uncle always wished you'd find?"

Tears flooded her cheeks as she nodded, choking out, *"Yes!"*

Cheers and applause rang out as Tegan threw her arms around him, her salty tears slipping between their lips as they said *I love you* in their kisses.

The cheers quieted as he slid the ring on her finger and said, "Canary diamonds in the shape of the sun because you are my sunshine. You can read all the reasons why when we clear off Berta to take her for a ride."

"Berta," she whispered through her tears.

"I've had her completely refinished, top to bottom. She'll last another fifteen years, and then we'll get her fixed up again, because when you told me you wanted to bury her in the garden, I knew just how much you needed *her* by your side, too."

A symphony of congratulations, whistles, and cheers rang out as he gathered her in his arms, and the clouds opened up. A streak of sunshine hit them like a spotlight, and as he lowered his lips to hers, he knew Harvey Fine was smiling down on them.

Your Next Bayside book is set on Silver Island!

Jock and Daphne find heart-meltingly beautiful and toe-curlingly sexy forever love in the first book in The Steeles at Silver Island, a Bayside Summers spin-off series.

A man who's lost it all and carries a torturous secret, a divorced single mother who has everything to lose, and the little girl who helps them heal.

Justin Wicked and Chloe Mallery finally get their happily ever after!

Set on the sandy shores of Cape Cod, the Wickeds feature fiercely protective heroes, strong heroines, and unbreakable family bonds. They're so fun, sexy, and emotional, you'll want to climb between the pages and join them!

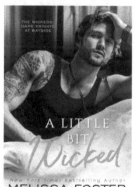

What do a cocky biker and a businesswoman who has sworn off dating bad boys have in common? According to Chloe Mallery, not much. But Justin Wicked has had his eye on her for a long time, and he is sure the inescapable heat between them runs far deeper than just physical attraction. Could their difficult pasts be drawing them together, or will his protective nature be too much for her independent heart to accept? Find out and fall in love in *A Little Bit Wicked*, a stand-alone romance.

Have you read Tegan's sister, Cici's, story?
Fall in love with Cooper Wild and Cici Fine today!

Four years ago at a film festival, Cici Fine met Cooper Wild, a man who turned her world upside down in the span of one deliciously perfect week. He was everything she'd ever dreamed of: sinfully sexy, intelligent, and incredibly loving. When the festival ended, they returned to their own hometowns with promises of forever. But Cooper disappeared, and Cici was left to raise the daughter he never knew about alone.

Cooper is finally thinking straight after years of being lost in grief from the tragedy that killed his father and left his mother blind. Now he's on a mission to find the woman he left behind—the only woman he's ever loved.

But Cici Fine is no longer a naive young girl. She's a savvy businesswoman with big responsibilities, on the cusp of a life-changing move. When fate brings the two together, they'll put the old adage to the test and find out if love really can conquer all.

READY TO BINGE READ?

If Bayside Fantasies was your first Bayside Summers book, you have many more Bayside and Seaside Summers love stories to catch up on. I suggest starting with SEASIDE DREAMS. That series leads into the Bayside Summers series.

Start reading ***FREE** with SEASIDE DREAMS!
(*Free in digital format at the time of this publication. Price subject to change without notice.)

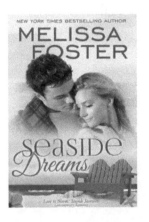

Bella Abbascia has returned to Seaside Cottages in Wellfleet, Massachusetts, as she does every summer. Only this year Bella has more on her mind than sunbathing and skinny-dipping with her girlfriends. She's quit her job, put her house on the market, and sworn off relationships while she builds a new life in her favorite place on earth. That is, until good-time Bella's prank takes a bad turn and a sinfully sexy police officer appears on the scene.

Single father and police officer Caden Grant left Boston with his fourteen-year-old son, Evan, after his partner was killed in the line of duty. He hopes to find a safer life in the small resort town of Wellfleet, and when he meets Bella during a night patrol, he realizes he's found the one thing he'd never allowed himself to hope for—or even realized he was missing.

After fourteen years of focusing solely on his son, Caden cannot resist the intense attraction he feels toward beautiful Bella, and Bella is powerless to fight the heat of their budding romance. But starting over proves more difficult than either of them imagined, and when Evan gets mixed up with the wrong kids, Caden's loyalty is put to the test. Will he give up everything to protect his son—even Bella?

Have you met Tru Blue & the Whiskeys?

If you think you know everything about bearded, tattooed men, get ready to be surprised—and to fall hard for Truman Gritt.

There's nothing Truman Gritt won't do to protect his family—including spending years in prison for a crime he didn't commit. When he's finally released, the life he knew is turned upside down by his mother's overdose, and Truman steps in to raise the children she's left behind. Truman's hard, he's secretive, and he's trying to save a brother who's even more broken than he is. He's never needed help in his life, and when beautiful Gemma Wright tries to step in, he's less than accepting. But Gemma has a way of slithering into people's lives, and eventually she pierces through his ironclad heart. When Truman's dark past collides with his future, his loyalties will be tested and he'll be faced with his toughest decision yet.

Fall in love with Grace and Reed, and the fun, feisty Montgomerys in EMBRACING HER HEART, the first book in the Bradens & Montgomerys series!

Leaving New York City and returning to her hometown to teach a screenplay writing class seems like just the break Grace Montgomery needs. Until her sisters wake her at four thirty in the morning to watch the hottest guys in town train wild horses and she realizes that escaping her sisters' drama-filled lives was a lot easier from hundreds of miles away. To make matters worse, she spots the one man she never wanted to see again—ruggedly handsome Reed Cross.

Reed was one of Michigan's leading historical preservation experts, but on the heels of catching his girlfriend in bed with his business partner, his uncle suffers a heart attack. Reed cuts all ties and returns home to Oak Falls to run his uncle's business. A chance encounter with Grace, his first love, brings back memories he's spent years trying to escape.

Grace is bound and determined not to fall under Reed's spell again—and Reed wants more than another taste of the woman he's never forgotten. When a midnight party brings them together, passion ignites and old wounds are reopened. Grace sets down the ground rules for the next three weeks. No touching, no kissing, and if she has it her way, no breathing, because every breath he takes steals her ability to think. But Reed has other ideas...

Love in Bloom FREE Reader Goodies

If you loved this story, be sure to check out the rest of the Love in Bloom big-family romance collection and download your free reader goodies, including publication schedules, series checklists, family trees, and more!
www.MelissaFoster.com/RG

Remember to check my sales and freebies page for periodic first-in-series free and other great offers!
www.MelissaFoster.com/LIBFree

More Books By Melissa Foster

THE BRADENS & MONTGOMERYS (Pleasant Hill – Oak Falls)

Embracing Her Heart
Anything for Love
Trails of Love
Wild, Crazy Hearts
Making You Mine
Searching For Love

BRADEN WORLD NOVELLAS

Daring Her Love
Promise My Love
Our New Love
Story of Love
Love at Last
A Very Braden Christmas

THE REMINGTONS

Game of Love
Stroke of Love
Flames of Love
Slope of Love
Read, Write, Love
Touched by Love

SEASIDE SUMMERS

Seaside Dreams
Seaside Hearts
Seaside Sunsets
Seaside Secrets
Seaside Nights
Seaside Embrace
Seaside Lovers
Seaside Whispers
Seaside Serenade

BAYSIDE SUMMERS
Bayside Desires
Bayside Passions
Bayside Heat
Bayside Escape
Bayside Romance
Bayside Fantasies
Tempted by Love

THE RYDERS
Seized by Love
Claimed by Love
Chased by Love
Rescued by Love
Swept Into Love

THE WHISKEYS: DARK KNIGHTS AT PEACEFUL HARBOR
Tru Blue
Truly, Madly, Whiskey
Driving Whiskey Wild
Wicked Whiskey Love
Mad About Moon
Taming My Whiskey
The Gritty Truth

SUGAR LAKE
The Real Thing
Only for You
Love Like Ours
Finding My Girl

HARMONY POINTE
Call Her Mine
This is Love
She Loves Me

THE WICKEDS: DARK KNIGHTS AT BAYSIDE
A Little Bit Wicked
The Wicked Aftermath

WILD BOYS AFTER DARK
Logan
Heath
Jackson
Cooper

BAD BOYS AFTER DARK
Mick
Dylan
Carson
Brett

HARBORSIDE NIGHTS
Includes characters from the Love in Bloom series
Catching Cassidy
Discovering Delilah
Tempting Tristan

Standalone Books by Melissa
Chasing Amanda (mystery/suspense)
Come Back to Me (mystery/suspense)
Have No Shame (historical fiction/romance)
Love, Lies & Mystery (3-book bundle)
Megan's Way (literary fiction)
Traces of Kara (psychological thriller)
Where Petals Fall (suspense)

Acknowledgments

If this was your first Bayside Summers book, you have many more Bayside and Seaside Summers love stories to catch up on. I suggest starting with SEASIDE DREAMS, which is currently free in digital format (price subject to change). That series leads into the Bayside Summers series. Chloe Mallery and Justin Wicked's love story will be the first book in the new series The Wickeds: Dark Knights at Bayside. I hope you'll enjoy that, as well.

The Bayside Summers series is not ending, but when I met Jock Steele and his family, I knew they needed their stories told. Daphne and Jock's book will be the first in The Steeles at Silver Island. I'm beyond excited about introducing you to this new family. Jock's family are the cousins to our original Steele family (Reggie, Jesse, Brent, Shea, Finn, and Fiona), who you might remember from CRASHING INTO LOVE, Jake Braden and Fiona Steele. You will be getting the love stories of each of those family members as well. I'm also looking forward to writing about all our Bayside friends, including Rowan and his daughter, Joni.

Books are never written in a vacuum, and I am blessed that the number of people who inspire and support me is vast and constant. I could never name everyone who has touched my life during my fifteen-hour writing days. I appreciate all of you. But

I must give a special shout-out to my friend who feels like family, Lisa Posillico-Filipe. At more than four hundred and fifty pages, Tegan and Jett's story is the longest that I have ever written. There were many talking-off-the-ledge moments, and, Lisa, you were there for every one of them with your kind words and support. I could not have remained sane without you by my side. Thank you for believing in my storytelling abilities and for not smacking me in the head when I said Tegan needed a trip to LA even though the story was already going to be long. I'm so glad we both loved it!

Nothing excites me more than hearing from my fans and knowing you love my stories as much as I enjoy writing them. Thank you to all who have reached out. If you haven't joined my fan club, you can find it on Facebook. We have loads of fun, chat about books, and members get special sneak peeks of upcoming publications.
www.facebook.com/groups/MelissaFosterFans

Heaps of gratitude go out to my meticulous and talented editorial team. Thank you, Kristen, Penina, Elaini, Juliette, Lynn, and Justinn for all you do for me and for our readers. And as always, I am forever grateful to my family and to my own hunky hero, Les, who allows me the time to create our wonderful worlds.

Meet Melissa

www.MelissaFoster.com

Melissa Foster is a *New York Times* and *USA Today* bestselling and award-winning author. Her books have been recommended by *USA Today*'s book blog, *Hagerstown* magazine, *The Patriot*, and several other print venues. Melissa has painted and donated several murals to the Hospital for Sick Children in Washington, DC.

Visit Melissa on her website or chat with her on social media. Melissa enjoys discussing her books with book clubs and reader groups and welcomes an invitation to your event. Melissa's books are available through most online retailers in paperback, digital, and audio formats.